"AS I UTTER THE WORDS NOW, WE WILL CONDUCT THIS TRIBUNAL IN FEDERATION STANDARD, IN DEFERENCE TO CAPTAIN RIKER'S PRESENCE," CONTINUED KASTIS, "AND IN THE INTERESTS OF OPENNESS WITH THE UNITED FEDERATION OF PLANETS."

The judicator said the word as if it was sour to her, ashen and alien on her tongue. She indicated the three shadowy forms around her. "Tribune Delos will observe for Major Helek. Tribune Nadei will observe for Commander Medaka and the Romulan Senate. And our . . . visiting advocate will observe for the human captain."

Riker shielded his eyes, trying to peer past the light from the glowglobes to get a good look at the person assigned to him, but it was impossible to pick out anything. The shadow gave him nothing, no face, no hint of gender, only uncertainty.

He knew little of Romulan legal practices. Was Riker's silent watcher his lawyer, his judge? Executioner, even? He banished that last notion with a grimace.

Will Riker stood foursquare behind his every decision, even after everything that had happened over the last few days. What that would mean here and now in this place, he couldn't know. But there would be no obfuscation from him, no wordplay and clouding of the truth.

And once again, something came back to Riker, something Picard had said to him, years earlier on their very first mission together. *If we're going to be damned, let's be damned for what we really are.*

STAR TREK™
PICARD

THE DARK VEIL

James Swallow

Based upon *Star Trek: The Next Generation*
created by Gene Roddenberry
and
Star Trek: Picard
created by
Akiva Goldsman & Michael Chabon
&
Kirsten Beyer & Alex Kurtzman

G

GALLERY BOOKS

New York   London   Toronto   Sydney   New Delhi

G

Gallery Books
An Imprint of Simon & Schuster, Inc.
1230 Avenue of the Americas
New York, NY 10020

First Gallery Books trade paperback edition September 2021

GALLERY BOOKS and colophon are registered trademarks of Simon & Schuster, Inc.

For information about special discounts for bulk purchases, please contact Simon & Schuster Special Sales at 1-866-506-1949 or business@simonandschuster.com.

The Simon & Schuster Speakers Bureau can bring authors to your live event. For more information or to book an event, contact the Simon & Schuster Speakers Bureau at 1-866-248-3049 or visit our website at www.simonspeakers.com.

Manufactured in the United States of America

10 9 8 7 6 5 4 3 2 1

Library of Congress Cataloging-in-Publication Data is available.

ISBN 978-1-9821-5406-6
ISBN 978-1-9821-5407-3 (pbk)
ISBN 978-1-9821-5413-4 (ebook)

For Kirsten, because she's m'r-f'n awesome

Historian's Note

This story takes place in 2386, seven years after the events of *Star Trek: Nemesis* and one year after the "Mars Incident" and Jean-Luc Picard's resignation from Starfleet.

ONE

The Romulans kept William Riker in the cell for several hours, ignoring all of his attempts to communicate with them.

He knew he was being observed and scanned every second of that time, by sensors hidden in the walls or some mechanism in the chamber's only illuminator.

The glowing globe, no larger than an apple, floated deliberately just beyond his reach on silent antigravs. It threw weak, jaundice-yellow light down around him, and when Riker moved about the small, narrow cell, it followed.

If he spoke out loud, Riker's voice echoed off the gray metal walls in odd, flat tones, almost as if the noise was being stifled. He snapped his fingers a few times and sang the first couple of lines from "Fever" to test the acoustics.

He let the sound bounce, listening to the shape of it. The deadening effect was completely uniform. His captors had him in a sensor blind, and nothing—not even his voice—would be allowed to escape.

They hadn't taken his communicator badge, and clearly that was because they didn't need to. It gave a dispirited chirp when he tapped it, the tone signaling total disconnection. The device's internal chronometer still kept time, though, and he set it to mark the duration of each standard hour.

When it became clear his captors were in no hurry to return, he spent a while exploring the confines of the chamber. Like everything Romulan, it was a puzzle.

No clearly indicated controls to extend a sleeping pallet or reveal a 'fresher unit, nothing to dim or brighten the glow-globe. Eventually, through a process of trial and error, Riker found that if he pushed at certain seams in the wall plates, a seat of sorts extruded out of the floor, and retracted if the process was reversed.

He sat, absently drumming his fingers. Riker had never been able to grasp the Romulan need for inessential obfuscation and complexity.

Sure, he could see the motive to keep things concealed from a perceived enemy, even the sense that some cultures had to protect themselves from members of their own kind. But was it really necessary to make every tiny little thing so damned cryptic?

As an Academy cadet, he'd once listened to a noted xenoethnologist give a lecture on Romulan civilian life, explaining how the simple act of turning the handle on the door to one's house might mean navigating visual riddles and a complex hidden locking mechanism.

How can they live like that? It was a question that nagged him for weeks afterward. A younger Will Riker mused on the answer, reaching for an understanding that was beyond him. What kind of life must you lead when your whole culture is built around the tenets of concealment, of complication, of *deceit?*

His old friend and former captain, Jean-Luc Picard, had once told him of an Andorian proverb regarding the citizens of the Star Empire: *A Romulan will scheme for ten years to have you bring them a cup of water, but never once admit that they are thirsty.*

He still didn't truly understand them, despite numerous encounters with them both in battle and in conversation. It was dangerous to apply Federation values to them. For the Romulans, the act of hiding one's self was as automatic as breathing in and out.

"And you've paid for it, haven't you?" Riker voiced the rest of the thought out loud, casting a sideways glance at the glow-globe above him, wondering what those monitoring him would think of that. "In the end, the bill comes due for every lie that's told."

But it wasn't just falsehoods at the heart of Romulan culture, it was more complicated than that. It was a matter of *trust*, and in that arena, the United Federation of Planets had fallen short.

Riker felt a bleak mood gathering like black clouds on a far horizon, and he blew out a breath, as if that would carry them away.

A few moments later, one wall of the cell dematerialized. The chamber didn't have a conventional door or a force-field barrier, and this was the only way in or out.

Standing on the threshold were a pair of sullen centurions, a light-eyed and olive-skinned female, and a paler male with heavier brow ridges, both dressed in what Riker recognized as Romulan uniforms. Black baldrics across their chests were highlighted with silver detail, indicating their ranks and positions. He thought they were low-level officer cadre, something equating roughly to that of a Starfleet ensign or junior grade lieutenant. Neither of them seemed particularly happy to have this duty.

The woman threw something at Riker and he caught it: a pair of heavy magnetic cuffs with a connecting chain.

"I don't really wear jewelry," Riker noted, making no attempt to don the restraints.

The Romulans said nothing, waiting, watching him silently. The moment stretched and became uncomfortably long.

Riker let the cuffs drop to the deck. "We can keep up the staring contest all day, if you'd like." He was pretty good, he had to admit. His record was a full two minutes without blinking, and that was up against the laser-like glare of his young son, Thaddeus. That thought pulled up the corners of his lips in a faint smile.

The woman glanced at the man, and an unspoken communication passed between them. She stepped back, making room for Riker to move out of the cell.

Was that some sort of test? he wondered. *Did I pass it or fail it?*

The male Romulan led the way, down through tapered corridors that all seemed identical. Riker spotted some symbols on the walls in certain places that might have been signage, but they could have been decorative for all he knew. The color palette was uniformly drab gray and faded tan, and he noted a recurring threefold motif in consoles and panels as they passed. One screen in every three would be a false one, another test, another layer of everyday riddles.

Riker could feel a faint vibration through the floor beneath him, and it gave him a point of commonality to hold on to among all this unfamiliarity. Anyone who had lived enough of their life on a starship knew that low hum, knew that it meant the pulse of a vessel at rest. So the warbird he was aboard was not currently in motion, and that was something.

Or is that hum part of an elaborate fiction? Unbidden, the question popped into his thoughts. *Are the Romulans faking that sound to make me think we're not at warp when in fact we are? And if that's so, then where is the* Titan—*?*

He smiled at nothing, catching himself before he went down the wormhole after that line of reasoning. This was what being around the Romulans did to people, he reflected. They dragged you into their mindset, the gravity of their ingrained cultural paranoia pulling you into the same thought process, whether you wanted to or not.

In recent days, William Riker had had his fill of half-truths and hidden agendas. These things were insidious, and hard to wash off once you got a little of it on you. He cleared his mind of such thoughts and concentrated on the moment.

Presently, the narrow corridor widened to reveal a heavy door, which drew back with a theatrical hiss as Riker and the centurions approached. The captain was two steps into the wide chamber beyond before he realized that his escorts hadn't followed him in.

Another glow-globe dropped down from above to hover over his head and illuminate him as he took in the space. The room was circular and empty, built so that those within it had nowhere to hide. Riker's first thought was of an arena, a fighting pit, and he flashed back to those old Federation briefings that had first equated Romulan culture to one of Earth's most ancient and militaristic imperiums. Were they going to make him fight like a gladiator?

He wasn't alone. Two more glowing spheres cast light on other figures. To his right, with her wounds dressed with dermal regenerator tabs, a female Romulan with metallic-red hair and sallow skin stood watching him. Major Helek of the Tal Shiar studied Riker with the same confident scorn she had exhibited on their first meeting. Perhaps it was beneath him to think it, but some part of Riker would have liked to find her defeated and fearful after all that she had done. Instead, she glared back at him with the air of someone who had already declared victory.

To his right, and as far as he could be from Helek while still standing in the same room, was Commander Medaka, the captain of the Romulan warbird *Othrys*. His teak-dark face was weathered and grim, and he threw Riker a warning look that gave the Starfleet officer his first sense of exactly how dire this situation was.

In a gallery up above the circular chamber, a group of figures in heavy robes moved in shadow, past the light cast by more floating glow-globes. Riker made out the silhouettes of four humanoids with the close-cut hair and pointed ears of Medaka's people. *A Romulan tribunal*, he guessed, *here to pass their final judgment on the three of us.*

"I am Judicator Kastis." One of the shadows gestured, and a stern female voice issued out across the chamber. "Know that in this place, I am the hearing eye and the seeing ear. The laws of Romulus speak through me."

Medaka and Helek bowed their heads briefly at this ritual intonation, but Riker remained where he was, watching for cues.

"As I utter the words now, we will conduct this tribunal in Federation Standard, in deference to Captain Riker's presence," continued Kastis, "and in the interests of *openness* with the United Federation of Planets." The judicator said the word as if it was sour to her, ashen and alien on her tongue. She indicated the three shadowy forms around her. "Tribune Delos will observe for Major Helek. Tribune Nadei will observe for Commander Medaka and the Romulan Senate. And our . . . visiting advocate will observe for the human captain."

Riker shielded his eyes, trying to peer past the light from the glow-globes to get a good look at the person assigned to him, but it was impossible to pick out anything. The shadow gave him nothing, no face, no hint of gender, only uncertainty.

He knew little of Romulan legal practices. Was Riker's silent watcher his lawyer, his judge? *Executioner, even?* He banished that last notion with a grimace.

Will Riker stood foursquare behind his every decision, even after everything that had happened over the last few days. What that would mean here and now in this place, he couldn't know. But there would be no obfuscation from him, no wordplay or clouding of the truth.

And once again, something came back to Riker, something Picard had said to him, years earlier on their very first mission together. *If we're going to be damned, let's be damned for what we really are.*

"The events of recent cycles in this sector are troubling to the Romulan people," said Nadei in a clear, basso tone. "Armed conflict at our borders. Unchecked aggression from alien powers. Insurrection and subterfuge. These three are at the heart of it. The facts of the matter are held between them."

Kastis inclined her head. "So noted. Commander Medaka, Major Helek, Captain Riker. You will be detained in this place until you have answered all charges and specifications put to you, in a manner that satisfies this tribunal. At that time, we will rule on sentencing and dispensation."

Medaka and Helek nodded, and at length, Riker did the same. He had agreed to participate in this process for the good of Federation-Romulan relations, and it was far too late to back out now.

But when Helek's head rose again, she was staring straight into the gallery and starting as she meant to go on. "I will save the honored tribunal their time and their effort with one clear assentation." She pointed in Riker's direction. "The human and his cohorts bear all responsibility for what has transpired. As the Federation and their Starfleet have always done, he has attempted to entrap our people and bring us low." She shook her head, and in the pause Riker was unsure if he was allowed to interrupt. For the moment, he let her carry on. "To my shame, I did not realize until it was too late that Commander Medaka, through weakness of his character and active subornment, was a factor in that plot."

"If the deck slanted as much as your utterances, we would all stumble." Medaka eyed her warily. "As is her way, the major views events through a lens that only she can peer through. And it is a narrow aperture indeed."

"Commander Medaka's reputation for operating in unconventional fashion is well documented," Helek insisted. "I'm sure the tribunal have viewed his military record. One need only consider the eclectic crew gathered under his command to see that he has never been one to follow the letter of Romulan law . . ."

"I took *you* on," Medaka countered.

"You may pretend that was your decision, if you wish," said Helek, from the side of her mouth.

Frowning, the Romulan captain looked to his human counterpart, giving him tacit permission to speak.

"There's a lot of blame to go around here," said Riker, opening his hands. "A lot of emotions running high, despite all the coolness on display. You want me to help you place that blame so you can move on and call it done? I'm not here to do that. But if you want to know the facts? I'll give that to you without hesitation."

Medaka offered him a tiny nod. "Good opening," he said quietly.

"Fine words." Delos punctuated his reply with a barely perceptible snort. "But let us hold no illusions as to what we have invited into this chamber. A representative of the so-called United Federation of Planets. Our benign galactic neighbor, as they would have us believe. The ones who offered us the helping hand of a friend in our darkest hour . . . only to snatch it away when their mood changed." Delos leaned forward and pointed at Riker. "Do not make the mistake of thinking you have any allies here, human. You are William Thomas Riker of the planet Earth, formerly crewman aboard the adversaries *Enterprise* and latterly of the battle cruiser *Titan*—"

"The *Titan* is an explorer, not a ship of war," Riker protested, but Delos talked over him.

"The Empire knows you well, Riker," said the tribune. "A man of the *Enterprise*, a vessel which, in and of itself, carries a name synonymous in Romulan history with acts of base trickery!"

Delos could only be referring to a mission from the era of the storied Captain James T. Kirk, when that earlier *Enterprise*'s crew had orchestrated the first intact capture of a cloaking device. Romulus had never forgiven Starfleet for the success of Kirk's clandestine operation. And Delos's history lesson didn't end with that.

"A vessel you served aboard as first officer," he went on, "in missions that accepted the Empire's traitors, interfering with our private, internal politics . . . and let us never forget, saw you participate directly in the bloody rebellion of the treacherous Shinzon of Remus!"

The silent advocate leaned close to Kastis and whispered something to her. Kastis accepted the hushed words and raised her hand. "I have been reminded that Captain Riker and his colleagues fought bravely to *oppose* Shinzon during the clone's brief reign of terror, not aid him. Let us not lose sight of that."

"But to what end?" Delos gestured at the air. "Only so the Federation might benefit from the confusion sown in the wake of that atrocity!"

"We defeated Shinzon at the cost of our dearest blood," said Riker, unwilling to let things end there. In his mind's eye, he saw his friend and shipmate Data, that most unique of beings, going out to willingly give up his existence, without a moment's hesitation. Had he not, a man like Delos might not be alive now to belittle that noble sacrifice, and Riker told him so, his jaw stiffening in annoyance.

The battle against Shinzon and his Reman allies, with the lethal thalaron weapon in their possession, had almost finished the *Enterprise*. While those events were seven years past and gone, the echo of them was still something Riker carried close. Delos's glib dismissal of that and past events such as the tragic defection of the Romulan admiral Alidar Jarok, and the plot by factions on Romulus to invade the planet Vulcan, was equally grating. Riker wondered if this was some deliberate ploy on the part of the tribune.

Was he trying to draw out an angry reaction, or was that how Romulans really saw those events from their side of the Neutral Zone? Not as the Federation's attempts to make the right choices in difficult circumstances, but as the schemes of an enemy who wanted to destroy their way of life? This intransigence fatigued Riker more than he was willing to admit.

There had been a time, in the war against the rise of the Dominion, when the Romulans put aside their enmity to join the Federation and the Klingons to defend against a greater foe. Riker had been one among many who dared to hope that from the ashes of that horrible conflict, something good might grow.

He wanted to believe that an accord might be found in the wake of their shared fight. The first mission of his new command, after his promotion to captain of the *Starship Titan*, had been to open a dialogue with the Romulan Empire.

For a time, they wanted to talk. The veil between two cultures held closed for centuries opened a measure. But only for a short while.

Now it seemed to have fallen again, becoming heavy and impenetrable. Riker studied Medaka, the closest in this place to his own rank and position. A fellow captain, who had walked the same path as Riker but on the other side of the Neutral Zone. If he expected to find support, it was no longer present. The Romulan's face was unreadable.

For a fleeting moment in time, there had been the real possibility of détente. But all of that had been pushed aside with one revelation. The first falling domino that was even now reshaping the geopolitics of the entire quadrant, with worse to come.

The supernova.

Like every other officer of captain's rank and above, Riker had first learned of it from a Starfleet priority-one message, transmitted directly to his ready room. He watched as a hologram of the fleet's commander-in-chief, Admiral Bordson, worked his way through a tersely worded briefing that sounded the death knell for a civilization.

It had become apparent that Romulus's star was dying, Bordson explained, and within a scant few years, it would detonate in a nova effect that would consume the heart of the Romulan Star Empire. It was a bleak and appalling pronouncement, and Riker's emotional response to it had been so strong that moments later his wife, Deanna, had raised him over the intercom. Five decks away, his half-Betazoid wife had sensed her husband's shock and feared the worst.

Later, while their son, Thaddeus, slept, they had talked it over. The boy dozed fitfully, picking up on the dismay of his parents even as he dreamed, and they spoke in quiet tones so they would not disturb him further.

Bordson's briefing presented the single greatest catastrophe in living galactic history, and Riker's first impulse was to ask: *What can we do to help?*

It came as no surprise for Will and Deanna to learn that Jean-Luc Picard had already taken that same intent to Starfleet Command. Of all the men Riker had ever known, there was no one more ready to take on the mantle of something as crucial and as difficult as this, and seeing his former captain's name attached to the endeavor brought him hope. If anyone could find a way to offer aid to millions of displaced Romulans, to former sworn enemies, it was Picard.

In days, Picard had given up command of the *Enterprise*-E to lead the gargantuan relief effort. Riker offered *Titan* and her crew, and there was work enough for everyone. More than they could manage, if he were honest.

For a year, *Titan* went above and beyond, covering the gaps as other ships were diverted into Romulan-controlled space on refugee rescue op-

THE DARK VEIL   11

erations, taking on more missions than they ever had before. His crew had made him proud, each of them rising to the greatest challenge of their generation.

But it all went away within a day.

Riker woke in the dead of ship's night to find his wife standing over him, her dark eyes shimmering. *Something awful has happened on Mars,* she said. *They're saying it was a terrorist attack by a group of rogue synthetics. Geordi was there . . . No one knows if he made it out.*

He held her for a time, and then they both shuttered away their fears like Starfleet officers and went to work. Riker's *Enterprise* shipmate Geordi La Forge would later be counted among those lucky few who had escaped the destruction of the Utopia Planitia shipyards as the atmosphere of Mars burned, but that tiny fragment of good news would be eclipsed by what came next.

With the new fleet gutted by the terror attack, the rescue initiative was beyond overstretched, and with Federation member worlds up in arms, the inevitable happened. Starfleet withdrew its aid and the Romulans were left to fend for themselves. Unable to carry on in the face of such an order, Picard resigned his commission.

Jean-Luc wasn't the only one who wanted to resign, of course. Will wrote a letter to Bordson that would have seen him follow in his former commander's footsteps, but he couldn't bring himself to send it. As long as he still had a ship and a crew, a ship as good as *Titan* and a crew as good as his, there was still a chance to do what was right.

I have to believe that.

Riker blinked, and his reverie faded, bringing him back hard to the moment as Tribune Nadei's booming voice rolled over the chamber.

"To find certainty, we must first ascertain the human's purpose here. What was his ship's mission so close to our borders? To conduct espionage against the Empire? Undoubtedly. But what else?"

"We're not out here to spy on you." Riker denied it automatically, and immediately regretted his abrupt retort. It was a lie. Every Starfleet mission within a few parsecs of the Neutral Zone involved scanning across the border to observe ship movements and intercept communications from the other side, and the Romulans knew it. He modified his reply. "We keep watch, but that's all. You do the same." *And more*, he wanted to add, but it would have been a cheap shot.

The weight of every word he uttered in this room was clear to Riker, and he knew he could not afford to waste them. Relations between his government and that of Romulus were on thin ice, tensions edging toward the same heights as in the days of the first interstellar war between them in the latter half of the twenty-second century. In the worst-case scenario, what emerged from this hearing could have negative consequences across the entire sector.

Riker had come here specifically to stop that from happening, and not for the first time he wished that his wife were standing beside him, lending him that bottomless well of empathy she possessed, and helping him navigate these difficult waters.

"Our mission in this sector was one of peace," Riker went on. "My ship was doing something very simple, when you cut to the heart of it. We were taking someone *home*."

SIX DAYS EARLIER

TWO

Deanna Troi's errant charge deliberately slowed his walking speed until they were practically going backward, lingering by the *Starship Titan*'s observation windows as they moved down the port side of the vessel. Elongated stars, distorted by the effect of faster-than-light warp speed travel, scudded past on the far side of the portals. The impression was that she was walking against some invisible wind.

Certainly, what she was doing right now felt like an uphill struggle. "*Thaddeus . . .*" She injected a note of warning into the boy's name, drawing it out to show him that her patience was starting to thin. "Stop dawdling."

"I'm not." It was a poor fib. Troi's son was, in point of fact, the dictionary definition of *dawdling*, literally dragging his heels as he followed in his mother's footsteps. It had taken an age just to get him dressed, an eon to march him out of their quarters, and now she was beginning to wonder if she would get the boy to his classes before the heat death of the universe. "I just don't want to walk fast," he added.

"Really?" She reached a slender finger toward her combadge. "I can have you beamed right to school, you know. I'm a commander, I can do that."

"No!" Thaddeus made an animated show of moving, somehow doing it without actually advancing that far. "I'll walk. I am walking." He let his shoulders slump melodramatically, as if this was the absolute worst imposition he could possibly have endured.

Troi hid a smile from him, admiring the performance. *Maybe he'll become an actor when he's older,* she thought. *He needs to learn a little more nuance, though.*

Her mother had been quite amused when Deanna mentioned Thaddeus's theatrics during their last holo-communication, and Lwaxana Troi took great delight in telling Deanna that the behavior of her grandson was the precise echo of hers at his age. Troi refused to accept that, of course, and offered the boy her hand.

He eyed it like it was poisonous, and did not accept. "Do I have to go to school today?"

"It's a school day," she told him. "What do you think?"

"*Urlak sek farah.*" He pouted, saying the words into his chest.

Troi eyed the boy. "In Standard, please." Since the age of three, Thaddeus had been refining his own invented language, a dialect he called Kelu, and sometimes he would slip into it just to make a point. His parents had first thought it was a phase the bright youngster was going through, but as he got older he added more and more to it, all too often scribbling down notes on it when he was supposed to be doing his schoolwork.

Other kids build model starships or plant gardens, Will had noted, with a smile. *Ours is writing his own language.*

Which was fair enough, but recently Troi had learned that some of the *Titan*'s junior crew was adopting Kelu words as a kind of informal shipboard slang, and she wasn't sure if she should be pleased or perturbed by that.

"Okay, fine." Her son made a face like a grumpy Lurian and finally fell in step with her, admitting defeat but still determined not to go gracefully. He made a grunting, wheezing noise with each footstep he took.

Troi nodded to a couple of lieutenants from the astrometrics division who passed them going in the other direction. She wondered if it would be detrimental to her reputation as ship's senior counselor to be observed as the mother of such a recalcitrant child.

She sighed, stopped and crouched so that they were both on the same level. "Is something the matter at school? Is that why you don't want to go today?" Troi reached out and straightened Thad's hair.

"It's just . . . My project . . . It's going to be boring now."

"But you like languages." Troi continued to be quietly impressed with her son's ability to soak up dialects of all kinds. Along with his Kelu project, he already knew enough French to read the copy of *Le Petit Prince* that Jean-Luc Picard had given him as a birthday gift, and only a couple of nights ago, he had burped the entirety of the Klingon alphabet and reduced Will to tears of laughter.

Suddenly, the floodgates opened, and her son began to talk a mile a minute. Thad explained he wanted to do something clever to impress his teachers in *Titan*'s kindergarten, as part of an assignment to pick a sentient species and learn all about them—and he had boldly chosen the Jazari as his subject.

"Ah." Troi gave a knowing nod. To a child, it must have seemed like a brilliant idea. But it was doomed to fail.

Titan's current mission was taking the ship to the Jazari star system near the Romulan Neutral Zone, and a party of Jazari diplomats were their guests down on deck eight. There was even a member of the species serving as an active crewman in the medical department, a young lieutenant named Zade, one of very few of his kind in Starfleet. The Jazari were not part of the United Federation of Planets, but they had an associate status, a kind of halfway house between unaffiliated independence and a formal application for UFP membership.

What Troi's son had failed to reckon with was the Jazari's strict rules about personal privacy. To call them reclusive was like saying Tellarites were stubborn: technically correct, but also a *massive* understatement.

The Jazari had shared practically nothing of their culture with the wider Federation, beyond details of their complex codes of personal conduct. Their home planet was off-limits to visitors, just like their quarters and private spaces aboard the ship; they never conversed in anything but Federation Standard; and they had extremely exacting guidelines about medical matters and death rituals.

They were an enigma, but a very polite one. In return for a modest trade in the mineral ryetalyn—a vital component in certain vaccines—the

Federation accommodated the Jazari's desire to see more of the galaxy and quietly held open the door of friendship. The prevailing hope was that as they saw more of what the Federation had to offer, they would let down their guard and come into the fold.

That hadn't happened, though, not in the century since their ships first made contact, not after trade and diplomatic missions had been set up, or even the inclusion of a handful of their people into Starfleet. It was widely accepted that the Jazari would come around when it suited them, if ever, and not before.

"I thought it would be really neat if I could learn some Jazari words," Thad concluded, his expression glum. "I asked Lieutenant Zade, and he was nice but he said he couldn't help me." He looked up at his mother, thinking it through. "You could order him to do it. You're a commander, you can do that. Or Dad? He's captain, and—"

"Sorry, kiddo, but that's not how it works. If the Jazari want to keep some things private from other people, we have to respect that. You wouldn't want everyone knowing every little thing about you, would you?"

"No," he admitted, reaching up to take her hand as they walked. "But we don't know anything about them at all!" Thad made the face he did when he was thinking hard. "Maybe they don't even *have* their own language."

Some theories about the Jazari agreed, speculating that they communicated telepathically, like the Cairn or the Aenar. But Troi had never once sensed even the slightest hint of a psionic aura from Zade or others of his kind.

"It is a mystery," she noted. "But remember what your father said, that's why we're out here in space, to learn things. We might not be learning much from the Jazari right now, but we are always learning something." She smiled at him. "Every day is a school day for the *Titan*. You're lucky, you get the weekends off."

"I suppose." Thad gave an elaborate sigh as they approached the kindergarten, where the rest of his class were gathering prior to the start of lessons.

The commander noted another parent with a similarly reluctant child across the corridor, an El-Aurian officer with *Titan*'s diplomatic team. The two mothers exchanged a brief look of mutual sympathy.

"How about this?" she said, thinking on her feet. "That's Lieutenant Commander Phosia over there. She's an El-Aurian, and they have a very interesting language structure. I could talk to her. She might be able to help you with your project."

Her son's eyes lit up at the idea. "Okay! That would be cool!" And in that instant, all his morose mood evaporated and he was beaming from ear to ear. Troi couldn't help but be taken by his infectious grin, and it filled her heart. She gave him an impulsive hug and he squirmed.

"*Mo-o-om*," he said, drawing out the word. "Don't be clingy."

She deliberately gave him an extra squeeze and then let go. "I'm a commander, I can do that."

As the children streamed into their schoolroom, Troi intercepted Phosia and put the request to her. The other woman was thin and lissome, with large eyes and hair in a short purple bob, and always with a warm smile to offer.

"I'll trade you," she said, indicating the little girl she had dropped off. "My daughter Hanee wants to study up on Betazoids for her project. She's fixated on the idea that your people run around naked all the time."

"Not *all* the time," said Troi, and as she spoke she sensed a background note of frustration in the other woman. It was a rare emotion to find in as good-natured a species as Phosia's. "How are things with you?"

The other woman gave a shrug. "Is it that obvious?" Phosia was in charge of the team assigned to making sure the needs of their Jazari visitors were all taken care of, and she explained that as much as she tried, the guests wouldn't let her. "Every day it's the same thing. I go to the quarters we assigned to them and meet someone in the anteroom. I ask them if they need anything. They tell me they don't. I ask if everything's fine. They say it is. I offer them a tour of the ship, some holodeck time, or a dinner with the command staff. They say *thank you but no, thank you*. And repeat."

"They haven't come out since we picked them up at Vega," noted Troi. "Perhaps the Jazari have a very high threshold for boredom."

"They're not even eating," said Phosia. "Or at least, not our food. None of the replicators in their rooms have been activated. I think they brought their own supplies."

"I suppose they could be stargazing."

"They're reading, I think. We can't exactly spy on them, but we've seen some use in the computer system, calls for database information, but nothing that isn't on the interstellar public record. Other than that . . ." Phosia made a vague motion with her hand. "Commander, I was seriously thinking about asking Captain Riker if I can offer them a spin in his chair. Anything to try and tempt them out of there."

"Don't take it personally. You only had a week. Federation ambassadors have been trying to get them to open up for decades."

"They're distant, but they're just so *pleasant* about it," said Phosia. "They're like Vulcans, if you replaced the philosophy of logic with one of . . . politeness." She exhaled, in a little gasp of exasperation. "I guess it doesn't matter now. They'll all be off the ship by day's end and that'll be that. I suppose it's a better class of problem to have, when you think of certain other diplomatic missions we've been involved in."

Troi sighed deeply. "No one is going to forget the Pakled delegation's visit in a hurry."

"Yes." Phosia frowned. "I confess, I don't understand how a species that achieved space travel couldn't grasp the basics of a rudimentary waste-management system."

A two-tone bosun's whistle sounded, cutting through their conversation. *"Commander Troi, report to the captain's ready room."* The crisp diction of *Titan's* Izarian first officer, Commander Christine Vale, sounded around them. *"Commander Troi to the ready room."*

"Duty calls," said Troi, and tapped her communicator to affirm she was on her way. She took a step toward the turbolift, and a thought occurred to her. She called after Phosia. "If in doubt, you could try offering the

Jazari a chance to sample the chocolate desserts up in the ship's lounge. Who could say no to that?"

Phosia chuckled. "If that doesn't work, then they truly are a species like none we have ever encountered."

Riker leaned forward, absently running his fingers through his beard. He'd been letting it develop, growing it a little longer these days, flouting the grooming regulations. Partly because he liked the way it framed his face, and partly because it gave him something to do while he was thinking.

"Chris, what are we seeing here?" He gestured at the holographic panel hanging in the air above his ready room's desk, like an untethered window into a dark sky.

"You already know the answer to that, sir." His exec stood on the far side of the desk, her slender arms folded across her chest. That hawkish look in Christine Vale's eyes gave her a severe air, the same no-nonsense glare that must have served her well in her original career in planetside law enforcement.

Vale was a fast-moving officer rising up through Starfleet security and into the command track, and Riker had selected her for the post of *Titan*'s first officer soon after getting his captaincy. He'd had to work to persuade her to take the role, a fact that, if anything, had convinced him she was the right one for the job. Vale would make an excellent captain herself one day, but she was determined to put the work in and earn it by merit. That was fine with Riker. Any officer who went for the shortcuts wasn't someone he wanted on his bridge crew.

"I'd like to hear you say it," Riker told her. "Humor me, Number One."

Vale reached a hand toward the hologram, her fingertips registering with the gestural interface, and made a widening motion. The image grew, focusing on a metallic green blob in the corner of the frame. The holo refocused and reframed, the blob gaining definition until it was visible as a sickle-like curve, blurred by motion.

"Romulan," said Vale, without equivocation. "A *Mogai*-class warbird. I'd hazard a guess and say a Type-1 variant."

"Clear as day," Riker agreed. "More or less. And that in itself is unusual."

"Long-range sensors picked her up twenty light-minutes past their side of the Neutral Zone border. Cruising close, but not uncommonly so." Vale prodded a virtual tab and a tactical graphic of the sector replaced the image, along with a digital model of the Romulan ship. Fully revealed, it was a slender and deadly raptor, easily the mass equivalent of the *Titan*.

"Nothing unusual about a Romulan ship in Romulan space doing Romulan things," said Riker. "But letting us see them from our side of the fence? That's not typical." The ready room's entry chime sounded and he called out, "Come on in."

As the door hissed open and his wife entered, Vale threw her a nod and carried on her train of thought. "This warbird dropped its cloak when we were well within detection distance. It executed a sublight course correction around a brown dwarf star and then we lost it."

"They cloaked again," said Troi. "But they wanted us to know they are there."

"We're sure it couldn't have been some other reason?" Riker threw out the question. "System malfunction? Interference from the dwarf star?"

"Romulans don't make mistakes like that." Vale glanced at Troi for confirmation.

Riker's wife knew the Romulan character better than anyone in the room. She'd even lived as one of them for a brief period, taking on the identity of one of their Tal Shiar intelligence operatives during a clandestine mission behind enemy lines. "They're sending a message. *We're watching you.*"

"Watching us, watching them, watching us . . ." The captain frowned. "Nothing changes."

"With all due respect, Captain, that's not so." Vale took a breath. "The Romulans have always had ten agendas going at once, but now it's largely about one thing. The supernova. The clock that's ticking down on them."

"You're right," noted Riker. "It's an easy trap to fall into old thinking.

Five years ago, that warbird would have been out here patrolling the border, showing the Romulan flag. Now they're just as likely to be doing survey missions, looking for worlds they can send their refugees to before their star explodes."

The three of them fell silent for a moment, each considering the tactical map, but each of them thinking troubled thoughts.

A year ago, Starfleet's decision to withdraw from the Romulan rescue initiative had turned what was already a complex and fragile relationship into something far worse. Any hope of rapprochement seemed impossible to conceive of, but back in the core worlds of the Federation that matter was less important than everything else that was going on.

A year ago, a brutal and still unexplained attack by rogue synthetic worker androids at Mars's orbital shipyard complex had set that planet's sky ablaze. Dozens of vessels built to aid in the rescue mission had burned in their docks, perishing along with many people gathered from across the quadrant to work on them.

The shockwave from the attack resonated across the Federation, followed by the near-immediate ban on the construction of all synthetic life within its bounds. All practical research into artificial intelligence and android development was corralled, with only the theoretical still permitted, and even that was done under close scrutiny. It was a sweeping edict, echoing a similar choice made centuries earlier when the science of genetic manipulation had been decried.

The Federation and Starfleet had turned their gaze inward. Internal political schisms, many exacerbated by what some considered undue attention being diverted to the well-being of an old and bitter enemy, threatened the stability of the UFP. In the wake of the attack, Romulus was left to fend for itself, and out here on the fringes, the fracturing of the old order was already starting to make itself known. The minor interstellar powers, the criminal factions, and the smaller-scale threat forces were slowly realizing that Starfleet's presence was no longer great enough to stop them indulging their own ambitions.

As for the rogue synthetics, what had motivated them to commit such an atrocity was still unknown. No claim of responsibility had come, no manifesto delivered or threat of further attack made. All of the worker androids that had been at the Utopia Planitia yards were obliterated in the destruction they wrought.

At first, some in Starfleet thought it was the precursor to an invasion of the Federation—a ploy of the Dominion's shapeshifting Founders as retaliation for their enforced surrender, others bringing up the dire menace of the Borg Collective as a possible aggressor. But their predictions had not come to pass, and no one had made war on the Federation.

Some believed that the attack was actually directed toward the Romulans, in order to deny them any assistance in the face of their imminent disaster. The accusations flew, blaming the Klingon Empire, the Cardassian Union, and even clandestine elements within the Federation itself.

Or perhaps it was that the synthetics had decided to wreak this destruction on their creators. But it was hard for Riker to damn an entire form of life based on the actions of a few rogue elements, as horrific as they were.

As he often did when this matter came to mind, he thought of his friend Data and of Data's errant brother, Lore. The two androids as both sides of the same coin, one striving to know himself, the other consumed by darker motivations.

What would Data say if he were here to see this? Riker wondered. He imagined the android there in the room with them, cocking his head in that curious manner as his positronic mind analyzed the problem. Data's counsel would have been greatly appreciated.

There had been so many strong emotions in the days after the attack, but what stuck with Riker the most was the conversation he and his wife had with Thaddeus, as they tried to explain it all to the boy. He'd softened what he could of the terrible reality, but both parents knew they couldn't just ignore it. Thad's friends and teachers were talking about the events, and he was very perceptive for his age. Riker hated how he had been forced to steal a little of his boy's innocence too early because of all this, but to lie to him had never been an option.

That night, the three of them had lain in the dark and held one another, and Riker had not slept. For the first time in his life, he was caught by a true fear for the future his son would grow up in.

"Maybe we're coming at this the wrong way," said Troi, the melody of his wife's voice bringing him back to the moment. "Let's think of this as an invitation. We could hail them, offer them any assistance they might require on their mission."

Vale made an odd noise, like something had caught in her throat, and Troi shot her a look.

"Don't laugh, Commander. I'm serious."

"Wow, you really are." Vale raised an eyebrow. "Well, good luck with that. Let me know how it goes." Her tone made it abundantly clear how much confidence the first officer had in the willingness of the Romulans to converse with them.

Riker pressed a tab on the surface of his desk and the holograph vanished. "In practical terms, is this going to impact our mission?"

"Negative, Captain," said Vale. "But just to be sure, I've asked Lieutenant Commander Keru to increase sensor sweeps and maintain a higher operational tempo for the time being." The unjoined Trill served as *Titan*'s senior tactical officer, and Riker had come to consider him as one of the best in his crew. "If a cosmozoan so much as coughs three sectors away, we'll know about it," added the exec.

"Deanna." Riker turned to his wife. "Let's keep the circle small on this. We don't need to inform the Jazari unless it becomes an issue."

"I agree. They've practically been in seclusion all through this voyage, and I don't think we need to give them another reason to hide under the bed."

Vale blinked. "They don't actually do that, do they?"

"Your guess is as good as mine, Commander," said Troi. "But whatever they're doing in their quarters, it's quiet."

"It's suspicious," Vale corrected, her eyes narrowing. "I know it's my old peace-officer training talking, but someone making that little noise for that long has to be up to something."

"We can ask them on the way to the hangar bay," said Riker, glancing at his wife. "So, by my estimation *Titan* is about five minutes away from dropping out of warp at our designated intercept point. We're all prepped and ready to go?"

Troi nodded. In addition to her work as senior ship's counselor, she also maintained the post of senior diplomatic liaison, but with all the so-called reframing of Starfleet's mission going on, she played that role less and less, for the most part leaving it in Lieutenant Commander Phosia's capable hands. "Two shuttles are standing by in the main landing bay, the *Coltrane* and the *Holiday*. Engineering has rigged them to operate remotely from the bridge, so they can be piloted by instruments and use only the most basic sensors."

"A lot of work just for a taxi flight," said Vale.

"Well, we can't send them through our transporters; you've read the file," noted Riker.

"Yes, sir, I've read it," said the exec. "All two paragraphs of it."

Among the Jazari's rules of privacy was a moratorium on the use of any matter-energy transportation systems, which they claimed were fatal to their physiology. They were also touchy about allowing any of *their* shuttlecraft to put down on board a vessel like the *Titan*.

"Look on the bright side," said Riker as he rose from his chair. "When we're done here, we all get to file reports back to Starfleet Command that will read *Nothing Interesting Happened Today*."

The words had barely left his mouth when the intercom whistle sounded. He tapped the panel on his desk again.

"Riker here."

"Captain? Good day to you."

Riker's eyes widened. "Ambassador Veyen?" The last voice he expected to hear was that of the Jazari delegation's most senior diplomat, and he was briefly wrong-footed. "Hello, yes. Good day."

To one side, Troi gave him a wry smirk. "You jinxed it," she whispered.

"Your computer system has routed my inquiry to your office. I hope that is not an imposition."

Riker ignored his wife's comment. "Not at all, sir. Is there something I can help you with?"

"I wanted to inform you that we have dispatched a representative to converse directly with you about matters of transit and such. Please think of him as my proxy. I humbly request that you consider his requests to be made with the same authority as any of mine."

"As you wish," said Riker, after a moment. "Can I ask why—?"

The ready room's door chime sounded, interrupting him, and Veyen spoke once again before closing the intercom channel. *"That will be him now. Farewell."*

"Okay, then . . ." The captain tugged his uniform tunic straight and exchanged a look with his officers before calling out. "Come in."

The door hissed open and a humanoid in a Starfleet uniform with sky-blue trim entered. Like most Jazari, Lieutenant Zade was of average height and build, but thin in the limbs, giving him a skinny, almost gaunt quality.

His species were of a reptilian nature, with flesh tones ranging from the lieutenant's light green to dark emerald. Jazari were scaly and sported wispy feathery growths where humans had hair, along with tiny hornlike protrusions along the brow and neckline. Riker recalled that *Titan*'s chief of security had described them as "like a Jem'Hadar with all the angry taken out," and there was a superficial resemblance, but beyond that the character of the two races could not have been more different.

Zade fixed Riker with his wide, yellow eyes and came to attention. "Captain. Reporting as requested." He held a padd in one hand, clutching it tightly at his side.

"I made no such request, Lieutenant," said Riker.

"Not you, sir. Requested by my people." Zade's voice had a slightly nasal register.

Across the room, Vale was looking toward the ready room's window. "We're dropping out of warp, right on schedule."

Riker sensed the state change in *Titan*'s ubiquitous background hum as the distorted starlight outside collapsed back into normality.

"Ambassador Veyen asked me to take on this duty," continued Zade. "It was felt that as I had served aboard the *Titan* for an extended period of time, and I am therefore the most familiar to you, I should be the one to explain the circumstances."

"What circumstances?" said Vale.

Zade gestured to the ready room door. "If you will all accompany me to the bridge? Everything will be made clear."

Troi frowned. "You spoke with the ambassador? I wasn't aware the delegation had any visitors."

"He communicated his intentions to me," Zade replied, and didn't elaborate further. "Please, if you will?"

Warily, Riker followed the Jazari back out onto *Titan*'s command deck, with Troi and Vale close behind. Zade walked across to the main viewscreen, passing in front of the conn and ops consoles, where the helm officer and navigator both gave him a questioning look.

Vale spoke quietly at Riker's side. "Suspicious," she repeated.

"Commander, please be assured there is no need to be apprehensive." Zade was on the other side of the bridge, but he addressed Vale as if she had spoken directly to him.

"Good hearing," noted Troi.

"Yes, it is exceptional," said Zade.

In the middle of the bridge, Ranul Keru stood up from his temporary place in the command chair. "Captain, I was just about to signal you." He jutted his chin toward the screen. "Passive sensors are getting some strange readings."

"It is nothing to be alarmed about," said Zade.

"I'll be the judge of that." Riker was not enjoying the sense that the Jazari was leading them around by the nose. He glanced at Keru. "Report."

"The scans we have on record for the local planetary body, well, they don't match up, sir." Keru pointed at the screen. "Take a look and you'll see what I mean."

Riker stood in the center of the bridge and studied the view. Lit by the glow of a distant yellow star, a J-class gas giant striped with lines of dusky red and orange filled the majority of the view, and in orbit around it was the mottled globe of the Jazari homeworld. In the scant few images he had seen of it from Starfleet's files, the moon was rust red in shade, reminiscent of Mars or Vulcan; or, at least, it had been when those images were captured. Now it was a dead, ashen gray and streaked with dark outlines.

"Magnify that," he ordered. "Is it me, or does it seem . . . smaller?"

"It's not just you," said Keru. "Optical measurement shows nearly a ten percent reduction in planetary mass."

The pallid world grew larger and now Riker saw that the streaks were in fact kilometers-deep trenches sliced into its surface. Huge, continent-sized swaths of land had been cut out, leaving massive open-pit gouges in the landscape, valleys that went all the way down into the outer mantle beneath. The atmosphere seemed thin and insubstantial, and certainly incapable of supporting life. In addition, where the Starfleet logs had shown the glowing towers of Jazari arcology cities, there was nothing but bare rock. The sliver of the moon's visible nightside was an arc of blackness, showing no lights of any kind. The whole planet appeared as if it had been dipped in acid.

"No life signs down there," noted Keru. "No energy readings. It's been abandoned."

"What happened here?" said Vale, horrified by the transformation. "Who did this to you?"

Zade cocked his head. "I think you misunderstand, Commander. The alteration of my planet is not the result of any outside forces. *We* did this. The Jazari."

"Why?" Riker was aghast. A perfectly livable world had apparently been cut open and cored. That an intelligent species would do this to their birthplace was beyond him.

"In order to complete the work." Zade gestured at the screen. "We should be within detection range now."

Vale was at her station, peering at a console. "Captain, we're reading a massive object approximately zero point four light-minutes from our current location, along the plane of the ecliptic. It's an artificial construct, sir."

"A space station?"

"A ship," corrected Zade. "The Jazari have given up everything to build it. Our vessels, our cities, our world."

"Let's see it . . ." Riker gave a nod toward the helm, and *Titan's* viewscreen changed aspect, moving up and over the gas giant.

It was impossible to miss the craft. Space made it hard to gauge the size of the thing at first glance, but as they slowly approached, the scale grew clearer.

Beginning in conical prow as big as a mountain, a long cylindrical hull extended back for kilometers until it bifurcated into two shorter elements, giving the whole gargantuan construct a shape like a tuning fork. Nestled in the space between the two aft "tines" was an ovoid module bright with internal lights. The craft dwarfed the biggest vessels of Starfleet's inventory, its diameter large enough to swallow the great spindle of Starbase One's Spacedock; against it, *Titan* was a minnow alongside a whale.

In close formation around the great ship there were free-floating platforms, some lit by the lightning flicker of lasers. Riker could pick out the denuded hulls of Jazari-design starships within them, each of the smaller vessels stripped and gutted just like the planet.

"Those are the last few deconstructions," said Zade, noting the captain's interest. "They have been disassembled into their component parts, to be stored or repurposed for use in the ship."

A stream of smaller craft were passing through an open bay in the big vessel's flank, hundreds of them moving in a steady train. Coming ever closer, Riker saw glassy environment domes in the side of the giant, with glimpses of dark desert sands visible in some, lush greenery in others.

"What's the purpose of all this?" He had to tear himself away from the incredible sight.

"Departure," said the lieutenant. "The great ship is in the final stages of preparation for exodus. All Jazari have gathered to complete the work, and you have brought the last of my kind home, Captain." He bowed slightly to Riker. "I want to thank you personally, sir. You and the crew of the *Titan*. You have been good to me."

Zade offered the padd he had been holding to Troi, who took it. "What is this?"

"A message from the Jazari Governing Sept for the Federation Council, explaining what is about to happen," he said. "If you could please deliver that to them, it would be greatly appreciated." Zade reached up, and delicately removed the arrowhead combadge from his breast and the rank pips from his tunic. "You will also find the formal notice of my resignation from Starfleet, effective as of this stardate." With care, he placed the items on top of the helm console. He was silent for a moment as the bridge crew took in the import of his statement; then he continued, his manner briefly becoming less formal. "Sir, it has been my honor to serve on board this vessel. The conduct of *Titan* and her crew is precisely why my people chose to have you carry back the last of us."

A chime sounded and Keru glanced at his panel. "Message from shuttle-bay one," he said. "The Jazari delegation has assembled and they're ready to disembark."

"By your leave, Captain Riker," said Zade, "I will join them."

Riker was momentarily lost for a reply. It was within his power to refuse the lieutenant's resignation, but what value would that serve?

"Exodus." Troi echoed the word. "That term has weight, Mister Zade. It speaks to the migration of an entire population. Is that what is happening here?"

Zade looked down. "It is."

"But why are you doing this?" Vale frowned, unable to grasp the scope of it. "Where are you going to go?"

"Do not be concerned, Commander." Zade moved toward the turbo-lift. "This quadrant, these stars . . . They are no longer a place where my people feel welcome."

THREE

Troi took her seat in the *Titan*'s midbridge, her attention split between the words on the padd that Zade had given her and the activity all around.

Over the intercom, she heard Lieutenant Commander East report in from the shuttlebay. *"Security here. Shuttles are away. The Jazari are officially off the ship."*

"Understood." Vale leaned against her console, and Troi could sense she was too tightly wound to sit down. "Jonathan, take a team and do a sweep of the quarters they vacated. Just for the sake of thoroughness."

The Irish security chief gave a low chuckle. *"Already under way, sir. You'll be the first to know if anything irregular comes up."* Troi had often noted that East and Vale had a similar mindset when it came to matters of shipboard security, even if by her reckoning they veered a little too much toward the paranoid.

"Steady as she goes," said her husband. Riker stood behind the flight control and operations consoles on the lower bridge, watching the bright dots of the smaller craft zoom away in perfect formation.

"All systems nominal, Captain." Lieutenant Cantua kept her eyes on her panel, and the Denobulan helmswoman's thick fingers moved deftly across the slaved controls from the two shuttles.

"Hold us at station-keeping, Mister Westerguard." The captain gave the nod to the young, ochre-skinned human at the operations manager post. Westerguard was a recent transfer from another ship, and was as eager to perform well as he was nervous.

"Aye, sir," said the ops manager. "Holding at this marker."

Troi paged through the padd's contents, frowning as she read on, then she paused to check something in the Starfleet database. She could feel Ranul Keru watching her from the nearby tactical station.

"I can't believe Zade just quit like that," the Trill said quietly, offering the thought to the air. "He never said anything."

"You knew him socially?" said Vale.

"We got on okay. He played a few hands of tongo with our regular Friday-night card game. He never seemed that into it." Keru sighed. "But you would think he might have mentioned something about resigning."

"I get the feeling this is much bigger than we know," said Vale.

"Zade wasn't alone in what he's done." Troi nodded to herself as the data from Starfleet confirmed what she had suspected. "According to this, there were six Jazari officers on active service in the fleet, and every last one of them has resigned their commission in the last two months."

"No one picked up on that?" said Vale.

"I suppose it wasn't deemed important," she replied. "They all left under amicable circumstances."

A tone sounded from the science station across the bridge, and all eyes turned toward the alcove where Lieutenant Commander Livnah stood. *Titan's* senior science officer was a tall, ash-white humanoid woman from a nomadic species, long limbed and willowy, possessing a fierce intellect. She habitually wore an aural relay module in one ear, accenting the black tattoos down her face, and now she toyed with it, listening as her console fed her raw data. "I detect energetic discharges in the vicinity of that Jazari behemoth. A lot of power they're putting out."

"Any hazard to us?" Riker took a step toward the science station.

"Not at current range or magnitude," said Livnah.

"I thought we're not supposed to be scanning them?" said a terse English voice. On the opposite side of the command deck, Chief Engineer Karen McCreedy pushed a wisp of hair out of her eyes and adjusted her spectacles, using them as additional data readouts along with her console. "Isn't that one of their privacy guidelines?"

"No rules are being broken, Lieutenant Commander." Livnah's reply was stiff and haughty, as if the engineer were somehow impugning her conduct. "Passive sensors are in effect only, but with the noise the Jazari are generating, it's hard not to hear."

"Confirming the science officer's readings, sir," added Cantua, her heavy brow furrowing. "I'm getting interference on subspace bands with the shuttle control signal. I'm compensating, but it's definitely there."

"Do we need to recall our boats?" said the captain.

"No, sir, I've got it," said Cantua. "As long as it doesn't get any thicker . . ."

McCreedy mirrored Livnah's reading to her own station. "That energy pattern, it's a phased-tetryon waveform." Troi sensed the engineer's immediate apprehension. "That's potent stuff, Captain. A ship of that mass using a tetryon matrix as a power supply . . ." She trailed off for a moment. "I wouldn't want to try it!"

"They've built a generation ship," said Troi, the term coming to her from a half-recalled lecture during her days at Starfleet Academy. "A giant colony vessel, designed to seek out a new world and populate it." She held up a padd. "According to the message from the Jazari, they are forsaking their home planet and Federation space, and they intend to make a voyage to the far side of our galaxy." It was an unimaginable distance, and she found it hard to hold the idea in her mind.

"Even at high sustained warp, that would take hundreds of years," said McCreedy.

"My people's first interstellar explorers had their crews sleep in suspended animation," noted Livnah. "The Jazari may intend the same. Their population is small, a few million individuals at most."

"It's their world and their species," said the captain. "And it's their right to go wherever they want." He shook his head. "It just seems like such a wasted opportunity. We've never really been able to learn anything about the Jazari, to *know* them. And now we never will."

"Shuttles are docked with the main ship," reported Cantua. "Passengers are disembarking."

"Counselor, do they say why they're leaving?" Westerguard cast a quick look back over his shoulder. "I mean, they must have a pretty strong reason to gather up their whole population and light out for the deep sky."

"Do they know something we don't?" Vale added darkly.

Troi read aloud from the statement from the Jazari Governing Sept. "*We no longer wish to be a small domain amid larger galactic powers, whose manner grows increasingly hawkish and insular as time passes. There is no place for us here.*"

"What is that supposed to mean?" Vale's tone was immediately defensive. "They're judging the Federation for being guarded about our own interests? For protecting ourselves? They could have been part of that if they wanted to. They chose to stand separately from us."

"I think that's the point, Number One," said the captain. "The Jazari have always charted their own path and they believe that course and ours no longer intersect." He met Troi's gaze. In the privacy of their quarters, both of them had quietly shared similar thoughts about the changes affecting their society. "Starfleet and the Federation have had to make a lot of hard choices over the past couple of years," continued Riker. "I believe wholeheartedly in the ideal of the United Federation of Planets, and I know everyone on this ship feels the same. But we're moving in a direction that could take us away from our core beliefs, if we don't keep an eye on the winds that are pushing our sails."

The bridge fell silent, save for the soft beeps and chimes of the control panels. Riker had everyone's attention, his words coming from a place of honesty and sincerity. But his wife was the only one who heard the regret that marbled them.

He went on. "I believe we'll course-correct, in time. The Federation and Starfleet have a duty to everyone who lives under our aegis, whatever world they come from, whatever species they are. But that's never been the sum of it. We are also dedicated to reaching beyond the boundaries of what we know. Our first, best impulse should always be to hold out the hand of friendship. Not close our doors and bar the gates." He indicated the huge alien ship on the main screen. "The Jazari see us doing that, and for now they're right. And if they don't want to wait around until things change, then we bid them farewell and hope to meet again one day."

"No one wants to be where we are right now," said Vale, after a moment. "But it's not like fate has given us much of a choice."

Troi nodded. "It's a pity we couldn't have this conversation with Zade's people. We might have convinced them to stay."

"I don't think that's likely," said Keru. "Look at that vessel they've built, and those ship-breaker platforms. Look at what they've done to their planet. The Jazari had to have been planning this for a long time. Like Commander Vale said, they've made their choice."

"Shuttles are clear," said Cantua. "I'm bringing them home."

Livnah's panel sounded a tone and she made a negative noise. Riker caught it immediately. "Something else, Commander?"

"Unclear," said the science officer, glaring at her console as if it were defying her in some way. "There's an intermittent radiation pattern centered on one of those . . . what did Keru call it? Ship-breakers. But I can't get a clear reading, not with passive sensors at this distance."

"Is this an effect from the tetryon matrix?" said Troi.

Livnah shook her head. "No, this is something else. It's delta-wave energy, coming in random pulses."

Everyone on the bridge hesitated at the mention of delta radiation. It was a particularly virulent form of energy that was lethal to almost all sentient life-forms.

"Captain? If I may?" Lieutenant Cantua raised a hand, as if she were a child in a classroom. Off a nod from her commander, she went on. "I could easily extend the return course of the shuttles by a few degrees, take them on a wider arc that would pass closer to that platform. The *Holiday* and the *Coltrane* are both running passive sensors, but they're closer—"

"I could tie their readings in with *Titan*'s," said Livnah, catching on. "That would work."

"And technically it wouldn't break the Jazari's privacy rules," added Keru.

"Proceed," said Riker. "But gently does it."

Out in the dark between the vessels, the *Holiday* and the *Coltrane* executed a leisurely turn that briefly brought them prow-on toward the nearby Jazari dock platform. The unoccupied shuttles moved in perfect synchrony, their automated systems keeping the craft in close formation, as onboard computers channeled the readings from their sensors back over subspace to the *Titan*. For a moment, the auxiliary craft became substitute probes, taking in all the readings they could from their closer proximity to the ship-breaker.

The information streaming back showed the delta-wave output with damning clarity. Whatever was happening aboard the Jazari dock, the lethal radiation was growing in intensity, coming in jagged, irregular pulses.

Inside the empty cabins of the shuttles, red caution indicators blinked on screens and warning tones began to sound as alert subroutines activated.

Livnah's dark eyes widened as she watched the telemetry from the shuttles overlap with the readings gleaned from *Titan*'s passive sensor grid. "Mc-Creedy," she snapped, shooting a look across the bridge at the engineer. "Are you seeing this?"

"Bloody hell." The other woman cursed quietly as she read off the same data. "Confirming, a massive d-wave buildup on the breaker platform. What are they doing out there?"

"Captain, I think we're seeing an accident in progress." Livnah stared at the rising numbers on her screen. "Strongly advise we raise deflectors *now*!"

Riker didn't hesitate. "Shields up, yellow alert!"

"Can we reach the Jazari?" Vale looked to Counselor Troi, indicating the communications panel at her side.

But the message would never be sent. "Something's happening . . ." Westerguard pointed at the viewscreen, where a mote of brilliant, searing green-white light had appeared amid the skeletal frame of one of the Jazari spacedocks.

As the lieutenant spoke, the numbers on Livnah's panel suddenly spiked, far beyond the red line into the critical region, and a human epithet she had learned in her cadet days fell from her pale lips. "*Oh, shit.*"

Then the light came and hit them like a hammer.

Starship warp drives were intricate and complex systems that operated at a level where the laws of physics became fluid and malleable. Devices built to project into the fringes of spacetime, where dimensional membranes were at their thinnest, where energies of catastrophic scale collided, barely held these forces in check so that star-faring races could travel across the void in days rather than millennia.

So when those systems malfunctioned, it was rarely without ruinous results. Ships could be consumed whole in matter-antimatter reactions, dragged across event horizons into lethal subspace domains, or obliterated by the brief incursion of forces that should not have existed in this reality.

Inside the Jazari ship-breaker platform designated as Reclaim Zero Four, the last work on deconstructing a cargo sled's warp nacelles was under way. But a previously undetected anomaly in the artificial singularity that powered the sled was cascading, outpacing the ability of Zero Four's crew to damp it down.

Before they could stop it, the singularity tore free of its restraints, releasing an initial blast of subspace energy that rippled through the sled, the platform, and out into the vacuum.

The shockwave expanded outward in a perfect sphere of crackling emerald lightning, striking the *Holiday* a split second before hitting the *Coltrane*. The energy tore into *Titan*'s unprotected shuttles, overloading the onboard systems. *Holiday* spun out of control, colliding with its sister craft, and both vessels were lost as their micro–warp cores exploded.

The wave slammed into the Jazari generation ship with enough force to rock the mammoth craft like a sailing ship in a heavy swell, causing thousands of system failures across the entire length of the kilometers-long starboard side. Then milliseconds later *Titan* took its brunt, and the Starfleet ship's spaceframe rang like a struck bell.

There was a giddy moment when *Titan*'s synthetic gravity envelope went away and everything on the bridge gave a sickening lurch.

Riker felt himself leave the deck, saw the overhead racing to meet him with frightening speed. Then the gravity came back and he dropped hard. He fell into a painful stumble and caught himself on the engineering console, finding McCreedy clinging to the edge of it for dear life.

"Hold fast, Karen," he told her.

"Aye, sir," she managed, wide-eyed behind her glasses.

Riker had still been half-dazzled by the flash of light when the shockwave had hit the ship and spent itself again the shields. Had Livnah's warning been a few moments later, they wouldn't have been ready to take the blow on the chin, and he dreaded to think of what might have happened.

"Damage report!" Across the bridge, Vale was picking herself up, snapping out the command as she rose, her voice carrying over the alert sirens.

Riker fought down the impulse to go to his wife's side, and silenced the immediate worry for his son. Troi gave him an *I'm okay* look, and he knew she was thinking the same thing. But Thaddeus Riker was just one person on a ship of over three hundred and fifty souls, and every single one of them was his personal responsibility.

"Shields are down to twenty-three percent," said Keru, unable to keep a growl from his voice. "All decks reporting in . . . No hull breaches."

"I have red flags on a dozen subsystems," said McCreedy. "Damage-control parties are being deployed."

"The shuttles . . ." Cantua's words were thick with shock. "Sir, both shuttles have been destroyed!"

"Let's be grateful they were on remote," Riker noted. "Cut those sirens, I can't hear myself think!" He glanced around as the noise abated. "Livnah, what hit us?"

"A high-order subspace wave," said the science officer. "Emission point corresponds with the location of the ship-breaker platform."

"It's still there?" Westerguard peered at the screen and found the shimmering gem of warped light. "How is that possible?"

"Unknown. I need to analyze the energy signature," continued Livnah. "Give me a few moments . . ." She bent over her panel, the black lines on her face twisting as she scowled at the readout.

"What about the generation ship?" Riker moved back to the lower bridge, wincing as he put his weight on the ankle he had twisted in his fall.

"I can't read much without an active scan . . ." began Cantua.

"Do your best," he told her.

The Denobulan worked her panel. "I'm showing an eighteen-degree displacement from her previous position. Surface damage visible." She paled. "Captain, I think they might have lost some of their smaller craft in the shock."

Riker turned back toward his wife. "Deanna, hail the Jazari. Ask their status and offer help if they need it."

She gave a nod and opened a communications channel. "Jazari generation ship, this is the U.S.S. Titan. We have suffered damage from . . . from the shockwave, but we are still intact. Titan stands ready to assist, if you require it. What is your situation? Please respond."

He expected that Deanna would need to repeat the message more than once, imagining that the Jazari would be dealing with their own aftermath of the chaos, but their reply was almost instantaneous—and given the situation, disturbingly even toned.

"*Good day,* U.S.S. Titan. *Your offer of assistance is appreciated but not required.*"

"They've closed the channel," said Troi.

Vale stepped closer, speaking in low, urgent tones. "If they don't want our help, I advise we back off, sir. Get out of range of that shock effect."

But Riker couldn't pull his scrutiny from the brightly burning ember on the main viewer, where the ship-breaker station floated in a cage of viridian lightning. Serrated arcs of unchecked energy lashed at the grid work of the spacedock with wild violence.

"They might be telling us they don't need any help," he said, "but I'm pretty damned sure whoever is on that rig right now doesn't feel the same way."

Tarsin's eyes went through an adaptation cycle so that he could manage amid the dazzling light-blaze of the deconstruction bay. He had already sloughed down to dermal baseline while working in Reclaim Zero Four, but even now he felt the seething radiation prickling at his epidermis, threatening to penetrate deeper into his body.

He could sense another displacement shock building, and the deck beneath him trembled. They were fast running out of options.

"We need to get away from here." Sabem had to physically vocalize the statement at great volume just to be heard over the roaring of the energetic discharges.

Tarsin found the other reclaimator engineer on the gantry above him, signaling urgently. "Where are the others?"

"Assembling for egress, if possible. We need to join them if we hope to survive this. Remaining here means certain termination!"

"Assent," Tarsin called back. "But there is no guarantee egress will be possible. Please review the progression of the damage."

Sabem blinked as he took in the data. "That is troubling."

Now both of them understood. Leaving the transport sled's damaged singularity module to continue to fracture would not only lead to the eventual destruction of Reclaim Zero Four, it was possible it would birth a far larger field effect that would become self-sustaining.

"What do you propose?" shouted Sabem.

"I will enter the deconstruction bay and attempt to seal the fracture."

Sabem grasped the plan immediately. "The muon projector." Inside the bay, among the many tools that the Jazari reclaimator crew used to deconstruct their ships for the grand project, was a particle generator. In theory, a sustained beam from the device might have the effect of reversing the fracturing effect, but the percentage chance of success was marginal at best.

Sabem did not need to communicate this, but still he did. They were friends and coworkers, after all, and Sabem had no wish to see Tarsin's existence come to an unplanned end.

"You must remain outside the bay to monitor radiation levels," Tarsin told him, ignoring the warning. "I am entering now."

"Your termination would be unfortunate," said Sabem as Tarsin passed into the airlock. "I would prefer you continue to exist."

"As would I." Tarsin's vocalized reply began to fade as the atmosphere drained from the chamber. "But these circumstances do not account for our wishes." He wanted to say more to his friend, but there was no medium in place to carry the sound of his voice, and the radiation was too strong for any other form of communication. Instead, he gave a wave of farewell and walked out into the airless space beyond.

The force fields enveloping the deconstruction bay had collapsed in the first few seconds of the accident, the decompression effect blowing six engineers out into the darkness. Tarsin was unable to determine if any of them had survived. The airless vacuum was relatively easy to deal with, but the first pulse shock would have had a terminal effect on any unprotected Jazari bodies.

He had seen the two Starfleet shuttlecraft explode and known then that this was a far more serious problem than first believed. It was going to cost his life too, he determined, but if that was so, he needed to make the sacrifice a worthwhile one.

Tarsin found the muon projector in its charging rack, still intact and ready to operate. Gathering it up, he moved out from behind one of the blast barriers and into the full and unimpeded force of the delta-radiation source. His skin began to cook off his face and arms, searing and cracking, blackening into ashy flakes that drifted about him in a cloud. He concentrated on the deed, forcing himself to block out the catastrophic waves of pain that screamed down his nerve endings.

It was an incredible effort to raise the projector. The radiation was cutting through him, into his internal structures and skeleton. He felt himself stiffening as the horrific emissions ruined the muscles and joints in his limbs. He was burning from the inside out, consumed by the nuclear fire.

Tarsin's eyes filled with light as they were dissolved by the delta energy, and he tried desperately to activate the muon device. But his hands would no longer work, and with a terrible dawning realization, the engineer understood that he had miscalculated. The next shock pulse was coming, building far faster than he'd expected, and the bow wave of precursor radiation was moving before it, slowly disintegrating him on a subatomic level.

Tarsin's body turned rigid as he perished, and he became a statue.

Sabem sensed the death of his friend and diverted the sorrow that came with it, collapsing the emotion, putting it away to deal with later. He studied Tarsin's frozen form through the thick, protective armor glass, allowing himself a fractional moment to dwell on the image of him.

There was no way for anyone on board the platform to stop the cascade effect from within, not now. They were out of time.

Sabem accepted that he too would soon perish, feeling the energy coming through the barrier, feeling it grow more powerful by the moment. There was only one possibility, one last act he could perform, and he hoped it would be enough.

The Jazari engineer left the compartment and began the short climb through the access crawlways to the communications tower on Reclaim Zero Four's uppermost surface, ignoring the calls from his crewmates as they begged him to gather with them.

Even with the adaptive filtering on *Titan*'s main viewscreen, Vale still had to raise a hand to shield her eyes as the bright light from the ship-breaker throbbed and intensified.

She had the horrible sense that she was staring at a bomb about to go off—a bomb that had already detonated once—and the commander's every instinct was screaming at her to pull *Titan* out of there.

The ship trembled around them, the lights of the bridge flickering alarmingly. Vale gave McCreedy a wary look.

"Gravitational distortion," explained the engineer. "Another pulse is building, and the magnitude is much higher than that first one."

"Shield status?" said the captain.

"Restoration in progress, but we blew some EPS relays, so it's slow getting it back up." McCreedy blew out a breath. "I can give you sixty, maybe seventy percent if we divert power from nonessential systems."

"Do it," ordered Riker.

"Captain." Vale stepped up to speak at his shoulder. "We might not be able to handle another hit. If we back off to a safe distance, we can regroup and let the Jazari deal with this."

"Look at that, Chris," Riker replied. "Do you think they're anywhere near *dealing* with it?"

They both knew the answer to that, but Vale's first instinct was to protect her ship and its crew. The more calculating part of her saw it in cold, precise terms: the Jazari were not Federation citizens, and they had refused *Titan*'s help. From any angle you viewed it, putting the starship in harm's way was an unwarranted gamble.

But another part of her was seeing it through Riker's eyes. What kind of person could stand back and watch others perish when there was a chance to do something about it?

"Captain." It was protocol to do so, but Deanna Troi rarely addressed her husband by his rank, not unless the situation was of grave importance. Vale and Riker turned to see her looking up from her console. "A subspace message is being transmitted from the ship-breaker station on all channels."

"Let's hear it," said Riker.

Troi tapped a panel and a garbled voice filled the air, riddled with screeching bursts of interference. *"This is Sabem of reclamation platform Zero Four."* The words had the precise diction common to all the Jazari. *"We are experiencing an ongoing critical damage event that exceeds our ability to contain it. To any craft receiving this signal, if you are able to render assistance to us, please approach."*

"That sounds like a mayday to me," snapped Riker. "Our obligation is crystal clear. Helm, take us in, all available power to the forward deflectors!"

"I guess that answers that," said Vale. "I hope we don't regret this."

"Yeah, me too," said the captain. "Deanna, inform all decks and divisions to secure for rescue operations. This is going to be choppy."

The deck rocked as *Titan* angled around in a sweeping turn, closing in on the ship-breaker. Vale grabbed her console for support, and felt the juddering vibration coming up through the framework. The closer they got, the shorter the gap between the gravity pulses became.

On the main viewscreen, she could see green flashes of discharge where the exotic particles radiating from the platform were interacting with the leading edge of the starship's deflector-shield bubble. It resembled atmospheric aurorae, but it was as lethal as it was spectacular.

"Captain, I think I understand what has happened here . . ." Livnah spoke up from her station. "It's not just a radiation leak. It's much worse than that." The closer they got, the more data the science officer had to work with, and Vale could see the concern writ large across her milk-pale face.

As with most of her highly practical species, Livnah was not one for unnecessary overstatement, something Vale had always liked about the woman. So as she explained the severity of the situation, the first officer knew it was an honest and clear-eyed evaluation.

"It appears that damage to an artificial singularity power source has caused a spatial scission inside the platform." Livnah pointed toward the ship-breaker. "As an analogy, imagine piercing the crust of a planet and striking a pocket of pressurized magma beneath. The resulting outburst is deadly."

"They tore a hole in subspace," hissed Westerguard. "And all that radiation on the other side is gushing through!"

"The lieutenant is correct," noted Livnah. "According to my readings, the fracture is unstable, and the dimensional aperture is varying wildly in size. But there is a good chance it will stabilize."

"And if that happens, we'll be in the clear?" said Keru.

"You misunderstand me, Lieutenant Commander," said Livnah. "If the fracture stabilizes, there will be a catastrophic inversion pulse and it will become a self-sustaining phenomenon. Anything caught in the pulse's radius will be torn apart and the fracture will remain open, bleeding other-dimensional radiation into this area at an incredible rate. Within days, this entire star system will be contaminated."

Vale felt the color drain from her face. "How long until that happens?"

"Minutes," said the other woman. "With each shock the fracture emits, it gains permanency—"

As if to underline her words, a new surge of energy flashed out into the darkness, slamming into the *Titan* and knocking them all off their stride.

"How do we close it?" said Troi.

Livnah gestured to McCreedy. "If I can have the chief engineer's assistance? Together, we may be able to come up with a solution."

McCreedy nodded. "Tell me what you need." It was no secret that *Titan*'s senior engineer and the science officer didn't play well together, but both women automatically put aside all of that in the face of a crisis.

Vale left them to it, turning back to the captain. "Sir, we need to warn the Jazari."

"Put me through to them," ordered Riker, taking a breath before launching in. "Jazari generation ship, this is Captain Riker of the *U.S.S. Titan*. We've analyzed the situation aboard your dock platform. You must remove all your vessels from this area immediately. I repeat, *immediately*. The gravitational shocks we are experiencing are the precursor events to a high-magnitude inversion pulse. It's imperative you leave now."

Once again, there was no delay in reply. *"That is not possible, Captain Riker. Regrettably, our great ship's main drive is not operational. It will take several hours to bring it online. At this moment we are . . . stranded."*

"Then evacuate whoever you can aboard whatever warp-capable craft you have!" insisted Vale. "In the meantime, we will attempt to assist your people on platform Zero Four!"

"Regrettably, all life functions of the reclaimator crew aboard that platform have now ceased," said the Jazari voice. *"We suggest you remove your vessel to a distance of one light-year from this location. We estimate our great ship will be able to survive the pulse effect with eleven percent functionality intact. Titan's survival percentage of the same incidence is calculated at zero."*

"We're not ready to give up yet," said Riker. "Stand by." He made a throat-cutting gesture and the comm channel was closed.

For long moments, no one spoke into the silence that followed the Jazari's candid estimation of *Titan*'s dire odds.

Then something the captain had said back in his ready room drifted to the front of Vale's thoughts. "So much for *Nothing Interesting Happened Today*."

Riker gave a nod. "Now all we need to do is survive long enough to make an interesting log entry."

• • •

The captain watched his officers work, and in those seconds he could only step back and stand in the eye of the storm, trusting wholly in his crew. There was absolutely no doubt in his mind that he had the right people on hand for this crisis, and Riker hoped that would be enough.

Throughout his career, aboard the *Pegasus*, the *Potemkin*, the *Hood*, more than one *Enterprise*, and now the *Titan*, Riker had served among exemplary Starfleet officers. Every challenge they faced, they met without fear, no matter how slim their chances might have been.

But now he felt the weight of command more keenly than he ever had before. *Is it because of Deanna and Thaddeus? Or is it something else?*

And then it came to him: *Was this how it had been for Picard?* Not just during the *Enterprise*'s missions, but when the Romulan crisis began? Knowing that they were about to put their all into a desperate gamble to save a civilization, with no guarantee that their endeavor would succeed.

But it had to be done. To turn away would be unacceptable. He pulled free of the thought, catching Deanna's eye. But before she could speak, Lieutenant Commander Livnah was addressing him.

"Sir, we have conceived an angle of approach for our problem. If I may proceed?"

"Lay it out," he told her.

"We can attempt to 'cap' the fracture using a static warp shell, projecting a field from the *Titan*'s engine nacelles." Livnah glanced in McCreedy's direction.

"It'll take every last spark of power we have, and then some," said the engineer.

Riker nodded. "Use whatever you need."

Livnah's hands danced across her panel as a new set of shocks thundered around them. "We're ready, sir."

Riker raised his hand and gave the order. "*Engage!*"

• • •

Spears of brilliant light flashed out from the starship and reached for the ship-breaker platform, enveloping it in a coruscating globe of energy.

Within it, the riotous nonmass of the fractured singularity seemed to tremble, momentarily shrinking back toward the rip in spacetime. The blinding spark of radiation dimmed, shimmered, diminished.

Every system aboard the *Titan* lost power as vital energy was rerouted. Heat, light, gravity, all of it faded to feed the warp shell, to constrict it ever tighter around the seething fire burning into this dimension from the depths of subspace. Degree by degree, the shell narrowed, forcing the fracture to contract.

On the far side of the tear, raw inchoate energy the like of which was found only in the heart of stars churned and seethed, seeking the point of least resistance. It had no intellect, no guiding force behind it, only the unchained power of brute physics to drive it on. Like lightning seeking the ground, like a wildfire spreading over tinder-dry land, it pushed back.

And it found a way through.

In the dimness of the darkened bridge, the only illumination came from the starscape outside and the glowing displays of the command consoles. Riker felt light in the reduced gravity, and his breath emerged in puffs of white vapor as the deep cold of space leached through the hull and into the ship.

He gripped the edge of his chair and his hand found Deanna's there, the two of them drawing strength from each other. "Status," he called. "Someone talk to me!"

"No . . ." muttered Livnah, but the refusal wasn't directed toward her captain. He heard it in her voice, the defiance and denial of what she was seeing on her panel. "No!"

"Captain, the warp shell . . ." McCreedy spoke as if she were uttering a death sentence. "It's collapsed."

Riker looked back to the viewscreen in time to see the energy beams projected from *Titan's* nacelles fade to nothing. The searing light at the heart of the wrecked spacedock bloomed with new force, leaving purple afterimages burned into his retinas.

"We don't have the power," said Livnah. "I'm so sorry, Captain, I thought we could do it. *Titan* is just not enough. We can't contain the fracture."

"Can we launch the rest of the shuttles, the captain's skiff, use them as well?" Keru threw out the demands. "Is there a Jazari ship close by that could help? Something!"

"No." McCreedy shook her head.

"Then we have to withdraw," said Vale. "There's nothing else we can do."

Riker stiffened, knowing that the failure was already a reality, hating the truth of it. He opened his mouth to give the command to disengage, but he couldn't form the words. He did not want to admit defeat.

A strident tone cut through his thoughts. "I have an incoming hail," said Troi. "From another ship . . ." She tapped a control, and a new voice issued out of the air.

"Attention platform Zero Four, we have received your emergency message and are approaching your coordinates, stand by."

"Who is that?" said Cantua. "A Starfleet vessel?"

"There are no other Starfleet vessels in this sector," said Vale, but her words were drowned out by a keening proximity alert.

"Captain!" At his station, Westerguard bolted upright in shock. "Off the starboard bow, got a ship dropping out of warp!"

Ahead of the *Titan*, the stars seemed to writhe and shimmer as a glassy shape appeared and took on solid form. It became a starship, a metallic-green raptor with sickle-like wings and bared talons, all sharp angles and danger.

"Attention," said the voice over the comm channel. *"This is Commander Medaka of the warbird* Othrys. *My crew and I are here to assist."*

FOUR

"You are making a grave error in judgment." Major Helek's tone was mordant, the words of the Tal Shiar officer carrying forward from her seat at the rear of the warbird's cramped bridge. "Crossing the Neutral Zone can only be perceived as a provocative act."

"She saw the same scanner readings as the rest of us, yes?" Commander Medaka deliberately did not address Helek's comment directly, and instead turned in his chair toward Decurion Benem at the sensors and shroud console. Medaka's dark, wolfish face and his searching gaze locked with that of his junior officer, and Benem gave an affirming nod.

"The major has been fully informed of the developing emergency at all stages." Benem's species was Garidian, an offshoot of the Romulan race with longer chins and larger skulls, which made them seem like a distorted mirror of Medaka's people. When she scowled, it had the effect of greatly exaggerating her displeasure, and Benem did so now, making little attempt to hide her dislike of the Tal Shiar operative.

"So unless she has not been paying attention," said the commander, "the major will be well aware that the spatial fracture you detected could represent a serious danger to the Empire."

"Indeed."

That made clear, Medaka finally looked Helek in the eye. "This ship will not stand by and do nothing when lives are at stake."

"Not Romulan lives," Helek noted, the expression on her pale face stone hard and uncompromising.

"But lives nonetheless," said Medaka, "and if this danger is not contained, we will have allowed a lethal radiation source to propagate at the Empire's very border." He paused. "If you wish, I will summon scientician Vadrel up from his laboratory and have him reaffirm the severity of this hazard."

"Three metrics to de-warp." Lieutenant Maian reported the time to target from his station at the helm. Maian was taciturn and utterly unflappable, a craggy older legionary from the subdecks who had risen to officer status by what Medaka understood was sheer doggedness.

"What ship posture, Commander?" Sharing the console on the right of the bridge with Benem, Sublieutenant Kort was acting combat officer on this shift, and his young, reedy voice held notes of both eagerness and dread. Kort was one of the breed of Romulan who had never fired a weapon in anger, a graduate from the wave of recruits who had joined up during the grim days of the Dominion War, but not soon enough to see action in it.

"Condition Dagger," Medaka informed him. That would keep the warbird's weapons in quiescent mode and their shields at standby.

"You would take us into enemy territory naked?" Helek gave a snort.

"I can forgive the sublieutenant's nervousness but not yours," said Medaka. "Are the Tal Shiar always so anxious?"

"The Tal Shiar are *vigilant*," Helek retorted. "We are *careful*. What you are doing now, Commander, is the very antithesis of those things. It is reckless!"

"Tell me, Major, how many times have Federation starships crossed the border to render assistance to vessels in the Neutral Zone?" Medaka didn't wait for her to answer. "It is fair for us to return the favor, just this once."

"Turn back now and I will consider this a brief moment of eccentricity on your part," said Helek. "If you proceed, I will be forced to make a report."

Her words made Medaka rise from his chair, turning to meet the major's scrutiny strength for strength. "And is that not why you are on my bridge and on my ship, to make reports? To observe and record everything my crew does? As if we do not have enough to occupy us with the urgency of our survey missions."

"We all have our work, for the glory of the Empire," replied Helek.

When the news of the coming star-death had broken across the Romulan Empire, there had been panic, outrage, and then—because of the nature of the Romulan character—there had been an equal amount of resignation to the inevitable and suspicion toward the cause of it.

In the Romulan fleet, veteran warriors blooded in wars with the Federation and the Klingons were forced to turn from their endless patrols and saber rattling, to vital exploratory assignments. There were billions of Romulans who would be displaced when the nova came, and they all needed somewhere new to live.

But the fleet had not been built to handle a colossal mission of colonization, or a mass evacuation on such a scale. Romulan ships were largely lean, spare vessels, agile and deadly, even the most commonplace of them designed for stealth and war. Their commanders were soldiers first and explorers a distant second, and it had ever been thus.

Medaka remembered the fiery conclaves of senior admiralty and captains, convened after the reality of the star-death became clear. To save the lives of the endangered, the entire mission of the fleet would need to alter, with warbirds diverted away from their watches along the Empire's borders, in order to chart hitherto ignored sectors where unmapped but livable worlds might be found.

Many of the admiralty recoiled at such demands from the Senate. What good was an Empire with weak, undefended borders? they argued. Was it worth diverting resources in order to save those displaced by the supernova, if that encouraged their enemies? Others—captains like Medaka—argued that to let their fellow Romulans perish would be tantamount to gouging out the heart of the Empire.

Factions formed and fought in the corridors of power, wasting precious time as the clock ran down toward the nova event. Some even spoke openly of defiance, a few officers threatening to take things into their own hands.

And so the Tal Shiar made themselves known. For the safety and security of the Romulan Star Empire, one of their officers was placed aboard every ship on "sensitive duties," to ensure that orders would be followed in this time of great crisis.

Medaka studied Major Helek. She was not the only Tal Shiar operative on his ship, that was as certain as the rise of the moons; but until recently, the secretive organization had been good enough to at least *pretend* they were not spying on their own people. Helek's presence was that lie forced into the light, and it galled the commander. Medaka's trusted first officer had been transferred so that Helek could take his place, and she was in no way the lost man's equal.

"Our mission is to complete the planetary survey of grid section nine-zero-six," said the major. "It is not to come to the aid of aliens." She paused, affecting a wounded tone. "Surely you do not prioritize the safety of aliens over your own kind?"

Decurion Benem's head jerked up at her words, the Garidian's eyes narrowing. Across the bridge, at the warbird's navigation panel, Sublieutenant Hade-Tah gave a low, rumbling growl of annoyance in the middle of its throat. The muscular, rangy navigator was a sentient from the Taurhai Unity, an alien power that had become a client state to the Romulan Empire in the past few decades.

Many Romulan commanders kept their ships crewed only by members of their species, but Medaka saw that as shortsighted, as a waste of valuable talent. As well as the Garidian and the Taurhai on the bridge, the warbird *Othrys* had a Reman as senior engineer and Norkanians among its support force. Using their diverse skills to best advantage was a lesson Medaka had learned from observing the Federation Starfleet in action. The benefits carried more weight than the sneers of dismissal from Major Helek and the more traditionalist commanders in the fleet.

"If that singularity is not prevented from consuming the Jazari vessel, it will stabilize and grow in potency." Medaka kept his tone even, so that the record would show his argument was built on logical choice. "The

THE DARK VEIL   57

toxicity that results will eventually penetrate the nearby Neutral Zone, even reaching the planets in grid section nine-zero-six. We are seeking to forestall a disaster that *will* affect the Empire. Do you understand?" He gestured at the air. "I can have Hade-Tah project a holographic star map for illustrative purposes, if you wish."

"Two metrics to de-warp," said Maian.

Medaka glanced at Benem. "Status of the Jazari space platform?"

"Deteriorating rapidly," she replied. "Sensor returns are garbled by radiation output from the fracture."

"Best estimation," said the commander.

"If they are not all dead," she told him, "then they soon will be."

He nodded grimly, reviewing what he knew of the stoic reptilian beings. Because of the nearness of their home system to the far side of the Neutral Zone border, the Jazari species were one of many whose worlds were under constant long-range surveillance by the Romulan Star Empire. Their secretive activities over the last few cycles had been carefully observed by the Empire's automated scanner outposts.

Outwardly, the Romulans gave lip service to the Jazari's requests for privacy, but they were fooling themselves if they believed the Empire would not watch them. Perhaps the Federation would ignore them, but not Romulus. Medaka's mission briefing had mentioned intelligence reports that the Jazari were engaged in some large-scale orbital construction project, but little more beyond that. The Jazari were deemed to be of minor concern, and for the moment, beneath the Empire's notice.

But the energy signature from the poisonous spatial fracture changed all that in a heartbeat. Like Romulan ships, the Jazari craft used captive singularities as a power source, so the telltale signs of such a lethal malfunction were well known to Medaka's officers.

This was not something that could be simply ignored. Medaka had lost friends in the monstrous implosion shocks caused by such containment failures, and he had no desire to see it happen again, to aliens, to anyone.

Helek was silent for a moment, measuring her response. "You will bear full responsibility for whatever transpires from this point forward, Commander."

Medaka gave a humorless snort. "You say that as if it is somehow uncommon, Major. *Othrys* is my ship, this is my crew, *of course* I am responsible."

"One metric to de-warp," intoned Maian.

Helek indicated a display on Sublieutenant Kort's console. "There is a Federation starship waiting for us at those coordinates. Have you considered this may be a deliberate attempt to draw us across the border?"

"The *Titan*." Medaka sounded out the human name of the Starfleet vessel. "I am aware of it. It has been assigned to this sector for some time. I believe its captain is noted as being quite . . . resourceful." He paused. "As to your question . . . If you believe this is some kind of ploy, what value would they gain from it?"

"Who can know how humans think?" she replied.

"They want nothing to do with us," muttered Kort, almost unaware he was speaking aloud. "Their actions have made that truth clear."

Medaka drew himself up. "*Our* actions will make *our* truth clear, Sublieutenant." He walked back to his command console in the middle of the bridge, placing one hand upon it. "Discard our cloak upon arrival."

Benem affirmed the order as Medaka activated a subroutine on his panel. The subspace communications band he had used a short time ago was reactivated, broadcasting across channels that both the Jazari and the Starfleet ship would be able to hear. *It would not do*, he told himself, *for either of them to think that the* Othrys *is the vanguard of an invasion force.*

The warbird rumbled as it slowed from faster-than-light velocity, and the stars on the forward holograph normalized. Medaka could almost feel Major Helek's glare burning into his back as he took a breath to speak; if she could have killed with that look, the woman would have been the Tal Shiar's greatest assassin.

A shimmer like rainwater across a window passed over the forward view as *Othrys* decloaked a few thousand spans off the bow of the *Titan* and the stricken Jazari platform. In the distance, a huge vessel of unknown design drifted in a haze of wreckage from surface damage.

"What in the Praetor's name is that?" hissed Kort.

"We will find out soon enough," he told his officers, and opened the comm channel. "Attention. This is Commander Medaka of the Romulan warbird *Othrys*. My crew and I are here to assist."

Riker took in the shape of the *Othrys*, the warbird's avian form. He knew this class of vessel well, having fought alongside them in battle years ago, against the renegade clone Shinzon. They were formidable, and not entrusted to just any rank-and-file captain.

"That's the one that we detected earlier," said Troi.

"Undoubtedly," he agreed.

At Riker's side, Vale folded her arms across her chest. "Okay, what do they *really* want?"

Troi's lips thinned. "Chris, they're offering to help."

"And if that doesn't make you distrustful of their intentions, then nothing will," Vale retorted. "Romulans: even their agendas have agendas."

The captain frowned. This wasn't the time or the place to have a discussion about the nature of Romulan honesty. "Like it or not, we need all the assistance we can get right now." He glanced toward Livnah's station. "You think the output of a *Mogai*-class warbird will be enough to reinforce the warp shell?"

"Likely," said the science officer. Her arm went out to grab her panel for stability as new gravity shocks radiated through the deck. "Time is of the essence, sir."

Riker drew himself up to his full height. "All right then. Put me through."

The viewscreen blinked and he was seeing into the metallic gray-green spaces of the *Othrys*'s command deck. A Romulan officer stood up to match him, a man with a head of ink-black hair and a face that seemed carved from teakwood. *"Am I addressing Captain Riker?"*

"You are."

Medaka gave a solemn nod. *"In the interest of alacrity, I will be brief. My ship intercepted the distress call from the Jazari reclaim platform and my officers have analyzed the inherent danger. Can I assume your people have done the same?"*

Riker returned the gesture. "We've detected an expanding subspace fracture inside the platform, leaking toxic particles into this region. If it stabilizes—"

"The results would be catastrophic," said the Romulan. *"Your reputation precedes you, Captain, so I imagine you have a plan of action?"*

In quick order, Riker outlined their failed attempt to cap the growing anomaly. "We need more power to make it work, Commander. Can I count on you to back us up?"

"A static warp shell . . . an intriguing solution." Medaka turned to one of his subordinates, and shared a few words Riker could not hear. In that brief pause, he caught sight of a pale, stern-faced Romulan woman staring intently back at him from behind the *Othrys*'s commander. Then Medaka responded. *"Yes, we can provide an energy source for this stratagem. But my officer informs me that we will be placing both our ships in harm's way. Are you prepared for that, Captain Riker?"*

"We are, Commander Medaka."

The Romulan showed a faint smile. *"Very well. Have your science officer transmit the matrix formulae for the warp shell to my ship. We will synchronize engagement in . . . one minute, by your reckoning. Do you concur?"*

"That works for us, sir," Livnah called out from her station.

"Titan concurs," said Riker. "Good luck to you, Commander."

"To us all, Captain. Othrys *out."*

The screen flicked back to the exterior view and Riker rubbed at his chin. "I'll be damned. He was practically . . . reasonable."

"He's also in violation of the Treaty of Algeron," said Keru. "Just putting that out there, sir, but a Romulan warbird crossing the border uninvited is a massive red flag."

"My point," said Vale.

"Arguably, they were invited," Troi countered. "By the distress call. The treaty does have some flexibility in such cases."

"If we all live through this, we can have that debate." Riker shut down the conversation before it went any further. "I'm not looking a gift horse in the mouth, even if it is a Romulan one. For now, we deal with the problem that's in front of us." He dropped into the command chair. "Helm, take us back in toward the reclaim station, position us at optimal attitude to feed power to the warp shell." The words had barely left his mouth before the worst shocks yet battered the *Titan*.

Keru gave a yell as he lost his footing and struck his head on the tactical panel. He swore a Trill curse beneath his breath, his hand coming up to press against a cut on his forehead.

"Ranul, are you all right?" Troi was half out of her seat, but the other officer waved her away.

"Just rattled me a little, Commander. I can still see straight."

"The *Othrys* has acknowledged receipt of the matrix data, sir," said Livnah. "We are powering up the warp nacelles for projection."

"Energy transfer status nominal." McCreedy reported the readings from her station. "The Romulans are doing the same, modifying their containment field. We'll be good to go in fifteen seconds, Captain."

"We've only got one more shot at this," he told them, giving voice to what he knew his crew was thinking. "You know your duty. Stay on task."

"Can I just say, when I woke up this morning," Vale said quietly, "this is *not* how I saw my day going."

• • •

By now, Reclaim Platform Zero Four's structural integrity had completely collapsed, turning the small spacedock and the remains of the tug vessel hull within into a clenched fist of tritanium, polymers, and other alloys.

The gravity waves had ripped it into pieces, but the force of the spatial fracture kept the broken remnants in a strange kind of equilibrium, holding the wreckage in a sphere around the anomaly's event horizon. The poisonous beating heart of the thing, bright as a dying star and spewing delta particles into the void around it, was visible through the storm of debris.

With each new shimmering pulse wave, the diameter of the event horizon grew a few more degrees. Very soon, it would reach a critical mass and then nothing short of a stellar-level event would be able to smother it.

The *Titan* moved to activation range and the starship rolled to present its underside to the fracture, reinforcing the ventral shields as the first streams of energy were emitted from the warp nacelles. On the opposite side of Platform Zero Four, the *Othrys* settled into its position and did the same. The Romulan ship spread its wings wide, the complex design of a hunting falcon visible etched across them. Lines of pale green fire swirled around the other vessel's warp engines.

Then as one, *Titan* and *Othrys* combined their efforts to bring the static warp shell into being. This time, the glowing orb of energy formed fully and completely in milliseconds, enveloping the ruined platform and the toxic anomaly at its core. Degree by degree, the shell began to contract, forcing the subspace radiation back on itself, robbing the fracture of the vital power it needed to stabilize.

Clawing at the inside of its cage like a living thing, the fracture vented surges of exotic particles, but with nowhere to go, they built into a captive storm.

The fracture's final dissolution began. With just one starship against it, the anomaly's incredible forces were too much to resist, but with two equally powerful vessels working in concert, the anomaly could not continue to exist.

And then, at a point of no return, the torn-open singularity that had caused the disaster lost all dimensional cohesion and *imploded*.

In subspace, the effect was like a star cracking open; here in this reality, it shattered the static warp shell in one final spasm of destruction, consuming the remnants of the Jazari space platform to fuel a last lash of violent energy.

A feedback pulse shrieked into the engine nacelles of the *Othrys* with enough force to throw the Romulan warbird into a vicious spin. Warp plasma gushed from the ship's wings in great streams of virulent green as it pitched away, out of control.

Titan, already damaged from the first failed attempt to contain the anomaly, fared worse. Her shields were battered down in an instant and the final shockwave hit the bare metal of her hull. The starship's structural integrity fields flexed and bowed, for one giddy second taking the spaceframe almost to the pinnacle of its material tolerances. Hull plates and support spars all through the vessel's fuselage were put under incredible strain. A lesser ship would have been crushed like an empty beverage canister.

Like the mythological beings that were the starship's namesakes, *Titan* weathered the impossible and survived.

But not without cost.

Major Helek picked herself up off the deck of the *Othrys*'s bridge, angrily pushing aside Decurion Benem's hand as the Garidian attempted to help her to her feet. The wail of alert tocsins cut through her skull like knives and she grimaced as her eyes focused on the main holograph screen.

Outside, the stars were tumbling wildly, and every few seconds the white mass of the Federation starship whipped by. The view made her feel light-headed and she looked away, finding Commander Medaka in a heap where he had fallen against his console.

Helek made no move to assist him. Instead, she found Lieutenant Maian at the helm and barked an order in his direction. "Get this ship into a stable attitude!"

"Report . . ." Medaka said thickly, pulling himself up the console. "Did it work?"

"It did!" Sublieutenant Kort almost shouted the reply, as if he could not believe that they had succeeded.

"How much damage was done to the Empire's ship in the process?" Helek demanded an answer from Kort, but he hesitated before replying, looking to Medaka for confirmation first. "I asked you a question!" Helek snarled.

"Evaluating," said Kort, blinking at his readout. "Warp drive is offline. I think . . . the impairment is severe."

"You *think*?" Helek repeated, lashing him with the words. "Talk to the Reman engineer! Bring me facts, not your assumptions."

On the hologram screen, the motion of the starscape settled as the *Othrys* slowly reoriented to the plane of the ecliptic, and the Federation ship's status became clearer.

What there had been of the reclaim platform was now no more than a cloud of charged particulate matter, but a new slick of wreckage was drifting out behind the *Titan*. Glittering white bits of tritanium caught the light of the Jazari star and Helek could not stop herself from smiling. Seeing the Starfleet vessel wounded kindled a fierce, angry delight inside her.

How does it feel? she wanted to ask them. *How does that pain taste?*

Behind her, Medaka ran his hands over the command console, running a sensor scan. "The leviathan, the large craft filled with Jazari . . . It appears intact."

"No doubt they will laud the heroism of the Romulan fleet and be eternally grateful," she snapped, but he ignored the comment.

"Riker's ship, however . . ." He sucked in a breath. "It appears they have taken the brunt of it."

"Oh?" Helek turned toward him and craned her neck so she could read the sensor returns. Even at this range, the scanners could detect multiple hull breaches, and what appeared to be a buildup of lethal toxins in the ship's environment. "How tragic."

Medaka eyed her. "That could easily have been us."

"Let me guess. Now you want to give aid to the Federation?"

"That would be the principled thing to do," said the commander. "Cold space does not care about a starfarer's origin. We are all equally at its mercy."

"*Principled.*" Helek had to stop herself from laughing out loud. She had been told that Medaka was practically antique in his thinking, beholden to old, fanciful ideals of honor and hidebound codes of morality. The Tal Shiar were far more flexible about such things. "We could let them all perish and then tow their vessel back across the Neutral Zone as salvage. I would be happy to affirm any claim you would make that we were providing *assistance.*"

"Is that a serious suggestion, Major?" Medaka's brow creased in a frown. "I find it difficult to tell when you are being flippant."

"My suggestion," she said firmly, "is that we make sure our own vessel is safe before we look to any other. As we all know, Starfleet is quite capable of caring for itself." Helek said the last with real venom, and it pleased her to note that both Maian and Kort nodded along with her words.

"Deanna?" Her husband's voice seemed to be coming from a great distance away. "*Imzadi?*"

She blinked and took stock of herself, mentally partitioning her thoughts. "I'm all right," she told him, but it was a half-truth at best. Her Betazoid ancestry was one of her greatest gifts when it came to the work of counseling the *Titan*'s crew or serving in a diplomatic role, giving her an empathic insight into the minds of those she was dealing with. But sometimes, it could be as much a curse as a boon. Troi had been caught unprepared by the final discharge from the collapsing singularity, unable to erect her mental barriers in time before the dying shockwave collided with the ship.

In that brief instant, she felt the panic and fear of hundreds of people all at once as they experienced the same gut-twisting moment of impact. She had no words to describe the experience to a nontelepath; the closest analogy Troi could come up with was the roar of an atonal chorus, where each strident voice was the alarm cry of a single mind.

Some of the mind-voices were clear because of proximity—those of Vale and the other members of the bridge crew, the officers on the deck immediately beneath the bridge—and others were loud because of familiarity. She heard Will give a silent shout as the *Titan* took the hit, but worse than that was the shriek that emanated from the mind of her son. Thaddeus, down in the refuge area on the civilian decks, cried out for her, and the psychic wail cut her heart open.

She willed herself to project an aura of love and strength back to him, hoping that the boy's part-empath mind would pick it up. *We will be all right, little one,* she thought, *your father and I will get us through this.*

Riker had his hand on hers and he gave her a nod, as if he had heard it too. "You need me?"

"The ship needs you more," she told him. "Go to work."

"I could use some help up here . . ." At the engineering station, McCreedy was waving away clouds of smoke from blown EPS relays, frantically trying to reboot her console at the same time. Troi pushed out of her chair and crossed to her.

"I've got it, Karen." She grabbed a hand extinguisher from a locker in the wall and used it to douse the small electrical fire.

"Thank you, sir." The engineer tapped out a string of code and the panels lit up with a slew of crimson warning sigils. "Oh. That's not good."

Troi saw an exploded deck-by-deck graphic of the *Titan*, sliced into horizontal pieces like the toy construction kits Thad sometimes played with. Dozens of sections of the ship were glowing red, like fire reaching up along the warp drive pylons and across the belly of the ship. Even as she watched, the glow was spreading.

"I need a status report, Chief Engineer!" The captain called out the command from the midbridge, seeing McCreedy's worried expression and knowing what it could mean.

"I'm reading multiple plasma-coolant leaks on the lower decks, sir. Force-field barriers are spotty, they're not stopping the flow. It's rising up the turbolift shafts and the Jefferies tubes . . ."

"Who's down there?" said Riker, paling at the thought. The heavy, greenish gaseous material that kept a starship's warp core from overheating was a class-one biohazard, acidic to almost all organic life. A single drop could burn right through unprotected flesh, and a serious leak would dissolve any living thing it came into contact with.

"Unknown," said the engineer.

"Why isn't it venting into space?" Riker's brow furrowed.

"Severe damage to the internal sensors," said McCreedy. "It's not registering! So the venting systems don't know the plasma is there, and they're programmed only to activate under the most extreme of conditions."

Troi stepped to the secondary damage-control station and set to work. "Information is coming in. Evacuation in progress," she reported. "Main engineering, both mess halls, and sickbay have been abandoned . . ."

Riker tapped his combadge. "Bridge to Doctor Talov, please respond."

A moment later, *Titan's* chief medical officer replied. *"Captain, I am rather busy at the moment."* The Vulcan was breathing hard. He seemed to be on the move, and Troi could hear other, frightened voices over the open channel. *"We are in the midst of an emergency relocation. Please stand by."* The signal fell silent.

"Sir, permission to seal off the contaminated sections?" McCreedy met the captain's gaze. They both knew what that would mean. If anyone was still on those decks, they would be locking them in with a toxic atmosphere. But the longer the emergency hatches remained open, the farther the leaking coolant could spread.

He gave a sigh. "Permission granted."

McCreedy set to work, and on the deck-by-deck monitor, blue indicators blinked on as the lockdown began.

"Sir?" Westerguard called out from the navigation console. "Uh, Captain? I think I have an idea that could help!"

"Spit it out, Lieutenant," said Vale, moving toward him.

"Well, uh, if *internal* sensors are out, we could try a reflection pulse from the *external* sensors? It'll be noisy and definition will be poor, but it might be enough—"

Vale nodded vigorously, catching on to the navigator's train of thought. "Enough for us to map the leaks and locate anyone still in the contaminated sectors."

"Do what you can, mister," said Riker, shooting his wife a look. "Deanna, how are our transporter systems?"

"Operable," she replied. "That's something."

"Scanning," said Westerguard. "I've got a reading! Six life-forms, all in one chamber off the secondary deflector bay!"

"Good work," said the captain. "Route their locations to transporter room two, get them out of there!"

A moment later, Troi saw a message flag appear on the panel before her. "Transport is complete. All six recovered intact. The officer on duty reports they have severe burns and respiratory distress . . ."

"Talov to bridge." The Vulcan's voice issued out of the air.

Troi could imagine the statuesque, olive-skinned man in his usual pose, both hands folded across his chest, his piercing blue eyes taking in everything around him. Like Westerguard, Talov had come aboard a few weeks earlier, but unlike the lieutenant, the doctor seemed anything but pleased to be aboard the *Titan*.

"Where are you, Doctor?" said Riker.

"Shuttlebay two," he replied. *"I have already assembled a detail to convert a section of the space for use as a temporary infirmary. Does that present an issue?"*

"No." Deanna's husband gave her another sideways glance. In the short time he had been aboard, Talov had shown a tendency to act first and ask permission afterward, something made more irksome by the fact that he was usually making the right call. "I'll have the displaced crew diverted there as well," he continued. "Give me a casualty report, if you can."

"At present time I am aware of three deaths. Ensign Scoville, Lieutenant Junior Grade Mazone, and Specialist Second Class Brote. All perished in the initial plasma leak event."

At Troi's side, McCreedy stiffened. Scoville and Mazone were two of her engineering officers from the warp-core team. Troi laid a hand on her arm and the other woman gave a rueful nod.

Talov continued. *"The injured are largely suffering from toxin inhalation, dermal burns, and similar maladies. Severity ranges from walking wounded to borderline critical."* He paused. *"Captain, I would like an estimation as to when sickbay will be vented so my staff and I may return there."*

"You'll get that when I do," said the captain. "For now, carry on. Riker out."

"I've stabilized the ship's attitude, sir," called Cantua. "Reading the *Othrys* off our starboard bow at a distance of twenty kilometers. They're venting drive plasma but they appear intact."

"What's their posture?" said Vale. She was really asking, *Are they going to take advantage of our situation?*

"Station-keeping, minimal deflectors, no weapons active." The lieutenant read off the report in rapid-fire order. "I guess they have their own problems to deal with, if they took the same hit we did."

"What about the Jazari?" Vale glanced back at the main screen.

"Negative contact," said Cantua.

"You'd think they might send out a rescue boat," muttered Westerguard.

"For what?" asked the Denobulan. "Their people out here got atomized."

If the captain was following the conversation, he didn't show it. "Karen." He crossed to McCreedy's console once more. "What do you need to get us back up and running?"

The engineer adjusted her spectacles. "The Jazari have still got a half dozen of those dock platforms out there. If we could use some of their facilities . . ."

"Given their previous behavior, let's assume not," said Riker.

"Ah. Thought so." McCreedy took a breath. "Okay then. Give me ten minutes, sir, and I'll spin up a full damage report for you."

Riker gave her a last glance, and the two of them shared a little of their strength in that glance. Then he turned away and both of them went back to the business at hand.

The observation lounge ahead of the bridge was sealed off for the interim, thanks to the damage caused by a shard of the ship-breaker that had speared through one of the ports, so Vale gave the report to the captain in his ready room.

Usually, she was the one who paced and Riker watched from behind his desk, but this time the roles were reversed. The first officer stood unmoving as her commander followed a short course back and forth across the cabin.

"If we could put in at a starbase, it would be as if nothing had happened," she said, tapping the padd with McCreedy's terse report on it. "Corps of Engineers could buff it right out. But that's not an option, so we've got at least six days of active repair work. But the big problem is access. The damage-control crews need to get into the toxified sections of the ship to work, and for that the vent controls need to be operable and the plasma-tank breaches sealed. But for that to happen, the main vent controls have to be fixed and they're inside a compartment filled with gaseous, acidic coolant."

"Can we beam in a team wearing EV suits?"

"That's the chief engineer's recommendation, sir. But it'll be slow work." She paused, chewing her lip.

"There's more." It wasn't a question.

"Even after the venting units are back online and we purge the leaked coolant, the sealed sections need to be decontaminated. That means we can't move people back down there until it's done. And right now we have all one hundred percent of the crew crammed into thirty percent of the interior spaces, with a damaged environmental system that's straining to manage. We can triple up crew bunking, convert the holodecks to temporary dormitories for the civilians, but that'll only take a little of the pressure off."

"What about putting some people down on a nearby planet?" Riker glanced out of the window. "We have temporary shelters in the cargo bay. We'll send them on a camping trip."

Vale cut that option down with a sigh. "You saw what the Jazari have done to their homeworld, sir. It's a mess over there, barely any breathable atmosphere and constant hundred-k winds. The next nearest habitable Class-M planet is two light-years away, in the middle of the Neutral Zone."

"We have nothing but bad choices," said Riker. "Can we send up a flare and get another ship out here?"

Vale gave him a level look. "You know what Starfleet will say if we ask, sir."

"I suppose so." After the attack on Utopia Planitia and the body blow the fleet had taken there, starships were spread more thinly than ever before. Other shipyards in other systems were racing to make up the shortfall and replace the lost craft, but it was unlikely that a vessel would be diverted to aid the *Titan* unless the circumstances were extreme. "I guess we're on our own."

"We're always the ones who reach out," said Vale. "Seems like it rarely comes back the other way." They were alone, so she made no attempt to hide her bitterness.

The captain hesitated, searching for a reply, and in that moment the intercom on his desk chimed. *"Bridge to ready room,"* said Troi, *"we've got an incoming hail."*

"From the Romulans?"

"No. It's the Jazari. They say they want to . . . make amends."

FIVE

The holographic signal from the Jazari generation ship shimmered into a false solidity, forming two humanoid shapes in the middle of Riker's ready room.

In physical build and height, the Jazari were remarkably similar, but it was in the tones of their skin and the patterns of the scales on their faces that their individuality came through. The captain recognized the ambassador, Veyen, in the same plain robes he had worn when first he boarded the *Titan*, but the second figure took him a moment to place. The younger Jazari's face was out of context for him, and then he knew why—it was the former lieutenant Zade, no longer in a Starfleet uniform, now garbed in a simple tunic and trousers.

"Good day, Captain," he said, his image flickering as it settled. *"I confess I did not expect to be speaking to you again."*

"Same here," agreed Riker. "Ambassador, thank you for contacting us."

At the captain's side, his first officer remained silent, but her body language spoke volumes. Vale studied the Jazari with a cool, dispassionate eye.

"You have our gratitude and esteem, Captain," said Veyen. *"The selfless deeds of your crew will become part of our historical record. Every Jazari will know what you did for us."*

"Commander Medaka and his people should share the credit," Riker noted. "Without them, we would have failed."

Zade nodded. *"Indeed. And we are also communicating our thanks to them at this moment."* He paused. *"They showed remarkable compassion, at odds with our common evaluation of the Romulan character."*

"Did your ship suffer any damage?" Vale broke her silence, but not her watchful manner.

"Yes, but far less than we would have experienced had your static warp shell not succeeded in collapsing the spatial fracture." Veyen gave Zade a sideways glance. *"During our decommissioning processes, we suffered similar events in the deconstruction of some of our older craft, but none as deadly as this one. The exterior of our great ship was penetrated in several places, but its systems are . . . self-repairing."*

"Thanks to you, we will still be able to depart this system within our planned launch window," added Zade.

"You told Counselor Troi you wanted to make amends," said Vale. "Would you care to expand on that?"

Riker noted her tone, but said nothing. He was as interested in the answer as the commander.

"We are aware of the situation aboard the Titan," continued the ambassador.

"You've scanned us?" Riker raised an eyebrow. Clearly, the Jazari's rules about personal privacy were not a two-way street.

Veyen chose not to address that. *"We . . . wish to repay your kindness toward us."* He was finding it hard to say the words, and at length Zade stepped in.

"Captain, we would like to offer you the use of one of our great ship's ecodomes, as a temporary shelter for your crew. We have many of these compartments. Each is a self-contained biosphere holding samples of flora and fauna from our homeworld. The Ochre Dome is comparable to a temperate region on Earth, Izar, Rigel, and similar planets. We can give you sanctuary there, if this is agreeable."

Riker suddenly wished that Troi were here to lend him her diplomatic expertise. Of all the things he had expected to hear from the reclusive Jazari, an offer to come to their ship was not on the list. "You understand that our people would need to remain aboard your vessel for several days," he said carefully, his mind racing as he considered what this might mean.

This was an unprecedented proposal, and turning it down would not only insult the Jazari, it would close the door on something that might never happen again. Riker glanced at Vale, seeing his own surprise reflected on her face.

"We would have to bring across civilians and Starfleet personnel," Riker continued. "Support equipment and medical hardware. We have several casualties."

"That . . . will be permitted. It is the least we can do." Veyen's reply was so tight-lipped, Riker thought he might snap in two. *"Within reason, of course."*

The captain calculated the numbers in his head. With the civilians and the injured off the ship, and the demand on the ship's damaged systems reduced, *Titan* would be able to get back up to operational status in half the time.

"Can I ask," said Vale, "have you made this offer to the Romulans as well?"

"We have," said Veyen. *"Commander Medaka respectfully declined."*

"His vessel's repair requirements are not as urgent as those of the Titan,*"* noted Zade. *"His officers seemed quite uncomfortable with the idea of being our guests, in point of fact. But he has accepted an invitation to receive the thanks of Governing Sept in person. I hope you will too, Captain."*

"Of course." Riker straightened his tunic. Part of him was still catching up with what was going on, and suddenly he remembered that among the people who would go to that ship would be his son, as their family quarters was on one of the ship's still-contaminated decks. "This is very generous of you," he went on. "I know how seriously your species takes its privacy and for you to open your . . . your *home* to us, well, it means a great deal. On behalf of my crew, thank you."

"We would prefer you refrain from the use of matter transporters when boarding the great ship," said Veyen. *"The Governing Sept will transmit information on where and how to enter the Ochre Dome via shuttlecraft presently. Good day."*

The holograms dissolved into nothing, leaving Riker and Vale alone again. "That did just happen, right?" he asked her, after a moment. "Or did I bang my head during the shockwave and hallucinate that conversation?"

"One of the galaxy's most reclusive species just rolled out the welcome mat," she replied, "on the eve of the day they're about to leave forever for the depths of the Beta Quadrant. Nope, that pretty much sums it up, sir." Vale paused, thinking it over. "You know, the Federation Diplomatic Corps will hate us forever when they find out we fell into this by accident."

"Which is exactly why I am going to put my wife in charge of this thing immediately. If anyone can handle this, it's Deanna."

"No argument there."

Riker saw a familiar cast in Vale's eyes and made a beckoning gesture. "You have something else to say. Out with it, Commander."

She sighed. "I've been using the word *suspicious* a lot recently . . ."

"You want something different?" said Riker. "Iffy? Shady? Fishy?"

"Let's go with *all of the above*." Vale stood straighter. "Sir, I used to be security, and before that I was police, and those are jobs where you meet a lot of beings with ulterior motives. So, forgive me if I'm going with what I know, but right now I am on yellow alert up here." She tapped her temple with a fingertip. "And you should be too."

Riker smiled slightly. "You didn't trust the Jazari when they were closed off. You don't trust them when they're open."

"That's the rub, Captain," she replied. "I don't trust *anything* at face value."

"Link terminated," said the soft voice in the walls. *"Aura barrier restored."* It had a metered and gentle cadence that some beings would have gendered as feminine.

"Confirmed," noted Zade, addressing the comment to the air.

At his side, Veyen stood unmoving. "What we have just done is unprecedented. I am concerned that the full ramifications of it are not yet clear."

"That is a gargantuan understatement." Qaylan was one of the more vocal members of the Governing Sept, and he seemed about to prove so once more, his tone building toward the bellicose. "I am on record as opposing this in the strongest possible terms."

"With respect," said Zade, "bringing aliens among us is not wholly unprecedented. It has been done before."

Across the communication chamber, Yasil, the Sept's other senior representative, ran a hand through his barbs and smiled, emulating a very human gesture. "Zade, I respect the point you are making, but bringing up that part of our history will not serve you well. I was there in the days when humans first came to our planet, and it was chaotic, at best."

"We were very different then," noted Veyen.

"But the humans have not evolved, as we have." Qaylan seized on the comment. "And neither have the Romulans, or any of these aliens. They live too short a life. They lack our perspective. We cannot associate with them!" He gestured at the walls of the great ship around them, the high vaulted chamber extending away. "Here we stand inside a construct built precisely because of that very fact! Look at the data. Do we need to coordinate in order for you to accept this?"

"Leaving them to fend for themselves goes against everything at the core of our natures." The air itself resonated with the words. *"If we leave them, the tensions between the Starfleet ship and the Romulan ship are likely to grow. Probability of a negative outcome is high."*

"It is not our concern," insisted Qaylan. "Of course we appreciate their aid. But we did not ask for it."

"I did." The words came from a Jazari in an engineer's attire, observing from one of the galleries. "I sent the distress call."

"Sabem." Zade glanced in his direction. "You are not judged for that. You feared destruction. You did what you thought was right."

"You should have solved the issue yourself." For all of Zade's words, Qaylan seemed quite content to criticize the sole survivor of the reclaim station as harshly as he pleased. "That is *also* our way."

"Tarsin was destroyed attempting to close the fracture." Sabem looked away. "With his ending, I could not determine any other course of action."

"Would you rather Sabem had remained silent, Qaylan?" said Yasil. "We would have suffered great, great loss if he had."

"Perhaps," admitted Qaylan. "But some would have survived. Enough to reconstruct what was ruined."

"What is done cannot be undone," hummed the voice in the walls. *"We have a code. We live by it. The crew of* Titan *put themselves in harm's way for us, with no expectation of recompense."*

"As did the Romulans," snapped Qaylan.

"But the Romulans do not need our help," said Veyen. "Nor would they accept it, even if they did."

"We remember our obligations," said the voice. *"We have a code,"* it repeated.

"So we bring these beings aboard, we give them space in the Ochre Dome for a few day-cycles. What then?" Qaylan scowled. "They are overly inquisitive, disorderly life-forms. Has the Sept fully considered what they may discover about us, given such exposure? We must protect ourselves."

"And we will," insisted Zade. "I know these people. They are not our enemies or our lessers." He paused. "I have been clear in my opinions on the matter of the migration. I disagreed with it. Some might suggest my patterns of thought have been influenced by my exposure to these beings. Neither datum alters the truth. Captain Riker and his crew can be trusted."

Qaylan studied him coldly. "As the decision has already been made," he replied, "we have no choice but to hope that is so."

Keru kept his hands on the *Armstrong's* controls, guiding the shuttle up and away from *Titan's* landing bay, and over the ship.

Inside the small auxiliary craft, the air was cold but clean, a marked difference from the smell of anticontaminants that pervaded the interior of the *Titan*. The Trill welcomed the difference. For the last day or so, the smell of the decontamination process at work on the starship had collected at the back of his throat and left him with a nagging, unpleasant cough. It made it hard for him to sleep, and that was tough enough on top of working additional duty shifts *and* being crammed into a cabin with three other officers, two of whom snored. He missed his partner, he missed having a moment to just *breathe easy*.

Repair work on *Titan* was moving ahead, so that was a good thing, but the ship would not be back at optimal level for days more to come. Keru was quietly grateful for a chance to get off the vessel, if only for a few hours.

In the cabin behind him, Captain Riker and Commander Vale were going over the last few details before their formal meeting with the Jazari. The aliens had asked that no more than three officers attend, and given that they were already hosting a whole bunch more of *Titan*'s people, it seemed rude to protest.

Lieutenant Commander East argued that a security officer should have been the one to accompany Riker and Vale, but as the senior man, Keru had invoked his privilege and taken the assignment. He reasoned that if anything untoward was going to happen, it would have happened already.

Hope I'm right, he thought. *East will never let me live it down if I'm wrong.*

He angled the *Armstrong* toward the Jazari generation ship, the massive craft growing swiftly into a curved wall of silver metal that filled the view through the canopy. Small fragments of damaged hull flickered at the corners of his vision as they fizzed against the shuttle's deflector screens, but beyond that it was hard to see where the big vessel had taken any noticeable damage. Apart from some carbon scoring, it was relatively intact. Keru frowned at that. The Jazari had allowed others to take the brunt of the damage for them.

He pushed that uncharitable thought aside. Whatever the situation, the Jazari were helping *now*, and that was all that mattered.

Keru banked slightly so that the shuttle's port-side windows captured the giant hemisphere of the Ochre Dome. "Passing over the temporary camp," he called out.

Vale leaned close to the panel. "I see it, at three o'clock."

The spot the commander indicated was visible among the dun-colored landscape inside the ecodome, a cluster of white cubes around the dart-shape of another shuttle, the *Marsalis*. They were too far away to make out individual people, but the emergency bivouac seemed solid enough through the pentagonal panels that made up the arc of the clear dome. Disaster rescue pods and a fabricated tent "village" had been assembled within a few hours of the Jazari extending their invitation, and now it was a home away from home for *Titan*'s displaced crew. Counselor Troi was working as on-site administrator, and she had reported that all was well. She made it sound so inviting that some of the work teams still on the starship were making noises about asking for shore leave. Keru grinned at the thought, and then realized he hadn't actually smiled at anything for days.

The *Armstrong* sped past the Ochre Dome and over a series of other similar constructs. Clustered around the dorsal surface of the generation ship, the other neighboring ecodomes contained pocket environments of different sorts. Keru saw a lake, another with a lush forest, and a smoke-dark vault lit by peculiar bioluminescent glows.

"What do you think they have in there?" Captain Riker came up to peer over Keru's shoulder. "The animals in two by two?"

"Sir?" The Trill didn't grasp the reference.

"An ark, Ranul. These beings have uprooted their entire civilization and they're moving it wholesale." The captain looked up, taking in the size of the generation ship. "You've got to admire the scope of it."

"How many of them do you think there are?"

"Hard to know," admitted Riker. "The only population numbers we have for the Jazari are based on best guesses and what little census data they were willing to give the Federation Council. It's not a lot. Enough people to fill a major planetside capital city, maybe."

"Another mystery about them," offered Vale, from the cabin. "Why so few?"

Keru nodded to himself. A population that small was one major disaster away from an extinction-level event, and putting all their kind aboard a single ship seemed like a needless risk.

Riker gave Vale a frown. "Don't ask about that," he told the commander. "We've got our foot in the door with them, diplomatically speaking, and I don't want to turn it into an interrogation."

"I'll be the model of decorum," Vale replied.

"Maybe we just ask them what changed their minds about their privacy," said Keru as he brought the shuttle into line with the open maw of an illuminated landing bay. "Did they suddenly realize what it is they're going to miss?"

"Federation membership isn't for everyone," said the captain. "The Jazari have the right to choose their own destiny. It doesn't matter what we think about their decision."

An automated guidance signal locked on to the *Armstrong*, and with a shudder, twin tractor beams flashed out to snare the shuttle and draw it inside. They passed through the phase envelope of a force-field barrier and settled gently onto a wide landing pad.

Through the canopy, Keru saw Counselor Troi, his former crewmate Zade, and another Jazari he didn't recognize. "No sign of the Romulans," he noted. "Could be they're a no-show."

"They'll be here," said Vale as she stood. "They won't pass up the chance to poke around inside this vessel, as long as they get to do it on their terms."

Keru was the last out of the *Armstrong*, securing the shuttle before following the captain and the XO. He felt oddly underdressed without a sidearm and tricorder, but it had been made clear that the away team could carry nothing larger than a combadge on the generation ship.

He took in the landing bay as he walked. It was easily big enough to have comfortably accommodated a *Galaxy*-class starship, with the majority of the space given over to huge storage racks where medium-tonnage Jazari vessels hung from the overhead. Antigravity skiffs moved back and forth overhead, carrying octagonal container modules and sheets of repurposed hull metal. One whole quarter of the chamber was turned over to a ship-breaker platform like the one that had imploded, and as Keru watched, the construct began to fold in on itself like a giant origami sculpture, collapsing its structure for storage elsewhere in the great vessel.

He found Troi introducing the other, older Jazari male. "May I present Yasil? He's one of the key members of the Governing Sept."

"Good day." Yasil bowed and Keru attempted to do the same, a little stiffly. "Welcome, Captain Riker, Commander Vale, Lieutenant Commander Keru. I have heard much that speaks well of you." He inclined his head toward Zade.

Keru idly wondered if that included details of the Friday-night tongo games, but didn't mention it. Zade seemed different here among his own kind, still a little stiff and reserved, but in some way, more alive.

"Sir," began Riker, "your willingness to accommodate my crew shows a generosity that is, quite frankly, unexpected. But it is very gratefully received."

"Yes." Yasil cocked his head and gave a half smile. "I imagine you must think it very out of character for us. I will tell you this, Captain, not every Jazari wishes to follow an isolationist path." He glanced at Zade, sharing the thought. "But our people are a consensus, with all that entails."

"I am sorry that this meeting between us has come at this time, that it had to be a near tragedy that made it happen." Riker met Yasil's steady gaze. "But I'm glad we have the opportunity."

Yasil's smile faded. "We deeply regret that members of your crew were lost in this terrible accident. A number of our kind were also ended in the loss of the Reclaim Platform."

"We coordinate, and they are recollected," Zade said somberly. Yasil gave him a glare, as if he had spoken out of turn.

From the corner of his eye, Keru saw a flicker of blue light from the atmospheric barrier across the landing-bay entrance. A jade-green shuttle-craft with a bow like an eagle's skull floated into the chamber, pinned between the same tractor beams that had brought in the *Armstrong*.

The Romulan shuttle dropped smoothly onto the pad next to the Star-fleet craft and the beams snapped off. Presently, the jaw of the eagle-head cockpit module dropped open, becoming an embarkation ramp.

Keru stiffened as he saw the flash of a Romulan uniform. As a tactical officer, he was trained to think of Romulans as adversaries, and he had to work to rein in the instinct.

Commander Medaka led the way off the shuttle, followed by the red-headed female officer Keru had seen briefly during their communication with the *Othrys*. The last being to leave was a good head taller than Medaka, and he had to duck under the nose of the craft as he exited. While Medaka was of average build and the woman slight and athletic, the big guy was thickset and muscular, broad but well maintained. Under other circum-stances, he seemed the type that Keru might have bought a drink for in a shore-leave bar, but then their eyes briefly met and the pitiless glitter there killed that notion stone dead.

Yasil gave Medaka the same formal welcome he had to Riker, and the Romulan commander introduced himself and his cohorts. The woman was Major Helek, his executive officer; Keru was pretty sure he detected a sour note when Medaka described her as such, and filed that observation away for later consideration. Helek graced the Jazari with a haughty nod, but she didn't spare a glance for the Starfleet contingent. The bigger man was a centurion by the name of Garn, and he was clearly the muscle. Garn's eyes swept the landing bay like the nodes of a targeting scanner, evaluating everything in sight in terms of threat potential.

For their part, the Jazari did not appear to notice. "Our people wish to express their deep and heartfelt gratitude toward the United Federation of

Planets and the Romulan Star Empire," said Yasil. "As a duly designated representative of the Governing Sept, please know that your combined actions in containing the spatial fracture that threatened this ship saved countless Jazari from a premature ending. For that, we will forever hold the crews of the *Starship Titan* and the warbird *Othrys* in great esteem."

Medaka glanced at Riker, and then spoke. "I believe Captain Riker will agree with me when I say we did what any principled being would do. We may have our differences, but out here that does not matter."

"Well said." Captain Riker gave a nod.

Silence fell, and the moment stretched, becoming awkward. At length, Major Helek shifted her stance and eyed the Jazari. "Is that . . . all?"

Once again, Yasil and Zade exchanged an unreadable glance, and the older man went on. "I would like to show you what you saved. Many of our kind have lived their entire existence believing that we should shut ourselves off from other races, but not I. If you will come with us, we will show you our vessel, and you will grasp the magnitude of what this exodus means for us."

An antigrav craft came to gather them up, a slim cylinder with a clear canopy that reminded Riker of the air trams used on many Federation worlds.

It rose and entered a tunnel in the walls of the landing bay, accelerating past a blur of blank walls that suddenly fell away to reveal a transparent tube around them. And beyond, they saw into the terrain of one of the ecodomes.

"The Ochre Dome," explained Zade, gesturing toward a landscape of greenery and orange-red rocks. "As Counselor Troi is now familiar with. It is one of twenty such environment chambers of similar dimension."

"Reminds me of Colorado," said Riker, recalling childhood visits with his father to that part of Earth's North American continent. "Good spot for a vacation."

"It's pretty close," his wife told him. "I wish our visit came in better circumstances." Then Troi leaned in close so that only he would hear her. "I take it you saw the sigils on Major Helek's baldric? The placement sends a hidden message to anyone who knows how to read them."

He made an educated guess. "She's Tal Shiar?"

"Undoubtedly. And she wants us to know it."

Riker took that in. "I'll keep that in mind."

The transport flashed through another connecting tube and into a different environment. This one resembled an arctic tundra, and he caught sight of a herd of furred, yak-like animals roaming the landscape.

"Each dome contains a representative sample of plant life and other species from our planet and . . ." Yasil paused, reframing his words. "And other worlds."

"Two by two," Keru muttered to Riker.

"I understand the intent to preserve these beasts," said Helek, "but why do you require live ones? Surely gene samples placed in stasis would be a more efficient method of storage."

"We have extensive gene banks," said Zade. "But there is something to be said for a living example."

"Do you consume their flesh?" The heavyset centurion broke his silence for the first time, his voice a low rumble. He asked as if he was interested in sampling the meat himself.

"No." Yasil's expression became unreadable. "Ours is a mission of preservation and observation, nothing more."

The tube-way took them through a dome holding a pocket ocean and then another that resembled a desert of black basaltic sand, before emerging along the top of the great ship's central fuselage. They passed around the glowing orb of a massive tetryon power core, and the two Jazari deftly and politely deflected every query Riker and Medaka posed about it. Then the transport capsule flew out over open storage bays, where worker drones beneath them were busy placing reclaimed starship parts and the last few cargo pods, in preparation for the departure.

Troi engaged Yasil and Zade in conversation, and Riker found himself studying the view with Commander Medaka at his side.

"It is an impressive feat of engineering," offered the Romulan. "My civilization grew from colonists who once forged their way through the stars on ships like this."

"Humans from Earth did the same in the early days of space exploration, before the discovery of warp drive," said Riker. "But nothing on this scale."

"Yes, I am aware." Medaka caught Riker's curious expression and smiled briefly. "I'm familiar with Terran culture. You are quite open with your history, Captain. You make it freely available. Unlike our hosts, who seem to thrive on mystery."

Riker's lip curled. "Some might say the same thing about Romulans." Nearby, Centurion Garn gave him a cold stare that was almost menacing.

Medaka's smile became genuine mirth, a wry grin. "The Romulan people are an open book, Captain. You just need to know how to read it."

"I can't argue with that."

The commander's voice dropped. "I'm sure you notice that the Jazari are only showing us what we could have seen for ourselves with a cursory visual sweep. I confess, this sudden openness on their part feels like a token effort to me. A way to stop us asking too many questions. Do you agree?"

"Well, it's not about what they show us, Commander," Riker replied, "it's the fact that they're doing it at all that matters."

"And yet only Yasil and Zade are here to conduct us on this tour. I think you wonder, as I do, how the Governing Sept feels about the presence of aliens aboard their craft." Riker said nothing, but privately he had to admit that the Romulan's thoughts echoed his own. "How have your people been treated by them?"

"Politely," he noted, "but distantly."

"Little change from before." Medaka nodded at his own statement. "You know they made the offer to us as well? I declined, *politely*, of course.

Major Helek was quite upset by that. She felt a vital avenue of exploitable intelligence was being overlooked."

Down at the far end of the capsule, Riker saw Helek was interrogating Zade. "She has her chance now."

Their transport slowed, before turning on its own axis. It halted, then began to move back in the direction it had come, back toward the middle of the great ship. They passed by a section of the hull that had been raked with energetic pulses from the chaotic singularity, and patches of bright, new tritanium plate were clearly visible where they had been welded over hull breaches.

Both men studied the damage, both knowing full well what such scarring could cost a starship. "It could have been so much worse," said Riker. "It's fortunate the *Othrys* was close enough to render assistance."

Medaka eyed him. "You mean, fortunate that we were close enough to be spying on you."

"If you say so."

The Romulan gave that rueful half smile again. "I hope you won't be insulted if I tell you that observing the activities of the *Titan* is not at the top of my mission priority list."

"But it *is* on that list, right?" Riker decided to change tack, working to get the measure of his opposite number. "It occurred to me that you could have just let it happen back there. Your warbird was cloaked. You could have sat out the situation and watched the accident unfold. No one would have known. And I imagine Romulus would not have shed a tear to see a Starfleet ship lost."

Medaka gave Riker a sharp, searching look. "If I did that . . . what kind of person would that make me?" he asked. For a moment, he seemed to be caught between emotions, unsure if Riker was testing him or if the Starfleet officer genuinely thought the commander was capable of such a thing. Then it passed, and Medaka lost himself in the view across the Jazari vessel. "I grew up dreaming of being an explorer, of venturing to uncharted places such as our friends here will see," he said, taking a long breath. "But until very recently I have been a military man. Now, for my sins, it seems, I have been given the very thing I wished for in my youth." He gestured up at the stars. "I have a fine ship and the best crew available, beings from planets all across the Empire and its allies. We search for new worlds for the Romulan people. Such a laudable goal, and one I would delight in, were it not for the shadow cast over my mission."

"The supernova," said Riker quietly.

Medaka sighed. "We call it the star-death."

"Where are your people?" Troi noted that Major Helek was unable to voice any query in a way that didn't make it sound like a demand. "Do they fear us? Do they hide from outsiders?"

"No." Yasil's head bobbed. "The great majority of our people are in, or are in the process of entering, a state of suspension."

"For the journey," Zade clarified. "So that we might conserve our resources."

Troi's attention was split equally between the Romulans and the Jazari, so much so that had she not been watching carefully, she might have missed the split-second microexpressions on the faces of their hosts. She didn't see the indicators that most beings showed when they were skirting a truth. She only saw blankness, a nonexpression so bereft of meaning she could not parse it.

Helek, on the other hand, was quite readable, even if she believed she was not. Her manner was caustic and arrogant in equal measures, and Troi guessed that she wasn't used to acting within the realms of diplomatic niceties. As the Romulan secret police, the Tal Shiar and its agents moved unopposed through the Empire, with few willing to stand in the way for fear of incurring their wrath. It was plain Helek did not enjoy playing the role of a line officer, forced to feign interest in the Jazari's elliptical manners.

"What is your destination?" Again, Helek almost barked her inquiry.

"We have identified a number of viable star clusters deep in the Beta Quadrant," said Yasil. "The M-Class worlds orbiting those suns would be adequate for our needs, if we were to make a home there."

"You eschew the protection of the Federation and put yourself at the mercy of open space." Helek put acid emphasis on the word *protection*. "I wonder what they must have done to drive you away."

"The Jazari have never chosen to become members of the Federation," corrected Troi. "But we have always considered them respected friends and interstellar neighbors."

"The question still stands," Helek replied.

"Our destiny is not here," said Zade. "Our collective has decided to seek it elsewhere."

While the two Jazari remained empathically unreadable, Troi sensed the edges of the Romulan woman's emotional aura, felt them change and move. Helek was growing disinterested with the Jazari's gracious obstructionism and she sought her sport somewhere else. The major turned her attention fully to Deanna Troi, not even attempting to mask her thoughts.

She has to know I am an empath, thought Troi, *so she's deliberately showing her confidence.*

"How does your vessel fare, Commander Troi?" Helek asked, but gave her no pause in which to insert an answer. "You have civilian families and children aboard the *Titan*, do you not? Were any of them killed in the accident? Does Starfleet not consider such a thing to be irresponsible? How can such a policy do anything but impair the concentration of your crew?"

She took a breath and Troi could finally cut in, replying to everything with equal pace. "*Titan* fares well. Yes, we do. None of them. Starfleet does not, and we manage perfectly well."

"You have given that answer before, I think," said the major. "Your reply is well worn." Before Troi could challenge that, Helek switched gears again, back to the Jazari. "What is the maximum faster-than-light velocity of this great ship? Does it use a phased-array warp matrix or a standard field model?" The Romulan woman's practice of hectoring and changing the subject every few moments was wearing.

"I am no engineer, merely an administrator," said Yasil, "but I know our vessel can maintain a cruising velocity of warp seven. And I believe the field matrix is a hybrid model."

"You are a very well-informed administrator," Helek retorted. "It cannot be denied that your craft is an impressive creation. If Romulus and her sister worlds had a handful of vessels like this one, the *Othrys's* mission would be redundant." She let her eyes track back toward Troi and the other Starfleet officers, and her tone became harsh. "All those threatened by the star-death could be evacuated in weeks, instead of facing an uncertain fate."

And there it is, thought the counselor, *the bitterness and resentment that marbles everything in her manner, revealing itself in full at last.*

Helek locked eyes with Troi, and she was daring her to say something, the need to find an excuse to attack verbally seething behind that glare. A cloak of darkness fell over the clear windows atop the capsule as they reentered the transit tunnels, and it framed the pale woman like a revenant from some gothic holonovel.

The commanders of the *Titan* and the *Othrys* had picked up on the souring of the mood, and both men rejoined the group. Will gave Deanna a slight nod, affirming what she already knew, that he would back her up whatever was said next.

For his part, Medaka's silent warning was telling Helek to back off, but she ignored it. "In a way, we are kindred spirits, Yasil," said the major. "Romulan and Jazari. Both displaced by events beyond our control, leaving our homes behind for other worlds." At length, she broke eye contact. "The difference being that your species chose to do this. Ours did not have that option."

"We will initiate our departure in eighteen hours, Federation Standard." Zade offered the information unbidden, perhaps in an attempt to lessen the tension in the cabin. "The great ship will follow a sublight vector from orbit and then enter warp velocity on a heading out of this system, toward Sector 743-D." He glanced at Will. "Captain Riker, you have been granted permission for the *Titan* to travel with us on a parallel course for forty-seven hours."

"Will that be enough time for you to complete your repairs?" added Yasil.

"I believe so," said the captain. "Once decontamination is complete, we can start bringing our people back in stages. Then we can . . . go our separate ways."

"Forgive my interruption," said Medaka. "That Starfleet designation you used, 743-D. That area is known as a zone rife with plasma storms. You are aware of this, yes?"

"We are," said Zade. "But to avoid it would add a great deal of transit time to our voyage."

"The Star Empire has very precise charts of that region," Medaka continued, and both Helek and the centurion gave him hard, censorious stares. It was a well-known fact that the Romulans jealously guarded their astronavigational knowledge; just admitting they had detailed maps of regions near Federation space was akin to blurting out a state secret. "In the interests of continued cooperation," said the commander, "I will place the warbird *Othrys* at the disposal of the Jazari Governing Sept, and we will escort you through this area."

Yasil and Zade both showed that blank expression again for a moment. "A generous offer, but it is not required—" began the elder, but Medaka held up a hand to stop him.

"Sir. I know that zone well, and it can be treacherous to those unfamiliar with it. If we allowed your ship and the *Titan* to pass through it unescorted, we would be putting you in grave danger." He bowed slightly, and as hard as she pushed, Troi's empathic senses could not detect any pretense beneath his words. "Please. Choose to let us do this."

At length, Yasil gave a nod. "Very well. We will extend the forty-seven-hour vector to include the *Othrys* as well as the *Titan*."

Medaka gave Deanna's husband a smile. "I have never flown alongside a Starfleet vessel before. It will be interesting."

"I have no doubt," said Riker.

SIX

With Centurion Garn in the pilot's couch, the shuttle from the *Othrys* moved like a starfighter, peeling off the deck of the Jazari launch bay in a showy takeoff, speeding away and back toward the warbird.

Medaka remained the picture of indolent calm, even replicating himself a cup of hot *solok* tea to sip on the short journey. Helek decided that he was acting this part deliberately, in order to irritate her.

He was succeeding, but she would never allow him to know it. "For clarity's sake, Commander," she began, "will you remind me how many elements of your oath you have ignored?"

He drank his tea and shrugged. "I'm sure you will put them all in your reports, Major."

"There is a difference between creative interpretations of the requirements of military service, and naked disregard for them." She took the seat opposite and fixed him with a measuring glare. "You revealed secrets to an enemy power and a nonaligned alien species."

Medaka snorted. "I told them we have a map, that's all. I did not give them the key to the praetor's bedchamber or the command codes for our border stations." He eyed her. "The Federation knows that our charts of the Star Empire's borders are exacting in detail, even those of areas that by treaty we should never venture into. They ignore that truth the same way we ignore their listening posts disguised as astronomical observation platforms. The veil over these things is a convenience." He paused, watching her across the rim of his cup. "You would understand that if you spent more time on starship duty and less skulking in dark corners."

Helek ignored the jibe. "What does this gain us?"

He put down the cup. "We avert a potentially fatal contact between the Jazari, the *Titan*, and a plasma storm. Is that not enough?"

"And we do this . . . what is the Terran phrase, *from the goodness of our hearts*?" She could barely say the words without a derisive snort.

Medaka chuckled. "Believe me, Major, nothing will confuse them more than a Romulan displaying selflessness."

"That is a poor reward for so much risk."

He finished his tea as the shuttle slowed to enter the *Othrys*'s aft docking bay. "Helek, answer me this in honesty, if you can, when I say to you, *what is the right thing to do*, how do you reply?"

"The right thing to do," she repeated, "is whatever best serves Romulus."

"We agree on that, at the very least," he replied. But she had her doubts.

They disembarked and Hade-Tah was waiting for them, the genderless Taurhai standing stock-still as it waited for the commander to approach. Medaka led the navigator away, talking to it about the ridiculous offer he had made, and Helek glanced up at Garn.

The centurion said nothing, giving her a mute nod in return, and trailed after Medaka. There were a handful of officers and crew aboard the *Othrys* that Helek considered reliable, and Garn was at the top of that list. The ship's taciturn chief of security was known to the Tal Shiar, graded on the trust index of the secret police force as one who could be expected to follow orders instead of personal loyalties. The rest of them were largely at the malcontent end of the spectrum, some pureblood Romulan sub-lieutenants who nursed resentments at being passed over for alien recruits from allied races, others who would not dare to disobey and risk losing their positions. She could control enough of them, if the need arose.

And if there was one among the crew of the warbird over whom Helek had complete mastery, it was the gangly, narrow-shouldered scientist who approached her.

"Major Helek!" Vadrel gasped her name, his pale eyes darting around the shuttlebay. "I must speak with you, it is urgent!"

"Must you?" He was her age but he seemed old before his years, a skinny and ill-drawn Romulan male in the oversuit of an auxiliary crewman and the tool yoke of a scientist. "Proceed, then."

"Not here." He leaned in conspiratorially. "Somewhere *secure*."

Helek's lip curled, and she beckoned him to follow her. "I will humor you," she told him, "but make sure it is worth my time."

Vadrel trailed in her footsteps. He understood the need for secrecy, but he had no refinement about it. The scientist had the clumsy tradecraft of a civilian, his only redeeming quality being that he was, in his own field, a genius.

She led him to a storage compartment and shut them both inside, before pulling a masking module from inside her tunic. The device chimed, and emitted a small zero-surveillance field that would temporarily shield them from the ship's internal security sensors.

Satisfied the module was working, she gestured at him. "Out with it."

Vadrel drew his hands close and they moved as he spoke, his long fingers making complex shapes in the air. "The embedded scanners concealed in your uniforms," he began, indicating the black metal baldric across her tunic. "As ordered, I monitored the telemetry from them in real time while you were aboard the Jazari craft."

Although the Jazari had specifically requested that no sensor devices, no tricorders and the like, be brought onto the generation ship, Helek had paid no heed to that. While Riker and his people had obeyed like the credulous fools they were, Helek had ensured that she would be able to document every second they were inside the alien vessel.

On the returning shuttle, she had nursed annoyance over the lack of anything interesting shown on the brief tour, but now Helek wondered if that had been premature. "You found something worthy of notice?"

"Oh, yes." Vadrel smirked, and it made his appearance unpleasant, exaggerating the heavy northerner's brow over his eyes. The scientist had not been born with that face, nor with the name he had now; both were the dubious gifts of the Tal Shiar, given when they had provided him with a new identity.

Helek would always trust Vadrel's loyalty, not because he was a patriot, not because he was dependable, but because it was held in place by abject fear. Fear of who he had once been, and what he had done in that former life. Fear of what would happen if that information ever became public knowledge.

"The tetryon drive system they have, clearly that is of strategic value," he went on, slipping into the lecturing tone he was wont to adopt. "And I did gather some valuable readings from it when you passed by in the travel capsule—"

"Come to the point quickly," she demanded.

"I was quite alarmed at first," he told her, hands moving as he framed his reply. "I will need to run a deeper analysis of the data, of course, but it appears the embedded scanners detected the presence of multiple positronic energy matrices on board the Jazari craft! They are carrying some kind of artificially intelligent systems in the core of the ship. Deliberately concealing them, I believe."

An icy rush ran through Helek's body. "Are you sure?"

"As I say, I need to conduct a deeper analysis—"

She advanced on him, her eyes flashing. "*Make certain*," Helek growled. "Speak of this to no one. Conduct all investigations under most secure conditions. I will not hesitate to destroy you utterly if you disobey me, Vadrel. Do you understand?"

"Of course." His birdlike head bobbed on his thin neck. "I am aware of what is at stake."

"No," she said, silencing him with the cold menace of her reply. "You are not."

"*¡Madre!*" A small, tousle-haired tornado came rushing into the bubble tent, circling around Troi, waving his hands animatedly at the air. "*Las estrellas se mueven!*"

She gave her son a level look, putting aside the padd in front of her. "What have we said about knocking before you enter?"

Thaddeus Troi-Riker stumbled to a halt and took in the collapsible dwelling. "*Tenteu ya*," he replied, switching from Spanish to Korean, and then, mercifully, back to Standard. "It doesn't have a door to knock on."

"You know what I mean, young man. Don't just barge in, it's rude."

Thad's shoulders slumped. "Sorry. I just got excited." Then he was bouncing on the balls of his feet. "The stars are moving, Mom! Come and see! *Eínai apístefto!*"

"Is that Greek?" Troi sighed and surrendered to the reality that she wasn't going to get any more work done while her son was so animated, and she let him lead her outside. Thad's ability for parsing and storing away different dialects never ceased to amaze her. It did sometimes make things confusing, though, when his enthusiasm got the better of him and he started to babble.

He keeps this up, she thought, *Will and I will need a universal translator to talk to him.*

"Look look look!" Thad scrambled up on top of a packing crate and pointed toward the clear dome high above them. Through it, just as the boy had promised, the starscape was slowly drifting past, gradually picking up speed as the Jazari generation ship accelerated through space.

Troi experienced a moment of giddiness, and she wasn't the only one. Several of the other evacuees from the *Titan* had come out of their tents and temporary accommodations to watch the departure, and she heard nervous laughter from more than a few. If one lowered their eyes to the artificial horizon of the Ochre Dome, it would have been easy to believe they were on the surface of a planet, and Troi's subconscious clearly did so. But glancing upward made the truth apparent. The pocket ecosphere was just a small sliver of life clinging to the hull of a giant starship as it ventured out into the darkness.

The misty orb of the planet around which the Jazari's former home-world orbited passed across the "sky," and Thad gave a low whistle of appreciation. "Wow. See how big that is!"

"That is why it is known as a gas giant," said a precise voice. Doctor Talov approached from the direction of the infirmary tent.

"Does it smell stinky?" said the boy, in all seriousness.

Talov pursed his lips. "I am . . . unaware. I believe the odor would be redolent of certain organic hydrocarbon chains and—"

"You don't have children, do you?" interrupted Troi.

"I have yet to sire any progeny," admitted the Vulcan.

"I can tell." She switched subjects. "How are your patients?"

"Improving," he noted, and gestured at their surroundings. "I believe this environment is providing a positive influence on their well-being." Talov paused, searching for the right words. "It is . . . not unpleasant."

"I agree." Troi studied the low, leafy trees that surrounded the encampment's clearing, and the rocky ridges extending away toward the dome's perimeter. Even if the enclosure was an artificially engineered creation, it felt enough like the real thing. After days of being cooped up in cramped conditions aboard a damaged starship, this place was heavenly.

"I really, really like it here," announced Thad. "I think we should stay."

"We're just visiting," Troi reminded him.

"But we could build a house." Her son pointed out past the trees. "I even found a cool place. Near a stream, where we could swim!"

"Thaddeus," said Talov. "You and the other younglings should not venture too far from the camp perimeter without adult supervision. Has your mother not made this clear to you?"

"Lots of times," said Thad, rolling his eyes. "It's okay, though. I'm careful."

"That is a matter of perspective," noted Talov. "I have already had to prescribe anti-allergens to some of your school friends after exposure to alien plant life, as well as medication for the disagreeable effects on the digestive tract from eating too much of the local fruit."

"Listen to the doctor," said Troi. "We're guests here, remember? So don't go poking around where you shouldn't. Or eating strange things."

"I thought Starfleet were *explorers*," Thad said moodily. "I'm just *exploring*." He looked down at his mother. "Why can't we live here? We could ask the Jazari if it was okay. It would be a nice place to call home. And if they did let us, I'm sure I could learn their language and—"

"*Titan to Commander Troi.*" Will's voice issued out of Deanna's combadge, and saved her from having to shoot down her son's big ideas. "*How are things over there?*"

"We are in good spirits," she replied. "Doctor Talov has just informed me that our injured crew are healing well."

"*That's great to hear. I'm recommending you remain there until we pass through the storm zone. You may as well make the most of it.*"

"Hi, Daddy!" Hearing his father, Thad called out and waved, pointing back toward the dome. "I can see you!" Troi glanced back up and saw light glitter off a metallic white shape out in the darkness as starlight reflected off the hull of the *Titan.*

"*Hey, Thad!*" Will had a smile in his voice. "*Are you getting into mischief?*"

"No!" The boy's fib was so unequivocal that Troi and Talov both raised an identical, quizzical eyebrow. "I've been doing lots of exploration," he declared.

"*I don't doubt it.*" Her husband knew full well what that meant. "*Well, listen to your mom and make sure you pay attention to everything. I want a full report when I see you next, okay?*"

"Okay, Captain Dad." Thad slipped off the crate, catching sight of some of the other children. He dashed off, leaving the adults to their conversation.

"Sir, if I may?" Talov spoke up. "What is the status of the ship's sickbay?"

"*McCreedy's people are going deck by deck,*" he noted. "*Sickbay is top of the list for full decontamination, right after main engineering. Our repairs are on schedule.*"

Something else out beyond the glassy roof of the dome glittered in the glow of distant suns, and Troi caught sight of the *Othrys.* The Romulan ship moved with the *Titan,* both of them cruising alongside the Jazari vessel in a companionable formation.

"How about our colleagues from across the Neutral Zone?"

"Interesting times," admitted Riker. *"Ranul has caught them trying to run high-density neutrino-beam scans through our hull a half-dozen times now. They're not wasting the opportunity to give a* Luna-*class starship a good once-over."*

"Are we returning the favor?"

Her husband chuckled. *"I think if Commander Vale had her way, we'd have an EVA team out there scraping samples off their hull. For now, we're just keeping a weather eye on them."*

"I will confess," said Talov, "despite the fact that the Romulan people and my own share a common ancestry, I find their overly secretive behavior perplexing. Such a worldview can only, ultimately, be self-defeating. Given their changed circumstances, they should abandon it."

"A Romulan without an agenda . . ." Troi mused on the idea. "I don't think they could do without that."

"The Klingons changed their attitude toward outsider species when the destruction of the Praxis moon forced their hand," noted Talov, "and they have retained the character of their people. I believe the Romulans could do the same in the face of the supernova threat, if they so choose."

"And there's the rub," said Riker. *"If they choose, Doctor. I don't know if they could. Commander Medaka seemed genuine to me, but even he's holding something back . . ."*

Troi had sensed the same thing. "At least we can be clear about Major Helek's motivations. Medaka's executive officer obviously hates Starfleet and everything the Federation stands for."

"You think so? I didn't notice," her husband deadpanned, then he sighed. *"I think I need a different set of eyes on this, Deanna."*

She frowned. "What do you mean?"

"I'm going to call an old friend for some advice. Stay safe. Titan *out."*

"I do not follow the captain's intention," said Talov.

"Let's just say, we have a mutual acquaintance who has a lot of experience with this sort of thing . . ." Troi trailed off as she noticed that her son, and all of his friends, had vanished into the undergrowth.

Talov noted the same. "It appears your son has gone 'exploring' once again, Commander."

Major Helek returned to her quarters and locked the door, before sweeping the rooms for surveillance gear. This was a ritual she performed every night before going to sleep or—as now—if a matter of urgency had come to light.

Her scanner wand showed a solid blue glow, indicating no detections. She hid the device back in its secure compartment, behind a painting of the Gal Gath'thong firefalls, and activated her masking module once more, to be doubly secure. Then, with the lights dimmed, Helek went to the portable screen on her desk.

"Ready," said the voice of the ship's computer system.

"Recognize me," she ordered.

"You are Major Helek," it replied, *"first officer aboard the warbird* Othrys.*"*

Helek gave a series of commands that she knew by rote. "Access deep memory. Locate a subcluster with the identity nine-one-six-green-two and activate the contents."

"No such subcluster exists—" The synthetic voice suddenly stopped as a hidden ghost program was triggered. After a moment, it began again. *"Subcluster nine-one-six-green-two active and running. Root access now granted to ship systems, by the order of the Tal Shiar. What is your command?"*

The major smiled to herself. With this, she could remotely control all but the most critical of the *Othrys*'s primary functions. The Tal Shiar embedded these secret access codes in the mainframes of every Romulan vessel, in the event that their agents would need to influence the operation of a serving starship. They were a last-resort tactic, limited in usefulness and generally frowned upon as inelegant. But they could be a valuable tool.

"Tie in to the subspace communications array. Open a covert channel on this frequency." Helek manually tapped a string of digits onto the portable screen. "Block all indicators to other stations aboard this ship and erase all evidence of the transmission once it has been completed. Confirm."

"Stand by." A moment later, it spoke again. *"Warning! User-designated frequency has not been authorized by the Tal Shiar. No such receiver node exists."*

"Oh, it exists," she said to herself, then addressed the computer again. "Override and transmit. Authorization: Zhat Vash."

The device gave a strangled squeal as conflicting programs within it were nullified. *"Confirmed."*

For a long moment, the cabin remained dark and silent. Then a figure beneath a hood became barely visible on the screen, the vague outline of a Romulan face concealed in the gloom.

"What is the Admonition?" said a voice. It had been rendered genderless and unidentifiable, scrubbed of all indicators until it seemed more artificial than that of the *Othrys*'s computer system. That was, in a way, an amusing irony.

"It is the end of all we know," said Helek, speaking the response like a mantra.

"And what must be done to prevent it?"

She gave the next counterphrase. "Anything and everything."

The hooded head bowed slightly. *"Speak, sister, with clarity and alacrity. This channel will not remain open for long."*

With quick, spare description, Helek relayed what the scientist Vadrel had told her about the likelihood of artificial life being aboard the Jazari generation ship.

As she spoke, it was as if she were giving reality and dimension to this possibility. Helek's pale hands tightened unconsciously, her body tensing as if she were about to step into a fighting ring.

In her mind's eye she saw the horrifying potentiality of the thinking machines, their monstrous blank faces and dead artificial eyes. She remembered the nightmares she still experienced, of organic life erased from existence and a synthetic Armageddon consuming all of Romulan space and everything beyond. She re-experienced a shadow of the terrifying visions the Zhat Vash had shown her, there on the pallid sands of an alien world, and for a moment, Helek felt the faint pull of madness dragging on her. Others who had been there had not survived the experience, driven insane by it, preferring to take their own lives rather than live with what they had glimpsed. She had been strong enough to survive it—but something in her mind had broken that day, a fracture forming in her psyche that could never be mended.

In a way, there were two Sansar Heleks. The woman she had been before she experienced the power of the Admonition had been a dedicated, ruthless, unswerving patriot. The woman she was now still possessed those qualities, but with a zealot's willingness to cross any line and commit any act.

When her report ran out of words, the major found herself short of breath, her heart racing.

"This discovery, if true, is of grave import," said the hooded figure. *"The Zhat Vash cannot suffer the machine to live. If the Jazari are hiding synthetics aboard their vessel, we must take steps."*

"I am alone out here," she began. "How should I—"

"We are all alone," the voice replied. *"But we are united against the threat."*

"Yes, of course. What are your orders?"

"Act with care. You have trained your whole life for this moment, Sansar Helek, sister of the Zhat Vash. Confirm Vadrel's findings. If the scientist is correct . . . all trace of the synthetics must be destroyed. Whatever the cost."

"There may be complicating factors," she said, after a moment. "A Federation starship is in close proximity."

"Whatever the cost," repeated the voice.

"Very well." Helek inhaled deeply, moderating her breathing. "I will need disinformation to cover my actions."

"Provisions will be made," came the reply. *"We have done this many times. We are prepared."*

Helek nodded. "We will do what needs to be done. Anything and everything."

"It's the leafhoppers," said Moritz, drawing a big hand through his dark hair. "They're back in the top field. If we don't deal with them soon, they'll spread."

He was a portly man, with the kind of ruddy and rotund physique that would have you imagining him out of breath after taking ten steps, but he was fitter than he appeared. Throughout the morning, the affable Belgian agronomist had been at work all over the place, grubbing in the soil, popping up in between the growing lines of the vineyard. He seemed to have boundless energy, a quality that Jean-Luc Picard—if he were honest—found equally admirable and wearing.

Picard frowned, looking back in the direction of the chateau, finding the nearest of the gardener drones where it drifted on antigravs above the rows of greenery. "Do I need to change the mix in the spray again?"

Moritz gave a typically wide shrug. "It couldn't hurt, monsieur. Have you thought about using subsonics to discourage them?"

Picard tapped his earlobe. "Too bothersome. I hear it in my sleep." In truth, the noise reminded him too much of the low, ever-present hum of warp engines.

"Oh." Moritz stared past his shoulder at something. "And I suppose it is disturbing for your, ah, staff? With their, ah, sensitivity?"

"Romulan hearing is much more sensitive than that of humans," said a voice from behind him, and Picard turned to see Laris approaching, cupping a small electronic device in one hand. She was still a dozen meters away, but she heard everything they said. Back up by the main path, he could see her partner, Zhaban, taking in the day as if he were out on a constitutional. They were never far apart, those two.

Moritz colored slightly, and suddenly he didn't seem to know where to put his hands. Picard had often seen this kind of behavior in humans who were confronted by his offworlder friends. A directionless discomfort at close proximity to a being from a race humans had been raised to call an enemy. Moritz was a decent fellow, and Picard doubted he harbored any ill will toward Laris and Zhaban, but the man was still distinctly uneasy in their presence.

It is guilt, he thought. *It is easy to put the Romulan crisis out of mind when you don't have to meet one of them.*

"I'll, ah, put together some notes for you, and send them to your system. Suggestions." Moritz bent to gather up his geo-tricorder and soil samplers, and set off back toward his aircar with unseemly haste. "*Au revoir!*"

"I make him nervous," Laris said quietly as she stepped up to Picard's side. "I think he's a little afraid of me."

"Well, then he is a shrewd judge of character." Picard eyed her with mild amusement. The Romulan refugees who lived and worked at his vineyard were both excellent students of viticulture, but that wasn't their primary skill set. "You are one to be wary of."

The woman fingered some of the vines, returning his smile. "These days, my only adversaries are the leafhoppers, the little sods."

Not for the first time, Picard wondered where Laris had picked up her predilection for a certain Terran vernacular, but he decided that was a thread from the ex-spy's past he didn't want to pull on. Before Picard had offered them sanctuary at his home in the French countryside, both Laris and Zhaban had been agents of the Tal Shiar, engaged in a covert mission on a Romulan colony called Yuyat Beta. Nothing about that operation had gone the way it was expected to, not for the Romulans or for then-Admiral Jean-Luc Picard. But in the end it had borne out a new friendship—and that, Picard reflected, was far better than the alternative.

"Do you have need of me for something?" He was supposed to be working on the next chapter of his book, but the light of the day had drawn him away from the dusty corridors of history and out among the vines. Picard felt an impulse he couldn't put into words, a compulsion to be walking where things were growing and living, not hemmed in among the static tomes piled high in his study.

"You left your communicator back at the house," she told him. "An accidental oversight, no doubt."

"No doubt," he lied.

Laris offered him the device she was holding. "Someone wants to speak to you." It was a portable holographic emitter pod, capable of relaying a three-dimensional image from a subspace communications grid.

Picard's temperament soured. "I'm not in the mood."

"Mood's a thing for cattle and love-play," she chided. "Take it. You'll change your mind." Laris dropped the pod into his open palm and started back toward Zhaban.

He eyed the device warily, and almost stabbed the disconnect key the moment he saw the Starfleet delta indicator on the transmission header. But then he saw the originating location: *U.S.S. Titan, Beta Quadrant.*

Picard activated the connection and the pod floated up out of his hand, sketching in a human figure beneath it from its glowing holo-projector matrix. In a few moments, the haze of photons became a familiar face. "Will!"

"Admiral." Riker inclined his head. At his end of the communication, he was probably seeing a limited view of Picard's surroundings. *"I'm not interrupting you in the middle of something, am I?"*

"Not at all, not at all." Picard felt a surge of warmth at the sight of his former first officer. "Is everything all right? Deanna and Thaddeus—?"

"Both fine. They're on a field trip, you could say."

"This is unexpected," he admitted, "but welcome. Dare I ask how you got clearance for the energy cost for a call like this?"

"You know how it goes. Captain's prerogative, right?"

His smile turned bittersweet. "I suppose so."

"You look well. How's life in the country treating you?"

Picard made his way along the lines of vines, the holo-pod drifting obediently at his side. "Oh, the pace is hectic. I spend most of my days hunting down garden pests and avoiding my editor's calls about the history book I'm writing."

"History?"

"Yes. A study of the events surrounding the incident at Station Salem One," he explained. "If I ever get it finished. The most exciting thing I have to report is that someone sent me a puppy." He tried to keep his tone light, but the sullenness was creeping in. He changed tack. "How goes the mission?"

"That's why I'm calling," said Riker. *"I assume this is a secure line?"*

"Of course, but I doubt anyone is listening in on a grumpy old fool in a field."

"I need your advice on something, sir. I have a situation here and quite frankly, I'm not sure how best to proceed."

As Picard walked down the path between the ranks of vines, Riker sketched in an outline of the *Titan*'s current circumstances: the Jazari exodus, the accident, and the Romulan encounter. He took it all in, absorbing the information.

For a moment, the present fell away and he imagined himself on the bridge of the *Enterprise* in the same circumstances, facing the same challenges. How would Captain Jean-Luc Picard have handled it?

He eyed Riker's holo-image. "You've dealt with the Romulans before. What makes this time different?"

"It's them," said the other man. *"I can't articulate it, it just feels different. Things behind the scenes have changed on the other side of the Neutral Zone, and we're just seeing the ripples from it."*

"Indeed." Picard halted at the end of the row. "Their civilization is facing an extinction-level event. Some of them will dig in and become more Romulan than they ever were before, and others . . . like this man Medaka, they may become more open."

"If he's on the level, that is." Riker sighed. *"He could be playing us."*

"Good cop, bad cop." The other man frowned at the idiom, and Picard smirked. "Something I read in a Dixon Hill novel. Commander Medaka acts as a friend, while his executive officer is the expected enemy."

"But the reality is, they may both want to put us in jail." He nodded. *"It's hard to know what to trust. The Romulans have been our adversaries for so long, and we had the perfect opportunity to move past that and forge a friendship . . . But that moment was lost and I'm not sure we can ever get it back."*

Picard looked up, his face finding the glow of the afternoon sun. "You have to try, Will. They're not the monolithic culture they pretend to be." He found Zhaban and Laris off by one of the drone docks, and the two of them turned in his direction. Zhaban offered a wave, and he returned it. Picard's next words came from the heart, and their quiet power surprised even him. "I have to believe there's still hope. There must be." Then he cast off the moment and took a breath. "You know you'll be in the *merde* if Vice Admiral Clancy finds out you talked to me about this," he noted.

"Maybe so. But aside from Deanna, there's no one else I can go to who knows the Romulans as well as you."

"There's always Worf." Picard's response was wry, but only half in jest.

"He's got his hands full with the Enterprise. *He doesn't need another distraction."*

Picard nodded in agreement, pursing his lips as he thought on. "The Romulans will be up to something," he said. "The cardinal rule with the Star Empire: they're *always* up to something. But that doesn't mean we can't work with them." He paused, putting his thoughts in order. "If you want an edge, the best thing to do is be completely honest. If you can, give them the full, absolute, and unvarnished truth. You will wrong-foot them every time. They're simply not used to it."

Riker smiled. *"I'll keep that in mind."*

"And always look them in the eye." Picard gestured at the air. "Anything past that . . . Trust your instincts. That'll see you through." The sun vanished behind a cloud, and with it went the warmth that had first touched him on seeing Riker's face.

He was struck by a bleak sense of the distance between the two of them.

Not just in terms of the literal light-years, but of the chasm between one starship captain facing a stirring encounter and one old man standing amid rows of ripening grapes.

"Jean-Luc?" Riker saw the shift in his expression. *"Are you all right?"*

Picard felt the need to confess something to his friend. "Do you remember Anij?"

Riker nodded. *"One of the Ba'ku, yes. I recall you were rather taken with her . . ."*

A few years before Picard's promotion to flag rank, he and Riker and the *Enterprise* crew had visited the Ba'ku's planet on a personal mission that had revealed a conspiracy involving Son'a renegades and a rogue Starfleet admiral. While on the planet, Picard had experienced a profound moment of clarity that even now resonated clearly in his thoughts.

"Anij wrote to me," he went on, "an actual letter, ink on paper. She learned of my resignation from Starfleet and extended me an offer to return to their colony in the Briar Patch. To visit . . . or perhaps, to stay."

Riker's holographic form studied him carefully. *"Tell me you didn't refuse. The Ba'ku don't just allow anyone on their planet. And if you went there—"*

"Yes, the regenerative metaphasic radiation in the atmosphere would make me younger than you in a few years." Picard shook his head. "Of course I was tempted, who wouldn't be? But I couldn't accept. I couldn't leave this behind." He waved in the direction of the chateau. "I have responsibilities."

"That's not it," said Riker, cutting away the falsehood. *"You don't owe anyone anything. You've done the best that anyone could for the Federation, more than that, even. It's been over a year now since you . . ."* He hesitated, unwilling to say the word *resigned*. *"No one would blame you if you wanted to light out for a distant world, and find a new life."*

Despite the distance, Picard's old friend and former crewmate saw right through him. Riker took the thread of the other man's denial and brought it into the light.

"I have to be here, Will," he said, at length. "If for no other reason, to remind everyone in the Palais de la Concorde of the choice they made." Picard jutted his chin toward the west, in the direction of Paris and the seat of the Federation's government. "I want them to know I am here, a few kilometers away . . . like the ghost at the feast."

The words tasted ashen in his mouth. Hearing himself speak, he sounded petty and frustrated. The emotions from that fateful day in Admiral Bordson's office when he resigned his commission were still close to the surface. The wound remained raw and unhealed.

Riker took a moment before he spoke. *"Don't stay there just to spite them. Don't let yourself exist just for that, it's not enough of a reason. At the very least, play with your puppy, go write your books. But don't let resentment become your purpose, sir. It's a waste."*

"Always finding the alternatives," he said, with a rueful smile. "My friend, you are still looking out for me."

"It's what I do."

It felt like there was no more to be said, so Picard beckoned the holo-pod down to him. "Well . . . take care out there. And who knows, if you get tired of starship life and decide to put down roots, I can offer you some advice about retirement."

"Retire?" Riker chuckled. *"If I've learned one thing over the past decade, it's that whether you're on a starship bridge or not, once you're in this life, you never leave it."*

Picard laughed, and it was sincere. "What damned fool taught you that?"

Riker nodded his farewell, and the image of him faded into the sunshine.

SEVEN

Shelsa put his hands on his hips and drew himself up to his full height. "I am *not* going in there," he stated firmly.

The boy from Deneva was the oldest of the group and the tallest, so he liked to think that made him the one in charge. His gaze passed over the others, before settling on Thad, where the other child was crouching in the orange-red grass. They were close to the edge of the environment dome here. A few meters away, an oval tube protruded from the surface of the ground, half-hidden by the plants.

Thad felt compelled to reply. "That's okay, if you're scared."

"I am *not*!" Shelsa bellowed, predictably loud. "I'm not scared of any-thing!" He plucked at his jacket. "I don't want to get dirty in the mud like you do, that's all. It's icky!" He said the last word as if it was the absolute worst thing in the world.

"And we shouldn't." Hanee's hands knitted together. "We're already too far away. We'll get into trouble."

"Again," added T'Pir, arching her eyebrow. The short-haired Vulcan girl had the exact same manner as Doctor Talov, so much so that Thad couldn't believe they weren't related. "I have no desire to share once more in the penalties for your recklessness, Thaddeus."

"You said you liked exploring," Thad countered. "*I am curious*, you said that." He could feel the mood of the other kids shifting toward Shelsa's point of view. Thad had been able to convince them to come along on his latest adventure, and wander out into the wilds of the Ochre Dome, but the farther they got from the temporary encampment, the more tenuous his arguments became.

Ra'ag made the sort of barking-yelp noise that was his people's way of agreeing. "I'm all for it," he insisted, and Thad smiled. He could always count on the Antican boy to pick the more adventurous of any two options.

Min, who shifted nervously from foot to foot, wasn't the type to speak up unless he really had to, and Thad knew he could count on the other human child to follow along with the majority. "Min, you're with us, right?"

"Uh . . ." Min hedged, staring at the grass. "I don't know, Thad. Tee's got a point." He indicated the Vulcan girl.

Shelsa saw his opportunity and took it. "Remember when you said it was okay for us to play in the holodeck and it turned out you were making it up?" He sneered at him. "I was grounded and I had to miss dessert for a week because of you!" The boy jabbed an accusing finger in Thad's direction.

It was time to play his ace card, Thad decided. "My dad is the captain," he began, "and if he—"

But Shelsa and Hanee were both pulling exasperated faces before he could even finish the sentence.

"You always say that," snorted the young El-Aurian girl, "but it doesn't matter. Just because Captain Riker is in charge on the *Titan*, it doesn't mean you get to do whatever you want!"

Thad colored. He knew that truth all too well. "Okay, no . . ." He tried to backpedal. "What I meant was—"

"And we still get in trouble, even if you do not," T'Pir said levelly. "Your parentage has no bearing on that fact."

"Anyway, this isn't even your dad's starship!" added Shelsa. "It belongs to the Jazari, and they're not even in the Federation!"

Thad decided to make a last, desperate bid to keep the others interested. "Don't you want to know what is down there?" He pointed at the tube's mouth. "Don't you want to go . . . ?" He tried to remember the words written on the great big starscape mural on the wall of their schoolroom. "*Where no one has gone before?*"

"Thad thinks he's in Starfleet," Shelsa said to the others, his words dripping with sarcasm. "But he's too small. And too stupid."

"Je suis plus intelligent que vous!" Thad snapped back at him in French, knowing that the other boy couldn't understand him. But his display of linguistic skill didn't do anything to penetrate Shelsa's air of contempt.

"Something is coming!" cried Ra'ag, aiming a paw at the trees a few hundred meters distant.

From out of the canopy of greenery came an egg-shaped object made of translucent material, lit from within by blinking lights. The object dropped smoothly out of the air and dove straight toward the mouth of the tube. A low humming tone sounded as it came closer.

All of the children stood and watched as the thing flew straight into the tube, an iris hatch snapping open, then closed behind it.

"A monitor drone of some kind," said T'Pir, with a sniff. "It must belong to the Jazari. We should not interfere with its operation."

Thad rounded on her. "I think that tube leads somewhere. We saw a lot of other domes when we were coming in on the shuttle, didn't we?" He got some nods of agreement and went on. "Well, I want to follow the tube and see what's in the next ecodome!"

"Why?" Shelsa went back to his hands-on-hips pose again, and glared at Thad. "Who cares what's in the other domes?"

Thad didn't actually have a good answer for that, beyond his raw curiosity. "I do?" He swallowed hard. "We could find some Jazari. Find out all about them. No one knows anything about them, we could be the first!"

"I don't even want to *be* here," Shelsa went on. "I want to be back on the *Titan*. In my room, with all my stuff." With each sentence, the other children nodded along with him, and even Ra'ag joined in. "We're stuck down here because your mom and dad messed up the ship." He prodded Thad hard in the chest, with enough force to make him stagger back a step. "So we don't have to do what you say."

Thad's jaw stiffened and he stood as tall as he could. The last thing he was going to do was let Shelsa insult not only Starfleet, but his parents into the bargain. "Okay. Fine. Go away, then, if you're so afraid. I'm not." The low hum was sounding again, and as it grew louder, he marched over to the tube. "You keep your stupid jacket all clean and neat, and I will *boldly go on my own!*"

Ra'ag reached out to him as he passed. "Thad, you shouldn't. It could be dangerous."

With a click of metal on metal, the hatch opened to let another drone out into the dome. Thad shook off his friend's grip and launched himself at the tube.

"See you later!" he yelled, and slid headfirst into the yawning metallic tunnel.

The last sound he heard from the other children was Hanee Phosia calling out his name before the hatch snapped closed.

Inside, the tube was frictionless and smooth, and the boy sped away into the darkness, already regretting his impulsive decision.

From the ports of the *Titan*'s briefing room, the Jazari generation ship was a vast cylinder of steel-gray metal and black solar arrays, pushing on through the darkness at high impulse speed.

Riker found the shadow of his ship visible on the hull of the bigger craft, the outline cast by the diminishing light of the Jazari star. A second, avian silhouette drifted across the steel, thrown from the *Othrys*, but the Romulan ship wasn't visible from this angle.

The captain felt a prickle of tension over his skin. Seeing the shadow of the Romulans but not their reality was a blunt metaphor for almost every dealing Riker had ever had with their kind. Could he make today something different? He wanted to believe it was possible, but there were other shadows at play, forces that a single starship commander was too small to influence.

The door hissed open and he turned as Commander Medaka entered, with Christine Vale a step behind. "Here we are, sir," said the XO, and she indicated a vacant chair near the head of the table.

Medaka thanked her but made no move to sit. "Will you be joining us, Commander?"

"No, sir. I'm afraid I have other duties to attend to." Vale gave Riker a look that had a whole different answer in it, and she backed out, leaving the two men alone.

"Thank you for accepting my invitation," said Riker. "To be honest, I wasn't sure you would."

Medaka glanced around the room. "It would have been rude not to." The other man came closer and offered his hand. "I appreciate the offer, Captain Riker."

Riker paused. "I wasn't aware that Romulans shook hands as a greeting."

"We don't, as a matter of course," said Medaka. "It is too easy a way to exchange a contact poison or nanoweapon. But I have studied human customs, and I'm willing to make an exception." The commander's tone was deceptively light.

Riker accepted the gesture and the two of them took a moment to size each other up. Jean-Luc Picard's counsel to always look a Romulan in the eye rang through Riker's thoughts in that moment before they disengaged. "Would you care for some tea?"

"Thank you." Medaka took a seat—a different one from the chair Vale had indicated, Riker noted.

The captain settled down across from him, pouring out the steaming tisane. Medaka waited for Riker to take a sip before drinking some of his own.

"This is my first time on board a Federation starship," said the Romulan. "I must say, the differences are fascinating."

"Starfleet rarely has the opportunity to host officers from nonallied forces," noted Riker. "I imagine very few Romulans have had the chance to see our ships from the inside."

Medaka's lips quirked up in a faint smile. "Oh, you would be surprised, Captain. It's more than you think. Certainly more than you know about."

Riker didn't allow the comment to divert him. "I'll be sure to pass that on to Starfleet Intelligence."

"My lineage is heavy with officers," said the Romulan. "My ancestors first served on ships during the Great Stellar Progression, more than two hundred of your Terran years ago. And the Medaka name has been intertwined with the Romulan fleet ever since."

Riker tallied the numbers in his head. The so-called Stellar Progression Medaka mentioned was his people's name for the invasion in the twenty-second century that led to what was known by the Federation as the Earth-Romulan War.

"I had family in the United Earth Starfleet back then," Riker said carefully, uncertain of where Medaka's line of conversation was leading. "On the *Patton* and Station K-3."

"You and I have this meeting over a pleasant cup of tea, but our forefathers might have surveyed one another down the barrels of their weapons." Medaka took another sip from his cup. "We should toast progress, don't you agree?"

"We were enemies then, but we don't have to be that now," said Riker.

"A worthy thought." The Romulan was silent for a moment. "Do you know, Captain, you have quite an extensive file in our records. The Riker name is one of note for our intelligence gatherers."

"Should I be flattered?"

Medaka smiled. "So many important encounters, especially during your service aboard the *Enterprise* and its successor ship. Confrontations with my people in the Neutral Zone, at Galorndon Core, Devolin, Beta Stromgren . . ."

"And yet you're still a mystery to me," admitted Riker. "And I suspect, that's how you like it."

"You see, you *do* understand us!" The commander chuckled. "Captain. What do you hope to achieve from this meeting?"

Once more, Riker recalled Picard's advice about honesty and directness. "I want to know what you're really doing out here, Commander."

Medaka opened his hands. "The same as you. Helping the Jazari."

"Out of the kindness of your hearts?"

For some reason, that statement drew a hearty laugh from the Romulan officer. "Yes! Something like that!" He studied the Jazari leviathan. "What would you say if I told you that I have no ulterior motive?"

Riker decided to press on down the path of complete frankness. "With respect, I would suspect you are not being entirely truthful with me."

"And you would be right." Medaka gave a solemn nod. "I am using this opportunity to make a close observation of your starship and the Jazari, a species whom we know very little about." He looked back at Riker. "But you know that I am doing that. You should reward your tactical officers for their diligence, they have been very good at blocking our sensor sweeps."

Riker said nothing, but he made a mental note to tell Vale and Keru to double up their efforts to keep the Romulans from running deep scans of the *Titan*.

"But I would rather be elsewhere," continued Medaka. "This situation is taking time away from our primary mission to find habitable worlds for our population. Some of my officers have already made their displeasure over this diversion very clear to me."

"So why don't you leave?"

"Our warp engines still require some repairs," he replied. "But even if that were not so, if we did depart, I would be allowing your ship to pass close to the Neutral Zone border unmonitored. But more than that, I would be allowing sentients to go in harm's way, through the plasma storm zone ahead." He indicated the Jazari vessel. "And that is something I cannot, in good conscience, let happen." Medaka sipped the tea again and his enigmatic smile returned. "Does it surprise you to hear a Romulan say that? You in the Federation think of us as a ruthless society, yes?"

Riker gave a slow nod. "More often than not, that's been my experience."

Medaka frowned, his dark brow furrowing deeply. "Just as the mask you show us is not who you are, so the mask we show you is not all who we are."

The note of genuine regret in the commander's voice gave Riker something to reach for. "There's a lot of us who hoped your people and mine could move past such a thing. Once, the Federation and the Klingon Empire were intractable enemies, but the Praxis crisis planted the seed of an alliance that grew into something strong. The collaboration between the Romulan fleet and Starfleet during the Dominion War could have done the same for us. But now that ground seems barren. For men like us on the front lines, at the sharp end, we're left to deal with the consequences of that failure."

Medaka sat back, drawing away from the table. "I have observed, you humans are always pulled in two directions. You want so much to trust, but you fear that hope is a naïve one."

Riker leaned in, taking the challenge. "What do you trust, Commander?"

"Nothing." Medaka's reply was instant, automatic.

"Do you have family?" said Riker. "A child?"

"Yes."

"Do you love them?"

Indignation flashed briefly in Medaka's eyes. "Of course I do."

"Then tell me, sir. How can you have love without trust?"

The Romulan commander opened his mouth to reply, then closed it again. If he had an answer to that, he kept it to himself.

The boy's feet crunched on the dark-blue leaf litter on the forest floor, stirring up little puffs of bioluminescent pollen with each step he took. Above him, spindly azure tree trunks curled up away from the ground, forming complex helical shapes. At their tops, giant mushroom caps poured out a weak yellow-green glow, phosphorescing against the inside of the eco-dome's roof.

Thad called out every now and then, because the sound of his voice seemed to affect the peculiar fungal trees, making them ripple their colors along the blue end of the visible spectrum. The effect was magical, and it made him grin.

He fished a penlight from his pocket and used it to cast a pool of illumination ahead of him, picking his way through fallen branches and knots of growth too thick to climb over. Sometimes, furry things like six-eyed cats would be caught in the beam, and then flee into the deeper darkness. Thad could hear them moving around out in the gloom, and he imagined they were as curious about him as he was about them.

The boy absently fingered the communicator disc in his pocket, telling himself he wasn't worried, but it stayed resolutely inert. It hadn't worked from the moment he arrived here.

After being ejected at the far end of the drone tunnel into this alien woodland, Thad found himself sliding down a slippery wall that was impossible to climb back up. After a while, he realized that he would have to find another way out of this place.

He knew he could. Thad heard his mom telling one of the other adults that the Jazari had multiple ways in and out of these domes, so it was just a question of finding a human-sized hatch somewhere else. Part of the boy was afraid, and that part kept on clutching the disc in the hopes it might buzz back to life. But so far, nothing. Like the insignia badges worn by the *Titan*'s crew, Thad's disc was a combination of communicator, bio-monitor, and locator device—but none of those functions seemed to be active in here.

Thad sang tunelessly, making the trees react, concentrating on the story of his adventure, the tale he would tell to make stupid Shelsa and the others all so jealous. He'd been disappointed that Ra'ag didn't come along with him, but some missions had to be solo endeavors. Thad was an only child, so being alone didn't frighten him.

Well. Perhaps it did a little.

His hopes of stumbling onto a Jazari settlement and peeking in on their hidden lives had, so far, come to nothing. If there were any of the aliens in this dome, they were far away.

Or maybe they're hiding. He examined the forest around him. *Maybe they* are *the trees! They change into them when no one is watching!* The boy had heard of such wild things from bedtime stories his dad told him, incredible tales that both his parents swore on their hearts were true. Shapeshifters, rock creatures, and omnipotent tricksters, his parents had met them all, and the boy hoped that one day he would too.

Thad sat down on an exposed boulder in the middle of a small clearing and blew out a breath. He was getting thirsty, and regretted leaving his drink bottle behind at the camp.

All at once, he heard the cat-things in the undergrowth scatter in a panic, and a familiar low humming reached his ears. He bolted up as another of the egg-like drones wove its way through the tree trunks and drifted to a halt just beyond his reach.

Color and light blinked gently inside the device. It was as big as a soccer ball, and Thad immediately had the sense that it was observing him.

"Hello?" He waved at it. "*Bonjour? Nǐ hǎo? Oye?*" The drone didn't respond, so he tried something else. "*Guten tag? nuqneH? Hola? Oel ngati kame?*" None of the greetings in any of the languages seemed to have an effect, and the boy trailed off into an exasperated noise.

The drone moved and let out a soft blink of light. On an impulse, Thad brought up his pocket flashlight and duplicated the pulse of illumination.

It had an effect. The drone moved and blinked, moved and blinked. There was a pattern to the way it rose and fell, and the pacing and brightness of the light flashes.

Thad jumped in place, animated by a sudden realization. "Are you . . . trying to talk to me?" He moved his flashlight around, making shapes in the air, sending back on-off pulses toward the drone.

The humming tone of the machine changed, and the boy felt a thrill run through him. His parents had told him about this sort of thing: he was making first contact, learning to communicate in a whole new way with an alien intelligence.

It was so exciting that Thad temporarily forgot about his silent communicator disc and all the trouble he was going to get into. He climbed atop the boulder and concentrated hard on the movements and the lights. Slowly at first, then with growing confidence, the boy found a way to converse with the drone.

Grandma Lwaxana once told Thaddeus that every person had a unique ability, but some people went through life never knowing what it was. *The luckiest of us, little one, are those who figure it out early.* And Thad knew he was lucky, because he could parse languages like some people could understand math or play any instrument they picked up. *You're gifted,* his grandmother said. *So enjoy it!*

Soon he was laughing and dancing around, with the drone making loops about him, humming contentedly to itself. Thad lost himself for a while in the sheer delight of play and discovery. It was the most fun he'd had in ages.

And then, in a day that had already gone from one unexpected thing to another, something new came along.

"You are quite intelligent for an immature being," said a voice. It sounded female, and it emanated from all around.

Thad was so shocked he almost fell over. "Who said that?"

"Hello." The drone floated closer, coming within touching distance for the first time. *"Bonjour."* It allowed Thad to tap it gently with his fingertip. *"Hola."*

"You can speak." Although the voice wasn't coming from the floating orb, Thad assumed they were part of the same entity. "Why didn't you do that to start with?"

"I like the game," it said. *"Do you like the game too?"*

"Well, yes," admitted Thad. "I did. Hello. My name's Thaddeus Troi-Riker. What's yours?"

"I have no designation. You can call me Friend."

"Okay, Friend!" A million questions bubbled into the boy's thoughts and he tried to put them in order. "Are you a Jazari? Is this your home? Are you actually here or somewhere else right now?"

"The answer to all those things is yes, in a manner of speaking."

"So you're not . . . this?" Thad tapped the drone.

"Yes and no."

Thad paused, thinking hard. "Are you . . . the trees?"

"I am not the trees."

The boy laughed. "I think I understood better when we were flashing lights at each other!"

"I was testing you," said the voice. *"I hope you do not mind."*

Thad shrugged. "I'm the best at tests, my mom says so." He drew himself up, puffing out his chest. "And I am really good at languages. I'm sure I could learn Jazari if you'd teach me."

"Perhaps you could." The drone floated closer. *"You are interesting, Thaddeus. Your immature form is still growing and learning incrementally. That process is fascinating to me. I did not experience it. I learned everything I needed to know in a single moment, all at once."*

Thad frowned. He wasn't exactly sure what Friend was talking about. "Are you, like, a computer?"

"That description seems limited," said the voice. *"The word is insufficient."*

The boy leaned closer, his voice dropping to a conspiratorial whisper. "You know, I'm making my own language. It's not all done yet, though."

"Why?"

"So everyone can speak it!" Thad opened his hands. "It's clear and simple so there can never be any misunderstandings or . . . or insufficient words! Everyone everywhere will be able to talk to one another, and understand exactly what they mean, and they won't need a universal translator to do it!"

"That is an admirable idea. Communication is the root of harmony."

"My mom says things like that all the time." Dwelling on thoughts of his parents made Thad's good mood dip sharply. "Oh, she's gonna be sooo mad at me."

"You should return to the Ochre Dome," said Friend. *"Your parent is currently engaged in a search for you."* There was a pause. *"She is some-*

what agitated." The drone set off at speed, weaving back through the trees. *"Please follow, Thaddeus. I will guide you back."*

Thad set off after the drone at a run, calling out to the air as he went. "Can we talk again? Would that be okay, Friend?"

The reply came from all around him. *"I would like that."*

Riker watched Medaka get up and walk to one of the ports of *Titan's* briefing room, to the exact spot where the captain had stood earlier that day.

"Do you know what the Klingons said when we put out our call for help?" The commander answered his own question. "The high chancellor's reply was three words: '*Die well, Romulans.*' In their own way, that was a gesture of respect. But respect will not save lives."

Riker had the strange sense that he had crossed a line with the Romulan, that he had passed some kind of test. The commander had offered more about himself in their conversation than any Romulan Riker had ever spoken to, and he wanted to believe that it was authentic.

"I was on the far side of the quadrant when the news about the stardeath was announced," said the commander. "When I heard the message, I experienced a moment of the most desperate, depthless panic. Odd, that I can openly admit this to you, an outsider, but never to my own crew." He paused. "I think you know that fear, Captain. One cannot be a husband, a father, a leader, and not know that abject terror for the safety of those you care for."

Riker nodded grimly. "That dread . . . It's a familiar companion."

"I tell you now, it pales before the danger faced by Romulus. This is not just a threat against flesh and blood, it is the coming annihilation of our homeworld. The end of the heart of all we are." Medaka let his words settle for a moment. "And when the United Federation of Planets, an oath-sworn enemy to us, offered help? It was unprecedented." He turned back and strode across the room, the energy of the motion animating his words.

"Some among us thought it was a grand trick. Some believed that agents of the Federation or your Klingon cohorts had deliberately triggered the nova in the first place, to set this chain of events in motion." Riker opened his mouth to protest, but Medaka held up a hand to hold his silence and continued on. "I knew that was not so. Your kind don't have it in you to do something so terrible on such a scale."

"Thank you. I think."

Medaka went on. "But many do not agree. And as we have seen, that leads to poor choices and decisions fueled by fury, not clarity."

Although Medaka did not say the names, Riker knew the commander was referring to incidents like those on the planets Vejuro and Nimbus III, and the attempt to capture the *U.S.S. Verity* at Yuyat Beta. Situations where elements of the Romulan government, and factions like the Tal Shiar, had interfered with rescue efforts out of fear, out of misplaced anger, even out of vindictiveness.

"Those acts were shameful," said the Romulan. "They were not, however, unexpected." He frowned. "But then came the revolt of your synthetics. And the subsequent withdrawal of Federation assistance."

"Not exactly our finest hour." Riker couldn't hold the other man's gaze. "We argued . . . *I* argued against it. The Federation Council and Starfleet Command made the choice."

Medaka watched the passing stars. "Members of the Romulan Senate have said that you reached out to us at our greatest moment of weakness just so you could crush us. They tell my people the breaking of Starfleet's promise was an act of utter cruelty, an old and petty revenge for the first war." He sighed. "I am told that some Terrans believe Romulans had a hand in what happened on Mars. As if we are so hateful that we would sabotage our own rescue just to spite you."

"What do you believe?" said Riker.

"I believe that unfounded rumors like these are part of the problem, on both sides of the Neutral Zone. But you must understand, Captain, the withdrawal cemented the worst fears and beliefs of the Romulan populace about your Federation. At best, you are considered incompetent and unreliable. At worst, they believe you want to see us all exterminated." He was silent for a long moment. "We can share tea and conversation, but beyond you and I, Riker, there is the void I fear we cannot bridge."

"I won't accept that. You must know we tried our best. Jean-Luc Picard lost his command over it—"

Medaka made a small noise of assent as Picard's name was mentioned. "Yes. And then he went home to his farm. Fortunate for him that he has the privilege to retreat from the galaxy at large when events turn against him. But not everyone has that option."

Riker bristled at the other man's tone, instinctively wanting to leap to his friend's defense, but he held back. Medaka's point hit close to home.

"After the warning of the star-death, I thought I might use what small measure of influence I had to relocate my husband and my daughter to a world on the far periphery of the Empire. But I was unsuccessful. Like me, many of the crew on the *Othrys* still have loved ones inside the threatened zone." Medaka returned to his seat. "It is why we are so dedicated to finding new worlds to home our people. This is not an abstract thing, it is personal."

"It's not easy to sit in the captain's chair," said Riker. "At times like this, even less so."

Medaka eyed him. "Is this conversation being recorded?"

"My first officer and my chief of security wanted to, but I refused. This is just you and me."

The commander smiled thinly. "On board a Romulan ship, that is not even an option." He paused, and Riker sensed he was choosing his next words carefully. "I know what you have been doing, Captain Riker. The *Titan* and the *Lionheart*, the *Enterprise*, the *Robinson*, and the other ships. Your quiet little conspiracy."

Riker became very still. "I'm not sure what you mean."

"For some time, Romulan ships have been coming across anonymous caches of survival resources and materiel, left near border worlds where the refugees have been relocated. Medicines, replicators, and the like. Deposited there by some unknown benefactors, who have diligently scrubbed out any evidence of their origin. Almost as if a handful of Starfleet captains have decided to provide what meager help they can, even if their leaders order them to do otherwise."

"I wish we could do more," Riker said quietly.

"I believe you."

Silence fell across the room, and in that moment, they were just two captains, two fathers and husbands, two men caught between the bounds of orders and their own codes of honor. Each of them knew that there were larger forces at work around them, political pressures and military strategies being decided on by others light-years distant.

But they were the ones on the edge of all this. Riker and the *Titan*, Medaka and the *Othrys*, they were lone outposts of their people on a deep and unforgiving ocean. It would be up to them to do better than those distant leaders, and to find common ground where they could. The alternatives led only toward darkness.

"He's been gone for hours," said Troi. She refused to say *missing*; it conjured up all the worst possibilities, and she couldn't allow herself to think those thoughts, not now.

"From what I have observed, Thaddeus appears to be a very resilient child." She knew that Zade offered the reply intending it to assuage her fears, but it didn't help one bit. The former Starfleet officer seemed to sense his mistake and gestured to his companion. "But of course, we will do all we can to locate him. My colleague Keret will interface with the great ship's systems and perform an area scan."

"Of course." From Troi's point of view, Keret was similar enough to Zade to be a sibling, with comparable patterns of facial scaling and body mass. He nodded to her, then removed a device from his pocket and stared fixedly at it. "This will take a few moments."

"I told him not to go in there," said Shelsa. The boy stood nearby with a cluster of Thad's friends, the children pinned under the watchful eye of Doctor Talov and Lieutenant Hernandez, one of the security officers from the *Titan*. "He didn't listen to me. He never ever listens to anyone."

"Thank you for bringing Thaddeus's actions to our attention," said Talov. "However, if you wished to obey the rules you were given, you should have turned back to the camp long before you reached the dome wall."

The sneer on Shelsa's face slipped off. The boy had a tendency toward tattling, but he clearly hadn't considered this time he might also get into trouble. Troi felt a flash of irritation, but she didn't let it show.

"Return to your temporary classroom," Talov told the children, getting a chorus of moans from the group. "You will remain there until your parents collect you."

As Shelsa and the other children walked away, Troi took a deep breath and concentrated on her son, picturing him in her mind. Her empathic senses were limited, but she knew in her bones that Thad was out there and he was well. The sensation couldn't be put into words, but she believed it wholeheartedly.

"Zade!" Her reverie was broken by an abrupt shout and she saw another of the Jazari approaching. His manner was brisk and irritable, and he barely gave Troi or the others a moment's glance. It was a marked difference to the usually courteous and even-tempered behavior she had come to expect from their kind. "How has this happened?" he demanded.

"Counselor Troi, allow me to introduce Qaylan, one of our senior thinkers—"

Qaylan graced Troi with a disinterested glance, then glared at Zade. "We were assured that our privacy would be respected. You made that guarantee!"

"Sir." Troi interposed herself between the two Jazari. "The blame for this falls on me. It's my son who left the dome, and it's my fault for not making it fully clear to him how seriously you take your boundaries. Please accept my sincere apologies."

She hoped that a polite admission of guilt might be accepted by the other Jazari. It wasn't.

Qaylan gave her his full attention, and the shift in his body language toward annoyance was enough that the security officer came a step closer, instinctively moving to defend the commander if the need arose. "Your progeny is undisciplined and disruptive," he snapped, giving the retreating children a withering glare. "Had the decision been mine alone to make, none of your kind would have been allowed to board our vessel."

"Thaddeus is an immature human, sir," offered Talov. "You must understand, at his age and development he has yet to fully grasp the effect of his actions on the greater universe."

"It's not uncommon," said Hernandez, in a deliberately chatty tone, trying to lighten the moment. She gave an affable *what can you do* shrug. "Some of the *niños* push the limit, it's the way they learn. You know how kids are, right?"

The seemingly innocuous query seemed to dismay Qaylan and the other Jazari. They exchanged glances and a sudden flash of insight came to Troi. *No*, she thought, *they really don't*.

In point of fact, since coming aboard the generation ship, she had seen no signs of any young Jazari—or, for that matter, any *elderly* Jazari. Their only encounters had been with males of the species, all of whom appeared to be in the same roughly uniform age grouping. It was difficult for her to estimate the maturity of their kind from anything other than mannerisms and behavior patterns.

"Huh." Hernandez seemed to sense the same thing. "Or maybe not?"

"I am sure my son meant no harm," Troi said. "He is curious about your species. That curiosity outstripped his caution."

"The boy is safe and well," Keret said suddenly, looking up from the device in his hand. Troi was uncertain how he could have determined that, but all the concerns she had and the small inconsistences preying on her mind went away when Thad walked over the shallow rise behind the medical tent.

He caught sight of his mother and gave a sheepish half wave. She wanted to run to him and gather him up, caught between the need to be sure her son was unharmed and the impulse to give him a serious telling-off. It took an effort for Troi to stand her ground and let Thad come to them. With each step he took, the reality of the boy's situation was settling in on him.

"Hello, Mom," he said, one hand rubbing at the back of his neck. "Um. Am I in trouble?"

Troi folded her arms across her chest and channeled the commanding voice she remembered her mother using when she was a girl. "Thaddeus Worf Troi-Riker." She used his full name to let the boy know that he was *indeed* in trouble. "What do you have to say for yourself?"

"I'm sorry." He turned to the Jazari. "I'm very sorry. I shouldn't have gone poking around where I wasn't supposed to." His lip trembled. He was trying not to cry. "But I didn't mean to do anything wrong, I was just . . . making first contact."

"You are grounded, young man, indefinitely," Troi said firmly. "And you are going to give your father an explanation. You are the son of a starship captain and a diplomatic officer. You're supposed to set a good example for the others."

"Yes, Mom." Thad blinked furiously, his eyes shimmering. Behind him, Talov stepped up to examine the boy.

"And that will be the end of it?" Qaylan said harshly. "It is not enough. I demand you all remove yourselves from our vessel immediately!"

"With respect," Zade noted, "you do not have the authority to make that request."

"We shall see," retorted Qaylan, and he marched away. After a moment, Zade and Keret made their farewells and followed in his wake.

"I am *really* suh-sorry." Thad barely got the sentence out before he burst into tears, and Troi couldn't hold off any more, letting her firm expression melt. She hugged him and he tried to talk, gasping out words between breathy sobs. "I . . . just . . . met a . . . Friend. Made friends, that's . . . what we are supposed to do . . ."

Troi caught Hernandez's eye and the lieutenant gave her a smile. "Hey, kid." She dropped to Thad's level, so they were eye to eye. "You know, I got into a lot of trouble with my mom when I was your age. But it was okay, I learned from it." She offered him her hand. "My name's Macha. Tell you what, why don't we walk back to your tent and I'll tell you about the biggest trouble I ever got in, okay?" She looked up at Troi, who gave her a nod.

"'Kay," said Thad, and suddenly he seemed like the little boy he really was as he took the lieutenant's hand and let her lead him away.

"Sometimes I forget, he's not even six yet," said Troi, watching him go. "He's so clever for his age, it's easy to think of him as a little adult."

"Quite." Talov raised an eyebrow, then held up the tricorder he had in his hand. "I conducted a medical scan of Thaddeus and I detected no issues of note, other than some dermal abrasions. However, there is a minor anomaly of which you should be aware. Specifically, with regard to bio-matter traces on his clothing."

"Something dangerous?" Troi's chest tightened.

"Negative," said the doctor. "Merely . . . unusual." He showed her the tricorder's screen. "Thaddeus's clothes and footwear show traces of a quadrilateral tetrad pollen, of a kind similar to that from trees native to worlds in the Lembatta Cluster and Pavonis Sector."

Troi frowned. "Those places are nowhere near this system."

"Correct. I believe your son has been in close proximity to plant life not native to the Jazari homeworld, or indeed anywhere within this sector." He folded the tricorder up and put it away. "The only logical explanation is that ecodome bordering this one contains a transplanted alien biosphere."

"Why would Zade's people have something like that?" Troi frowned.

"I have no answer for you, Commander. It is another unknown," said Talov. "The Jazari seem to . . . collect them."

EIGHT

"I think this is a miscalculation," hissed Vadrel, and his long-fingered hands found one another in an absent, nervous motion.

"Your reticence is duly noted," Helek told him. Her voice echoed off the walls of the dimly lit storage bay. The only illumination came from the glowing coils beneath the nearby cargo transporter and the idle-mode display on the operator's console. The rest of the chamber was filled with towers of container modules stocked with spare parts and nonreplicable materials. Seldom used by the crew of the *Othrys*, it was an ideal staging point for the mission at hand.

Helek adjusted the matte black shroud suit she was wearing, pulling it tight around her shoulders. The collapsible helmet mechanism sat like a heavy collar about the major's neck, and with a tap of her finger it could deploy and seal the suit in half a second. Once she was concealed, no sensor scans would be able to register her life signs. Helek would be a shadow, a dark phantom free to do whatever was needed.

It is easy to act without fear and compunction, she reflected, *when one becomes a ghost.*

That freedom was what had first seduced her about the Tal Shiar, but it had been only the first stone in the path to something greater. She weighed her disruptor pistol in her hand, before stuffing it into a seal holster. The weapon was perfectly balanced for her. She had killed with it quite often, and not always in service to the Tal Shiar.

The higher calling she served was worth any cost, any amount of shed blood and collateral damage. Such was the grave responsibility of the Zhat Vash, to protect a naïve universe from the threat of its own machine progeny.

"Perhaps I could send a remote probe instead," Vadrel went on. "Give me a day to engineer something, Major. I can make it work—"

"We do not have a day to waste," Helek snapped. "This opportunity may not come again. We act now. You have your part to play. Don't try to change your role now, Vadrel. It's too late for that."

He sensed the implied threat and bowed his head, admitting defeat. "Yes, of course. Do you wish me to remain here while you are . . . on task?"

She shook her head as the storage bay's door slid open and silhouetted figures entered. "Once the transit is complete, return to your lab and activate the surveillance mask. The target with be brought directly to you."

Two Romulan males stepped out of the shadows. The first was Centurion Garn, the other a low-ranked security guard from the noncommissioned ranks. "This is Hosa." Garn indicated the man with a jut of his chin.

"You know what to do," said Helek, gesturing at an open container near the cargo transporter. Inside were more shroud suits like hers, and as she watched, the men changed out of their shipboard uniforms and donned the stealth gear. She noted ritual scarification on the bare skin of Garn's back as he took off his tunic and wondered what it meant. Such marks were usually the indicators of a criminal upbringing, of prison servitude— was that how he had first come to the Tal Shiar's notice as a reliable thug? Helek filed the thought away for later consideration.

Vadrel moved to the control console and attached a small device to it. "This will divert the matter stream through the warbird's main deflector and conceal your transit. I have rigged it to automatically recall on voice command or, uh, after the cessation of an individual's life signs."

Helek leaned closer to study the targeting scanner. The location she had chosen was inside the environment dome where the Starfleet encampment was situated. It was uncomfortably close, but there was no other viable option. The other domes and interior spaces of the Jazari ship were impossible to scan clearly at this range, and Helek had no desire to materialize inside a bulkhead.

She moved to an intercom unit and activated it. "Command deck, this is Helek."

"Command deck responding, this is Maian." Up on the bridge, the taciturn veteran was the acting senior officer while Medaka was off the ship playing games with the human captain, and she was undertaking her own mission.

"I am returning to my quarters to meditate," she lied. "I am not to be disturbed until Commander Medaka returns from the *Titan*."

"Confirmed," said the lieutenant. Perhaps Maian suspected Helek was up to something, perhaps not. Either way, he was wise enough not to pry.

She closed the link and stepped onto the transporter pad, where Garn and Hosa were waiting. "Seal up." Helek tapped the helmet switch and the mechanism rose up to encase her head. The others followed suit, and she glanced toward Garn.

Vadrel considered the situation. If Garn had brought her this man, it meant he trusted him, and he knew if Hosa failed, he would pay for it as much as he did.

"Ready." Vadrel licked his lips.

"Energize," said Helek, and in the next second a buzzing wall of emerald fire enveloped her.

The transit was longer than usual, and painful with it—a side effect of the masking phase shift, she guessed—but then it was over, and they were standing in a woodland clearing. She saw the arc of a glassy dome far above.

Garn drew his weapon and pointed. *"Suit sensor is detecting a concealed hatchway in that direction."*

"Lead on," said Helek, her voice echoing inside the confines of the helmet.

• • •

The problem with adults, Thad told himself, *is that when they tell you they're listening to you, they're really only listening to themselves.*

Lieutenant Hernandez had been really nice to him, but she never gave the boy the chance to tell her what had gone on during his unauthorized venture into the forest dome. In the end, Thad glumly accepted his situation and now he sat alone in the prefabricated bubble tent where his mother and he were temporarily accommodated. He sucked on a squeeze pack of fruit juice and stared into the middle distance.

After the panic of the accident on board the *Titan*, coming down to the giant Jazari ship seemed like the start of a fantastic adventure. A camping trip, but more exciting than the tame experiences the family had on the holodeck.

But the Ochre Dome wasn't much better than a virtual simulation. It was real, but it was kind of fake as well. It wasn't the same as being on an actual planet, it was just a pocket of the outdoors trapped under glass.

Thad tried to tell Hernandez about what he had encountered in the other dome. He wanted to explain to her about Friend and the drones and the glowing trees, but in her nice and adult way she shut him down. He was told to wait here until his mother came to get him. *How long would that be?* He had no idea.

"Mom will listen to me," he said aloud. "Yeah. I'll explain it all to her."

"Who are you talking to?" A shadow by the tent flap resolved into Shelsa, and the Denevan boy squeezed inside. He made a show of looking around. "No one here."

"This isn't your tent," Thad said with a scowl. "Get lost."

Shelsa glared at the smaller boy where he sat on a gear case. "Make me." Thad heard a giggle from outside, and he realized that the bigger boy had probably come in here on some kind of dare. Some of the other children were watching the confrontation through the open flap. "Oh, you can't," Shelsa went on, "you can't do anything, you're *grounded*." He said the last word as if it were an eternal curse placed on Thaddeus's soul.

"You better go or I will get Lieutenant Hernandez and—"

"And you'll tell on me?" Shelsa sneered. "Like a little baby?"

Thad stiffened at the insult. He hated being smaller and younger than Shelsa, even though the other boy had barely a year on him.

"You got in trouble because you were stupid," he went on. "I came in here to check if you were still stupid now."

"That doesn't make any sense," said Thad, and he felt his cheeks redden. "Why are you always so horrible to everyone? Always pretending you're smarter?"

Shelsa blinked in surprise. "You are the one always doing that! You think you're so clever! Your mom and dad tell everyone that, but you're not! You're not special!"

Thad saw the other boy blink furiously and ball his hands into fists, and belatedly something occurred to him. Shelsa lived on the *Titan* with his dad, but the boy's mom had died a year ago, and it was something to do with the bad things that had happened on Mars. Shelsa seemed sour and angry all the time, but maybe that hadn't always been true.

"You're in deep shit," Shelsa insisted, grinning around the swear word, an unkind smirk forming on his lips. "And I think it is funny."

"I met an alien," Thad retorted. "Her name is Friend and you've never seen anything like her!"

Shelsa made a sneering noise. "You are such a liar. Always making things up, like your stupid stories and pretend languages!"

Thad leaped to his feet. "No!"

"Then prove it," Shelsa prodded him. "Where is your new friend?" He made a mock-thinking face. "Oh, I forgot. Thad doesn't have any friends because no one likes him." He leaned in. "People only say they like you because your dad is the captain."

For a second, Thad wanted to say something spiteful back, something about Shelsa's mom, but he couldn't do it. He could almost sense the other boy's anger, like a distant, flickering flame. He didn't want to be like him.

"You are mean and you are wrong." Thad pushed past the other boy and stormed out through the tent flap. He ignored the knot of children lurking nearby and set off in the direction of the tree line. His eyes were burning with brimming tears, but he refused to let Shelsa and the others see him cry.

"Thad is a liar-liar-liar!" the older boy called after him, singsonging the words.

"I am *not*," he said to himself, stalking into the undergrowth. "I'll *prove* it."

"I have something here." Hosa broke his silence, and Helek's head snapped up, finding the soldier crouched by a low boulder. *"Beneath this."*

She tapped controls on her stealth suit's gauntlet, double-checking to be sure their scattering field was still in place. Blue lights pulsed back at her, signifying that the masking aura hiding them from any Jazari internal sensors was working at optimal capacity. Satisfied, she picked her way through the knee-length orange grasses and approached him.

The short-range scanner in her helmet projected a warning into her visual field. Hosa had found a power node beneath the ground, doubtless feeding energy to the dome's environmental systems. The node pulsed softly, and Helek smiled. This was exactly what she needed.

"Log these coordinates," she told Hosa. "We'll make use of it on our departure." But Hosa didn't seem to hear her, and she snapped her fingers in front of his helmet. "Pay attention!"

"Apologies, Major." Hosa's head bobbed. *"I thought I saw something. Movement in the undergrowth."*

She saw only the grass and the thick trunks of heavy trees. "Probably an animal. Don't allow yourself to be distracted."

"Major Helek." A hundred meters away, Centurion Garn was in the shadow of a rock wall rising up to join the dome overhead. *"There is an egress port hidden here."*

"Show me," she ordered.

Garn dropped into a crouch and drew his disruptor. He carefully adjusted its settings, then fired a low-resonance beam into the stone.

Helek watched as a wide patch of the rock wall wavered and became insubstantial. Overloaded by the beam, the holographic mask winked out and revealed the steel hatch it had been concealing.

Helek and Hosa approached as Garn set to work on an oval control panel in a recess near the hatch. He had it open in short order, and the major was quietly impressed by the big man's efficiency. She wondered if Garn's criminal past had involved some kind of housebreaking. The hatch split along a diagonal line, retracting halfway before it halted.

"Make ready," she told them. "I want a prisoner, not a corpse. Understand?"

"Aye, Major." Garn holstered his disruptor and replaced it with a different weapon, a stubby baton with glowing tines at one end. Hosa produced a baton of his own, testing its weight. The devices were similar to those used by *warrigul* trainers to stun their animals into obedience, and on most unprotected humanoids they had an immediate and powerful effect.

Helek glanced at the chronometer display in the corner of her field of vision. So far, everything was running according to her schedule. "Move in," she ordered, and gestured into the corridor beyond.

Garn went first, with Hosa a step behind. Helek took a last look over her shoulder. In the distance, through the trees, she could make out the white cubes of the temporary Federation encampment. Content that her team had not been observed, she followed her men deeper into the Jazari ship.

Thaddeus hugged himself to stop from trembling, pressing his back into the void in the bole of the tree, hoping that the menacing figures in black suits would not come for him.

The boy's intention had been to make his way back to the dome entrance Friend had shown to him, and once there, attempt to contact the glowing drone. Thad nursed the fantasy of getting Friend to come back to the camp with him, so he could not only shut up Shelsa once and for all, but also prove to his mother, Lieutenant Hernandez, Doctor Talov, and all the other adults that he hadn't been making up stories.

But then he saw the figures in black and all his brittle bravery fractured. Thad couldn't put it into words, but just like he felt Shelsa's anger, he could *feel* that these people were not here with good intentions. The way they moved, keeping to the shadows, it set off all kinds of red alerts in the boy's mind.

He got himself as deep into cover as he could and watched them find the hidden hatch and force it open.

These people are not Starfleet, Thad told himself. *Starfleet don't sneak around!* And that left only one other option.

"Romulans." He whispered the word. Thad had never met a Romulan but he knew they looked a lot like Vulcans. Hanee Phosia had once told him that Romulans were what you would get if you made a Vulcan very, very angry, and Thad had no desire to see that up close.

But he also saw the weapons in their hands as he unconsciously read their intentions. They had come here to do harm to someone, he was certain of it.

Were they here to find Friend and hurt her? Or Zade and the other Jazari?

The horrible possibilities swirled through the boy's thoughts and made him feel ill. Thad pulled his communicator disc from his pocket and fingered it, but the device was still inoperative. In his haste to leave camp he hadn't thought to find a replacement.

What would Dad do? Thad squeezed his eyes shut and thought hard. Back on the *Titan,* there was a drill for things like this. *If you ever see anything weird on the ship, that seems like it doesn't belong there,* his father had told him, *go tap a panel and ask the computer to help you find someone who can help.*

But the nearest person who could help was back in the camp, and even if Thad ran home as fast as he could, the Romulans would be gone before anything could be done.

And he could imagine Shelsa sneering at him when he told the adults. They would think he was telling tales. No one would believe him.

Thad is a liar-liar-liar! Shelsa's words echoed through his mind, and once more his cheeks burned crimson.

The figures in black vanished one by one through the open hatch, and after a moment Thad rose out of cover. Perhaps he couldn't get back to the camp quick enough, but he could get to the hatch, and on the other side . . . He could find Friend or Zade and warn *them*.

If he did that, then everyone would understand. Mom and Dad would understand, and maybe the Jazari would be so grateful that they'd teach him some of their language after all.

Thad broke into a headlong run, dashing toward the open hatch.

After all, he thought, gathering his courage, *I can't get any more grounded than I already am.*

The interior of the Jazari generation ship was disappointingly unremarkable, Helek decided.

Illumination in the squared-off corridors came in a low purple-blue shade that did little to differentiate one passageway from another, and she noted how the design of the walls and floor repeated itself. A sure sign that modular technology had been employed to build the huge vessel, she thought, but it lacked an aesthetic quality. Romulan starships had a martial elegance to their construction, but the only visual signature Helek could see on this craft was a recurring motif of oblique angles in the form of support frames and doorways.

Still, the lighting and the structure cast plentiful shadows, and those they could make use of. Keeping close to the walls, Garn led the team down a long access way with Hosa a step behind. Helek studied the sensor scan projected onto her visor, watching for a viable target.

There! Motion detectors embedded in the surface of the stealth suit's black skin registered a mass moving up ahead, where the corridor branched, and Helek glanced at Garn. He nodded back at her, the centurion reading the same contact.

For a brief moment, the detectors showed something else, something behind them, and Helek hesitated. She turned in place, staring back into the gloom. The sensor return faded away and she listened carefully.

"Major?" Hosa leaned closer. *"Is there a problem?"*

Helek saw nothing, and she frowned. She was allowing her mind to play tricks on her. "Negative," she muttered. "Remain on mission."

"Target closing," whispered Garn, adjusting his grip on his baton.

The others fell silent, and Helek heard the sound of approaching footsteps. Presently, a Jazari male in a yellow coverall appeared around the corner, walking with an oddly rigid gait and a blank expression on his quasi-reptilian face.

Helek studied the alien as he came closer. The Jazari didn't seem to notice them, his thoughts elsewhere. He would soon regret his inattention to his surroundings.

"Now," she breathed.

Garn and Hosa burst out of the shadows, in front of and behind the lone Jazari, moving so fast that the alien was caught completely by surprise.

"What is—?" He started to speak, but whatever questions the Jazari had were cut short by the brutal application of the stun batons to his torso.

Flashes of bright blue lightning crackled around the alien's body and he let out a peculiar, atonal cry. Twitching and shaking, the Jazari didn't collapse all at once, so Garn hit him again with a second, heavier charge in the belly.

This time, all consciousness fled from the alien and he toppled like a felled tree, crashing hard to the deck.

Helek darted glances around, making sure there were no signs their attack had been detected, while Hosa knelt by the unconscious alien and secured a sensor-masking unit around his arm. It was imperative their quarry could not be tracked.

Garn peered at the tip of his baton before holstering it. *"How long will this keep one of them out of it?"*

"Unknown," said Helek. "So we must move quickly. Take the prisoner."

Garn bent and hauled the Jazari up over his shoulder with a grunt. *"Heavier than he appears."*

"We have what we came for," said the major. "Fall back to the transit site."

It took every ounce of the boy's bravery to trail after the Romulans, and Thad found his hands trembling and his stomach knotting. But still he dared to follow, keeping his distance and pressing himself into the same shadows the invaders were using to conceal their activity.

He'd hoped to find something like a public data terminal, with which he could contact Friend or one of the Jazari, but there was no evidence of anything like that along the length of the sparse, wide corridor, nor any sign of the floating drones. Aboard a Starfleet ship, there was a computer panel every hundred meters—but here, only bare walls and blank, sealed doorways. Thad reluctantly moved deeper into the ship, following the curve of the corridor and hoping against hope to find what he needed.

He was terrified that the Romulans would spot him, so he made himself as small and as silent as possible. Once or twice, the tallest of the three figures stopped and looked in his direction, as if it could sense him there. Thad held his breath and held statue still, each time wondering if his luck would run out.

And then, to the boy's openmouthed shock, he saw them ambush the lone Jazari and knock him out. He couldn't understand the reason for this act of cruelty. It would have been easy to let the Jazari pass them by where they were hidden, but instead they deliberately attacked.

Thad saw the biggest of the trio gather up the limp body of the fallen

Jazari as if he were a sack of supplies. *They're abducting him*, he realized, *they're going to take him back to their ship!*

For an instant, Thad hated that he was just a boy, too small and too weak to do anything to stop this act of aggression. Indignation burned in him. *They have no right to do this!* But he could not stop them, and Thad's fear came back tenfold when he realized that the Romulans would take him too if he was discovered.

They started in his direction, and Thad took off like a rocket, sprinting as fast as his legs would carry him. He didn't dare to look back, dashing through the shadows, back toward the spill of artificial daylight coming through the gap in the open hatch.

He fairly threw himself over the threshold and back into the Ochre Dome, tripping over his own feet, scrambling back up again and running into the undergrowth. Thad made it to his hiding place from before, in the bole of the big tree, and he flattened himself on the ground, wishing the earth would open up and swallow him. His breath came in quick, panting gasps, and he covered his mouth with both hands. *If they hear me, they'll kidnap me.*

A moment later, the tall and thin figure stepped through the open hatch, quickly followed by the other two black-clad Romulans. As one of them closed the diagonal doors and restored the illusion of the fake stone wall, the big one carried the lifeless Jazari back toward the large boulder in the middle of the clearing.

They were so close that Thad could have hit them with a thrown stone.

Suddenly, without warning, their unconscious prisoner stirred and tried to break free of the big figure's grip. He writhed and struggled, casting desperately around—and he locked eyes with Thad, crouching there among the thick grasses.

The Jazari's expression implored the boy for help, but there was nothing that he could do. The big Romulan pulled out his baton and threw his captive onto the dirt before shocking him again. Thad had to turn away, the violence sickening him.

When he dared to glance up again, the other black-suited Romulans were standing around the fallen Jazari. One of them removed a cylinder of some sort from a backpack, while the tall one—who seemed to be in charge—used a slim probe to draw a blood sample from the prisoner. The probe went into the cylinder and the second Romulan placed it at the foot of the boulder, before stepping back.

A dull, humming buzz filled the air, and the green shimmer of a transporter whisked the Romulans and their prisoner away.

Gingerly, Thad got to his feet. He was alone in the clearing, but the cylinder still remained.

"Friend!" Thad yelled the name at the top of his lungs "Can you hear me? Friend, please, I need you to come here right now! Something very bad is going on!"

He had no idea if the disembodied voice heard him, so the boy approached the boulder, craning his neck to see the device the Romulans had left behind.

When Thad was half a meter away, he heard a low rhythmic pulse emanating from the cylinder. He could see it more clearly now, a thing like an hourglass inside a metal shell, within it swirling chains of glowing energy and the vial of fluid taken from the kidnapped Jazari. With each passing second, the speed of the pulse increased and the glow grew brighter.

The boy felt a sense of imminent threat as the glow inside the device took on a menacing crimson aura. Everything in him screamed to *run away* and Thad surrendered to the impulse, taking big, loping steps over the uneven ground to put as much distance as he could between himself and the Romulan device.

Then a flash of light behind him turned the world blood red for one dizzying second, and a vicious wall of heat slammed into the boy, picking him up off his feet and tossing him into the air.

Grassy ground and domed sky wheeled around him as Thad was flung away by the shock of the device's detonation.

He clipped a thick tree trunk and fell in a heap amid its roots, lost to darkness.

NINE

Vadrel stepped back from securing the restraints around the male Jazari's wrists and ankles, then threw Helek a wary glance. "How long do we have until they are aware this one is missing?"

Helek folded her arms. "As far as the others of his kind know, he is dead. Vaporized in the blast from an overloaded power node."

The scientist scowled, looking around the dimly lit space of his laboratory. At the only door, the security guard Hosa stood as an impassive sentinel, his face a blank.

"You laid a false trail," said Vadrel. "The Tal Shiar do have their clever ways." He paused. "How was it done? Wait, don't tell me, let me guess. A genetic sample from the prisoner in an undetectable explosive matrix, yes? So anyone who scans the blast site will pick up just enough trace organic matter to believe there was a victim."

"Your intuition does you credit," she allowed.

"Not really." Vadrel seemed irritated with himself. "I've seen it done. They used the same method to falsify my death when I had to leave my old life behind. It's very effective, if one does not dig too deeply."

"Fortunate that the Tal Shiar had use for you," she replied. "If not . . . there would have been no fiction about your ending."

Vadrel studied the unconscious Jazari. "So you'll terminate this one when you are done with him, is that the intention? It's not as if we can return him."

"Are you becoming squeamish in your later years?" She approached the angled chair on which the comatose alien was lying. "Disappointing."

"Death without purpose is always disappointing," he countered.

"Oh, this one will serve a purpose, Vadrel. Of that you may be certain."

Without warning, the Jazari's eyes snapped open and he was instantly awake. He jerked against the restraints, shock written across his broad, scaled features. "What is going on?" He looked wildly around the room, finding Helek and fixing on her. "Why did you attack me? I am no threat to you! What is this place? Where am I?"

"Remain calm," said Vadrel. "You are . . . safe."

"I do not believe I am," retorted the Jazari. "I am Redei, a technician of the Sixteenth Sept, and you have no right to hold me captive! Release me immediately."

Helek came closer, letting her voice drop. "Redei, I regret that these methods were necessary, but I am afraid I must compel you to provide certain answers to me. And I do not believe you or your people would do so willingly. So I am obliged to use coercive methods."

"If you intend to threaten my life and use me as a bargaining chip, I warn you that the Governing Sept will not negotiate—"

The major smiled coldly. "No, no. You misunderstand. We didn't take you to ransom you back to your people." She picked up a photic probe from a tray of tools nearby and switched it on. "We took you because we're going to interrogate you."

Helek picked a fleshy spot on Redei's throat where his scales were thinnest and touched the probe to his skin. A web of energy leaped from the tool's tip and into his body. The Jazari went into spasm, his mouth locked open wide in a silent scream.

Vadrel made a disgusted noise and backed away a step. He worked a medical tricorder, aiming it in the alien's direction.

Helek moved the probe away and let Redei recover from the surge of pain. "I think you understand the situation now. No more questions. Only answers."

The shudders running through the Jazari faded and he recovered quickly. She made a mental note of that. The reptilians had a stronger constitution than expected.

Redei took panting breaths and his head rolled as he tried to take in the whole room. Helek knew this kind of behavior pattern. She had seen it in other interrogations, with other species. He was searching for an escape route, or for someone who would give him respite from the source of the pain. But there was only the grim-faced scientist, the silent security guard, and her. Helek waited for him to grasp the reality of the situation.

"There is only one way out of this," she told him, "and that is to tell me what I want to know."

"The ways of the Jazari are our own," Redei replied. "We do not speak of them to outsiders. For your sake as well as ours."

Helek wondered what that last comment meant, but now wasn't the time to pursue it. She knew that Commander Medaka would soon be back aboard the *Othrys*, and the last thing she wanted was for that fool to find his way down here to the lab and interfere.

"I don't care about your *ways*," she told Redei. "I have only one simple query for you to answer. Do so honestly and I will free you." Helek made a show of dialing up the power on the photic probe. "Tell me where your people are hiding the synthetics."

Redei flinched as if she had struck him. "Hiding . . . ?"

"We detected the presence of positronic systems on board your great ship. Synthetic minds, Redei. Artificial intelligences, androids and the like. The Jazari's attempts to cloak their existence are commendable, but ultimately futile. You have them concealed somewhere in among all those decks and domes. You are going to tell me where."

"I . . ." The Jazari shifted in place, lost in the middle distance. "I see." He paused for a moment, then spoke again. "You are acting on a misconception. There are no artificial life-forms on board our vessel. Your detection was in error."

"Was it?" Helek looked to Vadrel, and the scientist shook his head.

"No. The additional readings gathered remotely when you were over there with Garn and Hosa confirm it."

"I know nothing about these synthetics you speak of," insisted Redei. "Release me! Your abduction of my person is an act of gross criminality, and it will not be permitted! Let me off this ship!"

"Did the Jazari build the synthetics themselves?" Helek circled the captive. "Are they your serviles, or does your society have an equality with them? Is that why you are so determined to maintain your privacy?"

Redei made a visible attempt to compose himself. "The Jazari people have no quarrel with the Romulan Star Empire. We have never been your enemies. Your actions are unwarranted!"

Helek halted. "If you believe the machines are to be trusted, you are mistaken." She adjusted the probe. "Once again, I implore you. Answer me."

Vadrel hesitated. "Major . . . His physiology is unfamiliar, it makes it difficult for me to establish a threshold for identifying false statements. We should consider that he may be telling the truth. He may not be aware of the location of the synths."

"No." Helek had been the lead investigator in hundreds of invasive interrogations like this one, and her experience had seen her dig out answers for the Tal Shiar from all kinds of subjects—not just Romulan malefactors, but Terrans, Vulcans, Talarians, Andorians, and more. She had a sixth sense for obfuscation and mendacity. Her clarity of vision was the reason the Zhat Vash had chosen her to become one of them.

Helek used the photic probe again, and the Jazari writhed in horrible silence once more. She kept the device there for long and agonizing seconds, enough that it would have made a human's heart burst from the strain. Then she relented and wandered back to the tool tray.

"There are no artificial life-forms on board our vessel," rasped Redei. "Please do not continue to harm me."

"The probe's damage is temporary," she explained, ignoring the prisoner's words. "I have devices here capable of stimulating organic nerves while keeping them physically undamaged, allowing me to hold a subject in a state of intense pain virtually forever." Helek picked through the tools, selecting a curved blade. "But those techniques can take days to break a prisoner's will, and I am impatient. Sometimes the more direct methods are the best ones."

"I cannot give you the answer you want," said Redei. "This is senseless!"

"You continue to lie to me and I am going to punish you for it," she replied. "I will do harm to you, and continue to do it until you answer truthfully. Even if I have to carve the information I want out of your brain matter."

Helek leaned forward, and with the care of a fisher slicing bones from a fresh catch, she cleanly cut Redei's right eye from its socket.

As a concession to the urgency of the situation, the Jazari allowed the shuttlecraft *Armstrong* to pass through a force-field barrier in the arch of the Ochre Dome and the small craft put down a few hundred meters away from the temporary encampment.

Riker didn't wait for the drop ramp at the rear of the shuttle cabin to open fully, and he scrambled out and broke into a run. He didn't care how it looked. At that moment he only cared about his son.

Deanna rushed up to meet him, flying into his arms. His wife's beautiful face was streaked with tears and they held each other tightly. Riker felt his eyes burning and the bleak, fathomless panic he was struggling to keep in check began to rise. He forced it away, desperate to remain strong for himself, for Deanna, and for Thaddeus.

He had been on the bridge, talking with Commander Vale, when it happened. *Titan*'s course had it directly over the environment dome, and Riker had actually seen the flash of light inside it, a momentary blink of crimson out by the hemisphere's edge.

He immediately knew something was wrong, but the cold realization of that soon turned into the most terrible of any parent's personal horrors.

"Talk to me," he said softly, fighting to keep his voice steady.

"He's alive," managed Deanna, around a sob. "But it's bad, Will. Oh, it's very bad."

Our son. The shape and power of that concept was heavy in Riker's heart. The thought of their boy being taken away from them would overwhelm him if he allowed it, and that couldn't happen.

Alone in the shuttle, in the few minutes it took to fly down from the *Titan*, Riker had allowed himself a moment of pure, unguarded fear—just so he could meet it head-on, so he could try to be ready for the very worst. But now he needed to lock that away. He had to be the captain as much as the husband and father.

He pressed Deanna's head to his chest and they held each other for a moment. Then Riker heard a discreet cough and found Doctor Talov standing a few meters away.

"Captain, Counselor," said the Vulcan. "If you will both come with me?"

Talov led them to the infirmary tent, past knots of *Titan*'s displaced crew and civilian complement who stood around in worried silence. Riker briefly met Lieutenant Hernandez's gaze, and the woman gave him a nod of support. Her dark eyes were shimmering.

"Macha feels responsible," Deanna said quietly. "But it wasn't her fault."

It's mine. The words formed in Riker's mind, weighing him down. Thaddeus and Deanna and all the rest of them were only down here because of the choices he had made. *I've put them in harm's way*, he told himself.

His wife sensed the turmoil in him and she took his hand. He squeezed it back, grateful for her presence.

Thad was on a collapsible biobed, his small frame beneath a life-support arch. The boy's usually pink complexion was sallow, drained of vitality. A breather mask covered his nose and mouth, and a neural monitor band sat across his pale, sweaty forehead. Riker had to fight down the primal urge to gather up his son and carry him away.

To where? The traitorous voice in his thoughts sounded out the question. *What good would that do?*

"Thaddeus is in a medically induced coma," began Talov. His tone was surprisingly gentle, and not what Riker had expected from the eminently logical physician. "It was the safest choice given his condition. He has suffered serious bodily trauma, resulting in broken bones, tissue damage, and, most critically, an injury to his skull." He paused to let them process his report. "I have done what I can to alleviate the pressure to his brain, but I am afraid my options are limited."

"There was an uncontrolled explosive event," said another voice. Riker turned to see Zade standing in the infirmary's entrance vestibule. Drifting above and behind him, a small glowing orb appeared to be monitoring the conversation.

"An accident?"

"It appears so, Captain," said Zade. "The great ship's systems use a series of distributed power nodes throughout the vessel, and one of them suffered a critical overload. It may be a remnant effect from the subspace fracture that damaged our vessels . . ." He trailed off. "I am truly sorry, sir. Thaddeus must have been playing nearby when the node overloaded. He was caught by the edge of the blast."

"Was anyone else . . . ?" Deanna tried to speak, but her voice caught.

"Yes." Zade anticipated the rest of the query. "It appears that one of my people perished in the event. He may have been attempting to stop the overload when it occurred." The Jazari glanced at the floating orb, then away. "The details are unclear at this time."

Riker listened to his son's weak breathing and the gravity of it drew his attention back to the boy's pale face. "Doctor, what's your prognosis?"

Talov took a moment to choose his words. "There is hope, but I must be clear to you. Thaddeus's condition is critical. How he progresses through the next few hours will determine if he survives."

"Can we get him back to sickbay on the *Titan*?" said Deanna. "If that would help?"

"It would not," Talov replied. "Moving him, via shuttle or transporter, is not recommended. In my opinion, it presents too great a risk to the child. I strongly advise that Thaddeus remain here for the time being."

"We will help if we can . . ." said Zade. He trailed off again, once more looking to the orb.

Talov stepped away, and motioned for Zade to follow. "We can discuss it outside."

Zade gave a wooden nod, and left with the Vulcan. The orb drifted silently after them.

When it was just the three of them, mother and father each took one of their son's hands and held it.

"I let this happen," said Deanna, her words thick with emotion. "Thad wanted my attention, but I was so focused on keeping everyone here in good spirits, I neglected him." She took a shuddering breath. "Will, before this happened, I told him off. What if that's the last thing I ever get to say to him? He misbehaved and I was annoyed about it—"

She couldn't say any more, and fresh tracks streaked down her face.

"No." Riker's voice broke and he felt his own tears come. "Deanna, no, don't say that. He knows you love him, he knows we both love him. You're not to blame for this. Please tell me you believe that."

"How could it happen?" His wife's question was so plaintive that it cut into Riker's heart like a dagger. "Did we do this? By staying out here, did we do this? Should we have left Starfleet when Jean-Luc did?"

He couldn't answer that, not without spiraling into a gulf of self-doubt and *what might have been*. His wife's thoughts echoed his own, blame coiling inward, becoming corrosive.

"We are here for him," he said firmly, holding on to that single truth. "And Thad is the best of you and me. He'll get through this, and we'll be here to help him back. We have to believe that."

She said nothing, and Riker leaned in close to hold her tightly.

• • •

Hot, acidic bile rose in Vadrel's throat and the scientist turned away, forcing himself to choke it back down. His fingers whitened around the medical scanner in his grip, his palm slick with sweat.

Vadrel heard the guard, Hosa, give a low and sneering grunt at his queasiness. Behind him, Major Helek deposited the flesh she had sliced from the captive Jazari on a sample tray, without the slightest flicker of emotion. After the eye, she had removed part of Redei's nasal canal and several facial nubs.

Since the day the Tal Shiar had placed him in Helek's service, Vadrel had nursed the fear that his "handler" possessed sociopathic tendencies, and now he belatedly understood that the reality was far worse than that.

On the examination platform, the Jazari was trembling with pain response, and a half mask of bright blood covered the side of his face around his ruined eye socket. His breath came in tight, short gasps.

"I will keep asking," Helek was saying. "And I will keep cutting. I will stop when you reply." She repositioned the curved blade in her hand, studying her subject as she considered what she would remove next.

"Major!" Vadrel couldn't help himself, and the words spilled out of him. "Is this really . . . the most efficient way to conduct this interview?"

A shadow of irritation briefly passed over Helek's features. "What is the subject's condition?"

Vadrel said nothing, unwilling to give her the information she wanted.

The woman stepped away from her captive and came closer. With one gloved hand, Helek snatched the medical tricorder from Vadrel's fingers and considered the data on the device's readout. "He has only been lightly maimed," she noted. "Life signs remain strong." She toyed absently with the bloody blade in her other hand. "Our friend here is doing well, given the circumstances."

Doing well. Vadrel scowled at the way Helek said it, as if she were complimenting a child taking its first steps. "I am not comfortable with this. There are other methods," he insisted, "less messy—"

She spoke over him. "You find my technique unpleasant?" Helek showed her teeth. "Why would I possibly care about what *you* find comfortable?" She shoved the tricorder back into his hand. "For a moment there, Vadrel, it almost sounded as if you were challenging me. But that can't be right, can it? I must be mistaken. Because a man as intelligent as you, in a position as tenuous as yours, would never do something so unwise."

Helek glanced in Hosa's direction, and the veiled threat was there.

"Do you want your guilt to be revealed to everyone?" She barely breathed the question, so only he would hear it. "Would you like the crew of this ship to know what you and your colleagues are responsible for?" She leaned in until her lips were almost touching the high curve of his ears. "There are many like Hosa aboard the *Othrys*. They have so much to lose in what is coming. I think they would like someone to blame. Don't you?"

The roiling churn in Vadrel's belly was replaced by an altogether different variety of nausea—the horrible sickness that came from knowing there was no escape from one's own mistakes. In his life before this one, the man who was now Vadrel had been a part of a project so secret that it defied even the most byzantine of Romulan schemes. But the fires of its failure had condemned billions to certain death, and he shared a great deal of the responsibility.

"We both understand the magnitude of your crime," whispered Helek, and she gestured toward the twitching Jazari technician. "This amount of bloodshed is tiny in comparison." She leaned back. "You will help me. And you will not challenge me. Yes?"

"Yes," he said, admitting defeat once again.

She put down the blade, narrowing her eyes. "Let us try something more potent. Bring me a neural fractionator."

Vadrel removed the device from its container. A hemispherical object little bigger than a Kaferian apple, the fractionator was capable of projecting energy fields through bone and flesh, directly into cerebral matter. Correctly attuned, it could dechain or reorder neurons in certain parts of the brain, even down to the most basic autonomic physiological functions. Set one way, it might make a person forget how to breathe. Set another, and it could rewire pain centers to create endless storms of agony.

He offered it to her, but the major was no longer paying attention to him. Over by the doorway, Hosa had a finger pressed to a communicator clip in his ear.

"Centurion Garn reports that Commander Medaka returned from the Federation ship a short while ago," said the guard. "He seeks you, Major."

Helek let out a frustrated hiss and walked to an intercom module on the wall, tapping an activator stud. "Find me the commander."

A moment later, Medaka's voice issued out. *"Major. You're not on the bridge."*

"I'm dealing with an issue belowdecks," she replied. "Do you require my presence?"

Vadrel found himself hoping that Medaka would summon Helek away and put at least a temporary stop to this horror, but that did not happen.

"There's been an incident on board the Jazari generation ship. A fatal accident."

"How terrible." She sounded like she was going to yawn.

Medaka didn't seem to notice. *"They appear to be dealing with the aftermath. But in addition, it seems a civilian from the* Titan *was badly injured. In the interests of continued amity, I have made an offer to Captain Riker of medical supplies, should they be needed. Have Vadrel put something together for them."*

"I will attend to that immediately." Helek's expression showed her intention to do no such thing.

"The civilian is a child. Riker's son," noted Medaka. *"See to my orders, Major."*

"Your compassion does you credit, sir," said Helek, and she closed the channel.

Vadrel hesitated, casting around. "I will have the infirmary prepare a package of—"

"Don't be foolish." Helek snatched the fractionator out of his hand and gave him a withering look. "We have far more important work to do here."

"'Captain Riker and his crew can be trusted.'" Qaylan said the words in a pitch-perfect imitation of Zade's voice, throwing the quote back across the council chamber to where the other Jazari stood silently. "It would seem *not*."

Zade found the faces of the diplomat Veyen, the elder Yasil, and his old friend Keret among all the others in the Sept's gathering. Only Keret gave him the support he was searching for. The others stood in silence, waiting for him to respond to Qaylan's statement.

"Your implication is unclear," he began. "Do you mean to suggest our guests from the *Titan* are responsible for the incident in the Ochre Dome?"

"I mean to question the motives of these Starfleet people entirely," retorted Qaylan. "I mean to show that having them on board our great ship is a huge error! We must deport them all immediately. If not, we risk further such 'incidents' and perhaps greater losses."

"Our preliminary findings suggest that the overload of the energy node was accidental," said Keret, stepping up to be heard. "A great misfortune, we all can agree. The loss of our kindred Redei is keenly felt, and the injury to the human child is saddening . . ."

"Did he cause it?" snapped Qaylan. "The boy? Riker's son is a perfect exemplar of their lawless behaviors! The boy got into the Azure Dome even though he knew it was forbidden, and interfered with the growths within it!"

"*His name is Thaddeus.*" The air vibrated, and the bodiless voice hummed from the very walls around them. "*He did no harm, I saw to that. He was merely curious.*"

"I wonder if that curiosity was responsible for this accident," said Qaylan. "And the ending of Redei! Not through malice, of course, but through ignorance! This child should not have been where he was, and yet his parents and guardians allowed him free rein on board *our* vessel. It proves what I have always said, the humans and their like are supremely undisciplined!"

Yasil's normally mild expression was downcast. "It is regrettable that nothing of our kindred survived the fatal discharge."

Zade had seen the datum from the drone scanners that surveyed the damaged zone inside the Ochre Dome. Anything caught in the field of the node's critical failure would have been atomized instantly, including poor Redei.

Keret shifted uncomfortably. "It is correct that bio-traces from the site correspond to the presence of Technician Redei there at the time of detonation. However, drone coverage of that dome was down-cycled due to the presence of the *Titan* evacuees, so no direct observation of the blast was recorded." He paused. "There are some anomalies in our readings."

"If you will please elucidate?" said Veyen, breaking his silence.

"I am reluctant to theorize at this juncture," Keret replied. "I am . . . looking into it."

Keret's evasive answer gave fuel to Qaylan's argument. "I will go further," he said. "I believe there is a clear and present danger to us as long as these so-called evacuees remain on board our ship, and as long as their vessels continue to shadow us. They stumble about, interfering and asking too many questions, and we cannot predict what other accidents they may cause."

Zade saw others in the gathered group nodding in agreement, some of them with the blank-eyed stare that showed they were already coordinating together. He felt compelled to counter Qaylan's argument before it could sway others.

"You are committing the error of processing a conclusion from incomplete data," he said, and the other Jazari flinched. "I do not believe that a human child is responsible for what happened. I know Thaddeus Riker. The boy is intelligent for a being of his age. Overly inquisitive, perhaps, but not malevolent or thoughtless."

Yasil glanced toward Veyen. "Kindred, you too have lived among these beings. Is Zade's evaluation accurate?"

"I do not know the boy." Veyen answered without hesitation. "I have found individual humans to be agreeable. But in a group they are unpredictable, even dangerous."

"We have seen how they *think* in what they *do*," insisted Qaylan. "In the laws they pass and the edicts they live by. Am I incorrect in that?"

At length, Yasil gave a shake of the head. "You are not."

Zade sensed the mood of those in the council chamber shifting further and further toward Qaylan's point of view. He thought of the friends he had made on board the *Titan* and the beings he had come to know during his years in Starfleet. Not all of them were the finest examples of their species, but most were striving toward that goal. They hoped to become the best they could, and for that he admired them greatly. They deserved better than to be characterized as lesser, immature beings.

But he was also one of his kind, not one of theirs. Zade's entire mission, every single day that he had spent in Starfleet, had been so that he could observe and understand the peoples of the Federation—and then report back those findings. His first duty was to his fellow Jazari, and it always would be. On the scales of significance, the future of his race outweighed the fate of a handful of aliens.

"Perhaps it would be best to have our guests depart," said Veyen. "In light of what has happened."

"Removal by force, if necessary," Qaylan added. "If it comes to that."

"We offered our aid to them and now we take it back?" Zade frowned. "We send them to an uncertain fate, with an injured child among them? What does that make us?" He glared at Qaylan. "You believe we are superior to them. How are we so if this is how we behave toward beings in need?"

"We have a code." The voice came from out of the air once more. *"Have some of you deleted that information? We have avowed responsibilities, laid down by the Makers thousands of solar cycles past."*

"In the past," insisted Qaylan, looking up at the vaulted ceiling overhead. "Times have changed. The galaxy is a very different place now. The fact that we have engaged in this migration is proof of that!"

"We have abandoned our outpost world and repurposed all our technology to craft this vessel," said the voice. *"So now a new question must be asked: Will we also abandon what we are, abandon our code and our core?"*

All around Zade, the chamber fell silent as his kindred went inward to find their answer.

"Tell me where your people are hiding the synthetics," said Helek as she moved the neural fractionator over the trembling Jazari's forehead.

She wondered what the pain caused by the device felt like. It wouldn't be the commonplace, ordinary agony she had inflicted with her blade. It would be something exquisitely pure and perfect, generated by the reformation of the captive's brain matter.

But he was not responding the way she had expected him to. In previous uses of this tool, Helek had only needed to apply the lightest of power to get her subjects to comply. She remembered breaking a battle-hardened Nausicaan reaver in just a few minutes, using a setting six gradients lower than this one. This simple civilian technician should have been a drooling imbecile by now. But he *resisted*.

The Jazari's face was locked in a shuddering rictus, his one undamaged eye staring past her toward the ceiling. And still he did not speak.

"How is he enduring this?" She demanded an answer from Vadrel.

"I . . . may have missed something on the scan," ventured the scientist. "Perhaps there is a quality of Jazari neural structure that makes them resistant to the fractionator."

"Impossible." She turned the power all the way up, to a setting she had never used before, and returned to work. On one level, Helek was infuriated by the device's failure to provide her the results she wanted, but on another she was grotesquely fascinated by the prospect of turning the Jazari's brain tissue into a jumbled, knotted mess.

"He must be in incredible agony," breathed Vadrel.

"Are you?" Helek leaned over the shivering form of her captive, where his wrists and ankles juddered against their restraints. "It can all end with a word. Just answer me, Redei. It will stop if you answer."

With monumental effort, the Jazari forced out a reply. "Never."

A flare of hot fury surged through Helek at the alien's continued defiance and she briefly lost command of her self-control. The major struck Redei with a vicious backhand blow across the face, biting back a gutter oath.

It was as if the physical blow triggered something in the prisoner.

With a high-pitched *ping* of breaking metal, the wrist restraint closer to Helek broke open and the Jazari's right arm was suddenly free. His hand flicked out and grabbed her around the throat, lifting her off the ground. Boots kicking at air, she clawed at Redei's fingers, but they were iron-hard and immovable.

Vadrel stumbled back in open shock, and across the chamber, Hosa belatedly responded to what was going on. The guard went for the disruptor holstered at his hip.

The Jazari's other hand came free, and in a single fluid motion, he snatched up the photic probe from the tool tray and threw it across the lab. The improvised missile struck Hosa in the soft tissues of his throat and the guard fell to his knees, dropping his weapon before he could even fire it. Hosa made wet, choking noises as a gush of emerald blood flowed from a punctured artery in his neck.

Still dangling from the end of the alien's grip, Helek could only struggle to keep breathing, her eyes widening as she watched the Jazari free himself from the last two restraints. He cast around, his expression oddly vacant. "You gave me no other option," he said flatly, then shoved her away.

Helek fell into a storage rack and barely kept her footing. Coughing and wheezing through her bruised throat, she tore her own weapon from its holster, but the Jazari was on his feet. He pulled the disruptor from her hand, breaking two of her fingers as he did so.

"I am leaving. Where is the nearest matter-transporter unit to this location?" The Jazari stared blankly at her, his red-purple blood dripping down his scaled face and off his barbed chin. Despite his condition, he gave no outward sign of distress or pain. He gripped her weapon as if he was unfamiliar with it. "Answer me."

"How . . . ?" It was hard for Helek to speak.

A brief flicker of confusion passed over the Jazari's reptilian features. "I regret this. But the ways of the Jazari are our own." He moved toward her, and Helek knew the kill would come next.

The skirl of an energy bolt cut through the air and a green flash momentarily dazzled her. Helek blinked and saw Redei stagger away a few steps, his hands coming up to probe at the massive exit wound that had suddenly appeared in his belly.

Behind him, on the floor near Hosa's bleeding corpse, Vadrel crouched with the guard's disruptor in his trembling grip, the emitter tip still aglow.

The Jazari seemed to freeze in place, and then he toppled over, turned rigid like a statue.

Warily, Helek recovered her weapon and approached the dead captive. His eye was open, staring at nothing, and his blood still seeped over his face. But Vadrel's close-range shot had opened up Redei from back to front, the blast disintegrating a good portion of his torso. Wounds like this were not unfamiliar to the major, and she did not shrink from the sight of it. But as she looked closer, she saw something amiss.

Redei's epidermis was fused from the disruptor hit, and the beam had cored through him. What she could see inside his chest cavity was not burnt meat and bone. "Look at this," she hissed.

"Must I?" Quaking, Vadrel put the pistol down. "I . . . I have never killed a living thing before . . ."

"And you still have not." Helek beckoned him closer. "Look!" she repeated, making it an order.

Vadrel did as he was told, and she watched the horror on his face turn to confusion and then amazement.

Beneath a layer of organic skin tissue, the skeletal frame and internal organs of the dead Jazari were entirely artificial. The destroyed remains of complex arrays simulating lungs and micropumps distributing processing fluids were visible through the gaping wound. Bones made from spun polymers crackled and cooled as the spent heat from the energy blast faded.

Redei was no more a living thing than the gun in Helek's hand.

"They're not concealing synthetics aboard their ship," Vadrel breathed. "They *are* the synthetics."

Helek had her answer, at last.

TEN

The Ochre Dome had moved into a night cycle, with the overhead illuminators dimming to simulate the end of the day, but Deanna Troi barely
noticed.

Her world had contracted to the space in the corner of the temporary
infirmary, where Thad lay on the biobed, his breath coming in shallow
stutters. She watched her son and time seemed to slow. She had been there
for hours, keeping a vigil after her husband had reluctantly returned to the
Titan.

Will had wanted to stay, to give over command of the ship to Christine
Vale and sit here with Deanna, but that would have solved nothing.
He was captain and he had a crew to supervise, a vessel with repairs to
oversee—and Deanna knew well enough that Will would be better off
with something to distract him from worrying about Thad.

She took on the burden because she knew she could bear it. Countless
times, Troi had been there to guide other people through their own crises
just like this one, and she knew how to cope.

Don't I? She took a deep breath that almost sounded like a sob. *Counselor, counsel thyself.*

Not since her father died when she was a little girl had Deanna faced
the specter of losing someone so precious to her. She had wept for Tasha
Yar and again for Data when death had snatched her dear friends away, but
despite how close she had been to them, they were not her blood. Thaddeus was hers, the child she brought into the world, he was the bright,
amazing son she had watched blossom and grow over these past few years.

In these times, when there were so many trials and darker moments at hand, Troi always sought out the good and the light. She found it every time in her son's laughter and inquisitiveness, and the terrible possibility that she would see that extinguished filled her with a dread like no other.

She took Thad's limp hand in hers and gave it a gentle squeeze. More than anything, she wanted him to react to her presence. "Come back to us," she said quietly. "If you can. Please come back."

The soft rustle of the tent's flap drew Troi's attention, and she used the heel of her hand to wipe away a tear.

Zade stood hesitantly in the collapsible vestibule, and at his shoulder was the floating drone orb she had seen earlier.

"Commander Troi," said the Jazari, inclining his head. "May I enter?"

"Of course."

Zade approached, and the drone followed, maintaining a respectful distance. He offered her a Starfleet ration pack. "I thought you might require sustenance."

"That's very kind." Releasing the child's hand, she took the pack, and found a water sachet inside to drink from.

"Has there been any improvement in Thaddeus's condition?"

"Doctor Talov has done all he can. We need to wait and see if my son can heal on his own."

Zade's expression was full of sorrow. "The advent of the migration was meant to be a great event for my people. A new beginning. Instead it has become a mire of tragedy. I am so sorry that Thaddeus was caught up in this."

"Did you know the technician who perished?" Troi couldn't stop herself from taking on the role of therapist, even at a moment like this. She saw someone in distress and she was compelled to reach out to them.

"I was acquainted with Redei," said Zade. "His loss is keenly felt, so soon after those we lost on the reclaim station during the spatial fracture. There are few of us in real terms, so the ending of any one of our kind is cause for great sadness."

Something that had nagged at Troi before drifted back to the forefront of her mind. *No sign of any young or elderly Jazari on board the generation ship.* It was believed that they were quite long-lived for a humanoid species, but as with much about them, that was more theory than proven fact.

It wasn't the only unknown about the Jazari that Troi had dwelled upon. She had never seen a female of their kind, and she wondered if they were a monogendered species. Perhaps reproduction was difficult for them, and that might account for the comparatively small size of their populace, and the graveness of Zade's reaction to the death of one of his own. *There are so many things we don't know about them.*

She drew upon all of her abilities to try to read Zade. Her empathic senses were ineffective where the Jazari were concerned, reading nothing but a void where others projected an emotional aura—but Deanna Troi's skills also included xenopsychology and neurolinguistics, and she searched his expression and his posture for every last clue as to his true feelings.

To her eye, he seemed to be what she expected of him: a young man, troubled by loss and frustrated by events outside of his control. But there was something else beneath all of that, a faint disconnection that she could not quantify. Her instinct told her something was *off*, but she could not have articulated exactly what it was.

Zade seemed to sense her scrutiny, and once again he gave the silent drone a look. Was the device watching him, or watching her? She couldn't be certain.

"I should leave," said the Jazari. "Please let me know if there is anything I can do—"

"Why do you hide so much from us?" The question slipped out of Troi's mouth before she was aware of it, and once it had, she didn't want to call it back.

Zade's manner shifted, his lips thinning. She had seen this from the Jazari before, the standard response mode they went into whenever anyone asked something they didn't want to answer. But now it seemed false to her, too practiced, too much of a performance. "The ways of the Jazari are our own," he said, after a moment. The statement had a tired, rote quality to it.

Now that she had crossed the line, the faint sense of disquiet Troi had always nursed about the Jazari came to a head.

"We have only ever wanted to know you," she continued. "To be your friends and your allies. But your people have always held us at arm's length. Why?" And then Troi found the core of it, the element of this relationship that had until now escaped her. "What have we done that makes us unworthy of your trust?"

Zade's expression shifted again, the false front briefly falling away, and beneath it, something else was revealed. Was that fear she saw?

"I . . . cannot . . ." Zade frowned, unable to find the words.

But then the drone drifting behind him glowed brightly and surged forward, over their heads, halting sharply over Thaddeus's silent form.

Troi heard her unconscious son give a strangled gasp, and in the next second the boy was in the throes of a seizure.

"*Summon aid,*" said an urgent female voice, coming from the halo of vibrating air around the drone. "*The boy is in danger.*"

A conundrum always had the same effect on Vadrel. It detached the scientist from the common, routine reality of the world around him and plunged him into something exciting. It was the only time he truly had purpose, when the exhilaration of a problem to be solved was put before him.

Without a challenge, Vadrel felt as if he were sleepwalking through life, just marking time. He sometimes wondered how his fellow Romulans of lower intellect and incurious natures lived their lives without such stimuli. It had to be a dismal and tedious existence.

When something unknown was before him, when a mystery was there to be unpacked and solved, Vadrel felt *alive*. Nothing was greater than burying himself in theorems and experimentation, opening up the secrets of the universe and mastering them.

In his life before this one, he had done exactly that. He had been part of an elite cadre of thinkers who crossed the limits of what was possible, while other scientists had wrung their hands and bleated about ethics and accountability. Unshackled from all restrictions by the personal command of the praetor himself, for the advancement of the Empire, they had been at the cutting edge of Romulan sciences.

Forbidden, volatile technologies like omega particles, protomaterials, time-active substrates, even red matter, all of it had been at his fingertips. But then there had been *the error*, and everything else that followed.

It cost him his life; that old life, at any rate.

And now he was here, sentenced to eke out his days with a new face and a dull name, with a psychopathic Tal Shiar agent holding his leash.

Thus, a new challenge—a conundrum that none before him had ever laid eyes on—was a cold draught of pure water to a man dying of thirst.

Dissection of the Jazari-thing took a few hours, and interestingly, his earlier reticence vanished once he knew that he was examining an artificial, manufactured device rather than an organic life-form. The mechanism was intricate and beautiful. A work of engineering genius, clearly far in advance of anything commonly known in the Alpha or Beta Quadrants.

The complexity of the cybernetic form was darkly fascinating to him. The Romulan Star Empire had always eschewed the development of artificial intelligences, reasoning systems, and androids, barely tolerating those few iconoclasts on the fringes of the scientific community who studied such things. To have this knowledge was to be branded at best a wild-eyed crank, at worst a dangerous radical. But the lure of the forbidden enticed Vadrel, and the truth was he knew more about these kind of machines than anyone was supposed to. It was his sordid little transgression, now eclipsed by a far larger, far more toxic secret.

With each piece of the Jazari-thing he cut away, Vadrel discovered something new about it. A clever biomorphic sheath around the synthetic's core frame and organs was durable enough to be accepted as ordinary skin and bones, but in reality it was a cloak. Threaded through the simulated muscles and nerves, on a virtually undetectable level, the Jazari had a nanoscale mesh that generated an adaptive scattering field. Any tricorder scan or sensor sweep passing through it reflected back with what appeared to be readings showing an organic being. Beneath the fake epidermis and the pseudoreptilian countenance, the true nature of the Jazari synthetic was forever hidden.

He grinned as he examined a mechanical hand, now stripped down to the bare metal bones. The structure seemed woven rather than cast, an elegant design that made other similar forms he had seen appear crude in comparison. Vadrel recalled fragments of outlawed documentation he saw on the Soong-type android that had served in the Federation Starfleet. The Jazari machine was a generation beyond that style of synthetic, an evolutionary step along a path that might one day lead to a fully biological artificial being.

He explained all of this to Major Helek, becoming more animated as he went on. Vadrel didn't notice that she was only half listening to him, her expression fixed in a cold, hateful grimace as she watched him cut up the deactivated android.

"I need you to be certain," said Helek. "If this is a single machine masquerading as one of them, if there are more—"

"No, no." Vadrel interrupted her, waving his hand. Normally, he would never have dared to do so, but he was so enrapt by his new discovery, he temporarily forgot to be afraid of the Tal Shiar agent. "I have compared the secret telemetry you gathered while you were on their ship with the reading from this . . ." He aimed the laser scalpel in his hand at the gutted android. "It is exactly the same! The bioreadings from every Jazari you came into contact with, they're identical in form." Helek seemed doubtful, and Vadrel pressed on, his voice rising. "Don't you see? It fits with what little we know about them! They hide their true natures, they forbid anyone to deep-scan them. They refuse to use transporters because that would leave a molecular record of their physical makeup!" He threw a gesture in the direction of the ship's walls. "Did you wonder why it was that we found no sign of Jazari bodies in space after the destruction of their reclaim station?"

"They recovered their dead."

"Of course!" Vadrel put down the scalpel with a sharp clatter of metal on metal. "To hide them from us!" He reeled at the consequences of his own statement.

Helek glanced toward the polymerized body bag on the floor of the lab, where Hosa's corpse had been stowed. "It kept up the pretense, even while I was interrogating it. It was only when the risk of the discovery of its actual nature became too great that it used its superior abilities."

Vadrel's enthusiasm waned as he realized something. "The android would have killed us all to conceal the Jazari secret."

"Of course it would," she snapped, as if he were stating the obvious. "They are abominations. *Destroyers*. It is in their nature." Helek stepped closer to him, and Vadrel unconsciously backed away, bumping into the partially dissembled corpse of the fallen machine. "You understand the seriousness of this, yes?" Her voice dropped to a breathy, dangerous whisper. There was a light in her eyes that Vadrel had never seen before, a fanatic glitter that would brook no disagreement, no disobedience. "We have uncovered a grave threat, you and I. A danger even greater than the star-death that threatens our homeworld. These machines are a threat to *all* organic life, everywhere. Those simplistic dolts in the Federation have given these things free rein to go where they will and build their plans against us. The machines want nothing less than to replace us." She took a shaky breath, as if she were remembering something terrible. "To make all flesh extinct."

Vadrel wondered how Helek could know that with such ironclad certainty, but he did not dare to challenge her resolve. He had no doubt that Helek believed what she was saying with every fiber of her being, and the scientist was too scared of her to do anything but agree.

"We must move quickly. They may already have been alerted to our discovery. They must be dealt with before they can move against us," she concluded. "The Zhat Vash cannot allow this nest of synthetics to exist."

That name meant nothing to Vadrel, and he did not draw attention to it. "As you say."

Helek tapped the dead machine's forehead. "Open it up," she ordered. "You understand the operation of positronic matrices."

"Th-that knowledge is restricted—"

"Don't insult my intelligence, Vadrel. I want you to plunder the android's memories." Her smile turned feral. "Show me what it knows."

Talov cleared them away from Thaddeus's biobed and the Vulcan doctor went into a swift and efficient process, scanning Troi's son, attending to him with various devices and hyposprays.

She could do nothing but stand a few meters away and watch helplessly. Troi's Betazoid empathic senses were bombarded by the confused, chaotic feelings leaking from her son's unconscious mind, and she had to clasp her hands together to keep them from shaking.

I'm here for you, she thought, projecting that intent as hard as she could, hoping something in her boy would pick up on it. *It will be all right.*

But Troi had no way to know if Thad could sense her presence. His inchoate fear roared silently around her, and any attempt she made to push back against it was like shouting into a storm.

"Counselor . . ." Zade stood nearby, his face fixed in an expression of terrible, almost childlike sadness. "Perhaps we could wait outside."

She turned toward him, and saw the drone that had spoken earlier drifting near the infirmary's entrance. "What is that device? How did it know my son was going to have a seizure?" The Jazari glanced toward the drone, and Troi's patience broke. "Zade. Answer me!"

"We would never do anything to harm him," he insisted. "Please believe that."

The orb floated closer to them. *"I will speak, Zade,"* it said. The feminine voice hummed in Troi's ear, and she noticed that no one else in the tent seemed to hear it. *"You may call me Friend, Counselor Troi. I am of the Jazari, and I am not a danger to you or your kind."*

Troi wondered what *of the Jazari* actually meant, but there was too much going on to consider that fully right now. "What do you know about my son?"

"I encountered Thaddeus in the Azure Dome, the chamber bordering this one. We played a game, and I guided him back to you after his . . . exploration. I am concerned for the boy's well-being."

"Are you an artificial intelligence?"

"Thaddeus asked a similar question. That definition is insufficient."

Zade gave the drone a worried look. "Counselor, please do not speak of this. If the Governing Sept were to learn—"

"I don't care about any of that." Troi spoke over him, heartsick and filled with dread. "All that matters to me right now is my son. I respect your people's right to your privacy, but if you know something that can help Thaddeus, you must tell me!" She felt tears welling up and swallowed a sob. "Please."

"Commander." Talov's voice cut through the moment, and the Vulcan approached, his neutral expression betraying nothing.

Behind him, a Bajoran nurse was applying another neural monitor to Thad's temple, and mercifully the boy's seizures had halted. Her son was pale and drawn, his usual lively color and warmth faded down to a ghost of itself.

"Thaddeus suffered an attack of severe synchronous neural activity," said the doctor. "This relates to the damage inflicted on him earlier. I have been able to temporarily halt the effects, but I am afraid this seizure has severely impacted his chances of recovery. Even if I had the full capabilities of *Titan*'s sickbay at my disposal, I am uncertain more could be done to improve his condition at this time."

Talov's clear and unequivocal evaluation of the situation turned her blood to ice. She waited a moment for the doctor to offer some thread of hope, but when he did not, the trembling in her hands began again.

"Perhaps Thaddeus could be placed in stasis?" said Zade. "I believe the Federation has a dedicated neuroscience center at Starbase 88. The staff there would have the greatest chance of being able to assist him."

"I am aware of that facility," said Talov. "However, the neural shock of entering and later reviving from stasis would put the patient at greater risk. And I am uncertain we could reach Starbase 88 before his condition deteriorates beyond the point of any logical progress." The doctor addressed Troi directly. "Commander, the decision is ultimately yours and Captain Riker's."

Troi reached up to touch the combadge on her chest, but faltered before her fingers tapped the gold arrowhead.

What could she say to her husband, how would she break this to him? Could they abandon their mission and their responsibilities here and now to race across the light-years to the distant starbase?

"There is another option." The drone spoke again, and Talov jerked in surprise, clearly unaware that the floating orb was capable of doing so. *"The Jazari possess expertise in biotechnology and neural sequencing that could be employed to heal a human."*

Talov recovered quickly, raising an eyebrow. "I have no knowledge of this. No Jazari medical techniques have ever been shared with the Federation Science Council."

"That is so," said Zade. "We have kept our . . . advances in this field to ourselves." He frowned, glancing at the drone. "With good cause. The Jazari neural structure is very different from that of a human."

Once again, Troi sensed that Zade was holding something back. But if there was any hope in what the entity called "Friend" was offering, she had to consider it.

"Theoretically, neural sequencing of the affected areas of the patient's brain would mean a greatly improved survival ratio," allowed Talov, "but it also carries the inherent probability of complications in later life. The effects are . . . unpredictable."

"You are correct," said the voice from the drone. *"There are risks, both at this time and to Thaddeus in the future. But the issue before us is the boy's immediate existence. I would like to see that he does not end before his life has had a chance to truly begin."*

Troi felt light-headed. This was all moving so fast, but she knew that time was a factor. Delaying a decision could mean the worst for her son. She took a deep breath to center herself. "How would it be done?"

"Thaddeus can be transferred to one of our reparation capsules," said Zade. "Essentially, it is a self-contained bioengineering pod that will restore his function."

"The process can be completed within a few hours, if you will agree to it," added Friend.

Troi gave a slow nod, and once again, she reached for her communicator. "I would like some privacy, please. I . . . I need to speak to my husband."

The dead machine's brain was a work of art, if Vadrel allowed himself to think of it as such. A symphony of positronic neurons, encapsulated inside a core module that not only replicated the model of an organic brain, but excelled it.

He wanted to take his time over the dismantling of it, and he cursed circumstances for forcing him to attack the device in a crude, incautious manner. The scientist was certain that some of the dead Jazari's memory engrams and knowledge chains were being lost in the process of peeling back the machine-brain's layers. In an ideal world, Vadrel would have taken weeks, months even, to ease apart the structure of the core module he had pulled from Redei's poly-alloy skull.

But he did not have that luxury. Every so often, Helek came back to the lab to demand a report on his progress, and he could see her patience growing thinner with each subsequent visit.

Now she stood over him again, her dark eyes glaring imperiously from a face rendered wraith-pale in the greenish light of the laboratory. "I want results," said the major.

"I have something to show you," he replied, reluctantly offering up the information. "You may find it alarming." He tapped a keypad and a holographic screen appeared above his work space.

Flickering, ill-defined images filled the screen, but none of them were coherent enough to make visual sense. "This is meaningless," Helek began, but Vadrel made a halting motion with his hands.

"Let me explain." He showed her where the detached android brain was now connected to an isolinear processing unit, allowing him to crudely interrogate the contents of the synthetic's memory centers. "There are gigaquads of data stored there. The equivalent of a planetary database's worth of material. It would take a hundred thousand hours just to catalog it all."

Uncertain of where to start with such a mountain of data, Vadrel had experimented by searching the memory for something specific. On an impulse, he told the processor to scour the dead machine's mind for anything relating to Romulus.

"See what I have found." The scattered, indecipherable images on the screen became clearer as the memory core gave up a specific recollection.

It showed a busy city street on a sunny day, as seen through the eyes of someone walking among crowds. The point of view paused as a face appeared in front of them.

A Romulan face. An older man, working behind a mobile server cart. He looked directly through the screen and although there was no sound component, Vadrel could almost hear him say the words *Jolan tru* as he mouthed them, before accepting a few coins in exchange for what appeared to be a cup of *solok* tea.

Then the view moved on. The memory continued to unfold, the viewpoint moving to pass over buildings and pedestrians. "Watch carefully now," said Vadrel. Helek had not spoken since the footage began to unfold, and he knew he had her full and complete attention.

The view tilted up to take in a particular pillar—a tall, narrow construction ending in the giant sculpture of a raptor made of old, greenish copper. Helek let out a gasp and Vadrel froze the image.

"You recognize it, of course?"

"That is the terminus obelisk on the Avenue of Right. Outside the old Dartha wall in Ki Baratan."

"This machine possesses a memory of being on Romulus," said Vadrel. "In our capital city."

Helek peered closely at the image, then pushed Vadrel aside so she could operate the holo's controls herself. She ran the footage back a few seconds, then isolated a section of the image and enlarged it. A narrow building made of yellow stone lay in the center of the frame. "This is the Fejek Gallery. It was destroyed in a fire twelve years ago. I know because I was in the capital on that day. I saw it burn and collapse. It was never rebuilt." She paused. "Could this be a simulation?"

"Possibly," he admitted. "But if so, the level of detail is unparalleled. I believe it is authentic." Vadrel added Helek's bit of information about the date to what he had already learned, and gave her an encouraging nod. "There's more. Let the memory continue onward."

The major did as he asked, and presently the footage caught a moment when the path of the viewpoint passed a mirrored wall near the Second Circular. Helek froze the image again and found the reflection of a face framing the eyes that had captured all these scenes.

A young Romulan woman stared back at them. She had a plain, unremarkable aspect and the kind of garb favored by islanders from the White Sea territories. She was utterly commonplace, a person who would be instantly forgotten by most who saw her, easily lost in the crowd. The perfect appearance for a spy.

Helek went back to the dead Jazari and plucked at the skin of his face. "This flesh is as much a cloak as the masking field that hides their true nature. I wonder, did they pick this reptilian aspect at random?" She gave a grunt of grim amusement. "They can cover their machine forms with any skin, appear as any gender, from any race."

"I've scanned several hours of memory from this period," noted Vadrel. "She . . . I mean, *it*, visits several museums and libraries. Sites of historical significance. Over a two-day period, it observes six different plays at an open-air theater."

"No military or strategic locations?"

"None that I have seen." He paused, considering. "If I were to hazard a guess, I would say the machine was conducting an ethnological and cultural survey."

Helek gave a dismissive snort. "A spy is a spy," she replied. "Are you certain this memory belongs to this particular android?"

He frowned. "There is a possibility it may be from another one of its kind." Vadrel moved to the gutted machine corpse and used a penlight to illuminate a component inside the android's braincase. "Observe. This appears to be a near-field communication array. I believe the Jazari synthetics can use it to transmit data instantaneously to one another over short distances. This Romulus memory could have been shared via that mechanism." Vadrel took a moment to phrase his next words carefully, wary as he always was of antagonizing the Tal Shiar agent. "Major, I know I don't have to state that our discovery here is of grave military importance. I feel we must bring this to Commander Medaka immediately and inform the fleet. There may be Jazari infiltrators at large throughout the Empire at this very moment!"

"The Zhat Vash will determine what must be done with this intelligence," said Helek, invoking that strange name once more. "And *I* will decide what course we will pursue in the interim." A slow, cold smile emerged on Helek's pale, bloodless lips. "Compile all the data you have recovered and secure it, Vadrel. You will speak of this to no one but me, on pain of death. Clear?"

He nodded. "Very well."

"You have given me exactly what I require." Helek's eyes glittered with that murderous, fanatic light once more, and it frightened Vadrel more than anything else he could conceive of.

"Why do you hate these things so much?" He blurted it out before he could stop himself.

Helek turned a terrifying glare on him for a brief instant, and it was all he could do not to shrink into the bulkhead at his back. "Your error, Vadrel, is that you are always the thinker. The scientist and theoretician. You see everything as a puzzle to be solved. If you can resolve it, it is done. But you are so wrong." She ran a finger over the bloody, inert face of the dead android. "And that is why you will never understand how great a danger we face. Or how far we must go to stop it."

The boy's dreams were made of fire and darkness, and he could not grasp them as anything more than storms of cruel pain and voids full of nothingness. He drifted in the shallows of unconsciousness, unable to sink deeper or rise to the surface.

Time was an unknown. All he had that was familiar was the fear. Sometimes, he felt like there was a force trying to bring him back, but he was too weak to respond to it. The injured boy was lost.

Then, slowly, the fire began to recede and the void ebbed away. Light and color and sensation returned. Thad felt softness enveloping him, and a careful warmth.

"Thaddeus?" He knew that voice. *"Thaddeus, this is Friend. Can you hear me?"*

He tried to reply, but it was hard to form the words. Instead, the boy concentrated all his energy on waking up back into the world.

"Don't be afraid," said Friend. *"You are unwell, but I am going to correct that."*

For the first time in many hours, Thad opened his eyes. He saw a curved ceiling low above him, and his hands touched a spongy material at his back. He was lying inside a narrow tube lit with shimmering pink light, and behind the translucent material of the curved walls, he could see glowing forms moving back and forth.

"Where . . . ?"

"This is a reparation chamber," said Friend. *"Like your sickbay on board the* Titan, *but more advanced. Do you understand, Thaddeus? We are going to heal you."*

"I hurt myself." Recollection of the flash of light and the pain of his injuries raced through Thad's small form and he tensed. "I want my mom. I want my dad." He started to cry. He felt tiny and afraid.

"Your mother is close. Can you sense her?"

Thad took a breath and tried to reach out with his thoughts. He knew he had a little Betazoid in him—*just a dash of magic,* as his father liked to say—and what slight empathic ability he possessed allowed Thad to feel the vague shape of his mother on the edge of his thoughts.

She *was* there. He choked back a sob, wanting more than anything to hold her hand.

"I understand this may be disorienting for you," Friend went on, the soothing voice coming from all around, *"but you must be brave. Your parents have agreed to allow the Jazari to help you. Soon you will go back to sleep, and when you wake, you will be at optimal functionality once more."*

Thad tried very hard not to be scared, but he couldn't do it. Back in the woods of the Ochre Dome, when that terrible blast of light and noise had struck him, some instinctive human sense told him he was broken inside. He was petrified that nothing would be able to put him right, and that he would never be able to go exploring again.

"You are safe," said Friend, after he let all that out in a tearful moan. *"I am here to talk to you, Thaddeus. Concentrate on the sound of my words."*

Myriad points of warmth lit up all around Thad's neck and skull, and a comforting numbness crawled through him. "What is that . . . ?"

"I have begun the reparation process."

Thad remembered the lullabies his parents sang to him when he was smaller, and his tears came. "Mom sings to me when I can't sleep."

"I do not possess that skill set," Friend admitted. *"Perhaps I can occupy you in a different way. Would you like to play another light game?"*

"Can . . . can you talk to me?"

"I am *talking to you."*

"I mean, in your own language? In Jazari?"

Friend was silent for a moment, as the warmth moved slowly down the length of Thad's body. He could see tiny glowing fronds growing out of the material around him, entering his skin and fixing all the bits of him that were damaged.

"We do not have a linguistic construct as you would understand it," said Friend. *"But I can render an audial representation of our communication pool."*

A new sound filled the capsule interior, a low rolling rush somewhere between the gentle tinkling of crystalline chimes and soft waves lapping at sand. Thad laughed, despite himself. "It sounds like music. It's nice."

"I am pleased you enjoy it. You are listening to the shared information transfer of thousands of Jazari individuals on board the great ship. They are talking to one another, and to me."

"How can you do that . . . all at once?" Thad's thoughts were becoming sluggish, and he felt sleep reaching out to him, but he wanted to stay awake. He needed to know more about Friend and the Jazari.

"I am in many places at once, Thaddeus. Here, talking to you. Elsewhere throughout our vessel and in several of the drone orbs."

"You're in the ship," said the boy, with a thrill of sudden understanding. "No, you *are* the ship!"

"In a way."

Thad felt himself becoming weepy again, despite Friend's best efforts to keep him from sorrow. "I miss my ship. I want to be home."

Friend's reply was not what he expected. *"We want that too."* He could hear true sadness in the voice. *"We understand that need."*

"I . . . I have never had a home, not a real one," admitted Thad. "We have . . . a nice cabin on the *Titan*. I have my own . . . my own room." It was getting harder and harder to think straight. "But it's not the same. Not like being on a planet."

"Our home is a very great distance from here," said Friend. *"We seek to return to it. To find peace and security."*

"I'd like that." Thad's eyes drooped. "Mom and Dad and me. Like to live . . . on a planet one day . . ." The thought brought an image to him, of a planet like the forest in the Ochre Dome, but with no glassy ceiling and a horizon of distant mountains. A world like the one in the pictures of Earth his dad had shown him.

The dream image followed him into the stillness, and Thaddeus fell silent.

"Rest," said Friend. *"You will be well soon."*

"Thar she blows," said Westerguard as the *Titan*'s proximity sensors sounded an alert.

"What is blowing?" At the neighboring console, the Denobulan helmswoman threw the dark-skinned navigator a curious look.

Lieutenant Westerguard made a gesture with his hand. "It's a historical human idiom. It means, *holy crap, look at that thing.*" The navigator indicated the main viewer that dominated the forward quarter of the bridge.

On the screen, a huge swath of energetic cloud blotted out most of the starscape. Lit from within by exotic radiation and infernal fires, the plasma storm cell dominating Sector 743-D resembled a gigantic pool of molten metal, and the *Titan* was heading straight for it.

"Cancel that alarm." Commander Vale rose from her seat and stepped into the midbridge. The captain had withdrawn to his ready room, leaving her the conn, and the mood on the command deck was still subdued.

Lieutenant Cantua silenced the trilling alert. "Fifteen minutes to outer boundary, sir," she reported, anticipating Vale's next request.

Vale went to Livnah at the science station. "Do we have the course heading?"

Livnah gave a sharp sniff. "Confirmed. Transmission from the helm station of the *Othrys*. The Romulan transit path has been uploaded."

"Better double-check their math," said Keru, eyeing her from the security station. "Just to be certain. It only needs one vector to be a single decimal place out of line and we could sail right into a plasma plume."

"Commander Medaka made his offer to guide the ships through this zone in good faith," said Livnah. "He would not sabotage that."

Vale couldn't be sure if the tattooed science officer's words were a question or a statement, and although she hadn't voiced them, the first officer's own concerns echoed those of the Trill at tactical.

Keru shrugged. "Maybe not. But there's a lot of Romulans who are angry with Starfleet over our withdrawal from the rescue efforts. One of them might want to do something about it."

Livnah gave Vale a quizzical look and she sighed. "Lieutenant Westerguard, tie in to science console one and take a pass over the Romulan navs before you input them. Just to be certain."

"Aye, Commander." The navigator followed her orders, and Vale's gaze went back to the plasma storms.

On the screen, the Jazari ship was already making a turn toward a corridor of clear space between two great pillars of superheated gas. The winged form of the *Othrys* kept pace with the *Titan*, moving like an avian shadow. If everything went to plan, the passage through the storm zone would be over in a day or so, and past this sector would be clear space. Beyond that, the Jazari would leave the edges of the frontier and pass into unknown territory.

And that will be the last we ever see of them, she thought. Vale studied the Romulan warbird. *Then it'll be just the two of us out here. That'll be an interesting journey back.*

"Crossing outer boundary in ten minutes," reported Cantua.

"Contact all decks and divisions," said Vale, "caution all department heads to secure for transit. These storm zones are unpredictable. We're likely to encounter some rough seas ahead."

"Course passes muster," said Westerguard. "Ready to proceed."

Vale gave her assent, and the *Titan* shifted to follow the Jazari generation ship.

Across the bridge, the door to Captain Riker's ready room stayed resolutely shut, and after a moment Vale made a snap decision. "Keru, mind the store for me."

She marched across the room and tapped the lock. Riker didn't order her in, but the door hissed open and she entered.

Inside, the ready room's lighting was down and the window out into space was flat black, turned opaque.

The captain sat in a low chair, a silhouette leaning forward, staring out at nothing. "Problem, Chris?" Riker sounded gruff and distracted.

Of course he is distracted, thought Vale. *His only child is over on that alien ship, facing life and death, while he's up here watching the clock.*

"We'll be pushing into the plasma storm zone soon," she reported. "Medaka's people sent us the safe path through the sector and the course is laid in."

Riker nodded once. "Good. Carry on."

As Vale's eyes adjusted to the dimness, she noted something else. There was a bottle of real, nonreplicated bourbon and a single empty glass sitting on the desk in front of him.

He sensed her hesitation. In the gloom, Will Riker seemed haunted, and Vale felt a sharp pang of sympathy for her commanding officer.

"Sir, if you want to go back across . . ." He shook his head, so Vale tried another tack. "There's still a window of opportunity, Captain. I talked to McCreedy, she can have the *La Rocca* stripped down to bare bulkheads and boosted for high warp in thirty minutes." The captain's skiff was *Titan*'s fastest auxiliary craft, and with the chief engineer's modifications, Vale knew it could be even swifter. "We can get your son to Starbase 88 in half the time—"

"He's already gone under," Riker broke in. "All I can do now is wait."

Vale studied the bottle. It was in violation of every regulation in the book for a Starfleet officer to drink a nonsyntheholic liquor while on duty, but Christine knew what Riker had to be feeling and she found it hard to judge him. "Sir, I can take the rest of the watch from here." She was offering to let him go below to his quarters and deal with this in private, but Riker refused.

"I haven't opened it," he said, indicating the bottle. "I thought I might, but I can't."

"I wouldn't blame you."

He turned away. "When I was a kid, my dad was fearless. At least, I always thought he was. But years later he told me that the only time he had really, truly known what fear felt like was on the day I got thrown from a horse and he thought I might die." Riker reached for the neck of the bottle and turned it in place. "He'd never touched a drop of this stuff until then. And the truth is, an inch of bourbon doesn't make the fear go away, not really. I hear him telling me that right now, that the worst of it was sitting in a medical center and not knowing if his son would ever wake up again." Riker looked back at her, and Vale felt the echo of the pain her captain and friend was going through. "It's worse than he told me, Chris."

"We're here for you and Deanna, Will," she said. "Whatever you need."

Riker got to his feet, gathering up the unopened bottle and the unused glass, placing them back in a cabinet. He pulled his uniform tunic straight and drew himself up. "I know," he told her, "and for that, I will always be grateful."

Then he moved past his first officer, becoming the captain once again, and strode back out onto the bridge.

ELEVEN

The door to the observation chamber slid silently open, and framed in the opening, Commander Medaka saw Major Helek's thin, angular form. She was a hard-edged shadow, and he couldn't help but think of her like a predator, waiting for the right moment to strike.

Out in the corridor, Centurion Garn stood guard, as impassive and menacing as ever. He was hard to read, Medaka thought, but efficient in his duties. However, a seed of doubt about the security officer's ultimate loyalties lodged in the commander's thoughts. *I have not looked too closely at Garn's past,* he considered. *I may regret that oversight.* Medaka resolved to correct his error when the opportunity arose.

Helek did not wait for permission to enter, and she slipped inside. The door whispered closed and then the two of them were alone in the glass-walled compartment atop the warbird's bridge. Orange light cast from the plasma storms filled the room with shifting waves of fire color, and when it caught the major's pallid face, it gave her a strangely un-Romulan aspect. She carried a cloth bag in one hand, holding it close to her side.

"I do not care to have my time wasted," he began. "Master Engineer Dasix has informed me that our vessel is back at optimal status, and I want to run drills to make sure all is well. This conversation prevents me from doing so, and I will not be pleased if I discover you have delayed vital ship's duties for nothing." Medaka fixed her with a measuring eye. "You asked to speak to me alone, and I have agreed to it, despite my better instincts. What is it you want, Major?"

"The Tal Shiar is not your enemy, Commander."

Medaka scowled. "That is what you begin with? A half-truth, at the very best."

"We all serve the Empire in our own ways," she replied. "Is it impossible for you and I to be allies in this?"

"In my experience, the Tal Shiar only does what is best for the Tal Shiar. Your masters would burn the homeworld to a cinder if they thought it would make them stronger."

"I am saddened to hear you say that." Helek took on a demure aspect. "As I am sorrowful that Romulus will indeed burn, and neither you nor I nor the Tal Shiar can prevent it." She came closer. "I know you dislike my methods. But we want the same thing."

"Your methods?" Medaka pointed toward the closed door. "Cultivating spies aboard my vessel and suborning my officers? Scouring every word I utter for the smallest trace of sedition to hold over me? Absolutely I *dislike* them!"

"For the record, Commander, I have no doubt you are true to your oath to the praetor and the Empire. But sometimes that is not enough."

"I will not apologize for how I conduct myself. And I refuse to let it limit me."

Helek took that in, musing for a moment. "What would you do to keep our people safe, Commander? And not just those aboard this warbird, but all Romulans, everywhere?"

Medaka stiffened at the veiled challenge in her words. "I am here, now, when I should be standing together with my family in the face of the coming disaster! Does that not make my dedication clear?"

"It does." She gave him a nod. "Commander, I asked for this private discussion to make you aware of a most grave discovery. And I assure you, it will not be a waste of your time and attention." Helek produced a padd from inside her tunic. "It is my determination that the *Othrys* has stumbled upon a conspiracy of great proportions. The Federation captain, Riker, is manipulating you. He is in league with the Jazari, working with them against the Romulan Star Empire."

Medaka folded his arms across his chest. "Riker's wife and child are on the Jazari ship and his boy may die from injuries he suffered there. I doubt his father has the time to plot against us."

"One could admire the strength of will it would take to use one's first-born as a tool of such deceit," said Helek.

"Perhaps *you* might, Major," Medaka retorted. "I find the suggestion abhorrent."

"Then let me give you clarity," she told him, tapping out a code on the padd. A holographic panel formed in the air between them, a glowing green frame enclosing a series of scanner images and captured footage. "The Jazari have been lying to us from the very start, Commander. Everything they have told us about their origins and their nature is a fabrication."

"What are you talking about?"

"They are *machines*." Helek loaded the last word with venomous menace. "Synthetic life-forms with no soul and no emotion. They fake everything about themselves, and they have done it in order to conceal their true intentions."

"Show me proof," said Medaka. Like most Romulans, he had always found the idea of artificial beings to be unsettling. Their society was rife with myths and old stories of evil mechanical duplicates and false beings, ancient cautionary tales woven into the tapestry of Romulan culture. But Medaka was also a scholar as much as he was a warrior, and he knew enough not to dismiss the idea of a civilization of alien synthetics out of hand.

The holoscreen cycled through deep-sweep sensor scans of what appeared to be a Jazari male, revealing—as Helek stated—the metal and polymers beneath a sheath of cultured flesh.

Medaka's thoughts reeled as he tried to process the torrent of information, and dozens of questions demanded answers. *Does the Federation know of this? Are the Jazari's stated intentions truthful, or is there another agenda? Are these machines a threat to us?*

As if she read that final thought in his eyes, Helek's lips compressed into a thin grimace. "It is my sad duty to report that the Jazari have already acted against us. In the past few hours, one of their agents boarded the *Othrys* and it killed a crew member. Vadrel and I almost suffered the same fate."

"*What?*" Medaka could hardly believe what he was hearing. "Why was I not informed immediately?"

"I had to be sure the ship was secure," she told him, tapping another control on the tablet. "As your second-in-command, that was my primary responsibility."

The commander's chest tightened as he watched the moment Helek described play out. The holoscreen showed a robed Jazari in one of the ship's laboratory work spaces as it savagely attacked the major and the scientist Vadrel. He saw it stab crewman Hosa through the throat and then attempt to choke Helek to death. Beside him, the major absently rubbed at a line of yellow-green bruising around her neck.

Shocked silent, Medaka watched Vadrel scramble for a fallen disruptor and shoot the murderous alien in the back. As it collapsed to the deck, the android's synthetic innards were clearly visible in the footage, through the horrible wound in its torso.

"It boarded by remotely co-opting one of our cargo transporters," Helek went on. "I believe it came here to terminate Vadrel and wipe out all evidence of the scans we took aboard their generation ship."

"What scans? I specifically ordered—"

Helek bowed her head, becoming sorrowful again. "I disobeyed that order, sir. For the Tal Shiar. I forced Vadrel to conduct covert scans while we were on the Jazari vessel. Somehow, this android discovered what had been done and it moved to erase the gathered data. And now Hosa is dead, and the responsibility for his loss is mine."

Medaka forced himself to stop reacting to what Helek was showing him and consider it dispassionately. It was easy to falsify holographic footage, especially for someone as well trained in deception as a Tal Shiar agent.

Even the digital watermark in the corner of the frame signifying its authenticity was not enough to convince him.

But what if this is *genuine?* The secretive nature of the Jazari was well documented, and if they were indeed synthetic beings, their mere existence in these troubled times was a volatile possibility.

"You want proof, Commander," said Helek, offering him the cloth bag she was carrying. "Here it is."

Warily, Medaka reached inside the bag and his fingertips touched a curve of cold metal. He drew out the object within; it was a distended silver skull. The intricate mechanism grinned up at him, and he could not prevent a crawling shudder passing over his flesh.

The moment Helek was waiting for finally came.

From the second she entered the *Othrys*'s observation chamber, the major's every word and motion had been a carefully judged and nuanced performance, designed to maneuver Commander Medaka into the emotional state he was now experiencing.

He doubts, she thought. *Even as he hates me and the Tal Shiar, he still doubts.*

That tiny crack in his contempt was the weakness she needed to exploit him, to bring Medaka around to the path that the Zhat Vash had laid out. Helek needed the commander to see what she saw, to understand that the machine life hiding under their grotesque skin masks was fit only to be eradicated. But to get him there would take finesse.

Helek pushed on. The foundation stones of the conspiracy were already in place. All she needed was to build upon that solid base.

Vadrel's work in altering the security footage from the laboratory was exemplary, and for the majority it was unchanged from the actual holo-scans. Helek's new narrative simply adapted what had already taken place.

She explained away her clandestine use of the cargo transporter by reframing it as an invasion by a Jazari spy. Making an honest admission of her disobedience over the secret scans helped to cloak the rest of the lie by giving it an element of truth. And feigning guilt over Hosa's death pushed the commander ever closer toward Helek's desired outcome. If she could bring him under her sway, Medaka would do the work for her.

A Tal Shiar agent would never admit an error. They would deny, dissemble, decry, but never accept the possibility that they had failed. This was what Commander Medaka expected of Major Helek, and so she disarmed him and gave him the exact opposite.

"My orders from the Tal Shiar were to learn all I could about the Jazari. But I never suspected . . ." She paused, building the tension. "Commander, what Vadrel's scans discovered on board that craft is nothing less than a weapon of interstellar mass destruction."

"That is an extreme accusation," said Medaka, frowning. "Can you back it up with evidence?" Helek showed him more scans, this time of the giant power core at the heart of the Jazari ship. He peered at them. "I see an exotic drive system and nothing else."

"You see what you are meant to see," countered Helek. "Do you recognize the core's energy signature?" She didn't wait for him to reply. "It uses an isolytic form of tetryons. Incredibly powerful particles . . . and in the right quantities, a highly potent stellar inhibitor. Deployed correctly, a tetryon pulse can arrest all fusion within a star." She let him dwell on that grim possibility. "It is a star killer."

"What you say is so," he admitted, "but tetryons can also be used for benign purposes."

"Few but a fool would dare to," she snapped. "And these machines are not fools." Helek gestured at the steel skull that Medaka still gripped in his hand. "Vadrel interrogated the memory bank of that one and what he learned confirms our worst suspicions."

She had to act swiftly now, to cement her narrative in Medaka's mind as the true, real version of events. Helek brought up a tactical plot on the holoscreen, shifting the display to a map of the local sector of space.

"The Jazari ship does not intend to travel out into the unmapped regions of the Beta Quadrant," she explained as a course projection sketched itself across the display. "Their vessel's actual path will take it past the edge of the Neutral Zone, where our forces are most thinly spread . . . and into Romulan space."

"To what end?" demanded Medaka.

"To burn every habitable world they find with their tetryon weapon." She kept her voice pitched low, laced with fear and fury. This was the fullest part of her lie, and she had to sell it to him. "They will deny the refugees from the core worlds a place to start their lives again." She touched her throat. "They will *strangle* us."

"I cannot accept this," said Medaka. But he was wavering, and Helek knew it. A lifetime of knowing the Federation as an enemy, and synthetic life as against the order of nature, was in every Romulan born. That cultural inertia was on her side.

The major saw her opportunity and took it. "The Tal Shiar have been monitoring the Jazari for some time, Commander. This collusion with Starfleet confirms they are our enemies. Tell me, did you not wonder about the origin of that spatial fracture, the so-called accident that first brought us here? I believe it was a weapons test that went wrong!"

"The Jazari called for help."

"One of them did, and that was against the wishes of their Governing Sept. It seems the Terrans and their machine allies underestimated the power of their killing tools."

"You cannot know that."

"The Tal Shiar knows," she insisted. Now Helek went for the final step, and she schooled her expression to appear contrite. "It goes against my pledge to say this, but I cannot remain silent. You must know what I know. The Tal Shiar have long suspected that the star-death is not a natural phenomenon. We believe it was engineered by the enemies of the Empire." She jutted her chin in the direction of the *Titan*, moving off to their starboard side.

"I have heard these stories," said Medaka. "They are nothing but base-less paranoia and conspiracy theories."

"Are they?" countered Helek. "Is it so hard to believe that the Feder-ation would rather see our kind become extinct?" Again, she pressed on before he could offer a reply. "A decade ago, the Empire stood strong and unassailable. But then the war with the Dominion came, a war that Starfleet brought here from the Gamma Quadrant. And we were forced to fight in it."

"We had no choice." Medaka had crewed a warbird during that con-flict, and he knew it all too well. "The Dominion took the Cardassian Union and they would have eventually taken us, given time."

"But the war sapped the Empire's strength," Helek continued. "And then Shinzon and his Reman allies took advantage of that to stage his coup. Romulus was made weaker still . . . and our enemies saw it."

"I know our history," Medaka snapped. "I was a part of it! And as much as the Federation are our adversaries, I know *them*. In three centuries, they have never initiated military hostilities without provocation. What you suggest is beyond them."

Helek let her lip curl into a sneer. "Yes, you know Starfleet. So do I. They have to be the heroes of every story, don't they? No Starfleet captain would ever be so ignoble as to attack us openly! A war would get their delicate hands dirty. Better for them, cleaner for them, to let us choke to death on our own." Helek snorted. "With a little push, of course." She gestured around, taking in the infernal, amber-red skies around them. "Put yourself in the place of their leaders, Commander. You see your most ancient enemy hobbled by losses against the Dominion, with a Senate riven by internal conflict. It is the perfect moment to *accelerate* the rot. Then word of the star-death comes, and your enemy asks for help. But you cannot be seen to refuse! That would tarnish your perfect, unblemished self-image." She held out her hand. "So help is offered, only to be snatched away because of a terrorist attack." She made her open hand a fist, walking away to the nearest port, to stare down at the vast Jazari ship. "A *synthetic* terrorist attack."

"I cannot accept that Starfleet would attack their own shipyards," Medaka insisted. "They would not collude against their own people."

She heard the hesitation in his voice, and like a disruptor cannon locking on to a target, she homed in on it. "A Romulan state with its heart torn out, its armada in tatters, and its people scattered with no new worlds to live on. That is what our enemies want. You know it, and I know it."

Medaka made an effort to rebuff her line of attack. "Your theory is riddled with voids. The Federation have banned all synthetic life. If what you say about the Jazari is true, why would they ally with them? And why would the Jazari dedicate the whole of their race toward invading Romulan territory?"

"The Federation ban is a lie, like all the others they hide behind. And the machines . . . ? They act on cold logic. They crave resources to construct more of their kind, and those riches are more easily plundered from dead worlds than live ones. Their alliance with the Federation benefits both sides."

Every attempt the commander made to counter her argument had a retort. Helek suppressed a smile, savoring the anticipation of bringing Medaka to her side. He might resist, he might even believe that he was beyond all this, but he was a pureblood Romulan, and Medaka could never escape that.

The reality of living a Romulan life, reflected Helek, was that one was predisposed to believing all those around you were hiding dark secrets. *Because they always are.*

"If even some of what you say is true . . ." he began, and the major allowed herself that brief smile. "Then this is a grave matter indeed. I am compelled to act. For the good of Romulus and our people."

She gave a short bow. "I will order Maian to sound the call to battle stations and take the ship to Condition Scythe—"

Helek was a half step to the door when Medaka shook his head. "You will do no such thing. I said I would act. I did not say I would arm our weapons and make ready for war." He tossed the android skull back to her, and she caught it awkwardly. "Never forget that I am in command here, Major, and I do not take kindly to those who try to manipulate me with an arsenal of half-truths." He made a low spitting sound. "What kind of fool do you think I am?"

Medaka was furious at the Tal Shiar agent's arrogant, scheming behavior.

He guessed there was some measure of fact in among her words—the most convincing lies always had a grain of truth in them, after all—but the callous, unprincipled manner in which she had tried to corrupt him was insulting in the extreme.

"I didn't rise to the command of a *Mogai*-class warbird by letting your kind work me like a puppet," he snarled, finally allowing all his loathing for the woman to show. "If you want to stoke hatred and violence toward the *Titan* and the Jazari, then I have no doubt that is in your interest only, and not for any goal as grand as the preservation of the Romulan Star Empire." He was disgusted with her. "Even for the Tal Shiar, this is an underhanded tactic. You seek to ignite a war where no conflict exists, at the worst possible moment in our history!"

"We are at war," she barked, "we have always been at war! With the Terrans, with the machines! You are blind if you think you know what peace is!" It was as if a veil fell from Helek's face, and for the first time Medaka was seeing through to the real person beneath it. What he glimpsed there was ugly and full of hate. Not dedication, not duty, but something barely controlled. *An obsession.*

His hand dropped to rest on the pommel of the ceremonial commander's blade sheathed at his belt, a clear warning to Helek to stand down. "I will be the judge of when and how this vessel goes into battle," he told her. "Riker is an adversary, but he is also a man of candor, of honor. He and his fellow officers have been trying to *aid* us. I refuse to accept that he is poised to attack." Medaka considered his options. "I will speak with

Riker on this. I'll make my judgment then on who is the threat this day, and who is not."

Helek's anger waned and she gave a reluctant nod. "I have made an error. Mark this moment well, Commander, for it is rare to hear an agent of the Tal Shiar admit a fault. But I believed that my oratory would be enough to cut through that superior self-confidence of yours. I thought I could take a different tack, appealing to your patriotism and the innate suspicion of our kind, rather than doing something as clumsy as threatening you and your family. I misjudged." She chuckled. "You're even more obstinate than your files suggest." Her studied veil dropped back into place, and now Helek's expression became one of exaggerated disappointment. "Oh, Commander," she sighed. "Why do you have to be so difficult?"

Medaka had reached the end of his tolerance with the other officer. "This is over." He reached for his wrist communicator and began to speak. "Security—"

"I wouldn't do that," interrupted Helek, tapping a key on her padd. Medaka's communicator instantly went dead.

He slowly lowered his hand, tightening his grip on the blade. "Don't try to get in my way, Major," he warned. "My crew are loyal. If you move against me, you will fail."

"I would," she agreed, "and they are. But loyal to the Empire, yes? Not just to you." Helek tapped out a code on the padd. "If the great Commander Medaka was shown to be *disloyal*, I am sure they would do what was right."

"I am no traitor," he snarled.

"A moment ago, that was so," said Helek, and on the holoscreen new footage began to play. "But now the reality is different. And you will be whatever the Tal Shiar says you are."

The images were grainy and distorted, but suddenly it became clear to Medaka what he was seeing. A view from the eye of a tiny camera mounted in the clothing of an unseen figure, framing the interior of a cabin on a Starfleet vessel. And there, caught at the edge of the frame, was Captain Riker.

"I have studied human customs. I am an exception." Medaka heard his own voice, his own words but altered and edited.

"Yes," Riker replied. *"I'll pass that on to Starfleet Intelligence."*

The commander reached up to touch the Imperial insignia on his uniform. He tore it off and stared at the metal shape of the great raptor, with the globes of Romulus and Remus held in its claws. The eyes of the raptor were tiny pinholes, and behind them glittered the lens of a sensor camera.

"I had Vadrel do it," explained Helek. "He embedded a tracking module and a scanner. So I could surveil you wherever you went." She opened her hands. "And see what I found? Such treachery."

"Odd, that I can openly admit this to you, an outsider, but never to my own crew." Medaka recognized things he had said to the Starfleet captain while he was aboard the *Titan*, but now the context had been shifted to give them a different meaning. *"This is not an abstract thing, it is personal."*

"You've been very useful to us," said the fake Riker. *"Your defection will put us in your debt. We'll find a home and a new life for you and your family, far from Romulus. Far away from the devastation that will come."*

A bark of laughter escaped Medaka's lips at the ridiculousness of what he was seeing. "This is idiocy," he snapped. "Pure lies!"

"We'll need the ship too, of course," continued the Riker analog. *"Is that a problem?"*

"No. Does it surprise you to hear a Romulan say that?"

"The Jazari will deal with the crew for us."

"Very well."

Medaka pulled the blade and flicked it into a fighting stance. "I should slit your throat for this," he spat. "You've gone too far this time, Helek!"

She eyed him, unintimidated by his threat. "I wanted you to be a part of what will come next, I really did. But I knew there was a good chance you would remain the same intractable, iconoclastic fool you have been in the past. That's why I had Vadrel prepare a secondary option . . . If the

Jazari data was not enough to convince you, then I knew I had to discredit you, utterly." Helek brought her hands together. "What you have just seen has been relayed to every station on the bridge. The crew are all witnesses to your cowardice, Medaka. Your sad betrayal."

"It's a fake!" he snarled.

"Yes. But they'll never know it."

The door behind Helek hissed open and Garn strode in, flanked by Crewman Felle, another member of the warbird's security team. Both men had disruptors drawn, and Medaka knew if he made even the smallest threatening motion, he would be cut down where he stood.

The commander opened his fingers and let the ceremonial blade drop to the deck, signaling his surrender.

"Take this traitor into custody," ordered Helek, feigning regret. "Place him in isolation. As of now, I am assuming command of the *Othrys*."

The long, stifling silence on the warbird's bridge seemed to go on forever as the captured footage on the crew's screens lay frozen in its final moments.

It was Decurion Benem who found her voice first, and when the Garidian sensor operator spoke, it was in a hushed, incredulous whisper. "I do not believe it. The commander would never . . . He would not . . ."

"Betray us for himself?" growled Dasix. The towering Reman female lurked in the shadows at the rear of the command deck, close to the dim displays of the engineering console. "Are you certain of that?"

"Watch your tongue, Engineer," said Lieutenant Maian. As most senior officer on the bridge, the old veteran stood next to the commander's chair.

"You dispute it?" Dasix glared at him. "Medaka has always been willful, we all know that."

"The Terran captain forced his hand." Sublieutenant Kort nodded at his own statement. "Forced him to choose between his family and this ship. What kind of cruelty is that, I ask you?"

At the navigation console, Hade-Tah said nothing, staring fixedly at its screen. The Taurhai's sharp features showed no emotion, no clue as to its inner thoughts.

"Helek is behind this," said Benem. "It's the only explanation." She twisted in her chair, taking in all the other members of the bridge crew. "We have to act before—"

"Act?" Maian cut her off. "In what way, Decurion? Major Helek is now the ranking officer. This isn't some Klingon scow, you cannot challenge her to a death duel if you dislike her."

Benem was going to say more, but then the turbolift at the rear of the bridge arrived and deposited the subject of his ire before them. Helek marched into the middle of the compartment, but it escaped no one's attention that Centurion Garn had accompanied her. The security officer took up a post where he could observe them all, his thick arms folded over his chest.

Helek seemed to sense Benem's accusation still lingering in the air, and she gave her a long, neutral look before nodding to Maian. The veteran returned to his primary station at the helm, but Helek didn't take the command chair.

She let out a sigh of regret. "It is my duty to inform you that Commander Medaka has been relieved of his post. You have all seen the recorded evidence of his betrayal. He was a good officer, but with a weakness that our enemies preyed upon. He will answer for his failure."

Benem couldn't stop herself from muttering something under her breath, and Helek rounded on her.

"You wish to speak, Decurion?" The major stared down at the Garidian.

"I've served with Commander Medaka all my career," she said, the words coming out in a rush. "I'd like to hear his side of this."

"Understandable." Helek gestured toward the turbolift. "I would prefer you remain at your station, but report to the brig if you wish. There, you may speak to the commander for as long as necessary." Her tone was level, but the inference was clear. *Defy me and join Medaka in the cells.*

Intimidated, Benem turned back to her panel, and at length Helek settled into the command chair. She sat erect, like a monarch upon a high throne.

"I want each of you to understand what has happened here," she went on. "For some time, it has been suspected that Commander Medaka's loyalty was . . . wavering. I was put aboard this ship to observe him." Helek paused to let that sink in. "I did not expect to uncover a defection in progress . . . and worse still." She drew her padd, keyed in a code, and the main viewer began a playback of the footage Helek had shown to Medaka on the observation deck.

The bridge crew watched as the Jazari killed Hosa, drawing gasps of surprise from Kort and Hade-Tah; but then they all fell silent when Vadrel's disruptor blast revealed the true nature of the androids. Helek gave them the same narrative she had offered to Medaka, of a synthetic alien infiltrator aboard the *Othrys*, a Starfleet ship in league with these duplicitous machines, and a plot against the peoples of the Star Empire. None of them voiced a challenge.

"Many of you knew Uhlan Hosa," she said. "You know he was no weakling, so you understand the danger just one of those machines presents. And there are thousands aboard that ship. An entire army of soulless automatons."

"The commander couldn't have known . . ." insisted Kort.

"Of course," Helek broke in. "He deserves our pity, not our anger." Then she snarled. "It is the Federation who warrant our unfettered fury! It seems it is not enough for them to watch the Romulan Empire perish slowly from the coming star-death. They seek to speed along the process with the help of their machine allies."

"Major Helek." The veteran Maian was the linchpin of the bridge crew, and when he spoke, the rest of them listened. "What are our orders?"

She took a breath. "We are outnumbered by the Jazari. The Starfleet ship can match us for power and maneuverability. But we have the element of surprise. The androids have yet to respond to the termination of their infiltrator, so we must act swiftly before they realize their plan has failed. We must be audacious and show no hesitation."

Maian turned to Kort and Benem. "Combat officer, sensors officer. Present a battle approach to the Jazari ship. Target power and defensive systems."

The two officers accepted the commands, and presently a holograph flicked into being at Helek's side. She gave it a once-over. "Good."

"The *Titan* is the bigger threat," Dasix rumbled, her voice carrying from the rear of the bridge. "Even in its wounded condition."

"The master engineer's point is well made," said Helek. "Prepare a firing solution for the primary plasma weapon on the *Titan*, and bring all weapons to ready state."

"Setting Condition Rapier," said Kort, his hands dancing over his panel.

"As regrettable as the events that have brought us to this moment are," began Helek, "today we will affirm the one truth that can never be challenged or betrayed: *Romulus does not forgive*." She brought her fingertips together in a point and set her gaze forward, before giving Maian a curt jut of the chin.

"Execute attack," said the lieutenant.

TWELVE

"Steady as she goes," said Riker.

He felt the faint tremor through the deck of the *Titan* as the starship passed close to a towering pillar of churning energetic plasma, the massive continent-sized plume throwing a hellish glow across the bridge.

Of course, *close* was a relative term in deep space. Such was the size of the plasma column that it seemed near enough for Riker to be able to reach out and touch it, but that was an optical illusion. It was hundreds of kilometers distant, a vast tendril of unchained energies rising up and out of the main cell.

The storm zone filled the viewscreen off the *Titan*'s port bow. It was a great swath of slow-rolling plasma that blotted out everything in every direction. At the heart of that colossal interstellar tempest, plasmatic fires burned as hot as newborn stars, the radiation they threw off illuminating the dust clouds and inert ejecta that littered the rest of the sector.

It was a stunning sight to behold, and on any other day Will Riker might have found time to be daunted and fascinated by it in equal measure. But his mind was constantly being pulled away, toward the pronged shape of the Jazari generation ship framed as a long black shadow against the plasma storms, moving in sync with his vessel.

"Holding steady," reported Westerguard. "The Jazari and the Romulans are maintaining separation."

"Storm activity is within expected parameters, Captain," said Livnah, peering at her science console. "If we maintain this velocity, the flotilla should pass beyond the turbulent zone within fifteen hours, and reenter open space."

"Don't get comfortable," warned Vale. Seated at Riker's right-hand side, the first officer addressed her comment to the whole bridge crew. "Plasma storms are notoriously unpredictable. We need to take each moment as it comes."

Riker glanced at the empty chair to his left. Usually, his wife would be there, and he felt her absence keenly. She was over on the Jazari ship, facing the worst that any parent should have to experience, but the bounds of duty meant he had to be here, unable to be with Deanna when she—and their son—needed him the most.

Some days, I hate this job. The silent admission hung in his thoughts, and he absently ran a hand over his uniform collar, feeling the four gold rank pips pinned there. *Jean-Luc never told me how heavy these things could be.*

An alert tone sounded on the tactical console behind him, breaking Riker's reverie. The captain turned as he heard Keru give a low grunt. "Problem, Commander?"

The burly Trill's brow furrowed, accenting the patterning of dark spots down the sides of his bearded face. "I'm reading an aspect change on the *Othrys*. Alterations in their power curve."

"They're speeding up?" Vale asked, her eyes narrowing.

"Negative, the power isn't going to their engines." Keru's frown deepened. "Or deflectors, for that matter." He looked up from the screen. "Captain, this is a shift to an offensive stance."

"Toward what?" But even as Riker said the words, he had a horrible sense that he already knew the answer.

The timbre of the alert suddenly became shrill and insistent. "Sir, the Romulans are breaking formation!" Lieutenant Cantua called out the warning from the flight operations station. "Sensors now reading high-energy precursor events inside the warbird's forward hull!"

That could mean only one thing. "They're powering up their primary weapon," said Vale.

Ever since the days of the first Earth-Romulan War, the Star Empire had equipped their warbirds with a singular, deadly weapons system—a directed-energy plasma projector capable of unleashing a fireball of hyper-accelerated matter. Although it would never be as controllable as a photon torpedo or as flexible as phasers and disruptors, the plasma weapon was far more destructive, capable of burning through deflector shields and turning the tritanium hull of a starship to slag.

Like the storm raging off the bow, it was a force to be reckoned with, and it could kill an unprotected ship in a single strike.

"Shields up!" called Riker. "Red alert!"

"Aye, Captain." Keru gave a nod. A new shade of crimson light bathed the bridge as warning indicators lit up.

"Sir, be advised, our deflectors are coming on slowly," warned Mc-Creedy, working the panel at engineering. "Main energizer is still below optimal function."

"Work with what we have, Karen." Riker leaned forward in his chair, scrutinizing the fast-moving Romulan ship. "Where are they going?" He took a breath, formulating his next command. *I'll put us between them and the Jazari ship,* he decided, *then find out what the hell Medaka is doing . . .*

But Vale's reply cut that intention down. "*Othrys* is turning toward us. They're starting an attack run!"

"Cantua, warn them off," ordered Riker.

"Negative response to hails," said the Denobulan.

Keru gave a shout. "Captain, on the screen!"

Riker's head snapped up to see the Romulan warbird coming at them straight on, and there at the tip of its beaked prow, a sinister glowing shimmer formed as the plasma weapon was uncaged.

"Engineer, divert all power to forward deflectors," said Vale. "Ready for—"

"They're firing!" Westerguard warned as the plasma bolt burst from the warbird's beaked maw in a gout of hellfire, and streaked toward the *Titan.* In milliseconds it grew from a speck of baleful light into a blinding miniature star.

"Helm, hard to starboard!" Riker was suddenly on his feet, one hand gripping his command console to steady himself. He felt the deck pitch beneath him and the pull of the *Titan*'s structural integrity fields as the ship pivoted sharply.

But the damage his vessel had suffered was still evident, and the captain sensed it in the sluggish turn. *Too slow. Too slow!*

"Incoming fire, brace for impact!" Vale barked out the warning over the intraship as Cantua desperately tried to drag them out of the line of fire.

For one dizzying second, Riker hoped they might make it through unscathed, but *Titan*'s turn was too wide. The core mass of the burning plasma bolt streaked past the starship's starboard side, but the crackling corona of energy around it hammered through the weakened shields and seared a line of fire across the ship's saucer-shaped primary hull and over one of the warp-drive nacelles.

Titan reacted like a living thing, shocked into motion, veering wildly away. Riker fell back into his seat and held on as the ship shuddered, trying to right itself.

"Good work, Mister Cantua," said Vale, "that could have been a hell of a lot worse!"

"Damage report." Riker threw McCreedy a wary look and the chief engineer nodded grimly.

"Shields down to forty-seven percent, hull damage on decks six through ten. Phaser banks offline, working on getting them back."

"Damn it." Riker muttered the curse. "This makes no sense!" Had Medaka been playing him from the start? The captain thought back to the conversation they had shared in the *Titan*'s conference room and he couldn't make that possibility stick. Will Riker always trusted his gut, and that instinct was telling him the Romulan commander wasn't the kind of man to bury a knife in an unprepared foe.

"Are they coming back at us?" said Vale. "They hit *Titan* with that again, we might not shake it off a second time."

"Negative, the *Othrys* has altered course." Livnah read off the data from her sensors, and Riker's blood drained from his face at her next words. "The warbird has opened fire on the Jazari generation ship."

From the outside, the reparation capsule was a tube of translucent material resembling frosted glass.

Troi watched glowing trains of blue and orange light move around the circular walls in complex patterns, stopping here and there to gather into knots of color. The capsule was one among a dozen suspended on arms of polished marble, although the others were inert, and among them drifted a handful of the floating orb drones that had spoken to her back in the infirmary tent. Every few seconds, the orbs gave off blinks of illumination that reflected from the chamber's shiny walls.

She put out her hand and laid it on the side of the tube, feeling the pulse of warmth within the material. "Can he hear me in there?"

"I'm afraid not," said Zade. The Jazari stood close by, his head tilted at an angle as if he were listening to something that only he could hear. "But Thaddeus is aware of your presence."

"The boy is calmed by your proximity," said Friend, the now-familiar, disembodied feminine voice echoing around them. *"Curious. He exhibits a low level of tele-empathic potentiality."*

"He's part Betazoid, like me," said Troi.

"Does that comfort you?"

"It's something," she admitted. "I wish I could hold his hand."

Zade shook his head. "The capsule must remain sealed for the duration of the reparation program. The system uses nanoscale technology to repair damaged materials on a molecular level."

"Nanites?"

"Yes. But they cannot exist outside of the capsule's control field."

As the Jazari spoke, the light trains on the wall of the tube shifted to become a map of her son's nervous system. Blinking dots collected around injured areas of his brain, and the tiny molecule-sized devices swarmed to those locations to repair what was damaged.

"Do not be afraid, Commander Troi," said the voice. *"We are aware you have had undesirable encounters with nanite technologies in the past, during your time aboard the* Starship Enterprise. *Please know that our systems are wholly benign."*

She wanted to believe that, more than anything, if it meant getting her son back in one piece. "This is . . . how you heal your own people?"

"When reparation is required," it replied. *"The incidence is rare. Jazari are long-lived and we are cautious."*

Troi's unanswered questions came to her once more. "Exactly how old are you, Mister Zade?" She vaguely recalled that Zade's Starfleet record put him somewhere at the low end of his thirties in standard years.

"We do not measure time on the same scale as humans." The reply was a deflection, and he knew it.

Inside the tube, the light shifted again, and she felt her son's aura change and soften. His fear was waning. He felt safe.

Please let that be true. Troi offered the thought to whatever benevolent powers or fates might be watching over them at this moment. As an empath, she had always possessed some measure of belief in the numinous and the spiritual, and as her son lay on the edge of survival, she desperately wanted every element of the universe to be looking out for him.

"What are his chances?" It took a moment before Troi realized that she had said the words aloud.

"Thaddeus's chances are good," said Zade. "He will endure today." Then a shadow passed over the Jazari's reptilian face. "Beyond that, he will face the same challenges as all of us—"

Zade suddenly stiffened, falling silent. In the same moment, a low booming sound like a tolling bell echoed through the reparation chamber, and the floating drones reacted like frightened birds, darting away to the corners of the space.

"What's wrong?" Troi cast around, her heart racing. "What is it?"

"Danger, Deanna Troi," said Friend. *"A weapons discharge has been detected in close proximity. The Romulan starship escorting us has launched an unprovoked attack."*

"Will . . ." She slapped at the combadge on her chest, but the device remained silent.

A heartbeat later, the walls of the chamber trembled as something powerful impacted the great ship's hull with punishing force, and Troi fell against the side of the glowing capsule.

"Get me a tactical approach!" demanded Riker, jabbing a finger at the viewscreen. "We have to stop this!"

"The warbird has completed a sweep over the generation ship," said Vale, reading the monitor at her side. "Reading multiple disruptor hits. They've already lost a dozen shield emitters."

"Why aren't they firing back?" said Keru.

"The Jazari are pacifists, their ship is unarmed," explained Livnah. "They believe in using force only in the most extreme of cases."

"I'd say this is pretty bloody extreme," retorted the Trill. "Captain, photon torpedo launchers are still cycling up to active state but I can give you phasers now."

Riker's hand tightened into a fist, and it took all of his self-control not to give in to an aggressive reaction. "Hold your fire." He bit out the words. "And someone get me communications with that ship!"

"Warbird is extending away and turning," said Westerguard.

Riker saw the *Othrys* on the main viewer as a distant green-gray falcon, describing a lazy turn away from the damaged shape of the bigger Jazari vessel. Mass for mass, the Romulan battle cruiser was nowhere near the equal of the generation ship, but its weapons were still powerful enough to reduce the other craft to irradiated wreckage.

"Coming around," continued the navigator. "Heading back toward us."

"Good." Riker drew himself up. "The longer they keep their attention on the *Titan*, the better it is for the Jazari." *And all our people still over there*, he added silently.

The captain pushed away his own anger and fear, knowing that the next few moments could mean life or death. Glancing around, he saw his command crew follow his example. They were good people, every one of them, and Riker knew he wasn't the only person on the bridge fearing for the life of someone they cared for over on the Jazari ship. Both Ranul Keru's partner and Hal Westerguard's daughter were down in the Ochre Dome, and the tactical officer and the navigator had to be feeling every iota of the same dread coursing through Will Riker's mind.

"We won't let them down," said Riker.

"Captain," Cantua called out from across the bridge, "the *Othrys* has reopened hailing frequencies." She nodded to him. "You're on, sir."

Riker stepped up to the midbridge and set his jaw in a firm line. "Commander Medaka, this is Captain Riker. What you are doing is an act of war! Stand down immediately and explain yourself!"

The main viewer blinked from the image of the Romulan ship to the interior of its bridge, and Riker's explanation sat there in front of him, gazing out of the screen with a haughty, dismissive expression on her face.

"The commander is indisposed," said Major Helek, her pale lips twisted in a sneer. *"This vessel is now operating under my orders, Riker."*

"I want to speak to Medaka," he insisted.

"You are in no position to make demands," Helek snapped. *"We are no longer in Federation space and you have no authority here. I gave you the courtesy of a warning shot. If you value the lives of your crew, turn away now."*

Riker stood his ground. "We're going nowhere."

Helek rose to her feet. *"Do not interfere, Terran! You may be too blind to see it, but we know the Jazari are an existential threat to all organic life! Their continued existence cannot be permitted!"*

"What the hell are you talking about?" Riker's snarl sliced through the air like a blade. "They are no threat to anyone! My people, my family, are on board that ship! I won't let you endanger them."

Helek's mercurial mood shifted, her fury becoming scorn. *"Unfortunate. But then, these are the losses incurred when one makes pacts with destroyers."* She put hard emphasis on the last word. *"Unless you wish to lose more, Riker. Unless you wish to lose everything. You will take your wounded ship and flee."* Helek made a vague wave at the air and settled back into the command chair. *"Consider that my one and only grant of mercy. It's far more than you deserve."*

Once more, Riker bit down on his instinctive reaction and tried, one final time, to find a way through this that did not lead to violence. "What are you trying to achieve here, Major? You know I can't leave. And you're firing on a ship full of defenseless civilians. Since when is this the Romulan way? It's the act of a coward! Make me understand why you have done this." As long as he kept her talking, the *Othrys*'s cannons were silent, and every second that passed kept people alive.

Helek hesitated, and for a moment she seemed to be considering his words. But then she pressed on. *"If you understood, Riker. If you were actually capable of it. Then you would join me in annihilating these things. But your kind are too weak. You will never have the burden of the clarity I bear."* She glanced toward her weapons officer. *"And for that, I think you must perish along with them."* Helek signaled to her subordinate and the link was severed.

"She's insane," breathed Vale. "And if that crew blindly follow someone so irrational—"

"She'll make good on her threat." Riker threw a glance at Lieutenant Cantua. "Can we raise the Jazari?"

The Denobulan's face creased in a scowl. "Negative, sir. The Romulans are putting out a broad-spectrum jamming field; it's interfering with long-range comms. But I read increased power output in the generation ship's engines. They're trying to get away."

"New aspect change on the *Othrys*," called Keru. "They're turning back toward the other ship."

"Helm, intercept course, full impulse." Riker looked back at Keru. "I need those torpedoes, mister."

"Working on it, sir."

Vale leaned closer, her voice low and urgent. "Sir, what's our play here? That warbird's a match for us; we need an edge if we're going to neutralize it."

"I know," agreed Riker. "First thing we do, get their attention off the Jazari and keep it on the *Titan*," he replied. "We've got to hope Zade and his people can put some distance between us."

Ahead, the Romulan warship pivoted on one wing and entered a swooping arc that would end with its weapons centered on the huge mass of the generation ship. At this range, it would be impossible for the Romulan gunners to miss the bigger vessel.

Its impulse drive surging, *Titan* dove after the *Othrys*, gaining momentum and bringing its own weapons to bear.

"All phaser banks charging. Ready!" called McCreedy.

"Target their weapons and engines," said Vale.

"Manual targeting active," noted Keru. "Ready to fire."

"Make it count," Riker told him. "Take your shot when you have it."

"Steady," muttered the Trill as a spread of beam fire from an aft disruptor stuttered across the rear arc of the *Othrys*. "Steady."

Emerald lightning slammed into the *Titan*'s shields and crawled away as it dissipated. Ahead of them, the warbird began its next bombardment of the slow-moving Jazari vessel, raining down green death on the lumbering giant.

"*Firing!*" Keru held his nerve until the optimal moment came, and when it did he gave full release to *Titan*'s weapons. Lances of searing orange-yellow energy stabbed out across the distance and raked over the wings and warp nacelles of the Romulan ship.

The *Othrys* trembled, and it veered off sharply before it could complete its second attack run, ignoring its primary target to shoot back toward its pursuer.

"Another power surge on the Romulan ship!" said Livnah.

"The plasma weapon?" Vale's voice held a note of fear.

"No, Commander," said the science officer. "I'm detecting a focused neutrino surge . . ."

"They're cloaking." Riker saw a shimmering aura move over the warbird. The vessel became glassy, insubstantial—and it vanished.

"Active sensors, sweep all sectors," ordered Vale. "Find them!"

Keru gave a nod and Riker heard him mutter something under his breath. "Well, now we've got ourselves a game."

For a moment, Troi felt disconnected from the events around her, briefly dizzy, her thoughts a muddle.

She picked herself up, wincing at the echoing hum of the tolling bell as the sound resonated around the reparation chamber. She placed both her hands flat upon the side of the capsule. *Thaddeus. I am here. You will be all right.*

If her son could pick up on her intentions, she hoped it would calm him. Troi found Zade nearby, the Jazari staring blankly into space. "Can we open this? Get him out?"

The reply came from one of the floating orbs. *"Not yet. The reparation cycle cannot be interrupted. It would be extremely bad for the boy."*

Zade snapped back to awareness, as if a switch had been tripped. "Our systems are calibrated for Jazari, not humans. It takes longer to process the . . . the healing."

"What is going on?" Troi tapped her communicator again, but it was still inactive. "I need to raise the *Titan*."

"Your ship is currently engaged in combat," Friend said matter-of-factly. *"Observe."* The closest of the orbs emitted a flickering bubble of holographic light and it became a three-dimensional viewer, showing images captured from sensors along the outer hull of the Jazari generation ship.

Troi caught a gasp in her throat as she saw the low-slung, fast-moving shape of the *Titan* trading fire with their Romulan companion. "They . . . They attacked? Why would the Romulans suddenly turn on us?"

The image jumped to a view of the Tal Shiar officer Troi had glimpsed a day or so earlier, in what appeared to be a fragment from an intercepted transmission. *"This vessel is now operating under my orders,"* said the woman, then the image changed again. *"The Jazari are an existential threat to all organic life! Their continued existence cannot be permitted!"*

"Major Helek is attempting to destroy this vessel," said Zade. "We are working to evade her, but the great ship is large and it presents an easy target."

"Why is she doing this . . . ?" Troi trailed off. She knew the byzantine thought processes of the Tal Shiar about as well as any non-Romulan could, but even this sudden, unprovoked violence was unlike them. "She must have a reason, no matter how twisted it may be."

"I warned you this would happen!" Behind them, a hatchway had hissed open to reveal the Jazari councilor Qaylan, and the technician Keret. Qaylan pointed at Zade, as if this entire situation was his fault. "Now see what you have brought to us! Ruin and destruction!"

"I tried to stop him," said Keret, "but he would not relent."

"Leave me!" Qaylan shouted at the technician, and then his angry glare found Troi. "You should not be here! This place is not for—"

"I permitted it." Friend spoke over him. *"We are saving a life."*

"The life of one human child, valued over the privacy and safety of our entire civilization?" Qaylan's response was incredulous, and he glared at the nearest of the floating orbs. "You have allowed your imprudent fascination for these outsiders to cloud your judgment! You put us at terrible risk! We have no weapons, we cannot possibly fight a Romulan warbird."

"We will help," insisted Troi. "Whatever the reasoning behind this attack, the *Titan* will fight to defend you. We know the Romulans and the Tal Shiar, we've dealt with them many times before."

Qaylan rounded on her. "We want no part in your endless wars,

Betazoid! We do not wish to be dragged into the tangle of your petty disputes!" He gestured at the orb. "Our only course of action is clear, we must escape this madness at once."

"You can't run from someone like Helek," said Troi. "She'll keep coming. The Tal Shiar are relentless." But the Jazari were barely registering her words. Qaylan, Keret, and Zade each exhibited that same, blank-eyed stare, as if their minds were momentarily far away.

"The transit is not yet ready for deployment," said Zade, after a long moment.

"Transit?" Troi echoed the word, wondering. Was he referring to some sort of drive system?

"We cannot activate it," agreed Keret. "The situation is too fluid. Too many hazardous variables are present."

Qaylan's manner shifted, and once again he turned to Troi. Now the expression on his scaled face was steely and uncompromising. "I want you and all your kind off this vessel." He pointed at the reparation capsule. "The cycle is almost over. When it ends, take your progeny and go!"

"You cannot ask them to leave in the middle of an attack," said Zade. "Remember our code!"

"The code is in error!" retorted Qaylan. As the words left his mouth, the deck shuddered again as another series of impacts slammed into the hull of the generation ship.

"The Romulan warbird has reappeared," reported Friend. *"They are targeting the environment domes."*

Adrenaline spiked hard through Christine Vale, and the first officer's hands gripped the armrests on her seat, her fingers digging into the material. Every battle she had fought pivoted on a moment like this, when the second-by-second choices of the command crew set the path toward survival or destruction.

Part of Vale hated this. In a hand-to-hand fight, when she was sparring with a holographic opponent in a training program or against a real, live antagonist, she could call on muscle memory, ingrained reflexes, and her own senses to predict an attacker's moves. *Plant your foot there; block with this arm; strike with that hand.*

It was so much simpler, so much clearer. In this kind of fight, she could only ride her chair and call out the commands, hoping that those around her could act in unison and make the right play.

"The Romulans have decloaked!" Keru called out from tactical. "Target at one-five-one, mark six. Firing on the Jazari."

At her side, the captain took that in. "Intercept course."

"Intercept, aye." Cantua repeated the order and pivoted the ship back toward the other vessel. On the main viewscreen, Vale saw the green flare of disruptors.

"Multiple structural hits on the Jazari craft," said Livnah. "Hull breaches . . ." She swallowed hard. "Catastrophic depressurization events in several of the ecodomes."

Vale was horrified as the screen at her side showed her the same sensor readings. She saw the disruptor cannons blast open a series of glassy hemispheres on the generation ship's dorsal hull. As the domes were punctured by a beam of fire, the environments within were blown out into the unforgiving vacuum. Around one, she saw the shredded remnants of great treelike structures tumbling in the dark. About another, the waters of an ocean-like enclosure became a torrent of flash-frozen ice crystals.

This was not an attack meant to hobble or wound. Helek's intention was mass murder.

"Photon torpedo launchers are answering commands," said Keru. "Ready on your word, Captain."

Riker nodded, shooting Vale a sideways glance. Neither of them spoke. They had no need. They both knew what the stakes were.

"Launch torpedoes, full spread," said Riker. "Set for proximity detonation, and fire."

"Photons away," said the Trill.

Four coruscating balls of light leaped from beneath the *Titan*'s saucer section and raced forward, tracking the warbird.

Whoever was at the helm of the *Othrys* saw the incoming torpedoes and broke into a high-g impulse turn, hoping to veer off and avoid the lethal antimatter warheads, but Ranul Keru's targeting was on the mark. The first torpedo detonated in a brilliant flash of fire and the warbird bucked in the shockwave. In quick order, the other torpedoes exploded in a halo of light and Vale saw the Romulan ship take damage. Splinters of hull metal tumbled into its impulse wake, shed like lost feathers from its metallic wings—but the *Othrys* was still in the fight, and she couldn't help but curse when the vessel became a ghost and recloaked.

"Target lost." Keru's tone was bitter. "At least we gave them a bloody nose."

"Captain, the jamming field the Romulans were projecting. It's gone." Livnah scrutinized her panel. "Yes. Confirming that. The photon strike must have destroyed their countermeasures array."

"That's something. Livnah, contact our people on the generation ship," said Riker. "Get me a status report."

Vale kept her focus on the *Titan*'s sensors. Once more, the Romulan cloak had rendered the ship completely undetectable, and she scowled at the data.

"I've seen this tactic before," said the captain, glancing over Vale's shoulder. "The Romulans call it 'the shadow dance.' They make quick passes, decloaking and recloaking from different vectors to strike at their targets, never staying visible long enough for their enemy to get a weapons lock."

"We can run a predictive model," said Keru, "extrapolate their most likely attack pattern and try to get ahead of them. Hope we get lucky."

"If we don't, it's the death of a thousand cuts," replied Riker. "I'll gamble over poker but not this. No, we need a better option."

"Report from Lieutenant Hernandez on the Jazari ship," said Livnah.

"Some injuries among our people, but no serious casualties so far. They've evacuated the Ochre Dome."

Vale saw past the wallowing shape of the damaged Jazari vessel, to the hazy fires of the distant plasma storms. The hair on the back of her neck prickled as an idea came to her, the same instinctive reaction she felt whenever she stepped into a holodeck sparring program. "I've got something, but you're not going to like it."

Riker smiled. "I like all your ideas, Chris."

"Liar. *Sir*."

He showed a thin smile. "Let's have it."

"Here." Her long fingers tapped out a new course on her console, and she mirrored it to Riker's panel and the officers at conn and ops.

"Ah . . ." At the helm, Lieutenant Cantua made a worried noise. "Commander, is this correct? You are aware that this heading will take us through the outer nimbus of the plasma tempest and directly *into* that storm cell?"

"I did say it wasn't likable." Vale took a breath. "We make a fast burn at full impulse into the storm, and take the Jazari with us. The Romulans will immediately lose long-range tracking—"

"So will we," noted Keru.

Vale went on. "But the plasma fields will distort around the mass of their ship, even if it's cloaked, and we'll be able to see the effect. Like moving your hand through a cloud of smoke."

"We track the distortions and we can target them." Riker ran his fingers over his chin. "The problem is, every minute we're inside the storm cell, we'll be taking damage from the ambient radiation." He blew out a breath. "You're absolutely right, I don't like it."

Vale eyed him. "But we're doing it?"

"Of course we are." The captain straightened in his chair and gave out his orders. "Commander Livnah, contact the Jazari and tell them our intentions. Tactical and engineering, I want our shields at full power or as close as you can get them. Helm and navigation, input the XO's course heading and take us into the storm."

Vale took a deep breath to steady her racing pulse and drew up. "We'll make this work," she said aloud, half to herself and half as an affirmation for all to hear.

"We have to," said Riker.

A flood of relief washed over Troi as the reparation capsule eased open and she caught sight of her son. Thad was ashen, but he was awake, and that alone made his mother's heart soar.

"Mom . . . ?" whispered the boy. "*Zeeku.*"

"Hello to you too," she said, holding back her emotions. "Come on, we have to get you out of there."

"Quickly," added Qaylan, folding his arms over his chest. "We've done enough for you."

"You do not speak for all Jazari," said Zade, his temper thinning. "Don't presume to."

Qaylan snorted. "You would do well to think on your own position, Zade. While you were away dallying with these outsiders, I have been guiding the grand project. Your actions have put all of that in jeopardy!"

"Zade fulfilled the mission he was given," said Keret, the technician coming to the other Jazari's defense. "As each of us is tasked to do."

Qaylan gave Keret an arch sneer. "Some execute their tasks better than others."

Thad was on his feet now, and he took a few shaky steps. "Oh," he gasped. "Woozy. I feel a little weird."

"Please be careful, Thaddeus. Your body is still adjusting to the repairs." Two of the orb drones drifted closer to Troi's son, scanning him with sensor beams.

Thad gave his mother a weak smile. "Hey, Mom, have you met Friend? I was going to get her, to show her to you . . ." He blinked owlishly. "Shelsa said I made her up, but I didn't."

"I see that." Troi deliberately ignored Qaylan's glare and dropped down so she was level with her son. "Thad, do you remember what happened? Can you tell me how you got hurt?"

The boy's face clouded. "I . . . It's all fuzzy. There was a bright light . . ." He trailed off.

"Thaddeus's short-term memory has been affected by his injury and the resequencing process," said the drone. *"I am afraid he will have lost some recall."*

"You may have your family reunion aboard your own vessel!" snapped Qaylan.

"He's mean," muttered Thad, holding close to his mother. "I don't like him."

"You need to leave, before—"

Qaylan's words were drowned out by a grinding, screeching howl of tortured metal, and suddenly the chamber was shuddering. Thad's grip tightened in panic and Troi pulled her son up into her arms.

"The Romulans . . ." The closest drone uttered half a sentence, and then without warning, the female voice died off as the walls around them trembled.

"This way!" Keret beckoned them to follow, moving toward the doorway as a shower of fragments fell from the curved overhead above.

Troi saw an ugly fissure erupt at one corner of the chamber and race over their heads. The overhead fractured and began to collapse, ejecting pieces of support structure and severed, spitting cables down into the room.

"Qaylan!" In a furious burst of motion, Zade threw himself across the chamber as a jagged section of the overhead fell in, directly above the quarrelsome Jazari.

In horror, Troi saw Zade shove Qaylan out of the way, saving the elder's life at the cost of his own. In a shower of choking metallic dust, Zade was crushed beneath the falling debris and lost to sight.

"Move!" Keret shoved Troi forward, with more strength than she had thought he possessed. "You cannot aid him!" As he spoke, more of the overhead crumpled inward, flattening the orb drones caught beneath the collapse.

"Yes, move!" Qaylan stumbled past her, covered in white dust.

Troi pressed her son's face to her chest, holding him close to protect him, and fled the ruined chamber.

They staggered out into the corridor, and outside, the situation was just as severe. The clean, blue-white lines of the great ship's interiors she had seen on her way here were now marred by heavy structural damage.

"We can't leave Zade . . ." Troi choked on the dust-filled air.

"You brought this on us!" spat Qaylan, staggering past her. "What you want does not matter!"

Troi swallowed a sob, feeling her son's tears soaking into the front of her uniform tunic. The awful possibility that Qaylan might be right made her feel hollow inside.

Ahead of them, another of Friend's drones came speeding around the corner of the corridor, and it pulsed with urgent energy. *"Follow me,"* said the voice. *"We have evacuated your people from the Ochre Dome. I will reunite you."*

"And then you can leave and never return," snarled Qaylan.

THIRTEEN

"Damage report!" Helek coughed out the demand, scowling through the wisps of smoke in the air from a blown-out command panel.

Dasix, the burly Reman engineer, responded immediately. "Minor damage to countermeasures and hull armor in three sectors. Cloaking system, weapons, drives, and life-support remain battle ready."

"Good." The major shifted in her chair, glancing in the engineer's direction.

At first, Helek was disquieted by Medaka's choice to put a Reman on the warbird's bridge, flying in the face of the restrictions put in place after many of their kind had been instrumental in the coup led by the traitor clone Shinzon. But Dasix was fiercely competent, and more importantly, she knew her place. The hulking female understood that what little freedom she had was granted only as long as she served the Empire and this ship. Unless she obeyed Helek's every order, she would be sent back to the mines of Remus, to perish when the star-death came.

Fear is better than loyalty, Helek told herself, *and with Medaka in chains, everyone on this ship is afraid of me.*

She decided to test that hypothesis. "Benem!" Helek barked out the name of the Garidian sensor officer, and she jerked in visible shock. "Status of enemy combatants?"

The long-faced decurion bent over her panel, nodding woodenly. "The . . . the Federation vessel appears to have abandoned its search for our ion trail. It is moving into the outer edge of the plasma storm zone. The Jazari vessel is on a parallel course with it."

Helek stiffened. This was an unexpected move for the Terran captain. She had assumed that her earlier challenges would goad Riker into overextending his position and present the *Othrys* with a clear target. Instead, he had put his ship on a course leading directly into the hazardous storm cell—and the accursed androids were following.

"They are coordinating," she muttered. "Working together."

"Just as you said," offered Lieutenant Maian, eyeing her from the nearby helm station. The old veteran's tone was without weight, but somehow he still was capable of injecting a note of challenge into his words.

At length, he broke eye contact with Helek. The Reman, the Garidian at sensors, and the rest of the command crew were intelligent enough to understand that they served only as long as the major wished it. Whatever fealty these officers had for Commander Medaka, cold pragmatism and self-preservation now eclipsed it. But if Maian thought he was an exception, he would quickly learn otherwise.

"They cannot hope to escape us inside the storm." Helek gave voice to her thoughts. "That Jazari barge won't last a day among those plasma clouds."

"What are your orders, Major?" said Maian.

She ignored him, concentrating on the warbird's weapons officer. "Sublieutenant Kort. Lock all active-cycle disruptors on the drives of the Jazari vessel, and ready the primary weapon for firing."

"That will take a few moments, if we are to maintain the cloak," Kort said warily.

"Proceed at your discretion," said Helek.

"Major." Once again, Maian spoke up to attract her attention. "If we follow them into the storm zone, we put the warbird at risk of detection."

"I am aware of the situation, Lieutenant," she replied. "Perhaps your previous commander was reticent to make bold tactical choices, but I assure you, I am not."

"*Bold* is often a euphemism for *risky*," said Maian. "With respect, it is often more prudent for a starship commander to consider options offered by officers with greater tactical experience."

Helek showed her teeth. "When I want your opinion, old man, I will call for it. For now, mind your post."

From the corner of her eye, she saw Maian's craggy face turn stony. "As you wish," he replied.

"All stations, commit to attack vector," she ordered, the anticipation building in her. "Decloak and fire when ready."

"Warbird on sensors!" Keru shouted out the warning. "Aft port quarter. Coming in hot!"

"On-screen." Riker leaned forward in his chair, tensing like a sprinter on the starting blocks.

The main viewscreen snapped to an image from the rear of *Titan*'s primary hull, along down the sweep of the vessel toward its warp nacelles. Far behind it, forming out of nothing, came the *Othrys*. The malevolent glow from its main weapon glittered like a demonic eye.

"They're going for the Jazari," said Livnah. The black lines of her facial tattoos creased in annoyance. "Targeting those unable to fight back is the act of a weakling."

The ship rocked as a low rumble passed through the *Titan*'s spaceframe. "We've entered the storm nimbus," reported Westerguard. "The Jazari are right with us. Romulans are still coming."

The infernal glow of the raging plasma fields lit up the space around the *Titan*, and it turned the warbird into an ominous black wraith. Riker was reminded of a huge raven; the carrion bird was a fitting match for the incoming attacker.

"Range?" He glanced up at Keru.

"Optimal," said the Trill. "We won't get a better chance than this, sir."

"Shield status?"

Keru indicated the viewscreen, where sparks of energy were already flickering at the edges of *Titan*'s deflectors. "As good as we are going to get."

Riker looked to his chief engineer. "Are your people ready?"

McCreedy returned a nod. "Aye, Captain."

"All right. Execute tactical pattern Vale-Six-Delta." Riker gave the command, and *Titan* turned hard, impulse grids flaring crimson as it cut across the path of the oncoming warbird.

The Starfleet ship put itself between the Romulan vessel and the Jazari craft, and at the same moment Keru unleashed a coordinated salvo of phaser bolts and photon torpedoes from the aft launchers.

Caught between the momentum of its headlong attack run and the urge to evade, the *Othrys* wavered for a heartbeat too long and took glancing hits from the barrage.

"Good strike!" said Livnah. "They will feel that one!"

But they had no time to enjoy the moment, as Commander Vale gave a new warning. "Romulan's main gun has fired! Plasma bolt inbound!"

Once again, a streak of rippling star fire burst from the warbird's prow, following an arrow-straight course toward the slower-moving Jazari ship.

"Dorsal shields to maximum, now!" Riker called out the order, and McCreedy set to work. "Helm, put us ahead of it. We're going to take the hit for them!"

The lights on the bridge dimmed, and the captain felt himself grow lighter as even power from *Titan*'s internal gravity generators was diverted, reinforcing the deflectors across the upper surface of the starship.

The vessel pitched as Lieutenant Cantua stood the vessel on its port nacelle, relative to the motion of the Jazari generation ship. *Titan* interposed itself between target and weapon as the searing light of the unleashed plasma bolt closed the distance.

"All hands, brace for impact!" shouted Vale.

And then the blow came. *Titan*'s shields held for a fraction of a second, dissipating the initial contact energy in a massive flash of white fire, then they collapsed and the ragged remnants of the plasma bolt ripped into the starship's hull with a force so violent Riker was thrown to the deck.

Power conduits around the bridge blew out in spurts of smoke and fire, and the captain felt his ship moan beneath him, the metal frame howling like a wounded animal.

"Son of a—" Vale bit off the end of the curse and pulled Riker to his feet. She had struck her head on her console and a bruise was already forming along the side of her cheek.

"I'm all right." He waved her away and swallowed a gasp of air that reeked of burnt polymers. "Report!"

"*Othrys* has cloaked again." Keru held on to the tactical station's curved console like a drowning man clutching a life raft. "Same ploy as before."

"Only this time, we have an edge," said Riker. "Find them, Chris, before they can recover."

"Aye, sir." Vale dropped back into her chair, and Riker moved to the engineering station.

McCreedy adjusted her glasses and gave him a weak smile. "Bloody hell. Sir, please don't ask me to do that again." She worked her console, rerouting functions around damaged systems to bring the *Titan* back to ready status.

"No promises," he replied. "Can we still make this work?"

"I can give you half impulse and ten, maybe twenty seconds of sustained phaser fire. After that, we're down to bad language and throwing stones."

"That'll have to do." He moved back to the midbridge, wincing at a jab of pain from his leg, from where he had fallen. Riker forced himself not to limp. His crew was looking to him for guidance and strength in this moment, and he couldn't show an iota of weakness.

"I see a ghost . . ." Vale's voice was rough from smoke inhalation, but there was steel in it. She stared into her monitor's screen. "Yeah. There they are."

"Confirmed. Sensors reading perturbation of ambient plasmatic medium at zero-zero-six mark two." Livnah read off the location. "Likely source is a cloaked vessel. Confidence is high."

"Tactical, lock phasers on the middle of that motion," he ordered.

"Phaser lock is inoperative, sir," said the Trill. "I'll do it manually."

"Mister Keru . . ." Riker jabbed a finger at the air. *"Fire!"*

"We hurt them." Hade-Tah's odd, toneless voice cut through the quiet on the warbird's bridge. "They were willing to give their lives to save the Jazari."

"Save them?" Major Helek echoed the Taurhai navigator's words with acid, mocking emphasis. "That was just another empty gesture of false heroism. One more performative act of hollow virtue from the Federation." She leaned back in the command chair, smiling coldly, pleased with her own words. "Mark me well. If Riker and his band of fools desire some meaningless death that pretends at courage, we will give it to them. And when it is over, they will be ashes and we will be victorious."

"The Starfleet ship is turning toward us," reported Benem, a rising note of concern in his reedy voice. "Commander . . . I mean, *Major* . . . be advised that we are experiencing a degree of edge-effect disruption to our cloaking field."

"It's coming from the plasmatic clouds all around us," added Maian. "The ambient radiation level is greatly increased."

"I am fully aware," Helek snapped. The Tal Shiar operative had spent most of her career dealing with special-activities units on planet-side missions, and while the Romulan secret service had trained her to command ships as well as soldiers, she was less experienced with the latter—which was exactly what Lieutenant Maian had been driving at with his earlier comments.

Maian clearly did not think her capable of running the warbird, and if she were honest with herself, Helek was finding the task a test of her patience. She was used to subordinates who jumped when she spoke, and who did not talk back so freely. *More evidence of Commander Medaka's laxity with this crew,* she decided. *He allowed them too much freedom of expression.*

"Federation craft moving now," continued Benem. "Their forward arc is bearing toward us." He swallowed hard. "I advise we fall back beyond the storm cell's nimbus."

"Retreat?" Helek cursed him with the word. "When we have the upper hand?"

"Do we, Major?" Maian did not waste the opportunity to undercut her.

She raised her hand and did not look at the old veteran. "Centurion Garn? If Lieutenant Maian speaks out of turn once more, remove him from the bridge and do not be gentle."

Garn's reply was a grunt of assent. In the midst of the action, the crew had forgotten Helek's man standing at the back of the command deck, observing everything that went on there.

Maian bowed his head, finally accepting that silence was his better option.

Helek rose to her feet and drew herself up. It was clearly necessary for her to reinforce her position as the mistress of the *Othrys*, and there was no better way to do that than drawing the blood of an enemy. She pulled from within herself, finding the depthless well of seething hate and loathing that the Zhat Vash had nurtured in her, from the first day they had taken her into their secret cadre.

"Centuries ago, we carried the Romulan flag to the very gates of the Terran homeworld, burning worlds along the way and striking fear into the hearts of their alien cohorts. Now the Empire's fortunes are ill-starred and these old foes believe we are fragile, that we can be made to pay for the daring of our ancestors." Helek showed a vicious, predatory smile. She was finding her pace, channeling her rage. "These weaklings whose armada will not meet us in open war, who cannot even show the animal courage of a Klingon or the base cunning of a Cardassian!" Helek glared through the viewing screen at the *Titan*, seeing the damage-scarred saucer and glowing warp nacelles pivot in their direction. "They are a pestilence.

A canker, against the order of nature! The galaxy will be better with them removed from it." As she said the last few words, Helek thought of the synthetic abomination that Vadrel had terminated in the laboratory, and her gorge rose. In that moment, she could not have hated the androids more.

None of the other officers spoke, their faces set, unwilling to show anything that might be considered dissention. *Good. They are learning.*

"Prepare the primary weapon to fire once again," said Helek. "And this time we will turn *Titan* into a smoking wreck."

But the weapons officer did not respond. Sublieutenant Kort's gaze was fixed on his console and his eyes were wide, as if he could not comprehend what he saw on the readouts before him.

"*Kort!*" Helek spat his name. "I gave you an order!"

The sublieutenant jerked in shock at the sound of her voice. "Major, the Starfleet vessel is attempting a target lock! They could only do that—"

"If they see us," said Benem.

"Energy surge off the starboard wing," growled Dasix, peering at her station's hooded scanner module. "Plasma effect is causing photonic drag."

"They *see* us!" This time, Decurion Benem shouted the words, and it was as if an electric charge crackled through the atmosphere inside the *Othrys*'s bridge.

On the screen, Helek saw bright flashes of yellow-crimson fire gather at the ends of the *Titan*'s phaser collimator ring and race together. Where they met, a lance of light burst forth, seeking the warbird.

"Evasive maneuvers, now!" She gave the command, but not swiftly enough to matter.

To an outside observer, *Titan*'s phaser barrage would seem to strike nothing, meeting an invisible object caught among the flow and eddy of the churning plasma clouds. Then a millisecond later the hit stripped away the light-bending shroud of the warbird's cloak and the *Othrys* was suddenly revealed.

Major Helek experienced this as a colossal impact along the starboard wing and fuselage of the ship, a blow that rang through the spaceframe, rattling the deck plates, knocking her off her feet. Helek stumbled into the command chair and almost fell, clumsily catching herself halfway. Her cheeks darkened, an emerald flush coming up as rage and humiliation coursed through her.

"How can this be?" Hade-Tah was saying. "It is not possible . . ."

"The cloak was compromised," Dasix growled. "The plasma mass reduced its effectiveness by too great a margin. We squandered our advantage the moment we followed them into the storm cell."

"See to your tasks!" Helek resisted the urge to chastise the Reman with more than just words, and dragged herself back into the command chair. All about her, alarm tocsins brayed, signaling the damage the warbird had taken in the *Titan*'s retaliatory strike.

"Federation ship has our bearing, they're coming at us," said Benem.

"Your orders, Major?" Maian broke his silence, and once more he made a simple inquiry sound like an accusation.

"Fire back!" she demanded. "*Fire everything!*"

"Unable to comply, main weapon charge cycle has been disrupted," said Kort. "Secondary armaments are not at optimal power levels."

A second salvo from the *Titan* crashed into the warbird's half-raised shields and once more the vessel quaked like a palsied drunkard.

With nowhere else to direct her fury, Helek slammed her fist into a fold-up screen beside her chair, smashing in the display and cutting her knuckles on the device. Under her breath, she cursed Riker, that Betazoid witch of his, and their idiot child. *I will see you all suffer before this is ended.*

"If we cannot fight, then restore our shroud." Her savage glare turned on Benem, but the Garidian was too cowardly to meet it, worrying at the controls before her.

"The cloaking projectors are still inoperative," said Dasix, answering for Benem. "We will need to disengage if they are to be returned to function."

Helek drew in a breath of tainted air through her teeth in a low, feral hiss. The next words she spoke tasted foul on her tongue, but she had no other choice to make. "Reman! Put whatever power you can muster into impulse engines! Helm, set an escape pattern and fall back beyond the edge of the storm cell." She dared Maian to say anything. "Do it now!"

The lieutenant silently inclined his head, and turned the *Othrys* away, into a retreat.

"The *Titan* is reducing speed," said Benem, after a long moment. "Yes, confirming that. The Starfleet vessel is breaking off pursuit and moving away."

"They're heading back into the storm," added the Taurhai navigator. "Where we cannot track them."

Helek muttered an epithet under her breath, sneering at Captain Riker's cowardice. *The human does not have the courage to finish us off*, she told herself, regaining her lost poise. *He would rather risk a slow death from radiation in the storm than battle in open space.*

"They cannot hide in there forever," said the major, casting around the bridge. Most of the crew refused to meet her eye, and that pleased her. They were afraid of her now, and that was exactly what she wanted. "When Riker and his synthetic collaborators show themselves, we will be waiting for them. And next time, they will find only death."

Commander Deanna Troi hugged herself as a cold wind blew around the clearing, the air inside the Ochre Dome stirred up by the arrival of the cargo shuttle as it passed through a force field in the glassy hemisphere high overhead.

The *Monk* came down swiftly and settled a hundred meters from what was left of the temporary encampment from the *Titan*. Most of the prefabricated habitat modules and yurt-like bubble tents had collapsed when the Jazari generation ship was bombarded by the Romulan warbird, and the damage stretched beyond into the woodlands around them, where fallen trees and smashed support structures were visible.

Troi walked toward the shuttle as the thruster note dropped away to silence. Behind her, she could sense the other evacuees from the *Titan* watching and waiting. None of them understood why the *Othrys* had suddenly attacked them, and Friend's terse explanation had not been enough for Troi to grasp. She searched for any sign of a floating drone, but saw nothing. If the machine mind was observing her, it was doing so in secret.

A hatch in the cargo shuttle's flank dropped open, and Lieutenant Commander East was the first out, the security chief's watchful, hawkish eyes taking in the location before signaling that the landing site was safe. The dark-haired Irishman caught sight of Troi and he gave her a rueful nod. "Commander."

"Jonathan." She returned the gesture. "Good to have you down here."

"We'll keep you safe," he promised. Behind him, a tall and rangy Kelpien woman stepped out and one hand wandered to her neck, where her threat ganglia were visibly twitching. "Ensign Kono, you're with me," said East, and he led the other officer away to secure the perimeter.

"*Imzadi.*" Deanna's husband emerged and they drew each other into a silent embrace. "Here we are again."

For a moment, Troi's emotions ran so strong and so high she thought she might burst into tears, and she saw the same in her husband. With a deep breath, she swallowed that down and stepped back. "Will . . . when the attack began, I was so afraid . . ."

"Me too," he replied. "I don't think I've ever hated being so far from you and Thad." He almost stumbled over the name of their son. "Is he—?"

"He's all right," she told him, and Will changed right before her eyes, as if an invisible weight lifted from his shoulders. "It was touch and go for a little while, but the Jazari did what they promised. They've healed him."

Behind them, the *Monk*'s crew were opening up the shuttle's rear drop ramp and bringing out fresh supplies for the displaced civilians. Troi and Riker stepped aside, holding on to this brief moment, both knowing that they would only have a few moments to be husband and wife, to be parents, before the needs of the situation forced them back into being Starfleet officers.

"Can I see him?"

"He's with Doctor Talov." Troi led him toward one of the tents that remained standing. "We're lucky, Will. We didn't lose anyone down here." She sighed. "But the Jazari were not so fortunate."

Riker picked up on the sorrow in her tone. "Zade?"

"And others, as I understand it. Helek has their blood on her hands." Troi shook her head. "Why did she do this? It doesn't make any sense!"

"She seems to believe we're in league with the Jazari against the Romulan Empire," he told her. "I've got no idea what happened to Commander Medaka. He was someone I could reason with, but Helek . . . ? That woman is running on pure rage and little else."

"An unfortunate truth of her kind," said an arch voice, and they turned to see three Jazari males approaching. Troi's heart sank as the querulous Qaylan led the group to block their path, with the technician Keret and the former diplomat Veyen following on behind. "I have frequently observed that outsiders allow themselves to be governed by passions and not rational thought. It is why I advocated disconnection from other species." Qaylan inclined his head. "Today's events have proven me right."

"Not every outsider is—" Veyen tried to offer a different viewpoint, but Qaylan silenced him with a hard look and the diplomat let his sentence peter out.

"You've come to see us leave?" said Troi.

"That would be for the best." Qaylan's tone shifted, becoming an insincere parody of the formal politeness his fellow Jazari usually exhibited.

"I'll take my people back if that's what you want," said Riker.

"I do," Qaylan replied.

Riker went on as if the Jazari had not spoken. "I'll bring them back to the *Titan* if the Governing Sept rescinds their offer of sanctuary." Will let that lie for a moment. "Do you speak for all of them, sir?"

Qaylan's scaled face twisted in irritation, and he tried a different tack. "Putting your people on our great ship led the Romulans to attack us. We are victims because of you!"

"You've got it backward," Riker corrected. "Helek wants your vessel obliterated. We were the ones getting in the way."

"Why does she wish us destroyed?" said Keret, but the manner in which he exchanged glances with Veyen suggested to Troi that he already suspected the reason. While she might have been unable to sense the Jazari's emotions with her empathic abilities, she could still read other physical cues. "We have done nothing to her," Keret concluded.

"That's something I'd like an answer to myself," said Riker. He let out a weary breath. "You have to know, this isn't the end of this. Major Helek is a member of the Tal Shiar, the Romulan Star Empire's most dangerous agency, and they are by their very nature relentless. She won't give up and go home."

"So *you* say." Qaylan sniffed.

Troi tried a different approach. "Together we may be able to find a way through this, to get you to where you want to go. But going forward alone would be a serious miscalculation. We came to your aid with the spatial fracture and now again with the Romulan attack. But the danger is not over. Surely you can see, this is not the time to push us away."

"My first officer has deployed some of the *Titan*'s shuttlecraft to the inner edge of the storm zone," continued Riker. "We're using them as sentries, so when the *Othrys* comes back, we'll get advance warning. But before that happens, we need to work together to formulate a combined strategy."

"The Jazari are not students of warfare," said Veyen. "We only defend ourselves. We cannot attack another sentient life-form. It is in our code."

"Hopefully, it won't come to that," Troi assured him. "Armed conflict is always the last resort. If we can resolve this peaceably, we will."

Qaylan peered at the fallen trees and damaged hab-modules. "The Romulans do not seem to share your intentions!"

At her side, Troi heard her husband release a low sigh, and she knew he was reaching the limits of his patience. "I'm willing to discuss this situation in full, sir," he said firmly. "But first I want to see my son."

Qaylan gaped as Riker turned his back on him and marched the rest of the way toward the medical tent; Troi jogged to keep up with him. A comment about tact crossed her mind, but then she thought better of it. *For the moment, diplomacy be damned.*

Riker was reaching for the door flap of the bubble tent when it came open of its own accord, and Thaddeus was standing there. He blinked in the false daylight, still pale and shaky, but very much alive. "I heard your voices," he said. "Didn't want to sit around and wait . . ."

Riker scooped him up into a bear hug. "You're all right," he said, more to fix that certainty in his own mind than to tell it to their son.

"I guess," Thad said weakly. "I'm sorry. I made you worry, didn't I?"

"Yes." Troi heard the tremor in her husband's voice. "And you're going to be in trouble for it later, but right now your mom and I are very, very happy you are okay."

Thad looked across to Troi as she joined their hug. "I didn't mean to get into trouble."

"Riker boys never do," she said with an unstable smile.

"True enough," offered Riker.

Doctor Talov stood on the threshold of the tent, holding a medical tricorder, and he gently cleared his throat. "I have completed a neural scan and cursory physical examination of Thaddeus. The Jazari reparation process is remarkably efficient, and it appears to have fully healed all neurological and physical damage. I will need to run additional tests, but I believe your son will make a complete recovery."

"Friend fixed me," said Thad, but the boy began to cry. "Zade said she would, but he . . ."

"Friend?" Will asked Deanna. "Who's that?"

"It's complicated," she replied.

"Dad, Zade died." Thad buried his face in his father's shoulder. "I liked him and he's gone."

"I'm sorry, kiddo." Riker tried to comfort his son. "But sometimes bad things happen to people that we care about, and we can't do anything to stop it."

"That's not fair," said the boy, with such innocence and pain that his mother had to turn away. "Why can't Friend fix him too?"

"Maybe . . . she can." Troi saw figures approaching from the ruined tree line and it took her a second to process what she was seeing. East and Hernandez were escorting a third person back into the ruined encampment, a Jazari with a pained limp and an injured gait.

The new arrival raised his head. The Jazari she had seen crushed to death beneath tons of poly-alloy and marble stood before them. Zade, it appeared, was very much alive.

Thad called out his name and everyone turned, and Riker let down their son. "Why do I feel like I've missed a meeting here?"

"We found him at the edge of the dome," said Lieutenant Commander East. "He insisted on seeing your lad, wouldn't take no for an answer."

"I needed to be sure he was healed." When he spoke, Zade's voice had a broken, crackling quality. To Troi, it seemed as if she were hearing it over a damaged communications circuit.

"Zade!" Thad's first reaction was a burst of joy, and he took a step toward him. But as the boy took in the condition of the Jazari, that moment of happiness soured and became fright. "What's wrong with you?"

"I have been impaired." Zade was clutching at a wounded arm, hiding it from them, stiff with injury from the collapse that should have killed him—*that* would *have killed any other being*, thought Troi. He seemed unfocused, as if caught in a daze.

"No! Get back!" Qaylan came running toward them, waving his hands, frantic to put himself between the *Titan* crew and Zade before they could come any closer. "Get away from him!"

The diplomat Veyen and the technician Keret were a few steps behind, and on their faces Troi saw open shock. But was it because they, like her, had believed Zade was dead—or was it because they did not expect to see him *here*?

"Zade is badly injured," Veyen insisted. "Our codes forbid aliens to be present at such times. You must not see him like this, it is prohibited."

"I came . . . to find Thaddeus . . ." Zade muttered, his words stuttering with static. "I . . . wish the boy . . . to survive."

"Cover yourself!" Qaylan demanded, pushing Zade away, gesturing to Keret. "Take him from here, quickly!"

"If he's sick, maybe Doctor Talov can help him," said Thad, looking back at the adults. "Right?"

Troi and Riker exchanged a troubled glance, both of them uncertain how to proceed. If they intervened, there could be serious consequences, and matters were already complicated enough with the Jazari.

Zade angrily shook off Qaylan's arm, his mood shifting toward belligerence. "Leave me alone! You do not . . . command me!"

"Fool!" Qaylan did not relent. "You jeopardize everything!" Once more, he beckoned the other Jazari to him. "Keret, Veyen, coordinate! Remove him!"

"Hey, hold up there." Lieutenant Hernandez raised her hands, dropping into a stance that was half defensive, half warning. "There's no need to get grabby. Let's all just take a breath here and calm down."

"Zade." Troi drew on her skills, keeping her voice level, doing nothing that could be construed as a threat. "Why don't you tell us what you need?"

"I need him to leave me alone." Zade gave Qaylan a fierce glare, an expression Troi had never seen on the Jazari's face before. Then it faded, and his aspect was the open, friendly one she had come to be familiar with. "I need to know that Thaddeus is all right."

"I'm okay." Without warning, Thad ran across to grab Zade's hand, pulling on it to guide him toward the medical tent. The adults reacted, but the boy was too fast. "We'll fix you up."

But in the next second, Thad's bright expression became one of shock. The hand he took came forward, and Zade's forearm was pulled into the light.

The limb Zade had tried to conceal was a broken, twisted ruin. It was tatters of torn flesh hanging loose over bones made of bright, polished metals. Beneath them, bunches of sparking, artificial musculature twitched with damage done by the collapse of the reparation chamber's ceiling.

Thad let go in a surge of panic and fled to his parents, hiding himself behind Riker's legs.

"No." Zade's broken voice grated like metal on metal. "No no no. I am sorry, Thaddeus, I do not mean to frighten you."

"He is a synthetic." Behind them, Talov solemnly raised his tricorder and studied the readings. "Whatever mechanism was deployed to mask his nature has been damaged along with Mister Zade's body."

"How dare you scan him?" Qaylan was furious. "You have no right!"

And all at once, a hundred unanswered questions came together in Troi's thoughts. "I saw him crushed. No ordinary organic humanoid could possibly have survived that. He's an android . . . and he isn't the only one, is he?"

Keret raised his hand. "Please, you must not speak of this—"

"Be silent!" Veyen shouted, before the technician could go on, his moderated diplomatic persona briefly forgotten. "Do not worsen this calamity!"

"So this is the secret the Jazari have been keeping from us for hundreds of years?" Riker drew closer to his wife and son as East and Hernandez moved to flank them. "Are you all like him?"

"You . . ." Qaylan grimaced. "You do not know what you have done. Now the child has doomed us."

"No," Zade repeated, shaking his head woodenly. "He has . . . I have . . . freed us."

As one, the expressions on the faces of Qaylan, Keret, and Veyen became slack and distant. They became dormant, unmoving statues.

"What are they doing?" said East.

"Coordinating," replied Zade.

"Dad, Mom . . ." Thad pointed toward the edge of the Ochre Dome. "Friend is coming." The boy marveled at his own words. "A lot of Friends."

From out of the trees came two of the floating drones; then five, then ten, then fifty, each of them swarming toward the encampment, moving with unknown intent and ready purpose.

"Recognize me," said Helek, her voice resonating in the silence of her quarters. The ship's computer obeyed, and the major followed the rote process, once more accessing the hidden subcluster in the system's core memory. From there, she activated her clandestine communication link and spoke the secret name that would open the channel. "Authorization: Zhat Vash."

Something light-years distant analyzed her voiceprint and confirmed that she was one of the chosen, before reaching back to complete the link. Had the analysis shown a negative result, the returning signal would have contained a digital virus, and that in turn would have eaten its way into the warbird's engineering subroutines. A fatal breach of the *Othrys*'s singularity core would have occurred a few seconds later, destroying the vessel with all hands.

Presently, the image of a hooded face appeared before Helek. Dark eyes glittered in the shadows, and that altered nonvoice filled the cabin. *"Report, sister."*

"I took direct command of the ship." Helek made it sound like a simple matter. "There was an initial engagement with the synthetics . . . The Starfleet vessel intervened. We were forced to withdraw and regroup."

"The mission has not changed," said the shadow. *"You cannot return until the machine colony is exterminated."*

"I understand," Helek said bitterly. "They will not escape. I know where they are, and where they intend to go."

"There can be no miscalculation in this act. The destroyers must be destroyed. Utterly."

"I will do what must be done."

"Not alone," came the reply. *"Other assets are on the way. An end will be put to this."*

Helek watched the hooded face dissolve into nothing.

FOURTEEN

"Stay close," said Riker, and his voice echoed oddly off the wall of the vast audience chamber.

At his side, Troi took in the wide, high-ceilinged space. "You could fit a soccer stadium in here with room to spare."

He found the vaulting asymmetric curves that rose up and up, meeting in glowing points of purple-blue light. More of the orb drones drifted around in the heights, some in twos and threes, others in shoals that rippled with color and motion.

On the lower levels, the chamber became a series of tiered platforms that dropped to an oval dais that could be seen from anywhere inside the space. Riker was reminded of some great theater-in-the-round, and instinctively he walked in that direction.

Behind Riker and his wife, a quartet of pulsing drones acted as their escorts, each one floating at torso height, each one humming with quiet power. For all the Jazari promised that they eschewed the use of force, Riker was sure that if he made a sudden move, the orbs would converge on him. He had no desire to test the limits of their hosts' pacifism.

Troi read his thoughts in the expression on her husband's face. "We're doing the right thing," she told him. "We have to let this play out."

He nodded. "What have we let ourselves in for, *Imzadi*? Nothing about this mission has been what we thought it would be."

"I have a feeling we're finally going to get some answers."

"I hope you're right."

Other doorways opened up along the tiers, and through them came hundreds of Jazari, some in robes of office, others in work gear or non-descript tunics.

With so many of them assembled in one place, the uniformity of their kind was as clear as day. Although there was a small degree of variation in their aspects, in such a large group it became clear that there were only a dozen or so "types." Facial features and skin tone repeated over and over, and seeing it so plainly sent a chill up Riker's spine.

"All males," whispered Troi. "No young or old. Almost like they've come out of a factory."

"That may literally be the truth," he noted.

No one had forced them to come to the audience chamber, but the inference had been very clear. The drones—each seemingly an aspect of the mysterious intelligence that called itself "Friend"—had moved to surround the *Titan* encampment in the Ochre Dome and prevent Riker's team from communicating with their ship. It was almost but not quite an act of aggression, and Troi reacted quickly to the situation, seeking a diplomatic resolution.

And truth be told, without weapons or a way to contact Commander Vale on the *Titan*, there was no other way forward but to talk things out. The Jazari held all the cards. *At least until the Romulans come back for a rematch*, Riker thought.

Much to the annoyance of Qaylan, Friend directed them here, leaving the rest of the group under guard while the captain and the counselor agreed to discuss in private what might come next.

Here they stood, as more and more Jazari filed silently into the chamber to study them intently. Riker felt like an insect trapped beneath a glass instead of a respected visitor.

The doors closed and a low chime sounded through the air. *"We begin,"* said Friend's voice, the soft feminine tone carrying across the chamber. *"For the first time in hundreds of solar spans, organics are among us."*

"And we are repeating the errors of previous generations!" Qaylan stood on one of the nearby tiers, sparing a withering glare for Riker and Troi before turning a cold eye toward Zade. The injured Jazari was close by, at the edge of the dais where they now found themselves. He cradled his damaged arm as if it were something foreign to him, scrutinizing the broken metals and torn flesh.

Riker had seen the inner workings of androids before—he remembered holding a disconnected synthetic limb in his hands and seeing the fine mechanics of such a thing up close—but the Jazari were an order of magnitude beyond that. They were not machines made of hyperpolymers and alloy sheathed in imitation skin, and they were not some strain of organic forms constructed from component molecules. They were a stage between both of those extremes, outwardly flesh and blood, but inwardly artificial.

It's incredible, he thought. *If only we could know them better.*

He scanned the crowd, finding the diplomat Veyen and the technician Keret. Riker thought he recognized others from the consular party *Titan* had brought from Vega, but it was hard to be certain.

Another Jazari moved forward to speak, and he paid no heed to Qaylan's terse comment. "Zade, you should not be here. Go to reparation."

"He refuses," said the drone voice.

"I must r-remain," managed Zade. "I must speak."

"You have done enough already!" Qaylan fumed. "You have ruined our work, you have put our very civilization at risk of destruction with your reckless behavior!"

"We don't mean you any harm," said Troi, seeing the opening and seizing a chance to make a positive statement. "The Federation is not a stranger to the Jazari, you know us. You know we do not bear you any malice."

"It is true the Federation is not an enemy of the life-form they know as the Jazari," offered Veyen. "But they are in opposition to all synthetic life. If they suspected that we were one and the same . . ." He trailed off. "Your leaders prohibit any such sentient forms from existing in your coalition, do they not?"

"It's . . . complicated," said Riker. "But the counselor's words still stand.

We seek peace. We came to your aid, and we'd do that no matter what your origins are. That's not something an enemy could promise."

"You aided us because you thought we were like you," countered Qaylan. "I believe that had you known the reality, you would have let us perish."

"No, I won't accept that," Riker retorted. "The United Federation of Planets isn't perfect, but we're open about our record. Our coalition, as you call it, is founded on the ideals of friendship and cooperation among all sentient life."

The Jazari who had spoken before gave Zade a regretful smile. "Outsiders were never meant to see this reality. And now, Captain Riker, Counselor Troi, my people have been placed in a very difficult situation."

"There is no difficulty," said the drone voice. *"These beings are to be considered allies. For too long we have hidden what we are. The time of concealment should end."* The way it spoke, the brisk and simplistic nature of its reasoning, made Riker think of a child. *"Many feel as I do, Yasil."*

"Friend, your input is always valued," said the Jazari it had called Yasil. "But you were not in existence in the time before our change. You did not experience what others of us have experienced."

"I have extensive records from that period in our history."

"But you did not live it!" said Qaylan. "And forgive me for my bluntness, but you have not suffered as many of the rest of us did!"

Riker shared a frown with his wife. It was becoming clear that the unfolding incidents around the Jazari exodus were not just a matter of secrets coming to light, but of deeper divisions among their society rising to the surface.

He found Yasil studying them closely. "Your Federation considers all synthetic life to be a threat, Captain," said the Jazari. "Is that not so?"

"I won't lie to you, some among us *do* believe that. People who have been hurt, and who are afraid of what they don't understand." Riker knew he could only be completely honest. Any equivocation could have serious consequences. "I'm not one of them." He indicated Troi. "We both served alongside an android for more than a decade. We faced adversity together on many occasions. And I know I speak for my wife when I say that we both considered him a dear friend."

"Data," said Zade, concentrating hard, as if he were drawing the information to him across a great distance. "The . . . Soong-type artificial. He voluntarily ended his existence in order to destroy the *Scimitar*. Captain Riker and Counselor Troi were among many organics whose lives were saved because of that selfless act. Much information on this unit has been . . . uploaded to the communication pool."

"The Federation Council acted in an extreme manner after the attack on Mars, no one is denying that," offered Troi. "But they felt they had good cause. That doesn't mean we want to destroy you." She took a breath. "Yes, this revelation changes things between us. But it is what we do next that matters."

"*Revelation*." Qaylan repeated the word with a sneer. "I see it differently. Zade has clearly malfunctioned, his error exacerbated by too long an exposure to these organics. He has been corrupted by extended proximity to them! And Friend has exceeded her programming, compounded by her curiosity and immaturity." He made an angry gesture at the air. "Organics are trying to destroy us, and we are debating how to treat them? Am I the only one who processes the seriousness of this miscalculation? We waste precious time debating this, it is foolish in the extreme!"

"We're not the Romulans," Riker insisted. "Hell, it may not even be the Romulans who have attacked you, it may just be one misguided person! If you hold all of us to account for Helek's actions, you're no different from the people who would see your kind and think of the synths who attacked the shipyards on Mars."

"We have kept a truth from the galaxy for over one hundred of your years," said Yasil. "In order to carry out our grand project, and so we might protect ourselves, we created a fiction. We created this . . ." He indicated himself. "Now that veil has been torn away, for better or for worse, and we are left to decide what happens next."

"Yes," said Troi. "So let us do so from a place of openness."

"There is a clear solution," said Veyen, acting as if the commander had never spoken. "With the successful healing of the human child, we have evidence that our reparation technology can effectively resequence organic neural engrams. I propose that Friend create a process to . . . reprogram all those who are aware of Zade's revelation."

"You wish me to edit the memories of these beings." One of the drones drifted closer to the two humans. *"Calculating. It could be done. But the long-term effects upon them are unclear. They would be deleterious."*

Riker instinctively stepped back toward Troi's side. "We're not going to agree to that."

"What makes you think your permission is required?" said Qaylan. "A civilization is at stake! Be grateful we are not following the example of the Romulans. The energy cost of ending you would be far less."

"We do not take life!" said Friend, the voice booming about the chamber. *"Recall the code. It is ingrained in the core of every one of us!"*

"Are you willing to force us?" Troi let her words fall into the silence that followed, holding her tone steady. "I imagine it's in your ability to do so. But our people won't freely submit to having their minds tampered with, and we won't order them to accept it." She pressed on, before anyone could frame an answer. "And even if you did erase our memories of what we know now, have you . . . processed what would come next?"

"That Romulan warbird is still out there," said Riker. "The woman in command of that vessel is part of the Tal Shiar, and they don't easily accept defeat. When she returns, Helek will most likely bring reinforcements."

"You cannot know her intentions," said Veyen.

"I know the Tal Shiar," he countered. "If they want to put an end to you, they'll keep coming until they do."

"We need each other." Troi searched the faces of the Jazari in the chamber, ending with Yasil. "If we cooperate, we can survive this. You can complete your journey, and we can push back Major Helek."

"I will follow the will of the Jazari, if so commanded," said Friend. *"But I do not wish to inflict harm upon our visitors. I wish to ally with them."*

"It is not your choice," said Qaylan, drawing himself up. "It is decided. We will coordinate, every one of us, and the choice will be made by our collective!"

"Agreed," said Yasil, and a moment later, every other Jazari in the chamber repeated the affirmation.

Silence fell again in the great open space, and Riker watched as a wave of stillness washed over Zade and the rest of his kind. The Jazari became statues, static and immobile, their eyes glassy.

"What are they doing? Have they deactivated themselves?"

Troi gently waved a hand in front of Zade's face, but he did not react. "Will, I think they're communing somehow. Sharing information." She paused, considering. "I've seen them reacting like this before."

The only motion was a rapid blinking pulse emanating from the orb drones, and Riker wondered if that might be one of Friend's functions, acting as a kind of facilitator for the greater whole.

The concept of a networked collective of cybernetic organisms brought up unpleasant parallels to the rapacious hive mind of the Borg, and he frowned at the notion. Fortunately, nothing Riker had seen suggested that the Jazari had the same kind of group consciousness, where all individuality was subsumed into a combined whole—if anything, the disagreeable Qaylan proved that these beings were clearly capable of singular thought and action. It would remain to be seen if that made things better or worse.

Then, as one, the Jazari blinked back to full awareness, and Riker felt every eye in the chamber turn toward him and Troi. At the most, only seconds had passed.

"We have come to an accord and our course of action is decided," said Yasil. "We will once again accept the aid of the Federation *Starship Titan*. The majority understand that cooperation is our only viable option and moral alternative." He paused, finding Riker and giving him a nod of assent. "Any other choice would betray the code our Makers instilled in us."

"I wish to formally protest this choice," snapped Qaylan.

"That is your r-right." Zade looked to the other Jazari. "But you must abide by the decision."

"I shall." Qaylan bit out the words, folding his arms over his chest. "For now."

Yasil was already stepping down from the tier he had been standing on, approaching Riker and Troi on the dais at the chamber's lowest level. "True cooperation can only be born from a foundation of honesty and openness, do you agree?"

"Of course," said Troi.

"For more than one hundred of your years, the veil that shrouded the truth of our kind had been in place." Yasil spoke to them, but Riker sensed the Jazari elder's words were for all his people, not just those here in the chamber but throughout the length and breadth of the great ship. "It is our destiny to leave this space and never return, and we need your help to do that, humans. We cannot defend our vessel alone."

"We must leave everything behind . . . if we are to survive," added Zade. "Even our falsehoods."

Yasil raised a hand, and the orb drones rose with the gesture, glowing brightly. A holographic haze spread from each one, joining to form a wall of shimmering color. "We cannot move on without showing you the truth of what we really are. Without that, there cannot be trust," he told them. "Observe."

The white light became blinding, and engulfed them.

At the appointed time, Major Helek strode onto the command deck of the *Othrys* and advanced on the Garidian woman at the sensor station. "Report, Decurion," she ordered.

Benem's long, distended face creased in a frown, but she made a show of checking the warbird's scanners. "Negative detections," she reported. "Neither the Jazari nor the Starfleet ship have exited the plasma storms." Benem pointed toward the glowing field of fire visible on the main viewscreen. "We are alone here."

"Look again," demanded Helek, making her way to the command chair.

"Major, is there something amiss?" From the helm console, she sensed Lieutenant Maian's scrutiny as the veteran voiced what was on the minds of the rest of the bridge crew.

Helek's answer was only a smile as Benem's scanner began a shrill chorus of alerts.

"Contact!" called the Garidian. "Forward quadrant." She hesitated, her eyes widening. "Correction! Two contacts! Unidentified vessels decloaking around us, forward and ventral quadrants!"

"Go to Condition Scythe—!" Maian started to give the order that would bring the *Othrys* to battle stations, but Helek made a cutting gesture that halted him midcommand.

"Belay that," she told him. "Open a subspace channel."

On the viewer, the lead vessel became discernible as it shrugged off a shroud of invisibility, rapidly shifting from a ghostly outline to a menacing shadow. The ship was Romulan in design, with the raptor-like aspect common to all but a few of the Star Empire's vessels; but it had been altered with stealth technology, advanced weapons, and other systems beyond the grasp of any standard Romulan ship. Clawlike constructions and serrated talons emerged from the hull, giving the craft the aspect of a barbed weapon. Rumors suggested that these vessels used technologies recovered from other species, whispering the name of the dreaded Borg, and worse.

No one on the bridge spoke. Every one of the command crew knew what these ships were.

Tal Shiar.

Helek smiled thinly. The Empire's secret police rarely deployed the vessels in their covert fleet, and to warrant two of them showed how seriously the threat of the Jazari was being taken. But the Tal Shiar's obsession with secrecy extended to all things, and she imagined that the crews aboard those ships had little knowledge of the synthetic nature of the alien threat they were here to eliminate. Such information was not required for them to complete their mission, only obedience to the objective.

Those among the Zhat Vash would know the full truth, their terrible responsibility shared silently among them. In turn, they would use the Tal Shiar as their tools, just as Helek now used the *Othrys* and its crew.

"Incoming signal," said Maian, breaking the silence.

"Let me hear it," she ordered.

A voice scrubbed of all identity crackled around the bridge. *"Major Helek. We are here to assist you in your task. We are at your command."*

She gestured at Sublieutenant Kort. "Transmit all tactical data we have on the *Titan* and that Jazari hulk, including the sensor logs from our most recent engagement."

After a long silence, the voice from the ship returned. *"Analysis in progress. Targets verified. How do you wish to proceed, Major?"*

"Prepare your weapons for a full-scale attack." Saying the words sent a thrill down her spine. "We will leave no survivors."

"Acknowledged."

Helek leaned forward in the command chair, her dark eyes glittering with malice. "Let us begin."

Deanna shielded her eyes with one hand, and she felt Will grab the other. He gave it a welcomed squeeze and she returned it. Despite all that they were going through, it felt good to have him close to her. Together they were stronger, able to face anything.

The blinding light from the orbs dimmed and she blinked, finding a new vision before her. Her husband stood at her side, and a short distance away, Yasil was waiting for them.

They were no longer in the audience chamber. They were standing on the surface of an alien world with a spectacular landscape of yellow rocks and ochre deserts. In the sky overhead, the arc of a planetary ring system glittered in the evening, reflecting the light of a distant amber star. Thin, bamboo-like trees waved in the wind atop a nearby ridge, and Troi felt the breeze on her face.

It was an almost perfect illusion, and she might have thought it real if she hadn't reviewed the survey records of the Jazari homeworld a few days earlier. They were standing amid a three-dimensional image of the surface of the planet that *Titan* had scanned when they entered the star system, the sphere that had been gutted and strip-mined to build the huge generation ship—but shown here as it had once been, not as it was now.

"This is some kind of holographic projection," said Riker, catching on. "We're still inside the audience chamber on your vessel."

"I hope you will forgive the theatricality, Captain. But it will help you to understand more quickly if I illustrate our narrative." Yasil walked toward them, and a strange, smoky effect surrounded him. His body became hazy and ill defined, until he was a wraith-like form barely recognizable as a humanoid. "What you know as the species called Jazari does not exist. They never did. No reptilian form evolved to sentience on this planet, developed warp drive, and made first contact with your Federation. The Jazari are a fiction that we created so that our kind could move among you, observe you, and interact with you, all while keeping our secrets safe."

The smoke ebbed briefly and Troi saw a simple bipedal form where the reptilian alien had stood. It was made of a seamless silver material, bereft of any facial features or identifying marks, with arms and legs that ended in identical grasping hands. A clear component in the torso revealed what was probably a power source, filled with a placid swirl of energies. It was quite clearly an artificial being.

"Behold us in our pure aspect. This is how we were devised by the

Makers, the arrangement in which they dispatched us to this galaxy. As humanoid forms were determined to be the most prevalent sentient somatotype in this stellar quadrant, we adopted a similar structure to better comprehend you."

Riker exchanged a sideways look with his wife. "It would be fair to say I have a *lot* of questions," he said carefully.

"Absolutely," added Troi.

"At first, we intended to mimic you, the humans," Yasil continued. "We monitored your communications and watched you remotely." The smoke gathered, then parted again. Now the mechanoid was gone, and in its place stood a human male. Troi estimated his age at around thirty standard years, a Caucasian of average height with short dark hair and a blank, distant expression. He wore a nondescript oversuit of metallic material, and there was a small object around his neck, a glowing device of some sort. She stepped closer, but the smoke gathered again and the image was lost.

Yasil's voice issued out of the knot of turning haze. "We know now that we did not fully understand your nature. We misjudged human ingenuity . . . and your capacity for emotive response and illogic." The shadow figure raised one arm and pointed at the sky. "When our original program proved insufficient, we initiated a new one. Beginning with the relocation of our outpost world."

The artificial night displayed above them shimmered with distortion, and Troi's eyes widened as a yawning maw of energy opened up. It was a wormhole, vast and seething with exotic radiation. She experienced a moment of giddiness as the event horizon filled the sky and the planet was swallowed whole. A tunnel of light pulled the desert world across parsecs of space and placed it in a new orbit, around a different star the commander recognized from their arrival here days earlier.

"You moved a whole world . . ." said Riker. "That's incredible."

"We have the technology to create temporary spatial conduits, but it requires vast amounts of energy and extremely complex calculations." Yasil's smoky form moved toward them. "The Makers used it to send us here, and we will use it to return to them. But we could not shift our planet once again, lest the tidal stresses of the wormhole crush it. So we built the great ship instead, as a lifeboat." Up in the illusory sky, an object took form as an accelerated view of the generation ship's construction took place. At the same time, the landscape of the planet around them altered, the desert being stripped into mine works and even the planetary rings reducing as they too were sifted for minerals.

"Where did you come from?" Troi asked.

"The human name for our origin point is Andromeda. A galaxy two and a half million light-years distant. The Makers dispatched us as one among many exploratory groups tasked to learn more about the universe. We were created to search for intelligent life and gather understanding of them. This is our core code."

"A Prime Directive," said Riker.

"Yes. Our code resembles your Starfleet General Order One in many ways. So we might better perform our principal function, we improved ourselves and evolved. We externalized certain functions of our shared purpose into the form known to you as Friend. Each of us became more individual . . ." Troi thought she heard a smile in the voice. "We developed emotional responses and deeper understanding of sentience, exceeding our previous limitations."

"Our friend Data followed a similar path," she said. "He strived to become more than he was. He was always growing and learning."

"We wished to do the same." The smoke-shape changed again; the figure in the haze became a Romulan woman, then a Klingon male, a Bolian, a Nausicaan, Cardassian, Tezwan, Bajoran, and more; species after species flashed into and out of existence, each one speaking with Yasil's voice. "We sent our scouts to visit many worlds and many civilizations, to observe you in your natural environments."

Riker stiffened. "Without our knowledge."

"We believed that it was not the right moment to make direct contact with the sentient beings of this galaxy. We made errors in the past we did not wish to repeat." Yasil's wraith-like form began to coalesce, slowly reverting back to what he had been when they first met. "After considering many of the stellar powers in these quadrants over the decades, we determined that your United Federation of Planets would be the best candidate for us to reveal ourselves to . . . but only when the time was right. Your society was not ready to know us, and we did not wish to interfere with the development of your cultures." Yasil's Jazari aspect returned, with a flash of regret in his eyes. "The Makers warned us of premature contacts in millennia past, events that led to the self-destruction of entire civilizations."

"And that's why you created the . . . the *fiction* of the Jazari?" Troi nodded toward him.

"Yes," said Yasil. "We fabricated the idea of an organic species, an identity that we could inhabit and continue our work. The cultural limits we invented allowed us to walk among you openly but still maintain the secret of our true natures."

"Hence all the restrictions about deep scans, using transporters, medical issues, and explaining away your lack of any telepathic signatures," noted Riker. "You wanted to be sure we wouldn't find you out." He gave a humorless snort. "Part of me feels insulted, but another part of me can see your reasoning."

"We're guilty of the same thing," said Troi. "The Federation observes pre-warp cultures using remote probes, holographic hides. Even operatives disguised to appear as native beings." She glanced toward Riker. In their time on board the *Enterprise*, her husband had undertaken that exact assignment on a world called Malcor III, and together they had both disguised themselves as members of a proto-Vulcan species during a mission to a planet in the Mintaka system. "I must admit, it is a little chastening to know that another species has done that to us."

Riker opened his hands. "So if you know us, you know we strive for peaceful coexistence with other life-forms." He sighed. "I want to ask you why you chose to pick up your whole society and leave, but I suspect I already know the answer."

"The Federation's moratorium on synthetic life," said Troi.

Yasil gave a solemn sigh. "We hoped that this would be a temporary reaction, but it has proven otherwise. Veyen and the other members who lived among you have all reported the same change sweeping through the worlds of the Federation. A shift away from the openness of the past, toward a hawkish and isolationist mindset."

"It will change," insisted Troi. "Right now, people are afraid. When that happens, they cleave to the simple answers, to the things that will make them feel safer. But give us time. The pendulum will swing back the other way. I believe that in my heart."

"I have no doubt you do, Commander Troi. And perhaps you are correct." Yasil's reptilian face was heavy with sadness. "But we cannot risk the future of our people on that hope. We wanted the Federation to be a new home for us, but our kind are not safe there. As for the other interstellar powers, there are none among them we could trust with our secret." He paused. "There is no future for us among you. Once our great ship passes into open space beyond the plasma storms, we intend to generate one final spatial corridor and travel through it, leaving this galaxy behind forever."

Riker looked up at the artificial sky. "Where will you go?"

"Home." As Yasil said the word, the stars above shifted and changed into the alien constellations of a different galaxy. "The Makers may no longer exist, and we have no knowledge of others of our kind that may exist. But it has been decided, we will return to our point of origin and fulfill the end point of our coding. We came to your space to seek knowledge. We have learned that there is nothing for us here."

Troi reached out, placing a hand on Yasil's arm. "Are you certain? We could learn so much from you."

"It doesn't have to end this way," added Riker. "If you revealed yourselves, you could help people understand that the synth ban is the wrong choice. You don't have to leave. You've shown your truth to us. We can speak for you."

But Yasil was already shaking his head. "Data," he said, and as he invoked the name, an image of the android formed a short distance away.

Troi's breath caught in her throat at the incredible accuracy of the simulation. He appeared exactly as he had the last time she had seen him, during that fateful mission into Romulan space.

"Data is the reason we have been truthful to you, Captain Riker, Counselor Troi. We believe we can trust you, because you knew him, and you were close comrades."

"We loved him." Troi blinked back tears, suddenly struck by how much she missed her old friend.

"You bear us no prejudice because of our machine origins," Yasil continued, "but you two are not enough."

One of the distant alien stars in the sky dropped silently from the darkness, becoming an orb drone, drifting toward them like a wind-borne cloud.

"They understand." Friend's voice hummed in the air. *"It saddens them, but they understand."*

"You're a synthetic being like them," said Riker. "An artificial intelligence, part of this ship."

"I am a distributed consciousness," Friend offered. *"Part of my sentience exists in the great ship, yes. But elements of me also cohabit the drones and the network of minds in our shared communication pool."* The voice paused, and when it spoke again, Troi felt that sense of a childlike persona beneath it. *"In a very real sense, I was born in this galaxy, but I have never known our origin. I have never had a place to call home."*

It was impossible for Troi to hear Friend's words and not perceive the echo of her son's in them. "You have to do what is right for your people," she said. "And if that means leaving, we'll say our farewells and hope to meet again." She shared a look with Riker. "How can we help you?"

"As we speak, I am deep in the process of making final calculations for a transgalactic shift. Until those are complete, the great ship is vulnerable."

"Will you help us defend ourselves?" As Yasil spoke, the illusory panorama around them and the image of Data began to disperse as glowing streams of light melted away to reveal the audience chamber once more. "We will understand if you refuse. You have every right to take back your people from our ship and leave us."

"A year ago, Starfleet turned away from people who needed our help," said Riker. "We're not about to repeat that failure today."

A chime sounded from their communicators, and Deanna exchanged a wary glance with her husband. Will tapped the badge on his chest.

"Riker here."

"Vale here, sir," said the *Titan*'s first officer. *"We've been trying to reach you. Comms didn't seem to be working."*

"We were . . . in conference. What's the situation, Commander?"

"The shuttles we deployed toward the outer perimeter of the storm zone are picking up intermittent neutrino flux readings. Multiple readings, Captain. That can only mean one thing."

Troi frowned. "Cloaked ships."

"Major Helek has returned," said Riker. "And she's brought some backup."

Vale went on. *"Sir, the longer we stay inside the plasma storms, the worse it's going to be. Ambient radiation is eating into our deflectors every second we remain."*

"If we stay here, the storm cell will eventually devour us," said Yasil.

"And if we go out there, we face an unknown number of hostile ships," noted Troi. "There's no good option."

"No," said Riker. "So we'll forge a new one. Together."

FIFTEEN

Benem's console gave off a new warning tone, and the Garidian turned to face Helek in the *Othrys*'s command chair. "Sensors are picking up substantial mass displacements on the outer edge of the plasma storm cell."

"Show me," said Helek.

The main viewer altered to display the writhing field of plasmatic fire, and there, clearly visible in the corner of the image, was the bifurcated shape of the Jazari generation ship. The metallic hulk emerged from the flickering clouds, dragging wispy pennants of the fiery material along with it.

"Magnify." Helek narrowed her eyes as the image grew larger, the definition stronger. Now she could also see the silvery form of the Starfleet vessel moving in close formation with the much bigger vessel. "We have them," she said to herself. "It was only a matter of time."

"Attention." The shrouded voice from the Tal Shiar ships buzzed over the subspace link. *"We see the targets. Ready to intercept."*

Now that the moment was at hand, Helek hesitated. She wanted to savor this, to feel the weight of her deserved victory. Once she gave the order, the Jazari machine-things would be exterminated and the Federation ship giving them succor would die too. The major searched herself for any hint of doubt, any uncertainty toward these acts. She found nothing, only the dreadful echo of what she had witnessed in the Admonition.

No one who had seen what she had seen would ever dare to obstruct her mission. The erasure of these synthetics would be a great triumph in the long crusade against artificial life. She smiled inwardly, knowing that only a few would understand how important this deed was. Major Sansar Helek wanted no laurels or tributes for doing what had to be done. The act itself would be honor enough.

"They are powering away at full impulse speed," offered Benem into the tense silence of the bridge. "It is clearly an attempt to put as much distance as they can between their vessels and our ships."

The decurion's statement of the obvious irked Helek, and she gave the Garidian a withering sneer. "Scan for life signs. Make sure they are not attempting subterfuge of some kind."

Benem did as she was ordered, delivering her report a moment later. "It is difficult to accurately gauge the number of Jazari on board. Hundreds of thousands of them. I also detect a small group of other beings in one of their environment domes."

"Riker's people," Helek mused. "The civilians. Careless of him to leave them aboard that craft. He will lament that choice as he watches us destroy it." The cruel smile on her lips pulled tight. "But then again, he will not live to regret it for long."

"The Starfleet vessel is scanning us," said Sublieutenant Kort. "They see us and the . . ." He faltered over the words. "Our allies."

"Perhaps we should cloak," suggested Maian.

"No. The time for stealth is over," she retorted. "Now we will strike like the raptors of the mountains. Terrible, swift, and righteous." Helek tapped a panel on the arm of the commander's chair, and her next words were carried throughout the corridors of the warbird. "Crew to your battle stations. Prepare to attack."

"Enemy ships in our zone. Three marks at two-ten!" Keru called out the warning from tactical. "Reading the warbird *Othrys* and . . ." He frowned. "Two more *somethings*. They could be Romulan, but I've never seen anything of that design before."

"Those are Tal Shiar enforcer cruisers," said Vale. "We must have really pissed them off to get that much attention."

"What can I say? It's a gift," the captain deadpanned, drawing a wry smile from his first officer. "Mister Keru, time to intercept?"

"They're coming in hot, sir. Sixty seconds to attack range."

Riker didn't need to give Vale the word for the next command. "Shields up, red alert!" The first officer shot a look toward the conn and ops stations. "Keep us moving, stay out of their target lock."

"The Tal Shiar ships are taking the lead, *Othrys* is hanging back." Livnah read off the data from her station.

"Let's not give them the opportunity they want." Riker tugged on his uniform tunic, pulling it straight. "Helm, maximum impulse. Pick a target and extend toward it." He glanced back at the Trill. "Ranul, make sure you leave a mark."

"My pleasure, Captain," came the reply.

The *Titan* pivoted on one nacelle and thundered into a combat run, sweeping forward to meet the Tal Shiar cruisers before they found their optimal range.

Keru's hands danced over the weapons controls with quick, dexterous motions, and the starship unleashed a combined salvo of photon torpedoes and phaser fire from its forward emitter rings.

The leading enforcer ship broke into a high-g impulse turn, avoiding direct hits from the torpedoes but not the buffeting from the proximity detonation of the antimatter charges. Even as their shields buckled, the following phaser strikes hit hard, and the lead ship was staggered.

The second enforcer, mere seconds behind, reacted quickly and avoided the attack. It slid sideways through the darkness, pitching up to present its own torpedo tubes. Spike-headed ship-killer missiles launched in flashes of retaliatory fire, shrieking away from the trailing vessel, describing corkscrew trajectories as they homed in on the *Titan*.

At the helm, Lieutenant Cantua was already working to pull the ship out of the kill zone, making hard shifts with the impulse grids. The

Luna-class cruiser was bigger than the Tal Shiar warbirds, but she had an agility that most vessels her size did not. Still, Cantua could almost hear Chief Engineer McCreedy groaning in sympathy with the ship's hull as she stressed it beyond safe limits.

Titan's evasive motion avoided all but two of the missiles. The first ripped a brief tear in the starboard shields, and the second plunged in through the gap. The weapon's serrated tip slashed across the ventral hull like a knife at the exposed belly of a prey animal. Torn hull metal tumbled away along with gaseous clouds of flash-frozen atmosphere, and the missile's trilithium warhead blew, blasting apart critical subsystems. The injury vibrated up through the spaceframe as they pitched away, firing as they went.

McCreedy called out the ship's status and marshaled her engineers to do what they could to patch the damage, even as Keru directed another barrage of phaser blasts into the *Titan*'s wake.

The salvo struck the second enforcer, but like the leading Tal Shiar ship, the hits seemed to do little to slow their racing attacks. Both craft blazed past the *Titan* and ran in on screaming passes over the slow-moving Jazari generation ship.

"The power distribution curves on those enforcers are irregular." Livnah was glued to her scanner hood, her black tattoos twisting as her scowl deepened. "Their weapons and defensive systems are highly decentralized, difficult to negate."

"Find us a weak point if you can," ordered Riker. "Keru, Cantua, keep us on them and keep us firing."

"Where's Helek?" Vale asked from her console.

"The *Othrys* is maintaining distance," reported Westerguard. "I think we hit them pretty hard that last time, Commander."

"She's letting the enforcers do the work for her," said the captain. "Waiting for the opportunity to come in and deliver the coup de grace."

"I can't believe a man like Medaka would let this happen." Vale lowered her voice. "You think Helek killed him?"

"The Tal Shiar don't waste resources. If he's useful to her, then he's still alive," said Riker. "If not . . ." He let the sentence hang.

Vale considered that bleak possibility. "If we could cut the head off this particular snake, we might be able to end this before there's any more bloodshed."

"Believe me, Commander, I've been thinking the same thing. But without—"

Riker's words were torn away by the sudden thunder of disruptor fire slamming into the *Titan*'s deflectors. The enforcers changed course abruptly, bleeding off washes of energy into their impulse wake as they came back around and zeroed in on the Starfleet vessel.

Acting in concert, the attackers unleashed a torrent of viridian energy toward the *Titan*, piercing the shields and lashing at the unprotected hull beneath.

Cantua and Westerguard worked in sync, both of the young lieutenants fighting to keep their ship together as they threaded the needle through the firestorm. But it wasn't enough.

Born from one of the disruptor hits, a wild shock pulse raced through the hull, into the *Titan*'s systems, emerging in a blast of overload that concentrated in the ops console. Lieutenant Westerguard's panel exploded in a crack of noise and he threw up his hands in a futile attempt to protect himself from the discharge.

"*Hal!*" Cantua shouted his name, but he would never hear her. The navigator pitched off his chair and slumped to the deck, unmoving.

Snatching a tricorder from beneath her station, Vale ran to the still form of the young officer and paled as the device's scanner let out a mournful, continuous tone. "He . . . he's gone."

"No!" The Denobulan's wide, pale eyes brimmed with tears. "No, that can't be . . ."

"Someone get him below." Riker bit out the words. "The rest of you, look sharp. We'll mourn when we're done."

"Sir." Keru spoke up, pitching his voice to be heard over the alert sirens.

"Shields are down to twenty-seven percent, torpedo launchers are offline." He made an angry noise under his breath. "This fight is starting to go their way."

"That doesn't work for me," said Vale. "I'm damned if we're going to back off now."

"I concur." Riker moved to Cantua's side. "Lieutenant, I need you here. Are you with me?"

The helmswoman sucked in a breath and straightened, keeping her view dead ahead as two crewmen carried Westerguard away. "Yes, sir. I've got Hal's . . . I've got the ops controls mirrored to my station now. I can handle the additional work."

"I know." The captain put his hand on her shoulder. "But I need something else from you."

"Sir?"

"I need you to push that shuttle subroutine you used before to the XO's panel."

Cantua nodded. "Aye, sir, you'll have it."

Vale frowned. "What are you planning?"

"Watch and learn, Number One," he told her. "Open a priority channel to the Jazari ship. Patch us through to Zade . . . And tell him I need to talk to Friend."

The Jazari engineer named Sabem led the way from the environment dome, and Troi watched sadly as the hatches were shut behind them for the last time. The corridor around her was choked with the *Titan*'s evacuees, each of them carrying whatever gear they could manage, even the children. Everyone fell silent as the thick diagonal doors ground closed, and the last image of the Ochre Dome's interior was shuttered away.

Even for a brief while, living inside the dome had been something special to all of them, a fleeting reminder of life on the surface of a planet—even if it was a simulation of sorts.

At her side, Troi's son put on a brave face, but she could sense his sorrow and the bright, sharp lines of his fears. "We'll be okay, Thad," she told him.

He nodded stiffly as the evacuees moved deeper into the ship. "I really liked it there. I wanted to stay."

"I liked it too," she admitted, "but it isn't our home."

"Where is?" Thad grasped her hand. "Earth? Betazed?"

Troi had no answer for him. "When this is all over, we'll figure that out," she promised.

The boy drew closer to her as they moved quickly down the corridor. Ominous echoes like distant thunder rumbled through the decks and the walls, sending a ripple of fear through the group. *They don't understand why the Romulans are attacking,* she thought. *And I can't tell them.*

The Jazari had demanded a guarantee from Troi and Riker that neither of them would reveal the truth about the origins of the androids, and they had agreed to it. Some of the *Titan*'s complement had seen things that wouldn't easily be explained away, but a captain's command would ensure nothing would be spoken of openly.

But still, Troi hated seeing the faces of her crewmates and friends knowing that they might die here and never know the reason why.

"Counselor Troi!" She heard a voice calling her name and turned as Zade emerged from a side corridor. He was moving as swiftly as he could, limping from the damage to his legs, and it struck Troi how hard she found it to think of him as a synthetic being rather than an organic one.

She pushed away the thought. The difference was irrelevant. Nothing about Zade had changed. She still believed he was the affable, intelligent young soul she had met when he first joined the *Titan*'s crew at Deep Space 5.

"Captain Riker has contacted us with an urgent request," Zade said quickly. "The Romulan ships are proving difficult to engage. A new approach is required."

"And you need me?" Troi hesitated. "I'll do what I can, but I'm not a tactical officer." She searched around for Lieutenant Hernandez. "Macha might be better suited for a military—"

"Forgive me, Commander," interrupted Zade. "I don't need a soldier, I need a diplomat."

"My mom is the best at diplomatting," said Thad, with the kind of solemn gravity that only a child could muster. "Dad said she can talk a hurricane into being a spring shower."

She couldn't resist shooting the boy an arch look. "Your father said that?"

"Yeah. He also said it doesn't work on *me*, but that doesn't mean Mom isn't awesome at everything else."

"I've seen you speak, Commander," said Zade, "so I am inclined to agree with Thaddeus. I need you to accompany me to the audience chamber once more. We must convince Yasil, Qaylan, and the others to commit to this battle, or we are done for."

"But you don't fight," said Thad.

"No, we don't," admitted Zade, "but your father has suggested a unique solution that might still allow us to defend ourselves."

Troi crouched down to Thad's level. "Are you okay if I go? You'll need to stay with Doctor Talov and the others."

Her son chewed his lip for a moment. "I'm a bit scared, Mom. But I'll be okay. You need to go tell some people what to do." He grinned. "You're a commander, you can do that."

She drew him into a hug. "We love you to the stars and back, you know that?"

Thad nodded. "Same here."

Troi watched her son dash away toward Talov and the gaggle of children surrounding the Vulcan medical officer, putting aside the stab of worry that twisted in her chest. She turned to Zade. "Let's go," she told him.

"Major . . ." There was a note of open disbelief in Maian's voice that set Helek's face in a sneer. "We are being hailed. By the Federation starship."

"What possible reason could I have to speak to them?" She sniffed, as if there was something foul in the air.

"Captain Riker wishes to discuss terms of surrender," said the veteran. "Protocol states that any commander in battle should make the attempt to capture any enemy craft that may have tactical value to the Empire."

Helek beckoned Garn, where the burly security officer stood close to the wall, and he rocked off his post, stepping forward with clear intent to intimidate Maian into silence.

For a moment, she considered answering Riker's hail with weapons fire, but she hesitated. As stolid and hidebound as he was, Maian was right about the fleet directives, and there was a delicious amusement at the possibility of taking the *Titan* as a prize. *But no. Riker and his people may have some inkling as to the true nature of the Jazari. They must be silenced.*

There was an elegant solution to this; she would magnanimously accept Riker's surrender, have him lower the *Titan*'s shields—and then obliterate the ship.

After all, she thought, *Romulan mercy—if there ever was such a thing—is only for Romulans.*

"All ships hold fire. Let the human speak," she ordered.

The command deck's holographic viewer became a window on the bridge of the *Titan*. Helek noted obvious signs of internal damage on the walls and consoles with open satisfaction, and her eye was briefly caught by the face of a non-Terran at one of the forward stations. The alien woman glared at Helek with the naked ire of someone who hated her, and she wondered what she had done to her to forge such wrath.

Riker stepped forward into view. He was haggard, but held firm. *"Major. This can't go on. I implore you, cease your attack. Call off your dogs."*

She smirked at the human idiom. "What do you offer?"

Riker frowned. *"Offer?"*

Is he being deliberately obtuse? Helek wondered if it might be a ploy of some kind, a way to stall for time. "What do you offer in return for your life, Captain? Tell me what you will give me and I shall consider accepting your surrender."

"Ours . . . ?" Riker shrugged and then, to her annoyance, he actually *chuckled*, giving his crew an indulgent smile. *"I think there's been a miscommunication here, Major. I don't want to discuss the terms of* my *surrender. I'm here to accept* yours. *"*

Helek was briefly lost for words, but she recovered quickly. "It appears your arrogance is matched only by your stupidity." She rose from the command chair, glaring back at the human through the holoscreen. "I intended to destroy your scow no matter what bargain you might have made, but now I will do so *slowly*." She showed her teeth. "I will take my time. I will hear you plead for your life."

"Beg to differ," said Riker, the threats rolling off him. At his side, Helek saw a human female with dark hair throw him a nod. *"Last chance, Major. Have your ships stand down and let the Jazari be on their way."*

When Helek spoke again, every word she uttered was a razor. "Do you really think you can defeat us?"

"Do you really think we won't try?" He turned away, moving back to his chair. *"Ask Commander Medaka. Ask someone who has fought in real battles. Then maybe you'll understand."* The human gestured to one of his crew and the channel closed, the viewscreen flicking back to the stars and the ships outside.

"He dares . . . ?" Helek's long fingers contracted into fists. A distant voice in the back of her mind warned her that Riker was a clever foe, playing on her flaws, digging in the dagger where he saw the chinks in her armor.

But that voice was drowned out by the snarls of the zealot inside Helek, the believer empowered by the apocalyptic vision of the Admonition, the warrior fanatic of the Zhat Vash. Had she believed in such things as gods, Helek would have sworn her mission was a divine one—a mission where all horrors were permitted.

She sucked in a breath, preparing to bellow a kill command, but that dithering Garidian fool at the sensors station babbled out a warning.

"Multiple target detections across the hull of the Jazari hulk!" Decurion Benem's long head bobbed in agitation. "They're launching dozens of metallic objects!"

Helek saw it now. Along the line of the Jazari ship's forked exterior, tiny points of light were emerging from hidden hatches, streaking away into the vacuum. "Identify!" she demanded. "They can't be weapons . . ."

"They're not photon torpedoes, not missiles," said Kort. "I'm detecting energy readings at their core, but not enough for an active warhead."

"They are drones," said Maian.

As she watched, the orb-shaped objects raced toward the *Titan*, expanding into a wide shoal of flickering dots. "It's a trick," she hissed. "All ships, power to disruptors, destroy those things!"

"Targeting lock is inconclusive," Kort replied. "The objects are generating a scattering field."

"Then sweep the area with wide-angle fire!" Helek spat the command at the combat officer, her ire building. Would she have to lead these fools on the bridge by the hand through every single order?

It was then that she noticed the light. Her shadow, falling across the bulkhead behind her, grew sharper and more defined. When Helek looked back at the viewer, she saw a wall of white forming in space, obscuring the *Titan* and the Jazari vessel. The drones were projecting a photonic barrier of incredible, blinding intensity. From the back of the bridge, she heard Dasix let out an agonized screech as the Reman engineer's light-sensitive eyes burned with pain.

"Filter that image," Helek ordered. "Do it now!"

"Unable to comply, the effect is present across all spectra," said Maian as the viewing screen dimmed and brightened again and again, unable to dampen out the adapting surge of energy. "Not just visual, but every sensory band . . ."

"Our escorts are falling back," reported Hade-Tah. "They are suffering the same effects."

"Viewer off!" Helek's words were finally obeyed, and the bridge was suddenly dark. She loomed over Sublieutenant Kort and stabbed a finger in the air. "Fire an all-aspect disruptor spread! Fire blind if we must, but do it now!"

"But the other ships are in our weapons arc—"

Her patience snapped and she shoved him away from his panel, slamming the heel of her hand onto the firing pad.

"Romulan ships are retreating in poor order," said Keru. "It's working!"

"Well, I'll be damned," said Vale. Riker's first officer had privately admitted to him that she had her doubts about the captain's ploy to wrongfoot their attackers, but now she saw the effectiveness of it.

The intelligence controlling the Jazari drone orbs was communicating directly with Livnah's console in real time, feeding the energy frequency shifts to the *Titan* as the light wall blazed against the darkness. Matching the ship's viewer to the ever-changing photonic field state allowed the *Titan*'s visual feed to operate unaffected, as did their sensors.

"Lieutenant Cantua, stay behind the drone net," noted Riker. "Tactical, keep our shields at maximum. As soon as the Romulans figure out the blinding effect has a limited range, they'll extend away and we'll lose our advantage."

"Captain, all shuttle bays report ready." McCreedy relayed the data from her screen. "We're clear to launch."

Riker turned to Vale. "Over to you, Number One."

"Aye, sir." She swiveled the console at her side and her fingers raced across the panel. Green indicators blinked on as the shuttlecrafts *Mance*, *Marsalis*, and *Ellington* left the *Titan* and powered away toward the enemy ships.

Each craft was unmanned, run by the same software subroutines that

Cantua had used days earlier to transfer the Jazari diplomatic party to their generation ship. "All shuttles answering remote control."

"*Othrys* is firing!" Keru called out a warning as the Romulan warbird released a wild barrage of disruptor bolts in every direction across their forward weapons arc.

Most of the blasts went wide, but Riker saw several of the orb drones destroyed by random strikes, and some hits even clipped the lead enforcer cruiser, knocking it off course.

Working the shuttles in unison, Vale turned the *Ellington* on an intercept heading toward the damaged Tal Shiar ship, the *Mance* toward its companion, and the *Marsalis* directly at the warbird. The gamble was that amid the chaos of the energy put out by the drones, the smaller, fast-moving shuttles would be difficult to spot, and able to get close to the attacking vessels.

"You know the drill," Riker noted. "Target engines only, Chris. We want to disable them."

"The Tal Shiar would not grant us that courtesy," said Livnah with a growling snort.

"The Tal Shiar don't value life," said Cantua, and the captain saw her cast a sorrowful glance toward the empty ops station at her side. "We're better than that."

On the screen, the *Ellington* was first to break through the photon field and the lead enforcer reacted, spinning on thrusters to bring its guns to bear on the shuttle. Vale set it into a wild, jinking evasive pattern, swooping beneath the cruiser's black, serrated hull, firing a point-blank phaser blast into its portside warp nacelle.

"Direct hit!" called Keru, punching the air. "That blew out their entire intercooler array—I'm reading massive mains power loss across the whole ship!"

The lead enforcer's running lights flickered and dimmed; it was dead in the water, but there was no time to celebrate.

Riker watched as Vale shifted her focus to the *Mance* as it bore down on the other Tal Shiar ship, seeking the same target that had neutralized the first. The *Mance* responded nimbly, diving like a starfighter as the second enforcer opened fire, sensing the presence of the incoming shuttle.

"Word from the Jazari," called Livnah. "Drones will lose power in sixty seconds!"

Riker acknowledged the comment just as a glancing disruptor bolt clipped the *Mance* and sheared off its starboard drive nacelle.

The shuttle twisted into a spiraling motion, bleeding fire into the vacuum, and Vale made a split-second decision. The commander put the *Mance* on a collision course with the Tal Shiar vessel, and guided it all the way to a fiery end, striking the Romulan ship where its wingtip connected to its warp engine.

The shuttle was obliterated in the impact, but the blast sheared off a full quarter of the enforcer's wing, rendering it immobile.

Another flash of fire caught Riker's eye and he grimaced as the remote link to the *Marsalis* went dark. While their focus had been elsewhere, the *Othrys* had recovered and burnt the third shuttle out of the sky before it could close the distance.

"Tal Shiar ships both inoperative, one target still remaining, damaged but active," said Keru. "That's some nice flying, Commander."

Livnah counted down the last few seconds of their distraction. "Drones offline in three . . . two . . . one!" As the last word left her mouth, the wall of coruscating light faded away and the drones became cold, dead metal.

"Number One, get the *Ellington* on board." Riker turned away, back to Keru. "Ranul, open a channel." The captain took a breath and then spoke again. "Attention, Romulan vessels. We have no desire to prolong this conflict any further. Back off and let the Jazari go on their way. We are willing to render assistance to you if you comply. Respond."

Keru's broad face creased in a deep frown. "Captain, I'm reading new energy buildups on both the Tal Shiar ships."

"They're powering weapons?" Vale caught sight of the damaged vessels on the main viewer. "They're in no state to keep fighting."

"That is not their intention, Commander." Livnah's tone became grave. "Those ships have unlocked their singularity cores. What Mister Keru is seeing is the runaway effect of an overload."

Riker took an urgent step forward, suddenly aware of what was going to happen next, and desperate to forestall it. "*Titan* to Romulan vessels, stand down! This doesn't have to end with—"

In quick succession, powerful flashes of twin destructive force bloomed around the enforcer cruisers and consumed them. For a brief moment, the compact, captive black hole at the heart of each ship's power core was uncaged, and in the instant before they collapsed under their own super-gravity, the hulls of the vessels imploded. Riker felt the destruction like a gut punch, and for a moment, it robbed him of his breath.

McCreedy broke the long silence that followed. "Romulans never surrender. They must have believed we would take their ships."

Riker scowled, giving voice to his disgust. "I'm sick of this bloodshed, and for what? It's driven by hate and fear, and nothing more."

"They do hate us," Vale said quietly. "They do fear us. And this is what that gets us, an enmity that neither side is ever going to bridge."

The captain shook his head. "I refuse to accept that."

"Aspect change on the warbird," called Keru. "The *Othrys* is moving into an attack posture."

"Major Helek isn't going to give us that option," said Vale.

Vale felt the weight of her pronouncement like lead in her chest. As much as she maintained the outward aspect of the watchful, hawkish second-in-command to Riker's open and companionable captain, deep down she was an optimist, and she wanted to see the best in the universe. It was the reason she had joined Starfleet.

But Helek's brutality and the complicity of the Tal Shiar made it hard to find any thread of hope in all this. The confrontation could only end in destruction, and Vale was not willing to let *Titan* fall and the Jazari die, just to satisfy someone else's hatred.

"Power building on the warbird," said Livnah. "Not a self-destruct this time," she added quickly.

"It's the plasma reservoir," added Keru. "*Othrys* is charging their primary weapon."

"That thing mauled us all to hell last time it hit," said Vale. "Helek won't rest until she finishes what she started."

"I know." Riker took a breath. "So we have to stop her in her tracks."

"I have an approach, but you won't like it," she told him.

"I like all your plans," he replied, forcing a smile. "Go ahead, Commander."

Vale rose from her seat. "Helm, put us on an intercept course with the warbird, bow to bow, full impulse."

"Full impulse, intercept course, aye." Cantua took *Titan* forward, increasing speed in a matter of seconds. Ahead of them, the Romulan ship seemed to swoop toward them and grow larger, becoming a predator hawk diving at its prey.

"One flaw in those Romulan plasma weapons," Vale explained. "They need to reach a minimum criticality after launch to become fully lethal . . . But if we go right down their throat, get as close as we can before they fire . . ."

"We can take the hit and push through." Riker took that in, then called out, "Chief Engineer! Reinforce the forward shields, give them everything you can."

"For the record, I'd just like to say *I* don't like this plan." McCreedy carried out her orders nonetheless, and the bridge's illuminator dimmed slightly as power was rerouted.

"So noted." The captain settled back into the command chair, fixing his eyes on the Romulan ship. "Here it comes."

Vale saw the malevolent glow building in the prefire chamber on the *Othrys*'s bow.

"You *are* sure about this, Commander?" Cantua's voice was low.

"If I'm wrong, we won't have time to worry about it." She gave the Denobulan a pat on the shoulder. "Maintain heading, Lieutenant."

Vale dashed back across the bridge, falling into her seat as Riker called a warning to brace for impact. The *Othrys* was moving, and perhaps the warbird's helmsman had an inkling of what the *Titan* was doing, but the moment came and it was too late to veer away.

Fire the shade of volcanic lava blasted out from the warbird's prow, and Vale momentarily imagined it like some star-born dragon breathing flames upon them, the challenging knights.

The plasma bolt struck the forward shields and *Titan* lurched alarmingly. The blow rattled the teeth in Vale's head and she tasted blood in her mouth, as if she'd been punched in the face. The automatic safety restraint across her waist stopped the commander from pitching onto the deck, but still she hung on for dear life.

Jumping-jack sparks flew from panels around the bridge as overload breakers blew, and acrid fumes stinking of flash-burnt polymers stung her nostrils.

Someone cried out—it sounded like Livnah, making an animal noise that was more fury than it was pain, as if the science officer were giving voice to the *Titan*'s distress.

Then the fire faded and the ship righted itself, angling away as the *Othrys* veered into a steep climb to avoid a direct collision. The ships passed so close to each other that the edges of their deflectors touched, the faint glimmers of *Titan*'s battered shields burning weakly against those of the Romulan warbird.

"This is it," Vale called. "Keru, target impulse engines and fire at point-blank range!"

"Firing!" The Trill was ready for the order, and he sent lances of collimated energy through the enemy shields and into the hull of the *Othrys*, where the other ship's impulse grids glowed orange red.

Molten gobs of tritanium and sparking flares erupted from the warbird's belly as the *Titan* passed beneath the Romulan vessel. Vale saw secondary-effect power surges run wild over the metallic wings, crawling jags of lightning burning out vital systems as they spread. A tremor went through the *Othrys*, and she knew that the hit had been a palpable one.

"Their sublight drives are dead." Livnah gave the report with an air of triumph in her voice. "They are adrift."

"Helm, extend away," said the captain. "Put some distance between us in case Major Helek decides to follow her Tal Shiar friends to martyrdom."

Vale watched the damaged warbird grow smaller. "I didn't get the impression she'd give up her life for anything."

Riker frowned. "I'm not so sure. Fanaticism takes many forms, Commander. I know that hatred when I see it."

"Sir . . ." Ranul Keru's brow furrowed as a tone sounded from his console. "We're being hailed by the *Othrys*. It's Helek. Captain, she's asking to speak to you. Privately, commander to commander."

Vale couldn't help but let out a snort of bitter laughter. "Didn't we just do that whole song and dance?"

"No question she's stalling for time," said Keru.

"No question," agreed Riker, "but I still have to listen." He retracted his restraints and stood up. "Commander Vale, you have the conn. Relay Helek's signal directly to my ready room."

"Captain . . ." Livnah's voice held a warning note. "That subspace channel will not be secure."

"So you know what to do," said Riker. "Be ready."

"Understood."

"She's going to try something, sir," Vale said quietly. "She's Tal Shiar. Schemes and plots are what they do all day long."

"I know," said Riker as he walked away. "Matter of fact, I'm *counting* on it."

The door to his ready room hissed closed and Riker took a moment to straighten his collar. He wasn't about to let his adversary see even the smallest sign of weakness. Helek was a jackal, and she would be searching for every possible advantage she could gain.

He tapped a panel on his desk, opening the communication channel. Riker expected a screen to open, but instead a shimmering, low-bandwidth hologram appeared before him. An image of the Tal Shiar officer formed in the center of the room, her copper-colored hair in slight disarray, her pale face permanently set in a sneer. There was a trickle of green blood at the corner of her mouth, but she didn't seem to be aware of it. He couldn't help but wonder how much of that was for show.

"Riker." She said his name like a curse. *"I underestimated your tenacity. That last attack was positively Klingon in its recklessness."*

"I'll take that as a compliment."

"It isn't meant to be," she said in disbelief. *"Why do you do this, Terran? Why do you always interfere, showing your bleeding hearts and shouting your petty virtues at every opportunity?"*

Riker's jaw hardened. "There's nothing petty about compassion. The Federation is built on that value."

"You are fools. You waste your empathy on them?" Helek waved in the vague direction of the Jazari generation ship. *"What does it gain you? What is the point of it?"*

"It's not about gaining something." Riker felt disconnected from the demand. Helek didn't seem to be able to comprehend something that wasn't transactional in nature. "It's about doing what is right."

"I will tell you what is right," she said wearily. *"Those* things *on that ship you are protecting . . . They are destroyers, not innocents."*

Riker froze. Did the Romulan woman know about the true, synthetic nature of the Jazari? Was she trying to entice a confirmation from him?

"Why do you hate them so much?"

Helek eyed him. *"I am Romulan. We excel at hating what threatens us. And what threatens us is everything that is not Romulan. Those abominations most of all."* She hesitated. *"Do you know what they really are, Captain?"*

Riker remained silent, holding his best poker face, giving her nothing back. For a moment, he tried to put himself into Helek's mind-set, to see this situation the way that she saw it. If she or the Tal Shiar knew the Jazari secret, then they clearly saw them as a menace to be eradicated— and it shamed him to admit that there were many within Starfleet and the Federation who might agree with that.

He remembered the emotions that ran through him a year ago, after learning of the synth attack on Mars and the Utopia Planitia shipyards. *Fear*, for those in danger, for his friend Geordi La Forge, who had been in harm's way; *anger*, at a ruthless enemy who would strike at innocent people as they worked to save others; and *disbelief*, unable to understand the reason for such a terrible atrocity.

Those forces, if not resisted, could act on anyone and turn them to a darker path. And if one traveled far enough down that path, there might come a point where any action—even genocide—would seem justified.

But Will Riker had spent over ten years with a synthetic being at his side, through terrible dangers and great adventures. He had shared the worst and the best of his life with his friend and colleague Data. He knew, with unwavering certainty, that just like organic beings, artificial ones had the same capacity to bring goodness into the universe, as much as they could do the opposite. The nature of a sentient being's origin did not matter. It was the expression of that life that created light or darkness.

To abhor all because of the actions of a few was a calculation that Riker would never be able to make.

"*This battle is not over,*" Helek was saying. "*Our vessels will keep fighting until one is cinder and ash. But there is another way.*"

"I won't let you have them," he said firmly. "The *Titan* will defend the Jazari to the last man. I give you my word on that."

"*Imbecile!*" Helek growled. "*You have no idea what you are dealing with! There is no Jazari, there is only the lie of what they are! And the danger they represent must be expunged, before they bring doom to all life.*" Then her tone shifted, becoming desperate, imploring him. "*Haven't their kind done enough to you, Riker? If only you could know the truth of this . . . you would stand with me. You would help me."*

Disgust welled up in him at the thought of that. "You don't understand us at all, Major. And for that, I am deeply sorry."

"I will make certain of it." In an instant, Helek's manner changed again, and the shimmering hologram flickered and distorted. She smiled thinly, and wiped the blood from her lip. *"You should have guarded your ship's systems more closely, Captain. I have many weapons at my disposal . . . some more subtle than others."*

An alarm tone sounded from the monitor on Riker's desk. The screen filled with a garbled mass of digital code, the data shredding as Romulan intruder software, embedded in Helek's hologram, invaded the *Titan's* computers.

"In a matter of minutes, your ship, your weapons, will be completely under my control," she told him as the hologram faded. *"And then you will help me kill these things, whether you want to or not."* Helek became a ghost, and then vanished.

Riker held his shock in place until he was certain the communication channel was closed, then the expression fell off his face and he tapped his combadge. "Riker to Livnah."

"Science officer here, sir. Did she take the bait?"

"Hook, line, and sinker," he replied. "Bring Commander Vale up to speed and assemble a team." Riker glanced out of the ready-room port, finding the *Othrys* where it drifted off the starboard bow. "We don't have a lot of time."

SIXTEEN

Lieutenant Commander East adjusted the setting on his phaser as he stepped up onto the transporter pad. "Is someone going to clue me in on how we're going to get through their shields?"

Livnah did not look up from the transporter console, the black lines on her face twisted in concentration as she hammered in the pre-sequence coding. "Romulans are always too clever for their own good," she said briskly. "Helek's attempt to inject a software weapon into our systems via the holo-comm required her to maintain an open channel."

"She tried to hack us, but that's a two-way street." At East's side, Commander Vale drew her own phaser and checked on her tricorder.

"Ahhh." Kono, the third member of the away team, bobbed her head in understanding. "So while the comm channel was open, we were using the same ploy against the *Othrys*! Ingenious!"

"I'm glad you approve, Ensign." Livnah's reply was sharp. "Unfortunately, our knowledge of Romulan systems is limited. I was only able to alter a small fragment of their core coding, changing the refresh rate of their shield harmonics."

"That'll be enough. Our transporter frequency matches the harmonics," said Vale, "we pass right through and Helek is none the wiser." She tapped her communicator. "Bridge, we're ready to go. Tell the rest of the team to meet us at the transit site."

"They'll follow you in, Commander," said the captain. *"Good luck. We don't have long before Helek figures out her virus program hasn't done the job, so you'll need to work fast. Riker out."*

"I should point out that if the synchrony is off by any more than a few degrees, you may materialize inside a bulkhead." Activating the console, Livnah relayed that information with her typically dry delivery. "I'll do my best not to kill you."

"Wait, what?" East raised a hand, but he could already feel the tingle of the transport effect at the tips of his fingers. "Oh, *shite*."

The buzzing whine of the beam enveloped him and for a timeless instant, East and the others were transformed into nonmatter; then the process reversed and a new environment appeared around him.

They were in a metallic gray corridor somewhere on the lower tiers of the *Othrys*, the space lit by dim illuminators close to the floor. East jerked back a step as he realized he had beamed in unpleasantly close to a bulkhead. He took a breath of dry, warm air and felt the subtle shift in gravity, from a Starfleet norm to Romulus standard.

Kono was close by, the Kelpien's threat ganglia writhing like nests of worms at the back of her skull. "I've got a bad feeling about this," she muttered.

"Good," said Vale, scanning the corridor with her tricorder. "I'd be worried if you didn't."

East registered the hum of another beam-in as three more figures materialized a short distance away. Leading them was Lieutenant Hernandez, with two of the Jazari standing with her. East recognized Zade, but not the other alien male.

"Commander," said Hernandez. "Mister Zade insisted on coming along, and his buddy Keret here is a technician. I figured we could use them."

"You beamed over from the generation ship?" said Kono. "I thought matter transportation was fatal to Jazari physiology."

Zade and Keret exchanged glances. "We . . . may have overstated that danger."

"Whatever." Vale dismissed the comment. "Hernandez, take our friends here aft and find main engineering. You'll have to pull the plug on the warbird if things don't go our way." She beckoned to the security officers. "East, Kono, you're with me. If I'm right, the brig is a few hundred meters away." The teams split up and went their separate ways.

"So we find your man Medaka, bust him loose, get him back his ship." It sounded simple when East laid it out like that. "But if that's not possible, do we have a Plan B?"

Vale shrugged. "I've barely got a Plan A. We're making this up as we go."

Helek stalked across the command deck, to the secondary console where Vadrel was working. He hesitated in the middle of his work, blinking those large, watery eyes of his at her.

"The program is not responding," he offered.

She'd dragged him up here from the laboratory to supervise the deployment of the software weapon, but his lack of progress was infuriating. The longer this mission went on, the more Helek saw Vadrel's weaknesses as outweighing his value. He had brought her vital intelligence on the synthetics, he had even saved her life, but those things were in the past. All that mattered were results, and she needed them now.

"Make it respond," she growled. "If we cannot take control of the Federation ship, all this will be for nothing!" Helek made an angry sweep of her hand, taking in the debris from the destroyed Tal Shiar cruisers. "Our comrades will have died for nothing!"

In reality, she cared little for the Tal Shiar operatives who had sacrificed their own lives to preserve the secrets of their cadre. Once, she might have been like them, but the Zhat Vash had given her a higher calling. They were tools—no, they were *weapons*—to be used in the crusade against machine life, just like she would use Riker's ship, just like she was using Vadrel and the crew of the *Othrys*.

But they were failing her.

"Major, even I cannot achieve the impossible!" Exasperation finally overtook Vadrel's fear of her, and he threw back the exhausted retort. "The intruder program you attempted to insert into the *Titan*'s mainframe has been contained. Captain Riker has outmaneuvered you!"

"For the second time," muttered Maian. The veteran spoke quietly, but not so much that his words did not carry.

Helek turned on the gray-haired helmsman and drew her dagger. "I will not listen to your criticisms anymore, you old fool. I gave you every chance to show your loyalty to me, but I see you are still mired in the past, dedicated to that fool Medaka!" She advanced on him. "Are you ready to die in his name, Lieutenant?"

Maian looked toward Centurion Garn, who had already drawn his disruptor, ready to take an execution shot if Helek commanded it. "If you murder a serving crewman on the bridge of this ship, then you do it for your own cause, not in the name of the Empire."

"My cause *is* the Empire's cause." She bit out the words.

Helek shifted the dagger in her hand, presenting the killing edge, but before she could commit to the act, the ship's alert tocsin began to wail.

"Intruder alert," said Sublieutenant Kort. "Message from Chief Engineer Dasix in the drive core, she reports Jazari and Starfleet invaders on the lower decks!"

"You see?" hissed Helek. "I warned Medaka. They want to kill us all." She aimed her knife at Garn. "Centurion! Seal the bridge and secure all control systems. If they want this ship, they will have to pay dearly for it."

"But . . . what about Dasix and the other crew?" Vadrel watched in shock as Garn activated the autolocks and force field that would isolate the command deck from the rest of the *Othrys*. "If there are intruders aboard, if they are in danger—"

"You will obey me!" she spat. "Or your lives will end like theirs."

Helek sank into the command chair, holding the haft of her dagger to her brow. The cold, hard metal pressed into her pale flesh, and she imagined it as a channel down which her rage was flowing.

When she closed her eyes, she saw the vision of fire and destruction embedded in her memory, and she knew she was doing the right thing.

Felle's sensitive Romulan hearing picked up the sound of metal on metal, the noise echoing down the corridor to the holding cells. He pulled his disruptor and hesitated.

The security guard's orders had come directly from Centurion Garn, and Garn's from Major Helek, and both had made it clear that the low-ranked uhlan was not to leave his prisoner unattended. But the door behind him was sealed tight and his charge had no way to escape. Then the sound came again, a clattering, ticking noise that irritated him unduly.

Finally, with an annoyed snort, Felle advanced down the corridor, his disruptor out and ready. The ticking noise was slowing, and a glint of gold on the deck caught his eye.

There, he saw what resembled a brooch of some kind, a golden arrowhead set spinning like a toy top against the metal flooring. *A Starfleet communicator insignia.* He bent and picked it up, turning it over in his fingers.

Felle reached for his own communication unit just as the ship's internal address system began to bray a warning tone. *"Intruder alert,"* said an automated warning. *"Security compromised."*

"They're here!" Felle barked into his communicator. "Starfleet is here!"

"We certainly are," said a light voice from above him.

Felle jerked back in shock, seeing a gangly, long-limbed alien with a fleshy, skull-like face suspending itself in the shadows overhead, wedged between the support spars.

The Kelpien dropped on him, and before Felle could react, Ensign Kono struck a two-handed blow to the nerve plexus clusters in his neck. The Romulan's eyes rolled back and he passed out, collapsing in a heap.

"I'll take that back, thank you," said Kono, plucking her combadge from the guard's hands and returning it to the breast of her uniform. Lieutenant Commander East and Commander Vale appeared from around the corner of the corridor, and Vale took the Romulan's weapon as East surveyed the unconscious guard.

"Nice work," said East. *Titan*'s chief of security had taken some criticism in the past for having a Kelpien on his team—considering that their species were widely considered timid and nervous sorts. But Kono proved the lie of that. If anything, she seemed eager to sample challenges that brought out her fear response, to the point that he sometimes had to rein her in.

Vale moved to the single sealed cell in the brig area, running her hand over the locking panel. She paused, throwing a scowl at the braying sound of the alert siren. "This seems promising, but we need to get it open."

"I've got it." East pulled his tricorder and set a decoder program running, using the device to broadcast a signal to overload the security seal. The panel changed color and, with a hiss, the cell door retracted into the deck.

The prisoner inside came at them with a yell, brandishing a metal cup like a weapon, and East almost took a blow in the face before the man stopped short.

"Starfleet?" said Commander Medaka, raising his eyebrow in a very Vulcan manner. "Well, this is unexpected. I don't recall inviting you aboard my ship."

"We can leave you in there, if you'd prefer," said Vale. She was still holding the stolen disruptor, and that didn't escape Medaka's notice.

The Romulan tossed the cup back into his cell. He was fatigued, and clearly the security guards had roughed him up a little, but he was unbowed. "Am I your captive now?"

"That's not why we're here," said East.

"In the interests of interstellar amity, Starfleet would like to assist you in recovering your command." Vale flipped the disruptor around in her hand and offered it to Medaka. "You may need this, sir."

Medaka sensed her reluctance. "You find it difficult to trust me," he noted, taking the weapon, careful not to point it anywhere near the three Starfleet officers. "But you came anyway. I thank you for that."

Vale put aside her own misgivings. "If we don't neutralize Helek, she's going to kill every living thing on the generation ship and the *Titan*. I'd team up with Khan Noonien Singh himself if it meant stopping her."

"I don't know who that is," admitted Medaka as he moved to a wall console. "So I'm going to take it as a compliment." The Romulan's fingers bounded from panel to panel as he tapped into the ship's system. He made a short hissing sound. "Helek is on the command deck. She's activated a lock-down protocol. We can't access the turbolifts, the hatches . . ."

A garbled mutter of static sounded from the fallen guard's communicator, and Kono spun toward it, her ganglia flickering wildly. "We have company!"

The Starfleet officers raised their phasers as a squad of Romulan security troopers rounded the corner of the corridor, each of them wielding heavy pulse disruptors.

"No! No shooting!" Medaka forced his way past Vale and the others, interposing himself between her team and his men. The commander put the disruptor pistol in his belt and raised his hands. "Stop this."

"Stand down and return to your cell, sir." The lead trooper took aim. "You are accused of collusion with the Federation. We saw the holographs."

"You saw what Helek wanted you to see. She lied."

"Then explain why these Starfleet intruders are standing with you!" One of the other troopers couldn't hold his silence. "You are a traitor!"

Medaka turned to Vale, Kono, and East. "Drop your weapons. This won't work unless you do as I say."

Vale frowned, but then she did as he asked. Warily, Kono and East followed suit.

Medaka stepped forward, making himself the only target. "If I wished to sacrifice this vessel, I could have done so before now." He looked to each of the troopers one by one, singling them out. "I know all of you. You've been my trusted crew for years. Desseh, you have two daughters who are dressmakers. Hutor, you find a new lover every time we make port. Lebre there plays *zhamaq* so well than no one on the ship will game with her. Umbran sends most of his pay home to his sister, so she might buy passage out of the danger zone." He let them consider that for a moment. "Have I ever lied to any of you in all the time we have served the Star Empire?"

A ripple of doubt went through the security troopers, and their weapons wavered. "But you stand with them, Commander." The trooper called Lebre jutted her chin at Vale and the others. "They're the ones who let us down. The ones who promised to help Romulus, and then reneged. How can we trust them?"

Medaka glanced at Vale. "These people did not make that choice, their leaders did that. *They* are little different from us." He took a breath. "But I am not asking you to trust them. I am asking you to trust *me*. Major Helek has exceeded her authority and her mental state is uncertain. So decide now who you wish to lead you."

For a moment, Vale thought things might go the wrong way. But then, one by one, the Romulans put up their weapons, and the tension in the air faded. "What are your orders, sir?" said Desseh.

"We will start by getting our ship back . . ." Medaka picked up Vale's phaser and handed it to her. "Perhaps our guests from Starfleet can help."

Vale took the weapon. "Welcome back, Commander."

"Oh, I never left," said Medaka.

"Confirmed," said Garn, speaking in a half snarl as he read the data off a portable panel. "Contact lost with Felle and my men on the lower decks. It's likely that Medaka has escaped from the cells."

Helek swore under her breath. "I should have executed him when I had the chance." She raised her voice, growing louder so everyone assembled on the bridge would hear her. "You see? I am proven right! Even now,

Commander Medaka is colluding with Starfleet aboard this ship, scheming to take control of it! All to prevent our mission from succeeding." She looked toward Maian. "Do you understand? What I am doing is more important than his life, than yours, more important than mine."

Those last words left Helek's mouth, and a wash of cold went through the major's body. The vision of the Admonition was there, like a storm out at the horizon of her consciousness, always threatening to close in and engulf her. She would never be able to escape it. Perhaps she was not meant to.

The Zhat Vash had chosen Sansar Helek because of her single-mindedness, because of the bottomless, simmering anger that fueled her. Perhaps this was the moment in which she would fulfill her purpose.

Only she saw clearly now. Only she had the unbending strength of will. *What must be done?* Helek heard the voice in her head.

"Anything and everything." She whispered the rote reply to herself.

"Major?" Close by, Sublieutenant Kort was watching her with an air of alarm.

She ignored him and strode to the helm console, pushing Maian out of the way. The veteran moved to resist, but Garn came in and shoved him viciously toward the back of the bridge.

"I need weapons," she ordered. "I need them now!"

Vadrel spoke up from the engineering station. "Major . . . that is not possible at this time. The primary weapon's firing channel was damaged in the last attack. Disruptor grids are still offline. It will take time to—"

"We have no time," she growled, and Helek worked the helm, swinging the prow of the *Othrys* away from the *Titan* and toward the great Jazari vessel. The generation ship filled the image on the main viewer. "Every second we delay we give them an opportunity to escape us." She girded herself. "Engines, then. Impulse power."

"Thirty percent impulse velocity is available," said Vadrel, reading off the data.

"That will have to be enough." Helek studied the shimmering orb-shaped module between the tines of the Jazari ship's secondary hull. Their main power core was there, a singularity-based source generating the volatile tetryon field Vadrel had detected before. All it would take was an impact in the right place, an uncontrolled release of those energies, and the Jazari ship could be killed.

She thought of the synthetics teeming aboard the alien hulk, each capable of the same violence as the one she had trapped in the laboratory. Helek had been powerless against it, the fear it instilled in her real and terrible. *They can't be allowed to live.* But she could wipe them out if she was willing to take the ultimate step. If she had the courage to do it.

Helek's fingers seemed to work of their own accord as they manipulated the thruster controls and pushed the *Othrys* onto a new course. The warbird began to move, slowly picking up speed, aimed like an arrow toward the Jazari vessel.

Maian saw her intentions. "No, you cannot!" He surged forward, trying to stop her, but Garn was already there and he intercepted the veteran, grabbing him by the throat. The two men fought, struggling against each other.

"This is what must be done," said Helek, and an odd calm descended on her.

"Major . . ." Vadrel was suddenly close at hand. His face creased in panic. "You'll destroy this ship. You'll kill us all!"

"That is the price the Zhat Vash require," she said quietly. "We must pay it. For the future of our species." A smile crossed her lips. "Don't fear, Vadrel. This is your chance for redemption. To erase your debt to every soul on Romulus."

"I won't let you!" He took a step toward the thruster controls, reaching out to turn them away from the collision course. His chest met the double-tipped blade of Helek's combat dagger as she brought it up and pushed it into him, burying the weapon to the hilt in Vadrel's torso.

A gush of dark emerald blood flowed out of the scientist's mouth and his pale eyes went wide with shock. Helek, her hand still gripping the knife, gave the weapon a savage twist that tore open his heart. Then she released her hold on the handle and he fell back to the deck with a crash, choking and dying.

There was consternation on the *Othrys*'s engineering deck when Medaka arrived with Vale's away team and a contingent of security troopers. With the assistance of the two Jazari, Lieutenant Hernandez had overpowered the crew and taken the warbird's Reman chief engineer captive, but they were unable to take control of the ship's systems.

Hernandez stood on the access walkway, pointing toward the warbird's singularity core inside its spherical metallic shell. "We can't get into it, Commander," she explained. "There's a level-six force field surrounding the unit, controlled directly from the bridge. We don't have the firepower to burn through something like that."

Vale saw the crackling sheath of the field glittering around the power core, and nodded. "I'm not sure shooting off energy weapons around a caged black hole is a good idea, anyhow."

Below them, on the support deck, Commander Medaka had released the engineering team and he stood in earnest conversation with the female Reman towering over him, while Ensign Kono and the Jazari kept a wary distance.

Lieutenant Commander East approached, his expression grim. "I made contact with the *Titan*," he reported. "We have a new problem. The *Othrys* is under way and closing on the Jazari generation ship."

"Helek's going to renew her attack," said Hernandez.

East shook his head. "No, it's worse than that. Livnah predicts we're on a collision course. Helek intends to ram it."

Vale took that in, hearing boots on the maintenance ladder behind her. Commander Medaka appeared, with his Reman engineer following close behind. "I assume you have the same information I do?" Off Vale's brisk nod, he went on. "I think Major Helek planned for this from the start," he said. "She's been waiting for the opportunity to take my command. All the vital systems are protected by deflector screens, including the bridge. She used a Tal Shiar software weapon on my ship. Locked me out of it."

East frowned. "Probably the same intruder program she tried to deploy against the *Titan*."

"Time is against us," rumbled the Reman. "Commander, we must consider evacuating the *Othrys*."

Medaka raised his hand to silence her. "I'll not surrender my vessel to the Tal Shiar."

"Helek shielded your bridge . . ." Vale considered Medaka's words. "Using the same deflector matrix as your ship's defensive shields?"

The Reman made a terse sniff. "What of it? As long as those shields remain in place, we cannot transport onto the command deck."

Vale's lip curled in a slight smile. "Actually, we've got a way around that."

East snapped his fingers as he caught on. "Livnah's counterprogram got us on board, and it's still active!"

"Sir, I said we'd help you get your ship back," noted Vale. "I meant it."

Medaka made an *after you* gesture. "Then by all means, Commander, lead on."

With each passing second, the warbird's acceleration increased. The Jazari hulk loomed large before the Romulan vessel, the flanks of it growing until it filled the main viewer.

Helek's awareness became hyperfocused, as if each instant were captured in crystal, perfect and flawless.

She was filled with a certainty that she had never known before. She would succeed, and the great threat predicted by the Admonition would, at least for a while, be forestalled. *A good fate for a true patriot and daughter of Romulus,* she told herself. *A hero's death.*

Her hand was covered in sticky green blood, Vadrel's vitae cooling on her skin. His corpse lay at her feet, her dagger still protruding from his chest. The dead man's sightless eyes stared up at her, silently reproachful. Accusing her from the afterlife. Seeing into Helek, and the lies that made her hollow.

A cold shiver shocked through her. "Do not look at me."

"Major?" Centurion Garn came toward her, thinking her words were for him.

"Look *away!*" She kicked at Vadrel's body with the heel of her boot, and his head lolled, his face turning from her as if ashamed by her conduct. "I will not be denied."

A familiar buzzing cut through the air, and around the bridge columns of sparkling light phased into being. Helek saw human forms taking shape— Romulans and Starfleet, appearing at all points of the command deck.

Impossible! She ducked forward, desperate for a weapon, clutching at the dagger lodged in Vadrel's chest.

A phaser blast shrieked over her head and struck Garn before he could open fire, knocking the centurion down in a heap. She heard the bridge crew calling out in alarm, but none of that mattered. All that was important was the next second, getting the knife, staying alive just long enough to complete the Zhat Vash's mission.

Her hands closed around the haft of the blade, but it was slippery and she could not remove it. Helek spat in anger, and tore it free with a jerk as a shadow fell over her.

"This ends now," said Medaka, holding a charged disruptor on her.

She rose slowly, clutching the dripping knife. "Silence, traitor. You and your Federation friends have no place here. You betray everything the Empire stands for!"

"No one is listening to you, Helek." Medaka gestured with the pistol, and she looked around the bridge.

Maian was back at the helm, veering them away from her suicide heading. Kort, and those alien fools Benem and Hade-Tah, all stood away from their stations, hands raised, *disobeying* her commands. She saw the human woman Vale and a dark-haired male of her kind standing alongside Romulan security troops. Their weapons were all toward her.

"You are cowards and fools." Disgust filled her, and she glared at Medaka. "I will not surrender. I will never abandon my cause." She took a step toward him brandishing the combat blade. "You will have to murder me first."

"That's what you want, isn't it?" said Medaka. "The Tal Shiar, or whoever guided you, that is what they desire. Nothing but fear and death." He let out a hollow sigh. "Has Romulus not had its fill of that?"

"Then let me die!" she spat, pushing herself up against the muzzle of the commander's lethal disruptor.

"That is expected of me," Medaka admitted, "but I don't think I will." He pulled back his weapon, throwing a look at Vale.

The woman fired, and the phaser's stun blast overwhelmed Helek's nervous system with light and sound, turning her world to darkness.

The turbolift doors hissed open and Deanna Troi stepped out onto the bridge of the *Titan*, adjusting her uniform jacket. Despite the obvious signs of damage on some of the panels, it still felt good to be back among the familiar, after days aboard the Jazari generation ship. A sonic shower and some freshly replicated clothes had gone a long way toward making her feel human again.

The counselor had invoked the privilege of rank to put off Doctor Talov's demands that she report for a mandatory examination after returning to the ship, unwilling to miss what was about to happen. After everything they had gone through, she wanted to be here for the end of it.

Troi glanced down at her son, who dithered on the lift's threshold. "Thad, what is it?"

"Kids aren't allowed on the bridge of a starship," he said, chewing his lip. "That's what Uncle Jean-Luc always said."

"Well, consider this a special treat," she told him, offering the boy her hand.

Thad became very serious. "All right." He drew himself up. "I don't need to hold your hand, Mom. I'm good." And then, in a perfect imitation of his father, Thad pulled his little tunic straight and strode forward, as bold as any captain taking his first command.

"Master Riker." Keru gave Thad a wink as he passed by the tactical station, and then a smile for his mother. Troi trailed her son toward the front of the bridge, where her husband was waiting by the main viewer.

The screen showed the generation ship, now framed against the distant plumes of the plasma storms they had left far behind. Its conical prow pointed out toward uncharted territory, and beyond that, the deep void of extragalactic space.

"We're at a safe distance," said Lieutenant Cantua, at the helm. "Holding station."

"*Othrys* confirms same." At the ops station, Ensign Shae had taken Hal Westerguard's post, and the young Deltan male was all business, treating this moment with the seriousness it deserved. Troi didn't miss how Cantua gave the navigator a sad glance, recalling the loss of her friend. Westerguard and Cantua had been close, coming up together through Starfleet Academy, forming the kind of bonds that only shared adversity could forge. As the last shuttles carrying the *Titan*'s evacuees back from the Jazari ship returned, Riker had offered the Denobulan woman the chance to stand down for a few days, but she refused it.

Troi could see the Romulan warbird a few thousand kilometers off the port bow. Like the *Titan* and the Jazari ship, it was showing signs of damage, but like them it had weathered the storm and come through it stronger.

"Hey, kiddo." Riker gave his son a smile. "I thought you would want to see this."

Thad's expression crumpled. "Are we going to say goodbye to them?"

"That's right," said Riker. "We've all been through a lot these past few days, but now we've got to go our separate ways."

"Power levels building inside the Jazari ship," reported Livnah from the science station. "I read precursor effects initiating in several subspace domains."

"They're opening a wormhole," said McCreedy, the thought of such a thing stirring awe in the engineer. "Or something like it."

Keru glanced down at his panel. "Incoming hail from the generation ship."

"Open channel." Riker gave the order, and a holo-comm image formed in front of the screen.

"*Good day,* Titan." Zade stood in the middle of the ghostly image field, and Troi could make out the faint traces of other Jazari close by. She saw Keret, the technician she had met on their ship, the council leader Yasil, and scowling in the background, the eternally querulous Qaylan.

"And to you," said the captain. "Are you ready for departure?"

"*Indeed. The events of our exodus have been . . . complicated. On behalf of my people, I wish to thank you for your amity and your compassion. It will be remembered.*"

Yasil moved closer, becoming better defined. "*Captain Riker, Commander Troi. We are leaving, but our trust remains. I know you will keep the confidences we shared with you.*"

"You have our word, sir," said Riker.

"Mom, what does he mean?" Thad was confused.

"When you're older, maybe I'll tell you," she whispered. Troi thought of the hidden reality of the Jazari's true synthetic nature, and recalled their shared promise to hold that secret safe. No word of it would appear in the *Titan*'s logs, and anything Thad recalled or the other crewmembers had seen could be explained away. "Thank you for giving our crew safe harbor . . . and for what you did to save the life of our son."

"*It was our duty.*" Zade seemed to sadden as he looked toward the boy. "*Cherish the time you share together, and remember us when you do.*"

Riker took a breath. "I regret that we have to part ways here. I want you to understand that although the Federation may have strayed from the path we set out for ourselves, it will not be lost. We'll come back to it, we always do. And I hope that one day, your people and ours will meet again, as friends."

"*I hope for that too, Captain.*" Yasil gave a sorrowful nod and stepped back.

"*Until then, sir.*" Zade bowed. "*Good fortune to you, my friends. May you weather whatever storms lie ahead.*"

"Can I say something?" Thad whispered. Troi gave him an encouraging smile, and the boy raised his hand in the traditional Vulcan salute. "Live long and prosper. I hope I did that right. And please tell Friend I said goodbye."

"*I will tell her,*" said Zade. "*Live well, Thaddeus.*"

On the viewer, a swirl of blue-white was forming around the Jazari ship, and Troi recognized it as the same exotic radiation effect she had witnessed during Yasil's simulation in their council chamber.

"Shields up!" said Riker. "This is it!"

The holograms dissipated as the light from the building distortion grew brighter by the second. Thad clung to his mother as the shimmering energy surged, enveloping the kilometers-long mass of the Jazari generation ship.

Troi felt the *Titan* rock as waves of spatial disruption rippled outward. The very structure of local spacetime was being warped, transforming and re-forming in ways beyond understanding. Whatever great science had created the Jazari, whatever insights their Makers had gained into the functioning of the universe, it came into action now. Deep inside that blazing stellar fire, the doorway to another galaxy was yawning open.

What would we see if we went through with them? New worlds, new life, new civilizations?

The question pushed to the front of her thoughts, and she knew that it was echoed in the minds of her son, her husband, and the rest of the *Titan*'s crew. Like the Jazari themselves, it touched the impulse that lay at the heart of Starfleet's ethos.

The need to know, to seek out knowledge and friendship wherever it might be . . . in whatever form it might take.

Then, without warning, the brilliant spectacle of the transition vanished, light and energy imploding into nothing. Where the Jazari ship had floated, there was only empty space.

Thad sniffed, reaching up to press away a tear from his cheek with the heel of his hand. Behind her, Troi heard Shae and Cantua both let out the breath they had been holding in.

"Did they go?" said the Deltan. "I mean, did they make it to where they were headed? Is there any way for us to know?"

"We'll find out," said Troi, and she reached for her husband's hand. "One day."

After Deanna and Thad left the bridge, Riker retreated to his ready room to pore over the reports from his department heads.

Titan was operational, but the damage she had suffered in the accident and then the attack couldn't be ignored. According to McCreedy, she'd need a week in the nearest spacedock to get the starship back up to specification, and Riker consulted the charts, plotting out the orders he would give. Without the massive Jazari ship to escort, the voyage back toward the Federation-Romulan frontier zone would take a fraction of the time, and using the course plots provided by Commander Medaka would get them through the plasma storm zone quickly and cleanly.

Then they would go their separate ways, and the status quo would return. Riker frowned at the thought, glancing out of the ready-room port to find the *Othrys* cruising serenely off *Titan*'s port quarter.

In such a short time, the crews of both ships had gone through so much, working together and then in opposition, before finally stopping a threat that endangered them all. It troubled the captain that despite what had transpired, larger events would move on unchanged. Yes, together

Federation and Romulan crews had saved the remnants of a civilization from destruction, and overcome their differences to do so, but that wouldn't change anything else.

The Romulan star continued to die, counting down to a supernova that could potentially destroy billions of lives. The United Federation of Planets remained mired in internal political conflict, forbidding an entire class of life from existing, and turning its back on the wider galaxy to look inward.

He wondered if Commander Medaka thought as he did, if the Romulan shared the same doubts and fears. From a distance, starship captains could seem like powerful, invulnerable figures, masters of their crews and the incredible technologies at their disposal, able to cross the stars in the blink of an eye and face great challenges wherever they rose.

But some challenges are beyond our reach, Riker thought. *Faced with that, what can we do?*

The answer, of course, was to concentrate on what he *could* do. It would be easy to succumb to bleaker thoughts, to consider every action too small to matter in the face of something immeasurable. But the truth was, every tiny moment of selflessness, every iota of effort put toward something better, was a grain of light in an ocean of darkness.

Riker stood up and walked to the window. He watched the stars go by. "We move forward and we do what good we can," he said to the air, giving voice to the thought, reminding himself of his purpose. "Because if we don't . . . then there's no reason for us to be out here."

The panel on his desk chimed and he wondered if speaking aloud had triggered the ship's computer; but then Christine Vale's voice issued out. *"Captain. We've got a situation."*

Her tone told him that his first officer was deadly serious. "Report, Number One."

"Multiple neutrino readings detected ahead of us, sir."

That could mean only one thing. Cloaked ships. "Go to yellow alert." He strode briskly through the door, onto the *Titan*'s bridge.

Vale was in her usual place by the center seat, poring over the screen at her side. "Do we have confirmation?" she was saying.

"Aye, Commander," reported Livnah. "Four discrete targets directly across our heading."

"The *Othrys* sees them too," said Keru, eyeing his tactical plot. "They're dropping out of warp."

"We'll do the same," said Riker, throwing a look to Cantua at the conn. "We'll play this out."

The velocity-warped stars around them shifted out of motion and no sooner was the *Titan* at rest than a quartet of shimmering forms melted out of the dark, taking on familiar, predatory shapes.

"Romulans," said McCreedy. "Warbirds."

Riker immediately recognized the distinctive twin-hulled form of a *D'deridex*-class starship, a vessel type he had faced time and again during his service as first officer aboard the *Enterprise*-D. They were older craft than the *Othrys*, but no less formidable. If it came to conflict, four of them would make short work of the wounded *Titan*.

Grim scenarios rose in Riker's thoughts: *What if these are more Tal Shiar vessels, here to finish the job that Major Helek started? Or has the Romulan Star Empire come to clean up her mess?* This far out beyond the Federation frontier, a single starship could be lost and Starfleet Command might never know the reason why.

"I'm reading weapons powered on all new contacts," said Keru, and the Trill's brow furrowed. "Captain, they're targeting us *and* the *Othrys*."

"The lead ship is sending a general hail." Vale gave Riker a worried look. "Orders, sir?"

"Let's hear what they have to say."

Vale opened the channel, and a gruff, accented voice filled the bridge. *"Attention,* Warbird Othrys, *Federation* Starship Titan. *By order of the praetor, you are to stand down and immediately present your commanding officers aboard this vessel, where they will submit to tribunal. Failure to comply will be considered an act of defiance, and punished accordingly."*

"We're not in Romulan space," said Shae. "They can't order us around."

"You want to be the one to tell them that?" Cantua made it clear that she did not.

"They've sent transporter coordinates," said Vale. "The *Othrys* is showing its belly. They've dropped their deflectors and cut engines."

"Commander Medaka has no choice but to obey . . . and for now, neither do we." Riker turned back to his first officer. "Chris, you have the conn. I'm going over there."

"Not on your own—" she began, but he waved her off.

"They want to talk," said Riker, "and if they're talking, they're not shooting. If they're not shooting, then there may be a way through this that gets us all home safe."

"What if you're wrong?" She stepped to him, asking in low tones.

"I trust you to get our people home safe." He tapped his combadge. "Riker to transporter room one. Lock on to my signal. Initiate site-to-site transport to the Romulan coordinates."

The last thing he saw was Vale's determined expression as the *Titan*'s bridge faded out around him.

SEVENTEEN

Riker came to the end of the story, returning to the moment at hand beneath the watchful gaze of the Romulan tribunal. His throat was scratchy and dry from speaking for so long, but he had given them all he could.

The truth, more or less.

He recalled for them the events of the accident that had first brought the warbird *Othrys* across the border to lend its aid to the *Titan*, the brief unity of purpose shared between the two ships and the Jazari, and then the devolvement into conflict that had followed.

Once or twice, Major Helek made dismissive noises in her throat, as if she wanted to spit, but she did not interrupt him. For his part, Commander Medaka remained silent, as did the four watchers up in the tribunal gallery.

"As I told you from the start," Riker concluded, "our mission here was a peaceable one. I did my best to keep it as that." The low echo of his voice carried the words away, fading.

"How noble." Helek let the mordant comment drop from the side of her mouth. "The human stumbles in his untruth, as his kind are wont to do. He omits many important details."

"Commander Medaka." From the gallery, Tribune Nadei addressed the other officer. "Does the version of events presented by Captain Riker concur with your own experiences during this time?"

"It does," said the Romulan. There was a mutter of consternation from Nadei and the other watchers. Medaka went on. "Major Helek grossly exceeded her authority and forced me from command of my vessel. She directed my crew to attack unarmed civilians and a Federation starship without provocation. Her ambition was only to fulfill her personal desire for violence."

"Do not make assumptions as to the mental state of another petitioner!" Delos, the other tribune, interrupted before Medaka could say more. "Such matters are not for you to judge upon."

"Correct." Judicator Kastis, the leading voice among the group, nodded in agreement. "We will make such determinations, if required."

Standing silently next to Kastis, the advocate assigned to Riker said nothing, but the captain could just make out solemn eyes beneath their hood, measuring everything said inside the chamber.

"Major Helek, do you deny these charges of misconduct?" Nadei turned toward the Tal Shiar agent.

"Do I deny the actions I took? I do not." Helek spared Riker a dismissive glance. "Do I deny allegations of wrongdoing? Most emphatically, yes." The angry, bitter woman Riker had encountered before was gone, and now Helek was controlled, possessed of a self-confidence that bordered on arrogance.

Which of those personas is really her? he wondered.

"Everything I did was for the good of the Romulan Star Empire," continued the major. "I removed a weak and ineffectual officer. I drove off a craven and unworthy enemy." At that, she waved toward Riker. "And I sought to protect countless Romulan lives from a dangerous alien threat."

"When you speak of a threat, you refer to these Jazari," said Delos, offering her an opening.

"Indeed."

"Where are they now?"

Riker held his breath. Helek had been right about one thing: He *had* omitted key details about events. Keeping the promise he had made to Zade and the other Jazari, he said nothing of their inorganic nature.

How much did Helek know about the androids? What would she reveal now?

To Riker's surprise, the answer was *nothing*.

"Gone," said Helek, her lip quirking upward in a cold smile. "Dead. Lost to the void. The method matters not, only that my mission was a success. They are no longer a threat."

Riker studied her carefully, his mind racing as he tried to fathom out her intentions. He'd expected Helek to trumpet her crusade against the androids to the fullest, but she did not.

There could be only one reason why she might keep the Jazari secret—if there was a *greater* secret she concealed beneath it. Something she was hiding from her fellow Romulans, something so dangerous that not even they could be allowed to know it.

He frowned at the thought. *Every Romulan is a damned puzzle with no solution.*

Tribune Nadei offered a question. "Commander Medaka, is the major's description of the Jazari's fate accurate?"

Medaka gave a curt nod. "Their generation ship vanished after an unexplained energy wave enveloped the vessel. When it dissipated, nothing remained, not even their dust."

"A mass suicide?" Delos wondered aloud. "A catastrophic system malfunction?"

"The *Othrys* inflicted great damage on their ship," said Helek, without waiting for permission to speak. "Their fate was already sealed." She seemed quite untroubled, and willing to take the credit for the destruction of millions of sentient beings.

As Helek went on, Riker realized that the Tal Shiar officer had absolutely no fear of these proceedings. In point of fact, she behaved as if the tribunal had ruled in her favor, as if the mere suggestion of her transgressions were ridiculous.

That doesn't bode well, he thought. *If Helek's acting like she's already won, maybe she already* has. *And all of this is theater, a show trial . . .*

He heard Kastis say his name. "Captain Riker, do you have anything to add to Commander Medaka's response?"

He thought of the promise he had made. If the Jazari were believed to be destroyed, they would be free. "No," said Riker, calling on his poker face once more. "I do not."

"There"—Helek brought her hands together with a soft clap—"with the greatest of respect to the esteemed tribunal, may we conclude this now? I would seek a decision so that any remaining impediments can be dealt with." The look she gave Riker made it abundantly clear exactly whom and what she considered an *impediment*.

But then the insouciant half smirk on her lips became as brittle as glass when Kastis spoke the next words. "By the praetor's will, it is the judgment of this tribunal that Commander Joron Medaka, shipmaster of the warbird *Othrys*, be returned to his duties immediately. All charges and specifications against him raised in this investigation are considered null. The commander's record will reflect his conduct during this matter."

Medaka's stiff posture eased a little, and Riker heard him let out a weary breath. The sound was quickly blotted out by a growl from the other Romulan standing in the arena.

"You allow him to walk away without censure?" Helek was incredulous. "He is a Federation dupe. He is not worthy of his rank!"

"Your judgment is unsound," said Delos, silencing her with his reply. "You acted without reflection, you stirred conflict where none existed. You fabricated false data to misinform and misdirect." After his previous behavior, Riker had expected Delos to support Helek, but now the tribune was doing the exact opposite, continuing on with his terse tirade. "You summoned ships without authority, and you alone are responsible for their losses. You were acting on your own injudicious impulses, not for the good of Romulus."

"No." Helek shook her head, imploring Delos. "Tribune, you must—"

Delos spoke over her. "Your actions have been disavowed by the Romulan Senate and the Tal Shiar. Your rank is forfeit." He stared down at the woman with an air of disgust. "If you have it in you, try to accept your fate with a Romulan's dignity."

Helek stared at the deck in silent shame. Whatever confidence she had came apart, becoming splinters and dust. *This isn't another performance*, Riker decided, *this is the truth of her, at last.*

The two guards who had marched Riker from his cell returned and escorted Helek away, into the bowels of the ship. She did not resist. She seemed dazed by the unexpected turn of events.

Riker realized that the attention of the tribunal was now solely focused on him. Up in the gallery, he saw his silent advocate lean close to share a few words with Kastis and the tribunes. Whatever they were saying was too soft to reach him down on the floor of the chamber, and he caught only the faint hiss of sibilants as they discussed his fate.

How badly could this go? Riker had willingly surrendered himself to the Romulans to keep the *Titan*, his family, and his crew out of harm's way. If it came to his fate weighed against all of theirs, he would accept whatever the Romulans dished out, no matter what. Riker drew himself up, ready to take it on the chin.

"Captain William Riker," began Kastis. "By the praetor's will, and with the valued counsel of our respected advocate, it is the judgment of this tribunal that you and your vessel are no longer of concern to the Romulan Star Empire."

He hesitated. With the judicator's steely delivery, "no longer of concern" sounded like it might be a death sentence. But then the illuminators around the gallery went dark and the doors to the arena hissed open.

Medaka gave Riker a sardonic smile. "That means you're free to go. The Empire does not consider you a threat . . . at least for now. I would make the most of that, if I were you."

Riker tapped his combadge, and for the first time in hours, he got an answering beep. "Riker to *Titan*, come in."

"Captain!" Vale couldn't hide her surprise. *"Sir, we've been tracking your biosigns since you beamed over there, but we couldn't make contact. Are you all right?"*

"I'm fine, Commander. Stand by to bring me back."

"Aye, sir, standing by."

He studied his Romulan counterpart. "So this is how we end things? You and I go our separate ways, write our logs, sail our ships?"

"That was always going to be the way," noted Medaka. "One of my ancestors was fond of saying that men like us are creatures of duty. Those words were as true for him as they are now for us."

"Even after what we went through?" Riker pushed the point, trying once again to get a read on the enigmatic Romulan.

"Do you think the Jazari destroyed themselves in that energy pulse?" Medaka countered by asking a question of his own.

"I don't know." Riker answered honestly. "I hope not."

Medaka stepped closer, lowering his voice. "Major Helek had a peculiar notion about them. She said they were a threat. She insisted they were synthetics. But that sounds like an outlandish conspiracy theory, does it not?"

The truth caught in Riker's throat. For a brief instant, he was drawn to share the secret the Jazari had left him with. His gut instinct told him that Medaka was a man he could trust, and he wondered what would happen if he did. Would the truth build a bridge? Would it go a measure toward mending the gap between humans and Romulans?

It was a tempting choice, but he let it pass. There was too much at stake for the Jazari, whatever their fate might be, and as much as Riker might want to trust *this* Romulan, he could not trust *all* of them.

When Riker didn't reply, Medaka went on. "Helek was Tal Shiar, and their kind live in a maze of mirrors, where every breath of wind and creak of the floor is the harbinger of a plot against them. Perhaps she went too far down that path, into that maze."

"I thought all Romulans believed in conspiracies," said Riker.

"Only the real ones." Medaka glanced in the direction of the hatchway through which the guards had taken Helek. "She was so certain that her Tal Shiar masters would forgive her and protect her, it never occurred to Helek she might be abandoned by them." He sighed. "Some will sacrifice anything to keep their secrets, even their most zealous and loyal."

Riker considered that. "Thank you for your candor through all of this. I hope if we meet again, it will be as friends."

Medaka smiled. "We shall make the best attempt." He moved to walk away, and on a sudden impulse Riker took a step after him.

"Joron." Riker deliberately used his first name, speaking in a hushed whisper. "You and your family. We could help you. We can find somewhere safe for them."

The Romulan hesitated. "Thank you for that offer, William. But if you were I, could you accept it?"

"I might," said Riker. "If it meant saving Deanna and Thaddeus."

"Then you have a courage greater than mine, sir. *Jolan tru*, Captain." Medaka turned and left Riker alone in the arena.

He stood in the silence of the great, metal-walled chamber, dwelling on the admission he had just made. *Could I give up everything I have for my wife and my child?* The answer was marbled through every fiber of Will Riker's being. *I hope I never have to make that choice.*

He took a breath and reached up to tap his combadge, but before he could do so, Riker became aware of another presence in the chamber.

"Captain. I would speak with you."

That voice. Riker knew it, but he couldn't immediately place it. It was the deep and sonorous timbre of someone who had seen more of the universe than he might in a hundred lifetimes.

He found his hooded advocate standing behind him, the silent and watchful figure silent no longer. Riker hadn't heard him approaching.

"Do I know you, sir?"

In response, the advocate reached up with age-worn but dexterous fingers, and rolled back the hood to reveal himself. A patient face lined deep with wisdom studied Riker, one eyebrow arched in consideration. "Greetings."

"Ambassador Spock . . ." For a second, Riker felt utterly wrong-footed. Finding the venerable Vulcan here aboard this ship seemed almost unreal. Spock was a legend, not just to every Starfleet officer in the last hundred years, but to beings all across the Alpha and Beta Quadrants. He fumbled for an adequate response. "It's an honor to meet you, sir."

"I was compelled to conceal my identity earlier," explained Spock. "The Romulans enjoy an unnecessary degree of theatricality in their legal mechanisms. I hope my silence did not stress you unduly."

"No . . ." Riker said, his mind racing as he worked this new, unexpected revelation into the series of events. "I'm grateful you were here to speak for me. Thank you for intervening on my behalf."

"You labor under a misconception, Captain," said Spock. "I am not responsible for your release. That decision was made by the tribunal. I merely offered an . . . informed viewpoint."

Riker gestured at the silent, empty chamber. "The Tal Shiar really have left Helek twisting in the wind."

"Quite so. The Tal Shiar is a ruthlessly results-oriented organization. Helek's failure and abuse of their resources for her own crusade sealed her fate. If she had brought them some element of success, matters might have been very different."

Riker gave a crooked smile. "If you hadn't been here, I might have gone with her into those cells."

"When a matter regarding Starfleet comes to my attention, it is a priority to me," said the Vulcan. "More so when the name of a former officer from the *Enterprise* is mentioned." He gestured toward the darkened gallery. "When I became aware of this situation unfolding in the Neutral Zone, I decided to offer my assistance. Sympathetic voices within the Romulan government saw the value in that."

Riker considered that. "The last I'd heard of you, sir, was that you had left Romulan space."

"For a short time. I returned after the threat of the coming supernova event became clear. I have initiated a collaboration between the Vulcan Science Academy and Romulus, seeking solutions that might preserve the Romulan civilization." Spock paused. He seemed to be mulling something over. "I had hoped that I might converse with the Jazari before they . . ."

departed. Their technologies could have proven useful. I regret that we arrived too late."

"If there's any way that I can assist," said Riker, "you need only ask."

"I intend to." Spock studied him for a moment. "Your colleague Commander La Forge is a very gifted engineer and shipwright. I have read several of his warp propulsion theory monographs with interest. I would like to speak to him regarding a . . . technical conundrum I have been working on. Off the record, you understand."

Riker wondered what the Vulcan was referring to, but he knew better than to press the point. "I'll reach out to Geordi when we make port, I'll let him know."

"In addition, I would also ask you to pass on my gratitude to your former captain, Jean-Luc Picard. Circumstances have conspired to prevent me from speaking to him directly, but I would like him to know that his efforts with the refugee crisis were greatly appreciated." A subtle frown creased the ambassador's face. "Many of those who supported Vulcan-Romulan Reunification were left displaced in the early days, after the supernova threat was revealed. Picard's tireless work during that time has ensured that those people, and their hopes for the future, will survive."

"You'll be rejoining them?"

"No." Spock's frown deepened. "For the moment, my focus remains on seeking a solution that might end the present crisis. Perhaps, if I can achieve that, then the proof of my good intentions toward all Romulans will finally be affirmed."

"I don't envy you the task," admitted Riker. "Good luck."

Spock raised his hand in the traditional Vulcan salute. "Until our paths cross again, Captain. Live long, and prosper."

"Peace and long life," he replied, returning the gesture.

The ambassador drew his hood back up and walked away. Riker watched him leave, still feeling a little nonplussed at the whole encounter. After everything he had experienced in the last few days, the last thing he had expected was to find a Vulcan guardian angel looking out for him.

He tapped his communicator. "*Titan*, this is the captain. One to beam up."

Helek sat cross-legged on the floor of the metal cell, her eyes closed and her head bowed forward. There was no door, no air vents or other furniture in the space. Inside this iron cube, there was nothing but her captivity.

Her uniform was gone, taken from her along with her sash of rank, replaced with a common ship suit of bland, scratchy fabric fresh from a replicator. Her concealed weapons and tools, down to the needle daggers hidden in the length of her hair, were confiscated.

Outwardly, everything that had made Sansar Helek who she was had been stripped away. Within, the loss threatened to be greater still.

She passed the time by building scenarios in her mind as to what her fate would be, dispassionately evaluating each one, and ranking them according to probability.

In one, she sat here in this pose until she starved to death, until her lifeless body slumped forward and began to decay. In a second, she terminated herself by breaking her neck against the unyielding metal walls. In a third, she waited for the eventual arrival of a guard and killed him by biting out his throat. More possible scenarios branched off that opening action, each becoming less survivable the longer they went on.

In some, she would be freed by the Tal Shiar, and they would reveal to her that this whole chain of events had been a ploy, a way to declare her dead so the Romulan secret police might use her as a nameless, faceless agent in ever more clandestine missions. In others, they left her here as a grim object lesson to anyone in their ranks who might dare to take matters into their own hands.

But in none of these potential futures did Helek allow herself to think of the Zhat Vash. To even hold the idea of them, to grasp the shape of their name in her mind, that felt like a betrayal. She had risked everything to fulfill the mission they had given her, to rage against the terrifying danger of the Admonition. And even in this moment, despite everything she had said in the tribunal chamber, Helek was unsure if she had succeeded or failed them.

It was difficult to reckon the passing of time, but she was sure it was days before someone finally came. And with him was the answer.

One wall of the cell shimmered and dematerialized to reveal a sallow-faced Romulan man in the naval duty uniform of an uhlan. The low-ranked crewmember stood in the corridor outside and waited for Helek to acknowledge him.

"I want food and water," she demanded. In Helek's experience, the best way to deal with subordinates was to put them in their place from the outset, no matter what the situation.

"You cannot give orders anymore," said the uhlan. "They took that privilege from you."

"Then take pity on me," she snapped. "Or go away."

"I do have something for you," said the man.

"What is it?" Helek decided to indulge him.

"A choice." He stepped over the threshold and into the cell, but he was careful to stay well out of Helek's reach. "A gift from Aia."

Aia. The name turned her blood to ice. In ancient Romulan myth, it meant *the place of every grief,* and for her sins, Sansar Helek had once walked in its dust.

Those initiated into the secrets of the Zhat Vash knew of Aia as the world where the horror of the Admonition lurked. On that desolate planet, beneath the waning light of eightfold stars, the dread warning of the death of all organic life awaited the unwary.

Helek had experienced that warning and lived. Few did. Not all were considered worthy enough to risk exposure to it.

She peered into the uhlan's eyes to search for the truth of him. His flinty gaze had a haunted quality to it.

"You have seen it," Helek said quietly. He did not need to respond. *Like knows like*, she thought.

He held out his hand, offering something. "You drew too much attention to our cause. You allowed your ambition to outstrip your reason. For the work to be completed, it must happen in darkness. Too much is at stake." He dropped an object into her open palm. "You understand that, don't you?"

Helek studied the needle dagger she now held. The wire-thin blade had the telltale rusted orange sheen of a felodesine-coated edge. The poison was swift and utterly lethal to Romulan blood chemistry.

In the moment before the uhlan stepped back out of reach, Helek ran a scenario in her mind where she killed him with the weapon and escaped the ship holding her prisoner. She could do it. It was possible.

But there was nowhere she would be able to hide. She could escape the talons of the Romulan fleet, she might even be able to evade the Tal Shiar. But the Zhat Vash would not let her draw breath for long. They would be in every shadow, concealed in every crowd, they would find her no matter where she went.

Helek rolled the dagger between her thumb and forefinger. There was only one place the Zhat Vash could not go, and there only the dead had dominion.

"Atone for your errors, sister," said the guard, backing away. "And be assured that the crusade will carry on without you."

Thad sat on the floor of the Riker family's quarters and doodled on the sheet of paper in front of him. Rather than using a padd like Shelsa and the other children in his class, the boy liked the feel of something physical and real. There was something better about the way his colored pencils scratched and smudged as they moved across the page. With a padd, if you made a mistake, you could just erase it and start again. On the paper, you had to make it work.

Rough, sketchy forms were starting to come together, abstract things that grew from the motions of the pencils. Thad didn't have a plan for what he was creating, just the impulse to create it. He let the thing come together on its own.

He heard movement in his father's study. Thad's parents—and everyone else's—were back at work now that the *Titan* was at "full operational capacity," whatever that meant. Dad's duty shift was supposed to be over, but the boy had learned early on that a captain never really got a day off.

That didn't seem fair, but his mother had once told him that being the commander of a starship was a lot like being a parent, and parents never got a day off either. *It's called responsibility*, she said. *The older you get, the more you'll have.*

Dad had been talking to the ship's computer in his study, making his captain's logs to send off to Starfleet Command so they would understand what had happened out here in space. Thad had a log of his own, a diary, but it was mostly filled with more sketches and scribbled notes on his invented language.

"What are you drawing, kiddo?" Thad looked up to find his father standing over him. His uniform tunic was open and he seemed tired, but happy.

"It's a map," said Thad.

"Of what?" His father crouched to see it better.

"I'm making a planet," he explained. "It's gonna have continents and islands and seas. I'll draw maps for them too, and make languages for everyone who lives on them."

Dad grinned. "That's pretty cool."

"I'm gonna make somewhere we could live," he added. "Maybe an island, with a nice house. And somewhere for the Jazari too, in case they ever come back." Thad stopped, thinking of Zade and the others of his kind. "I think they made it wherever they were going, Dad. And they fixed me up, so I figure that would be a good gift."

"What's it called, this planet?"

"Ardani. That's Kelu for *home*."

"Good name." His father reached out and tousled his hair. "There's a lot of worlds in the universe. Yours could be out there."

"Ours," corrected the boy. "Our planet, Dad."

The door hissed open and his mother entered, and immediately Thad sensed that something was up. Earlier, she'd gone down to sickbay to talk to Doctor Talov, and the boy guessed it was because of him. The Vulcan medical officer had submitted Thad to an extensive battery of testing, scanning and poking and prodding him in all sorts of ways to make sure he was whole and well.

His dad sensed his mom's hesitation too, and he frowned. "Are you all right?" He glanced at their son, and then toward his study, a tell Thad knew of old. It meant *Shall we talk about this privately?*

A smile formed on his mother's face. "I had a conversation with Talov. He told me Thad is in perfect health for a boy his age, but he wants to continue to monitor him for a while."

"*Uuuugh*." Thad made a long, annoyed sound. "More tests?"

"You went through something no human has ever experienced," his father said gently. "We need to make sure you're okay."

"I *am* okay," insisted the boy. "Better than okay!"

"But that's not all he told me," said his mother, and she reached out to take her husband's hand. Her smile widened, and Thad stopped drawing. She seemed different somehow, suddenly more *alive*.

His dad's grin came back, wide and wild, as something unspoken passed between them. "No . . . !"

"Yes," said his mother, and she grinned too.

Thad had the sense that both his parents knew exactly what was going on, but he was out of the loop. "What is it?"

"That house on your island," said his father with a joyful laugh. "I think it might need to be a little bigger."

The sun was low in the sky, but the air was still warm as the late afternoon began to reach for the evening. Straw-gold light the shade of a good Chardonnay filled the study, and Jean-Luc Picard sat back in his chair.

He allowed himself the indulgence of reading back over the words on the holo-monitor in front of him, and he was happy with his writing. History could sometimes seem like a dry collection of facts and dates, but there was a kind of thrill in turning those truthful details into a narrative that would draw readers in, and make them feel like they were witnesses to something important.

He heard soft, sure-footed steps on the wooden floor and found Laris watching him from the door. The Romulan woman often peeked into his study to keep an eye on Picard, and now she raised an eyebrow as she found him with a satisfied smile on his face.

"What are you so happy about? Not that I'm complaining, of course."

Picard indicated the screen. "I've finished a particularly difficult chapter of my book. And if I do say so myself, I think I did a rather good job."

"Well." Laris put her hands on her hips and wandered into the room. "That sounds like cause for celebration."

"What does?" Laris's partner Zhaban called from the corridor.

"Jean-Luc's cheerful about something. We should put out the bunting."

"Oh, be quiet," said Picard with a wry snort.

Zhaban appeared a moment later with two bottles of wine and three glasses. "How about a drink?" He showed off the bottles. "The '84 or the '86?"

Picard shook his head. "Save the '86 for when I've finished the damned thing."

"The '84, then." Zhaban opened the selected bottle, and after letting it breathe, he poured out generous measures.

The three of them savored the wine, and as he often did when appreciating the product of his family's vineyard, Picard closed his eyes and felt the sense of home surrounding him. It brought him a peace he had found hard to hold on to in recent months.

"I feel a little churlish, enjoying this," he admitted, indicating the monitor. "Considering the sober subject I'm writing about." The attack on Station Salem One was a grave matter that had been a prelude to war, but it was also a compelling topic. Ever the student of history, Picard hoped his work in progress would bring new insight into the events that surrounded it.

"Don't be foolish," said Laris. "That's pride of authorship. Make the most of it."

A soft chime sounded from out in the corridor, and Picard recognized the sound of an inbound communication. Off a look from Laris, Zhaban abandoned his wine to dash out and answer it.

"It's my editor," said Picard. "He can smell me finishing a chapter, I know it."

Laris's lip curled in amusement. "Isn't the whole book supposed to be done by now?"

"Didn't I say something earlier about being quiet?"

A moment later, Zhaban returned. "It's Captain Riker on subspace."

Laris's manner shifted instantly. "We'll leave you to it." She ushered out the other Romulan, and Picard took a breath.

He tapped a key on his virtual panel and stood up as three figures were made real by holo-emitters hidden in the study's walls.

Will, Deanna, and their son stood before him, the illusion of them as solid as if they were there in the room. Picard smiled widely, quietly relieved to know that they were whole and well. "It's good to see you."

"Uncle Jean-Luc!" Thaddeus gave an animated wave. *"You wouldn't believe the adventure we just had!"*

"Oh, I think I might have an idea." He glanced at his former crewmates. "Everything all right?"

"We'll get to that," said Riker. *"Big news first."*

"You'll never guess!" Thaddeus was filled with excitement, shifting from foot to foot.

Deanna took a step forward. *"Jean-Luc, you're so important to us, so we wanted you to be the first person we told. We're having another child."*

"I'm gonna get a sister!" The words exploded out of Thaddeus. *"Isn't that great?"*

"C'est magnifique!" Picard felt a swell of joy for his friends. "I'm so happy for you!" He picked up the wineglass and toasted them with it. *"Salut!* Have you considered a name, or is it too soon?"

Deanna nodded. *"Kestra."*

"Ah. Beautiful. Congratulations! A child could not have a more loving family. I look forward to meeting her."

They talked for a while, around ordinary things and extraordinary ones alike, and presently Deanna guided Thaddeus away so the boy could lead them on a tour around the *Titan*'s decks to tell everyone else the good news.

Will remained to speak alone with Picard, and when it was just the two captains, the conversation turned to the events surrounding the Jazari exodus and the confrontation with the *Othrys*.

Picard listened intently, sipping on his wine, saying little, even when his former first officer described his ordeal by Romulan tribunal and invoked the name of the legendary Spock of Vulcan. In Riker's place, he would have found himself challenged to come through those trials with the same results.

He sensed something different in his old friend, and reached for it. "Will, there's something you're not saying. I'm happy to hear it, if that's what you want. Or, I will be happy to talk about anything else *but* whatever it may be. The choice is yours."

"I could never keep anything from you," Riker said with a rueful smile.

Picard made an educated guess. "The family."

The other man nodded. *"First Thad, and now Kestra is on the way. For a while, I thought having a wife and children with me aboard a starship could work. But after nearly losing my boy, all of a sudden that seems naïve."*

"Beverly made it work," said Picard, with not a little regret. "So did Miles O'Brien." Each of those fellow *Enterprise* colleagues had threaded the needle between serving Starfleet and the needs of being a parent. "You've done well so far. Thad's an amazing youngster. You and Deanna should be proud."

"We are," said Riker. *"But for the first time, I'm wondering whether* Titan *is the best place for the four of us."*

"She's a fine ship, and you've made it even better." Picard recalled that the *Luna*-class vessels had been ill-starred in their early years, and although the original intentions for them to range far into unknown space and carry hugely species-diverse crews had been put aside following the Mars incident, under the command of captains like Riker, the *Titan* and her sister ships had done amazing things. "I have no doubt there would be a planetside post for you, if you ever sought it. The flag ranks could use some new blood, now more than ever."

Riker chuckled. *"Me, an admiral? You're joking, of course."*

"Stranger things have happened." Picard shared his friend's good humor, then sobered. "Will. I want to thank you. When we spoke before, it reminded me that things were still painful. My resignation, and everything that led up to it . . . It's still raw. That wound hasn't healed and I'm not certain it ever will." He looked away. "But I wasn't admitting that to myself. I didn't accept it."

"You've been changed by what happened in the last year," said Riker. *"Everyone has. The forces acting on us can't be denied . . . Both of us are thinking of our past and the futures rolling out ahead."*

"And we are asking difficult questions of ourselves, yes." Picard considered that. "Where do we go from here?"

"Forward." Riker said it with such certainty that Picard felt the other

man's conviction, even across the countless light-years between them. *"That's all we can do. Seek out the right path, the course that takes us toward our truth. Our best selves."*

"That has become difficult for me over these last few months," he admitted. "I'm not sure if I can find that path again."

"Maybe not today. But you will. I know you, Jean-Luc."

Picard gave a regretful smile, feeling a bittersweet pang in his heart. "I admire you, Will. Your clarity, your insight . . . It never fails to amaze me."

"I learned from the best." Riker gave him a final, respectful nod. *"Until next time, Admiral."*

"Until next time, Number One." Picard saluted his old friend once more with the wineglass; and then he was alone with his thoughts.

ACKNOWLEDGMENTS

My thanks to Kirsten Beyer for giving me the opportunity to write this story expanding the narrative of *Star Trek: Picard*, to Una McCormack and Mike Johnson for setting the path to follow, and to Jonathan Frakes and Marina Sirtis for creating one of *Star Trek*'s most enduring couples.

Thanks also to the indefatigable Margaret Clark, for her ceaseless diligence in all things editorial; and to Ed Schlesinger, Dayton Ward, David Mack, Scott Pearson, David A. Goodman, and Michael Chabon, for support both collegiate and practical.

And as always, with much love to my own *Imzadi,* Mandy Mills.

ABOUT THE AUTHOR

JAMES SWALLOW is a *New York Times* and *Sunday Times* bestselling author and BAFTA-nominated screenwriter, the only British writer to have worked on a *Star Trek* television series. His *Star Trek* fiction includes *The Latter Fire*, *Sight Unseen*, *The Poisoned Chalice*, *Cast No Shadow*, *Synthesis*, *Day of the Vipers*, *The Stuff of Dreams*, *Infinity's Prism: Seeds of Dissent*, and short stories in *Seven Deadly Sins*, *Shards and Shadows*, *The Sky's the Limit*, and *Distant Shores*. His other works include the Marc Dane thriller series and tales from the worlds of *24*, *Doctor Who*, *Star Wars*, *Halo*, *Warhammer 40,000*, and more. He lives and works in London.